JUST LIKE GREY

(BOOK 6: SEAN CASHMAN)

JESSIE COOKE

WWW.JESSIECOOKE.COM

License.

Acknowledgements

This book is a work of fiction. The names, characters, places and events are products of the writer's imagination or have been used fictitiously and are not to be construed as real. Any resemblance to people, living or dead, actual events, locales or organizations is entirely coincidental.

CONTENTS

Jessie's Reader Group	v
Chapter 1	1
Chapter 2	9
Chapter 3	16
Chapter 4	23
Chapter 5	29
Chapter 6	35
Chapter 7	41
Chapter 8	48
Chapter 9	53
Chapter 10	59
Chapter 11	65
Chapter 12	71
Chapter 13	78
Chapter 14	84
Chapter 15	90
Chapter 16	96
Chapter 17	102
Chapter 18	108
Chapter 19	114
Chapter 20	120
Chapter 21	126
Chapter 22	132
Chapter 23	138
Chapter 24	144
Chapter 25	151
Chapter 26	156
Chapter 27	163
Chapter 28	169
Chapter 29	175
Chapter 30	180
Chapter 31	187

Chapter 32   193
Chapter 33   199
Chapter 34   205
Chapter 35   210
Chapter 36   216
Chapter 37   223
Chapter 38   230
Chapter 39   236
Chapter 40   241
Chapter 41   247
Chapter 42   254
Chapter 43   262
Chapter 44   268
Chapter 45   275
Chapter 46   281
Chapter 47   287
Chapter 48   293
Chapter 49   301
Chapter 50   308
Chapter 51   315
Chapter 52   321
Chapter 53   327
Chapter 54   333
Chapter 55   339
Chapter 56   345
Chapter 57   352
Chapter 58   357
Chapter 59   362
Epilogue   370

Thank You   379

JESSIE'S READER GROUP

Join my no-spam Reader Group and receive exclusive content and updates on latest books.

Details available on my website...

www.jessiecooke.com

1

LEXI

EMPTY BEER BOTTLES AND HALF-EATEN PIZZA CRUSTS ON PAPER plates littered her coffee table. It looked like they'd had a pizza party for eight instead of a pity party for one co-hosted by her best friend and roommate. Said bestie, Samantha, sat on the couch staring studiously at a book with a highlighter in hand.

"Here," Lexi said. "And you are so lucky that I like you, because this is the very last pint of Cherry Garcia I have." She dramatically offered a bowl of ice cream to Sam. "And this means I must rise from my bed of grief tomorrow and claw my way through the Saturday morning shopping crowds to purchase more."

"You don't like me," Sam said, staring at the book. "You love me. Since the first grade. So don't act like it's a big deal you're sharing your ice cream with me. And I'd do the same thing for you. In fact, I did when the idiot-who-shall-not-be-named dumped me for that skank-that-shall-be-named, Tiffany Whatever-The-Fuck-Her-Name-Is."

Samantha had met one of Lexi's co-workers when she dragged Sam to the company Christmas party. She disappeared that night with only a "met someone" text. But she wouldn't tell Lexi who it was because she didn't want her roommate to feel awkward around her co-worker. But she was equally as adamant in refusing to name the culprit when he dumped her a month later and left Sam an emotional wreck.

"Yes, we both put on five pounds in that first month. The things I do for you."

"Well, at least we had fun sneaking covert glances at the muscle boys in the gym, working off that five pounds."

"Which led me to date the barely lamented Trevor MacGregor."

Sam snorted. "Please, you don't bring out the Cherry Garcia for just any breakup. You had feelings for that guy."

"Yeah. Disgust. Scorn."

"Defenestration," Sam said with mock seriousness.

Lexi laughed. "That's an act, not an emotion, you dope."

"I know what it is. If I found my boyfriend humping a gym bunny in the women's shower, you can be sure throwing him out a window would be the first act in my playbook."

"It's a miracle then that I've haven't had to put out more bail money for you."

"More? When have you ever put out bail money for me?"

"Senior year, high school, when Morris Sever talked you into trespassing on city property to Acker's Hill where that old guard tower sat."

"Hell, it was city property."

"And the roads to it are unsafe, especially in the middle of the night. That's why there was a huge 'No Trespassing' sign at the beginning of the road."

"Okay," conceded Sam. "*Once* you laid out bail money

for me, for all the good it did. My parents found out anyway."

"Glad you remember. You still owe me that money."

Samantha huffed. "Girl, you start listing who owes what between us, we'd be here all night and find out we're even. Sounds like an unproductive way to conduct a pity party. I'd rather spend it trashing Trevor."

"He's not worth our time. Besides, I've made a resolution."

"A resolution? Hell, girl, it's summer, not New Year's."

"I'll renew it for New Year's then. But I've made up my mind. No more pretty boys like Trevor. I'm going to find Mr. Steady-and-Reliable, who wears sensible suits to work and earns a six-figure salary."

"Uh-huh," Sam said.

From the crook of her arm, Lexi dumped the whipped cream, caramel, and chocolate sauce on her coffee table. A few empty beer cans skittered from the surface.

"What made us drink beer instead of wine?" she muttered.

"Because you had the beer left over from Trevor and we'd have to go to the package store to get wine, and payday isn't until next week."

"Speak for yourself," Lexi said. She popped open the caramel syrup cap and squirted a stream on her mound of ice cream.

"Shush. You are saving your grocery money for the ice cream, remember? Give me that." Sam swiped at the caramel sauce and accidentally dropped the book she held. Lexi picked it up and stared at the title. *Fifty Shades of Grey?*

"What the—? Sam, are you reading this?"

"Hasn't every woman in America?"

"No. And why would you?"

"Because it's fun."

"It's about a guy whipping a girl."

"No. Really, it's not. It's about two people negotiating complementary needs."

"And what would you know about it? You don't own a stitch of leather. The raciest thing you own is a pair of edible panties."

"Not anymore," grinned Samantha.

Lexi held up her index fingers and formed a cross to ward off Sam's indiscriminate sharing of information.

"TMI, roomie. TMI."

"It was with—"

Lexi put her hand over her ears. "I don't want to hear."

Sam pulled one hand away from Lexi's ear.

"I was going to lie anyway. The expiration date passed, and I tossed them."

"Good. I'm glad my bestie and roomie isn't a pervert."

"Edible panties aren't perverted. And a little bondage and spanking can spice things up."

"I can't believe you said that."

"What? About the edible panties?"

"No. The bondage and spanking."

"We have to get you out more. Or at least upgrade your reading material. This is much better than those spy stories you read." Sam pushed the book toward her. "You keep that. Find out how the other half lives."

Lexi shoved the book back at the Samantha. "I don't want to read it."

"So are you telling me that if you meet someone as hot and rich as Christian Grey you wouldn't follow him into his Red Room?"

"Red what?"

"His S&M dungeon," Samantha said as her eyes sparkled with mischief.

"Oh, good lord," groaned Lexi. "No."

"But—"

"Just no. Mr. Steady-and-Reliable, remember? I hardly think that includes whips and handcuffs."

From under the pile of paper plates on the coffee table, Lexi's phone intoned the ominous sound of the ringtone she'd assigned to her boss.

"Oh, for heaven's sake," Lexi said. "It's what? Ten at night?"

"Eleven."

"That man needs some boundaries."

"You don't have to answer it."

Yes, she did. Attorney Givens was a demanding prick that unfortunately paid her well to put up with his nonsense. She had just got the promotion as his personal paralegal because his former one decided that motherhood and working sixty to seventy hours a week didn't mesh. Lexi needed the job so she could afford her half of the outrageous rent for their New York City apartment.

"Lexi," huffed Givens, "I need you to print off the contract I'm sending you and carry it to that ass Sean Cashman and get his signature on it. He's about to blow a billion-dollar deal because he has his head up his butt for some reason."

"Um, sure, Mr. Givens. I'll get on it first thing in the morning."

"You'll get on it now. The plane I booked for you leaves in five hours. That should give you enough time to get packed and to Newark to catch it. You can handle that, can't you?"

"But—" blurted Lexi. She didn't want to kiss off her

weekend only to drag herself into the office Monday to work another five days without a break "It's Friday night."

"So? Lexi, have you've been drinking? Get your head on straight. We're talking about our biggest client and money he'll blame us for losing if we don't get this nailed down."

"I'm just a paralegal. I'm sure one of the associates can handle this better than me."

"And none of the other associates have your assets, Lexi. So stop arguing with me and get to the airport. I'm sending your boarding pass and the documents now. And don't show up at work on Monday without a signed document."

The phone clicked off.

"What's that about?" Samantha asked.

"Another threat to my job security," sighed Lexi. "My assets indeed!"

"What?"

"He made an offhand reference to my assets again. What is wrong with him? He thinks because I have long brown hair and blue eyes that every man who sees me will be so overwhelmed they'll do whatever I ask."

"You're right," Samantha said. "It's not the hair and eyes. It's that spankable round butt of yours and your c-cup titties. Then you have that air of 'fuck me, I'm-so-innocent-I-don't-know-what-a-dick-is' look going for you."

Lexi rolled her eyes.

"Please, I do not look like that."

"You do so. That's why I get sloppy seconds out of your dating pool. Always have." Samantha sighed and leaned against the couch.

"Yeah, right," Lexi said with derision. "Get off that couch. I've got to print up that contract, take a shower, and make myself presentable. Please pack a weekend bag for me."

"Where are you going? What should I pack?"

"You know, he didn't say." Lexi stalked to her laptop on the desk in the living room and pulled up her work email. There she found the boarding pass. She popped the flight number into the airline web page.

"Holy cow. I'm going to the Virgin Islands."

"What! Squee! You lucky bitch. Sun, fun, and sand for the weekend and you're complaining! Can I hide in one of your bags?"

"No. After eating all that ice cream, you are over the weight limit."

"That's not fair. You forced me to eat that ice cream."

"Did not."

"But this is great. Maybe you can meet a cabana boy to take your mind off Trevor. I hear they love hot American women."

"Idiot. The Virgin Islands belongs to the United States. They're American too."

"No. Really. You can have some fun there. Pretend you are a rich heiress. No, wait, make good use of all those stories you read. Pretend to be a spy, like the CIA, FBI, or DEA."

"You're ridiculous. The FBI only does domestic work, and the DEA does not spy."

"Please. You just pointed out that the Virgin Islands are domestic. And the DEA does undercover work. Same thing. Where's your sense of adventure?"

"You mean like the time you talked me into filching Principal Egger's toupee?"

"You are so old-fashioned. People call them hair pieces now."

"I almost got expelled for that."

"Pish. You got two weeks' suspension. And it was the best two weeks we ever had."

"Best two weeks you ever had because you faked having mono and the teachers felt sorry for you up until your miraculous recovery."

"Hey, I wasn't going to let my best friend suffer two weeks out of school all alone. And admit it. It was fun."

"Yes, you goofball. We had fun."

"So you see, a little mischief is a good thing. And that, my friend, is what you need right now."

2

CASH

Several Hours Earlier

"This," Cash said, "is what you called me in here for?" Whiskey and derision twisted his words, but even in his slightly buzzed state, he perceived the merger proposed by Walker Givens was one Sean did not want.

When will I be able to hold my liquor?

Walker Givens was Cash's father's best friend, his college roommate, and eventually the family lawyer. Growing up, Cash called him "Uncle Walker," but those days were over now. Especially since the attorney didn't seem to have a grasp on the new direction in which Cash was pushing Cashman Aviation.

"Sean," Givens said, using Cash's given name, "this will make us a lot of money."

"It's not the direction I'm taking the company."

"Have you looked at the balance sheets, lately, Sean? We need the cash."

"No," Cash said bitterly. "What you need is the billable hours that such a merger will rack up for you."

Givens sucked in a breath as if he were staggering back from a blow.

"That's not fair."

"And it's not fair that you push a deal on me that will take control of my father's company out of my hands."

"Very few companies like Cashman Aviation can afford to remain private enterprises."

Cash crossed his arms.

"Why not? The Japanese do it all the time."

"And the Japanese build significant cash reserves with retained earnings over time to secure their companies. But your father, God rest his soul, didn't do that. We have our capital assets, of course, but cash on hand...not so much."

The lack of a financial cushion was another thing that ground Cash's cookies. Walker was a lawyer, not a financial advisor, and hadn't always provided Cash's father with the best advice. It was true that both his father and Givens made a ton of money together, but it was by floating a lot of debt, something that Cash wanted to change.

"What makes you think this merger would do us good?"

"We'd be on the stock exchange."

Cash bit his lips to keep from curling them. The first thing that Givens would do after the stock split would be to sell half of it to add to his cash reserves.

"We would be a division of Pittman."

"The stock would reflect the new name of the company, Pittman-Cashman."

That name made Cash cringe. Or vomit. The whiskey Uncle Walker had given him didn't sit right in his stomach.

"No."

"But—"

"Just no. It's one step away from a hostile takeover. I couldn't do what I want. I'd have to answer to Pittman's board, and who knows if they'd even fund the new projects I have on the drawing boards."

"They promised to support the new engines for space shuttles."

The engine project was Cash's pet. He wanted to build more efficient, less expensive engines for space shuttles. Cash saw a future where Cashman ones would be the go-to engines for emerging shuttle technology. Governments all over the world wanted to hop into the space race, but right now costs were too prohibitive. But if he could make a better, cheaper engine, he could blow the market wide open.

"And at the first bump in the road, they'll yank it, and all my work dissolves in a puff of smoke. No."

"Cash," said Givens in appeal.

Oh, now we go to nicknames, thought Cash sarcastically.

"You haven't even shown me the due diligence audit."

Givens sputtered. "Well, it's not finished yet."

"Then how can you know we need this merger? I want to see the numbers, Uncle Walker." *If he can pull out the nicknames then so can I.* "I won't do anything until I get that accounting."

"You've been working too hard," Givens said. "You should take a few days off and clear your head."

Cash tossed the last of his whiskey down in one swallow. It burned his gut much harsher than it should, but not as badly as his Uncle Walker's words.

"Now, where is that daughter of yours?"

"Out by the pool."

Cash grimaced because "out by the pool" meant Tiffany was not ready for their dinner date, and the reservations were in two hours. Tiff had her charms but, spoiled daddy's princess that she was, punctuality was not one of them. That annoyed Cash. When they first started dating Tiffany's flaws were minor compared to her gorgeous blue eyes, kick-ass body, and perky personality. Cash fingered the ring box in his pocket. It seemed only natural that they would marry. They'd known each other forever, understood each other, and had tons of fun.

Cash was all about the fun.

At least before his father died.

Pancreatic cancer is a death sentence. But the time Cash's father found out, they sent him home to die. In six weeks Cash's world jumbled like a load of wash in an unmerciful dryer.

Tiff, for her part, kept a respectful distance but didn't back away entirely. Cash wasn't in any condition to keep up his end of the relationship, and Tiff understood that. He was not fun and became all about his work. Oh, they kept up their weekly dinner dates and talked or texted daily. But now, a year later, Cash no longer caught his breath, or found a black hole opening up under him, when he recalled his father. It was time to push forward to the future.

Cash pushed open the sliding door just the breadth of his hand, conjuring up the right words to surprise her. He spotted the back of Tiffany's head. She sat on a lounge chair in front of the crystal blue swimming pool where a waterfall tinkled at the end. It was an idyllic place, one where Tiff and he spent many teenage hours.

"No, sweetie, I can't tonight. Cash and I are going out."

She must be speaking to one of her friends, perhaps Caroline.

"What? Jealous?" Tiffany said in a teasingly seductive tone.

Wait a minute. No one speaks like that to a gal friend.

"No, sweetie, I can't just blow off Cash. He's one of my oldest friends."

Friend? He was a *friend*? Cash felt like an idiot standing there listening. He should walk out to the patio, announce his presence, something, other than eavesdropping like a stalking fool.

He stood frozen in the doorway.

"You want to what? Oh, that's so cute." She giggled. "I'm looking forward to tomorrow night. I'll see you then."

Cash stepped back and slid the glass door open noisily.

Tiffany jumped as if caught in the middle of doing something she shouldn't. She turned and the surprise on her face dissolved into a bright smile.

"Hi, sweetie, how are you?"

Sweetie. Like she called her mystery caller.

Cash plastered a smile on his face and walked forward to kiss her.

"Not ready, I see," he said steadily.

"Oh, I fell asleep in the sun," she said. "You woke me up."

How easily she lies.

"Well, that's okay. I have some bad news, anyway."

"Oh?"

"I've got a last minute meeting with Pike, my head engineer. But I couldn't cancel over the phone. I couldn't do that to you."

"Cash, really, you don't have to—"

"Don't I?" he said. It took effort not to grit his teeth. "You've been very understanding this past this year. Sometimes I wonder if I took you too much for granted."

"Cash, of course, it has been a tough year."

"For me, yes. But has it been for you?"

Tiffany lowered her eyes.

"I've kept myself busy, Cash."

I'm sure you have, he thought bitterly.

"Look, I have to go. I'll call you, Monday."

"Sure, Cash," she said. She raised her eyes to his and put her manicured fingertip on his lip. "But don't think you are getting out of next Friday."

"Wouldn't dream of it," he said. She turned her face to his. Obviously, she expected he'd kiss her. Instead, he moved his head and kissed her cheek.

"See you later, Tiffany."

She turned and settled on the lounge chair again. Already her phone was in hand.

Is she going to call him, whoever "he" is? Make plans for tonight? The thought curdled sourly in his stomach. He shut the sliding glass door and took a step away.

The room spun, his breath hitched, the black hole beneath his feet opened again.

"Are you okay, Cash?"

The rough voice startled him, and he looked up into the gray eyes of Uncle Walker. He hadn't noticed before how many wrinkles folded the man's face or the redness of his eyes. From what? Worry? Alcohol? A combination of both?

Maybe he had good reason to need more money.

But Cash would be damned Walker Givens would siphon cash off his company as he did off his father all those years.

"You're right. I have been working too hard. I've decided to take the weekend off."

"Where are you going?"

"To the condo in the Virgin Islands. I haven't been there in a while."

Walker eyed the pocket of Cash's suit jacket, and Cash protectively covered the ring box bulge with his hand.

"Is Tiffany going with you?"

Cash's throat grew thick.

"No." His voice was as rough as gravel. "She has other plans for the weekend." He pushed past Walker and headed out the front door.

"What are you going to do?" called Walker.

He poked his head in the door.

"Have fun."

3

LEXI

THE PROBLEM WAS THAT MR. GIVENS HAD BOOKED THE FLIGHT out of Newark, which was an hour and a half out of the city. By a miracle, she caught an airport cab, but between traffic and pickups, it took two and half hours to arrive. Her heart thumped in her chest from worry that she'd miss the flight. By the time the shuttle bus reached Departures, it was only an hour until takeoff.

Lexi hurried to check in, waiting behind a mass of business travelers. It shocked her that at this hour in the morning the security lines would be so long. Lexi tapped her foot with impatience. She did not want to miss the flight, especially after the breakneck cab ride to the airport. Her insides churned at the memory. New York cabbies had no fear. But when she told him the gratuity she would give him to get her to the airport on time, he turned that attitude up ten notches.

After defying death at least five times in the cab, her heart still raced. Now she stood and waited.

As she dropped her carry-on to the floor, her eyes wandered jealously to the VIP security line. Men and a few women in impeccably tailored suits sailed through as calmly as if they were taking a Sunday walk through Central Park.

Incongruously, a man in cargo shorts, flip-flops, and a black polo shirt jogged through the line, earning a stop by a security agent. He smiled, showed the man his ID, and without a fuss the agent let him pass. Lexi sighed. The last time she flew she forgot about the water bottle in her bag. That earned her a full pat-down from personnel, who seemed dispassionate, but didn't hide their caution, as if she harbored dangerous pathogens on her body. What would happen if she ran helter-skelter through the line? Not walk through hale and hearty.

What made that guy so special?

He was handsome. Yes. He stood about six foot, tall and straight, broad shoulders and blond hair that had a touch too much product in it—the classic American pretty boy.

There you go. Just because you had a bad breakup doesn't mean that all men are douches. Her little voice, the intuitive part of her, scolded her skeptical thinking and Lexi didn't like it one bit. She had every right to be whiney after a breakup. Self-pity and the adamant damning of all male-kind was a time-honored female rite of passage. She wouldn't deprive herself of what inevitably would lead to healing of her fractured heart. She argued that point with herself and felt as if she was losing.

I'm not likely to get next to him, anyway.

Pessimist!

Damn straight! And proud of it.

"Next!" called the TSA agent.

With a jolt, Lexi realized this was her. She stepped forward and handed her boarding pass and ID to him. He scrutinized it and her license, and Lexi felt antsier than ever.

Her plane was boarding in a half hour, and that didn't give her much time to get to her gate.

"Something wrong, Miss Winters?" the TSA agent said.

"My flight is going to board soon."

"Go through," he said with a sigh.

Of course, that wasn't the end. Lexi had to take off her shoes, take her laptop out of the bag, and dump it all in a plastic tub. The second TSA agent shook her head and told her to get another tub and spread out the items.

At this rate, she wouldn't have to worry about showing up at work on Monday. She wouldn't even make it the Virgin Islands to get Sean Cashman to sign the contracts.

She repacked everything in a hurry and dashed along the hallways to get to her gate. Intent on getting to her destination, Lexi wasn't watching all the foot traffic around her. Just as she made the gate area, she heard the announcement.

"Ladies and gentlemen, Flight 1310 to St. Thomas Virgin Islands is now ready to board first class. Any passengers with special needs who have not boarded should see the attendant immediately. Please line up at the gate and present your boarding pass to the attendant."

Oh, god, they've already started. While she didn't have a first-class ticket, she did want to get in a good position to get in line. She'd just redoubled her stride toward the gate when another person marched into her path.

"What!" Lexi said as she tumbled backward. A coffee cup flew up and splashed on the floor. A hot pool of coffee seeped under her leg. "Ouch!"

"I'm so sorry. Are you okay?"

Lexi glanced up to see the crystal blue eyes of Polo Shirt Guy, and her mouth opened and shut. He was even more gorgeous up close. Then she shook her head. Lexi had to get to her feet, get to the gate.

"Ladies and gentlemen, last call for First Class to board. Please present your boarding passes at the gate."

"Let me help you up."

"No," she said. The coffee had seeped under her leg by now, and she was sure it reached her ass. She was one hell of a mess right now, and that ticked her off. The shock of the fall seemed to knock what little sense she had out of her head.

"Don't move. I'll get someone to help you." Polo Shirt Guy looked around, then strode to the desk. Lexi watched in horror as people flowed around her and she sat in the middle as the coffee soaked her bottom.

Suddenly a paramedic team appeared.

"Are you okay, miss?"

"I need to get on that plane."

"We have to check you out first."

Lexi groaned. "I can't miss my flight."

"We'll ask them to hold it few minutes."

Could they do that? Apparently, they could. The crew kept boarding the passengers. She wondered how she was going to make a six-hour flight cramped into a tiny seat with no legroom.

"Does this hurt?" the paramedic said as he gently rotated her ankle. She sucked in a breath.

"I take that as a yes."

"I really, really need to get on that plane. My job depends on it."

"Move your toes."

She did.

"Your ankle."

Lexi did that too.

"Okay, let's see if you can put your weight on it. But first—"

Gently, as if she were Cinderella, the paramedic slipped Lexi's heels off and stuck them in the bag at her side. A paramedic at each arm lifted her to her feet.

"Can you walk?"

She damned well would walk. Lexi took a step and tried not to wince. It was sore but not broken. She looked around and saw to her horror that the plane had boarded. An attendant stood at the door and looked expectantly at her.

"Get a wheelchair, and we'll load her that way."

His partner nodded and grabbed a wheelchair by the gate.

"No, really."

"Look, miss. It is better this way. We'll get you on much faster, and," he leaned over and whispered in her ear, "they have to render assistance to the disabled by Federal law. We'll get you on, you put up your foot, and here..." He pressed a cold pack in her hand, "keep that on your ankle. The flight attendants can replace it when it stops being cold."

"You're nice."

"I wish you could tell my wife that," he said and laughed.

Seated in the wheelchair and clutching her carry-on bag on her knee, she was taken to the boarding gate by the paramedics.

"Okay, miss," the first one said, "the plane's crew will help you now. Have a good flight."

The paramedics merged into the flow of people walking between the gates, and the gate attendant sighed.

"Let me see your boarding pass."

She fished it from her bag, and he looked it up on his screen. He scribbled a few things on it.

"You're upgraded to first class for this flight."

"I am?"

"Yes, miss. We're sorry you had a problem boarding. And this way you can put your ankle up."

Wow. If taking a tumble meant getting a first class seat, she should fall over more often. But, of course, she didn't fly often, and she wouldn't do anything like that.

The acrid smell of coffee rolled off her and the sugar from it stuck Lexi's skirt to her leg. She could only hope she could get cleaned up sometime during the flight.

A flight attendant waited for her at the door and took her carry-on bag and the large floppy beach bag Samantha had insisted she take. Gingerly she followed the attendant to First Class.

Amazed, she stared at the seat. It wasn't just roomier. Each set of two seats was a complete, self-sufficient cradle of luxury. The seats were leather and seemed like recliners rather than airline seats. Two televisions sat side by side, one for each seat, in the divider that stood between this and the next set of seats.

"Here, miss. Take this seat by the window."

"Can I sit on the aisle?"

"Sorry, the passenger who is sitting here is using the bathroom."

"Oh." But she wasn't going to complain.

Efficiently the flight attendant put her carry-on in an overhead compartment and tucked Lexi's beach bag in the cubby in the divider unit between rows of seats.

"I'll get some towels to put under you. I'll be right back."

The attendant returned quickly with a couple of towels and put them on the seat for her and then helped to pull the footrest up. Then she took the ice pack and wrapped it on Lexi's ankle.

"Wow," Lexi said. "Can I take you home?"

"I'd have to ask my husband first," she said and then winked at Lexi.

Damn. Why was everyone paired up?

As she pulled on the strap and looked for the buckle, she didn't see her row companion when he plopped into the seat next to her.

"Do you need help?"

No. It can't be.

Lexi looked up for a second time to the crystal blue eyes of Polo Shirt Guy. The corner of his eyes crinkled in amusement and his lips turned up slightly in a smirk.

4

CASH

THE AROMA OF HIS FUMBLED COFFEE WAFTED TO HIS NOSE AS he stared at the beautiful woman sitting next to him. Thick lashes framed her cornflower-blue eyes. However, they stared at him with anger.

"You," she hissed.

"Look, it was all my fault."

"Damn right, it was." The words shot out of her mouth like fiery bullets.

Cash drew back at the vehemence in her words. No one ever talked to Cash with such anger. It shocked him.

What also surprised him was that her fire-laced words made his cock twitch. Those blue orbs in her innocent face turned gut-wrenchingly sexy when they blazed.

"Sorry," he said again. "And about your ankle. Does it hurt much?"

"No," she said through gritted teeth.

"That's a yes then. When we get off the ground, I'll have the stewardess get you some aspirin."

"No need. I have Tylenol in my bag."

"I'll get it for you," he said reaching for it.

Her hand collided with his, and she snatched the bag hastily. "I can get it myself."

But she only grabbed one strap, and his hand smacked into the bag, upsetting the contents. Books, a wallet, an eyeglass case, and a phone tumbled out onto the floor of the plane.

"Damn," she swore.

Simultaneously a voice blared from the loudspeaker.

"Ladies and gentlemen, please secure your bags and personal items for take-off."

"I'll help you," he said. Cash leaned forward, and his eyes widened at the book lying at her feet. *Fifty Shades of Grey.*

He picked it off the floor and stared at it, then flicked his gaze to the innocent face of his seatmate.

"Give me that," she said. She snatched the offending book from his hand with the speed of a pit viper as her cheeks blushed prettily. So Miss-Oh-So-Pure wasn't. Interesting. Cash hadn't explored BDSM, and he didn't understand the appeal. But different strokes made the world go around.

"How can I make this up to you?"

"You can let me sleep." She quickly retrieved her items and shoved the bag back into its cubby, minus the bottle of Tylenol. She turned her back to him as the plane rumbled down the runway and pulled up into the sky.

Just below the clouds, the plane leveled off, and Cash took out his iPhone, found *Fifty Shades* on Amazon, and downloaded it. He sped-read it enough to get an idea of the story, and slowed down to the few actual BDSM scenes. Somehow he felt that the book was missing essential components of what others euphemistically called a lifestyle. He knew a lot of wealthy guys, and the male main character didn't seem like any of the driven, competitive, perfectionistic men he knew.

Oh, they might hide it behind a mask of congeniality and broad smiles, but most of them were heartless bastards. They couldn't care less who they fucked over as long as it improved the bottom line.

Cash stiffened in his seat contemplating this. Was he like that? Did people perceive him that way? Was that why he was all too eager to believe Tiffany was cheating on him rather than ask her who she spoke to?

He didn't like these questions, at all.

"Would you like a drink, sir?" the stewardess said.

"Yes, thank you," he said with automatic politeness. "Jack and Coke."

"Right away. And the young lady?"

"She's sleeping."

"Don't you think," said his seatmate stirring, "you should ask me?" She sat up and groaned. Cash glanced at her ankle. It looked more swollen than before.

"How about a glass of white wine for her and ice for her ankle?"

"Of course, sir. And the young lady's lunch? I don't have it on the manifest."

The young woman's eyes were blazing now. "Excuse me. I can speak for myself."

The stewardess blushed, and Cash felt embarrassed for her. He would never treat a person that served him rudely.

"Of course. Sorry. We have limited extra meals. I can offer you a Caesar Chicken Salad, or Chicken Cordon Bleu accompanied by a selection of roasted vegetables."

"I'll take the salad."

"Very good, Miss—" The flight attendant stopped for lack of a name.

"Lexi Winters."

"I'll be right back."

Cash made a little noise he didn't intend to.

"Do you have a problem?"

"No," Cash said. He picked up his phone again and entered BDSM into his search engine. He shook his head, cursing his innate need to learn everything he could about a subject before letting it go.

Perfectionistic.

Oh hell. The word rattled around in his mind. Was that him?

His father was the same way and could be hell to be around when busy with a big project. But overall, he was a loving father, more so than some of the parents of his school chums. While Cash went to boarding schools for his education, his father would schedule the time to spend with him when he was home for vacations and holidays. But as a businessman, his father was just as flinty-edged as any of Cash's classmates' parents.

Cash finished speed-reading the book while Lexi slept next to him.

The flight attendant's cart rattled down the aisle interrupting his reading. On a flight like this with first class passengers, there was one attendant assigned to their section. She handed out different meals from the back of the cabin to the front.

"Here you go, one steak sandwich and a Caesar Chicken Salad."

Cash pulled down the tray table, and Lexi did the same. The attendant handed them their drinks and then the food. "Do you need help with this?" she asked as she held up an ice pack.

"No. Thank you," Lexi said as she took the wrapped ice.

"Here," Cash said. "I'll put it on your ankle."

"No, thanks," Lexi said stiffly. She leaned forward and put it awkwardly on her foot. Cash glanced at the flight attendant and nodded his head indicating they didn't need her.

"Look," Cash said. He turned his attention back to Lexi. "I understand why you are tiffed at me."

She arched an eyebrow.

"Tiffed?" she said. "Is that even a word?"

"Is miffed a better word?" he said.

She rolled her eyes. "Who do you hang out with? Sorority Girl Barbie?"

"Maybe," Cash said. *But at least she has manners even if she is a lying cheater.* "But at least I tried to make it up to you. I upgraded your ticket to first class to give you a more comfortable flight."

"You?" She looked horrified.

"Yes. And I got you wine. So perhaps you can stop looking at me like I'm a stalker who is only out to torture you."

She shook her head and looked out the window.

Damn, she was difficult. Usually, Cash at this point had the ladies asking for his room key. But Miss Oh-So-Pure wasn't buying what he was selling.

"But it seems like that's your sort of thing anyway."

"What?"

"Your book. *Fifty Shades?*"

Her face flushed prettily, and she took her plastic glass and chugged the wine like it was in a shot glass. Cash watched in fascination as she swallowed the liquid. The movements of her throat were delicate and feminine. Despite the bravado she attempted to portray, an appealing ephemeral quality clung to her that captivated Cash.

"What?" she said harshly. She met his stare. "A woman's reading material is none of your business."

"And if I want to make it my business?"

"Then I'll call the flight attendant and ask her to find some fat, boring businessman to take my seat."

Cash snorted. "For one thing, seats are assigned."

"That didn't stop you from getting me to sit here."

"There's a reason for that. I always book two seats in case I find a friend at the last minute who wants to go with me on my jaunts. And if I can't find someone, then at least I can get some peace."

"Sounds like you worry that someone would flirt with you."

Cash took a sip of his drink.

"It's happened."

"Why? Because you are so gosh-darn handsome?"

"You think I'm handsome?"

"No. But you seem to think you are."

Cash shut down the emerging chuckle from his throat. She was trying so hard to push him away, and all it did was make him want to win her over. Good lord, she had a face that radiated innocence and a lack of pretense, even when she was disagreeable. As if she had the world and him figured out, and she wasn't buying any of it.

"You should eat your lunch. We won't get dinner, since we will land close to dinner time."

The flight attendant returned. "Do you need anything, sir?"

"Yes. Bring the young lady another class of wine please."

She glared at him, but Cash didn't care. He took another sip of his Jack and Coke then bit into his sandwich.

5

LEXI

LEXI COULDN'T BELIEVE MR. POLO SHIRT WAS SITTING THERE casually eating his sandwich while she fumed. It was bad enough that Mr. Givens yanked her away from her weekend. But now she was on a six-hour flight next to the most annoying man she'd ever met.

"How'd you score a steak sandwich?" she said.

He shrugged. "It pays to have friends in high places. How's your salad?"

"Okay."

He frowned. "Just okay?"

"Yeah. Okay. The usual. Pre-processed chicken, salad from a bag, a few shavings of parmesan, and a Caesar dressing."

"Can I try?"

"Sure." She watched as he speared a piece of chicken and lettuce from her plate and put it in his mouth.

"Good lord," he spat after he swallowed it. "That's horrible."

"Well, not awful."

"For what people pay for these seats, it had better be more than okay." He bolted from his seat.

"Where are you going?"

"To speak to the flight attendant."

"Please," pleaded Lexi, "don't make a scene. It's okay."

He shook his head, and he appeared so upset that smoke could have come out of his nose, but he sank back into his seat.

"Is there a problem, sir?" the flight attendant said. She held another glass of wine.

"Nothing you can fix, so don't worry about it. No. Wait. Tell me. When was this new Chicken Caesar introduced to the menu?"

"About six months ago, sir."

"Six? And how have the passengers reacted? Never mind. I'll find out myself."

"Yes, sir. Is there anything else you want?"

"Do we, at least, still have the cheesecake?"

"We have *a* cheesecake."

He groaned. "Okay, thank you, Adele. Could you bring me another Jack and Coke?"

"Yes, sir."

He sat muttering staring at his phone and Lexi couldn't resist.

"Is there a problem?"

He pushed back his sandwich and stared at it glumly.

"Let's just say this hasn't been my day."

Lexi bit back a sharp retort. Mr. Unflappable appeared genuinely flapped, though she didn't understand why he would care about the meal service on the plane.

"Sorry to hear that."

"You are?"

"Sure. I understand about bad days. For instance, I have to work on my weekend, and I hate that. But what can I do?"

"Exactly. So what is it that you do for work?"

Samantha's advice about making up a persona to have fun swirled in her brain. Sure. Why not? It wasn't as if when she got off the plane, she'd see this guy again.

"If I told you, I'd have to kill you."

Lexi delivered the words with deadpan seriousness, and at first, he gaped at her.

"So what are you, a spy?"

She lifted her eyebrows and raised her wine glass. "Like I said. That's on a need-to-know basis."

"What if I needed to?"

"Then I'd say you're exactly the type of man I'm hunting."

His eyes sparkled with mischief.

"Oh, you're a hunter? That's not what subs do, is it?"

Don't blush, don't blush. Lexi thought frantically. "I never know what role I'll be playing," she said. Unbidden, a hint of seduction crept into her voice.

Whoa! Wait! The sensible part of her brain sounded the alarm that she was getting ready to do something stupid. That part hadn't had to speak to her in a long while. It didn't even pipe up when she flung herself into Trevor MacGregor, who seemed harmless then. But now with Mr. Handsome Polo Shirt Guy looking at her with puppy-dog-fuck-me eyes, she wanted to have some fun too.

Or least torture him a bit. Not sex. But torture. Yes.

He deserved that.

Well, maybe he didn't deserve that, but no man had a right to look at a woman like he was looking at her. She swore that given half a chance, he would devour every bit of her. To her eyes, he was a man that had thirsted far too long and now stood at a water source trying to decide whether to drink or not.

He leaned over to his seat. "You know what?" he whispered.

"Do tell," she said in a husky voice.

"You don't lie very well."

Now a blush did steal over Lexi's face.

"I'm not lying," she protested.

His finger toyed with the ice in his drink. "Yes, you are. You wouldn't spot a role play or a scene if it wandered over to you and sat in your lap."

She lifted her chin in the air. "There you would be wrong."

"Let's see," he said. With a swift movement of his hand, he pulled a screen, hiding their seat bay from view.

"What are you doing?" she whispered in panic. Lexi grew afraid that she'd overplayed her hand. What was she thinking, pretending that she was some undercover femme fatale?

"Testing to see if you are a liar or not."

He drew his finger from his drink and held it to her lips.

"Suck on that."

Lexi's eyes grew wide. "I will not."

"Now what kind of sub are you?" he said. "Come on, show me how you role play, Ms. Winters. Or are you busted?"

Lexi felt a sting of anger, but also, as he leaned close to her, a flare of arousal. She caught a whiff of his smoky cologne left over from a hard day—of what? Though dressed like a bum, he had a hard edge in his eyes that said he spent long hours telling other people what to do. He might appear charming when he wasn't bowling people over in airports, but she perceived the raw power of the man under his affability. And it made her shiver. Butterflies gathered in her stomach as she contemplated what she would do next.

She closed her eyes and opened her mouth.

He placed his fingertip on her lip, and she caught the tang and sweetness of the Jack and Coke. His finger lingered on her bottom lip, stroking it softly.

An electric charge shot from his finger to her plump lips, sending a wave of desire through her that pooled in her panties. Slowly he edged his finger deeper to her tongue, and just that simple movement caused her to quiver between her legs. His finger invaded in slow and intimate moves. Lexi had felt nothing as sensual in her entire life.

He inched along her tongue until his finger was thoroughly in her mouth.

"Suck it," he said huskily.

Lexi pulled on it with her mouth, and she swore his breathing hitched. For good measure, she wiggled her tongue against the underside of his digit, and he took a deep breath.

He withdrew it, pushed it back in, pulled back, then in again.

Mr. Polo Shirt Guy was fucking her face with his finger.

Why was this intrusion so sexy that she wanted to put her hand under her skirt to touch herself? She lightly rocked into the seat, seeking some sort of relief from the heat this man stoked on her tongue and zinged to her nether regions.

Lexi opened her eyes to spot his shut, and enjoyment spreading over his face. She gave his finger a sharp suck, and he gasped. Then she pulled her mouth off.

"There," she said. "You can see I'm not lying now."

"What kind of sub are you?" he asked. Disappointment flitted across his eyes, but really, he had no right to expect anything from her.

"Not yours," she said firmly. And she turned her back on him and gazed out the window.

6

CASH

Cash struggled with his composure, and his erection strained against his zipper after Lexi turned her back on him. What the hell just happened? He'd meant to call her out on her obvious mendacity. She was toying with him, and she demonstrated that with the way she sucked on his finger.

He never thought such a simple thing could arouse him. But as she hollowed out her cheeks, and her tongue and the roof of her mouth tightened around his digit, his cock sprung to life. Cash was never so grateful for a tray table in his life because it seemed his cock would rip out of the light material and say, "Hi there, sexy. Let's get it on."

For the first time in a year, his blood pounded in his ears, and his cock questioned his sanity for not trying to touch the luscious woman.

But, of course, she made it clear she didn't like him.

Or was she playing hard to get? Women did that.

The flight attendant arrived again and peeked over the screen.

"Can I take your plates, Mr.—"

Cash held up his finger to his lips

"She's sleeping," he said softly.

She nodded.

"Bring her a blanket," he whispered.

When she returned, Cash took the blanket and handed the food trays to her. Gently he laid the blanket over Lexi. He took a deep breath as he took in the curve of her rounded butt and slopes of her hips tucking into a tiny waist. Damn, how he wanted to grab onto that ass and plunge...

No. No. No. He had a girlfriend, didn't he? A woman he was going to ask to marry him. That is, until suspicion made him walk away from her. What would Tiffany say if she saw him salivating over a stranger? She'd probably be angry and with good reason.

Cash checked his messages and found only one from Walker. Well, Tiffany didn't waste any time sending him a text, did she?

Perversely, he sent a message to Tiffany.

Cash: How are you doing, Babe?

He tapped his phone waiting for a response that didn't come. Maybe she was *busy* after all.

Cash opened the message from Walker.

WG: I'm sending someone with the papers for the deal. You need to rethink your decision.

Cash's jaw drew tight. Of course, Walker would send someone to dog him while he took time off. It wasn't the first time. And since Cash always took a Cashman plane, Walker could easily find out what flight he traveled on.

Peeved, he emailed the property manager of his St. Johns Condo warning her of his impending arrival. At least he'd enjoy a good soak in his hot tub to get the kinks out of his muscles and start to unwind. He did need this mini-vacation.

But the next message from the housekeeper didn't brighten his mood.

Mr. Cashman,

I'm so sorry. I told you when you ordered the shutdown of the electric and water services it would take several days to restore them should you visit again. Plus, I'm sure it needs significant cleanup too, since it's been a year since you visited. Do you wish me to restore services? I should be able to do that by the middle of the week.

Cash ran his hand through his hair. Who'd authorized this? Not him.

Sorry, he sent. *I'd forgotten. No. Don't restart services. I'll book a room at a hotel.*

He put his hand on his chin as he thought about this. Besides him, only Walker Givens, with his power of attorney, had that authority.

What the hell, Uncle Walker? Why would you do that?

But before he got himself worked up into a state where the weekend would suck, Cash decided to let all of it wait until Monday when he returned. And as for whoever Walker had sent to harass him, Cash would just avoid him.

By now he'd drunk two Jack and Cokes and felt relaxed. Lexi was softly snoring, and they still had another hour on the flight. Cash called up the erotic website again and perused the BDSM stories trying to understand why a beautiful woman like Lexi would find that lifestyle appealing. He opened a story and grazed it with his eyes but stopped at a particular passage.

His sub bent at the waist, her wrists now cuffed to the long bench below her. Her ass stuck up in the air, and her red and swollen sex glistened with her arousal. The Master tugged at the nipple clamps he had fastened earlier, and she made a little noise. Of course, she couldn't say more. He ordered her not to make any sound. But she did, and she trembled beneath his hand on her back knowing that he'd punish her for disobeying his orders.

The idea that he made her tremble, not at something he did, but something that he might do, filled him with a sense of power. Damn. She was so beautiful, so willing to do whatever it took to please him, that his cock filled to rock hardness. He'd take her, yes. Not now. But soon. He'd pound her so hard that she would break apart at his command.

He fingered the tickler in his hand. Yes. This. He didn't need to spank her bottom to torture her, though that was fun too. Sometimes it was the lightest things that made women squirm. And, of course, she couldn't squirm. That was against his orders too.

The Master started at the instep of her right foot, knowing that her feet were extremely ticklish. She sucked in a breath, and a tremor went up her leg. He trailed the feather with the gentlest of touches up her leg, swirling it on her calf and the sensitive spot behind her knee and up the side of her thigh. Her breath hitched.

"Careful, slut," he said. "Remember what I said."

She crooked her index finger on her shackled right hand, the signal they agreed on to register her understanding of his words. Two fingers meant he had to stop because she was about to lose control, and three was an absolute red light. Then he had to stop.

He'd never torture her without her permission.

This was the delicate dance of Dom and sub. How far could he push her before he lost control of her? Too far and both of them lost the game. Not far enough and neither would get satisfied.

They'd discussed this as any good Dom and sub would. Though the game was about breaking her resistance and his control, she told him enough times she enjoyed it.

"I like how you push my limits. I love how you hold me at the edge of orgasm until you give me permission to cum. It's so much

better to hold off because when you tell me to cum, my orgasm is more intense than vanilla sex. I love how you do that to me."

Vanilla sex. That's what others called it. Cash had heard the term and understood it as lovemaking that was plain and, perhaps, boring. But here they were holding it to a higher standard, a comparison of a unique technique of edging and release that made sex more enjoyable. Still, he didn't see what the guy got out of it besides a sense of power. All men felt that when they were fucking.

For his part, he enjoyed the waiting too. When he enjoyed his slut, as he lovingly called her, it was after a long period of jacking her senses. He'd take her to the point where all he had to do was to slap her clit, and she would break apart screaming his name. Then he was free to take her in any way he wanted. Because he'd done his part in ensuring her pleasure, there were no holds barred on how he took his.

Really? thought Cash. This was about unselfish self-ishness?

Her breathing evened out and he had to be careful. Some Doms and subs engaged in the BDSM play to take their pleasure from entering the high of sub and Dom space, but that was not him or her. No. Theirs was a very sexual relationship, and if she drifted into subspace, he had to take extra care he did not hurt her. Subs in subspace would do anything their Master demanded and most times had no capacity to use the safeword out of a painful situation.

He ran his finger up her leg, noting that her muscles remained taut. Good. She wasn't in subspace yet.

Deliberately rattling the keys of the shackles, he unlocked them both. Her legs trembled, so he twisted his hand in the pony-tail he ordered her to wear and put another hand just under her breast.

"Stand," he ordered sternly. And with his help she did.

"Drop to your knees," he commanded. "I'm going to fuck your mouth."

"Ladies and gentlemen, this is your captain. We are about to begin our descent."

The all-to-normal voice caused Cash to jump. Lexi turned sleepily in her seat.

"Are we there yet?"

7

LEXI

LEXI WAS NEVER SO GLAD TO DEBARK FROM A PLANE. OF course, at her seatmate's insistence, they took her off in a wheelchair, though her ankle was feeling better. In fact, two wheelchair attendants were there, one to handle her bags and another to push her. When she tried to tip them, they refused.

"The gentleman already tipped us, ma'am," said the young man as he hailed a cab for her.

"What gentleman?" she said.

But the cab came, and they urged her into it. "We have to go, ma'am. Other passengers wait." They disappeared seamlessly into the outgoing crowd at the terminal. The cab took her to a ferry, where she traveled across a bay to her destination, then caught another cab to her hotel. Her overworked nerves tied her muscle into a knot, and her stomach rumbled.

She had serious work to do, and she was hungry too. It was easy to check in since Mr. Givens had reserved a room for her. Now sitting on her bed alone, all she wanted to do was to go to sleep. If it weren't for the rumbling in her belly, because she didn't eat that awful lunch, she would have. Sleeping on the plane was a feverish affair, with her waking at every jolt of turbulence and then falling again into tortured slumber.

She tried the number that Mr. Givens gave her for Sean Cashman, but there was no answer, and his voicemail didn't engage. That was strange. Then she tried to text him, but the phone stubbornly announced that the message wasn't delivered. How would she find this man?

But at least Lexi satisfied the need to clean off the sticky coffee mess left by Polo Shirt Guy on her body and clothes. After a shower and a change of clothes, she gingerly walked to the hotel restaurant to find something to eat.

Seated in a nice booth, she debated the wisdom of a fruity island drink. It would ease her nerves and her sore ankle.

"Hey," said a now familiar and unwelcome voice.

Lexi looked up into the stunning blue eyes of Polo Shirt Guy. It struck her she didn't know his name.

"How are you doing?" he asked.

"I'm fine," she said guardedly.

"And the ankle?"

"It's okay."

"Good. I hoped to see you again. Imagine my surprise when I saw you walking through my hotel."

"Your hotel?" she said.

"What kind of spy are you? This is my hotel. My father bought it as an investment several years ago when we were into diversification. It's done very well for us."

He snapped his finger, and a waiter scurried toward their table. Lexi had never seen a server move so fast.

"Yes, sir."

"Please, bring Ms. Winters here a Painkiller."

"No really, I've had enough Tylenol."

He smiled at her, and she swore his eyes twinkled. "It's not Tylenol."

To the waiter, he said, "And I'll have a Dark and Stormy."

"Very good, sir." The waiter rushed off.

"So," Lexi said, "did you order enough liquor to get us both plastered?"

"One drink? Naw."

"But you had at least two drinks on the plane."

"I did."

"And now you're going to drink what?"

"A Dark and Stormy is rum and ginger beer."

"And mine?"

"A little more complicated. It has local rum, pineapple juice, coconut cream, orange juice, and nutmeg. It's one of the best-tasting drinks on the island."

"I take it you never had one."

"Nope. I'm addicted to the Dark and Stormy. It's my drink of choice when I'm on the island."

The waiter brought the drinks and then slid menus on the table.

"You're in for a treat," he said. Then he flipped open the menu, and his eyes darkened.

"Bring one of everything," he rumbled unhappily to the waiter.

"Sir?"

"And I want to speak to the chef."

"Yes, sir."

"Why? What's going on?" Lexi said.

"Nothing for you to worry about."

A man dressed in a white chef's uniform stepped up to the table.

"Yes, sir."

"When was this menu changed?"

"About six months ago."

"And who authorized it?"

"Sir, those orders came from the corporate office. Is there a problem?"

"Some of the dishes we were famous for are missing."

"Yes, sir. The ingredients became expensive."

"Well, look at the floor, chef. This is a Saturday lunch, and we are nearly empty."

The chef looked pained. "Yes, sir, Mr.—"

"Just make sure we get a sample of everything on the menu."

"Yes, sir," the chef said. "I will do that."

Like the waiter, the chef moved quickly away.

"You have that 'sir' thing down pretty well," said Lexi.

"Well, I should," Cash said. He took a sip of his drink, though his eyebrows were knitted together in consternation.

"Is something wrong with your drink too?"

"No," Cash said. "I have things on my mind."

"I can imagine you would, since you are an international man of mystery."

Cash jerked his head up from his drink.

"What?"

"Everyone calls you 'sir.' No one seems to know what your name is."

He gave her a wry grin.

"Do you have a name?"

"Edward Teach," he said hiding his smile behind his drink.

"Why does that name sound familiar?" she said.

"Because it is a nearly ancient name here in the islands. It was the name of one of my ancestors. He's fairly well known. His name was Blackbeard."

Her eyes widened. "I don't believe you."

He shrugged. "Why would I lie to you?"

"Why wouldn't you? You haven't told me the truth since I met you."

"Are you using your super-secret spy senses on me? You can tell when I am lying and I'm not?"

"Yes," she said. Lexi made her tone grave. She dug deep into her spy thriller reading for her next words. "There is such a thing as micro-expressions. They teach us to use them to figure out if someone is lying to us."

"What?" he said. "In spy school?"

"Yes. That is exactly what they teach in spy school, among other things."

"Like how to play in a BDSM scene?"

Her eyes narrowed. "They instruct us a variety of things, Mr. Teach. Like how to gain a target's attention or trust." She pitched her voice into a sultry tone, and she eyed him shifting uncomfortably in his seat.

"Oh, I'm a target now?" he said.

"I didn't say *you* were," she demurred.

"But you are here on business?"

"Oh, yes. I'm supposed to meet someone."

"Who?"

"That's on a need-to-know basis," she said coldly.

"But I gather you haven't met him yet."

"I just got into town."

"What. Like you have a rendezvous set up for tonight?"

"Yes," she lied. At least it was a lie for now. After dinner, she'd track down this mysterious Sean Cashman and finish the job. She'd like to enjoy a few hours on the island before she left tomorrow. Maybe she could lie on a luscious white beach under the hot Caribbean sun. That would be an awesome way to finish this unwelcome trip.

"Too bad. I'd like to take you out."

His words snapped her out of her daydream.

"Sorry. I'm on duty," she said sharply.

"Well, how do you have any life if you are always on duty?"

That, Lexi thought, was a superb question. But not one she would discuss with a man that didn't give her his real name.

The waiter and three others behind him carried a load of plates towards them. Appetizers, entrees, and side dishes quickly filled the top of the table, and they pushed another toward their booth to take up the rest. Lexi had never seen so much food in her life.

Edward, because she had nothing else to call him, scanned the dishes before them.

"Take whatever you like," he said. "I just want a bite, though, so I can tell what it is like."

Lexi chose the marinated shrimp, which tasted good, and she said so.

"The shrimp are too small," he said after he took her offering from her fork. "In the past, they were extra-large, not medium."

"What are you? A chef?"

"No," he said. "Just a. . ." He stopped, and his mouth formed a grim line.

"What?"

"Perfectionist," he spit out as if it were a curse.

"Here," he said offering her a bite of steak, "what do you think?"

She took it and when it lay on her tongue, wrinkled her nose. "Over-marinated," she said.

"That's what I thought." He took out his phone and tapped in a few words.

They ate through the various appetizers, salads, steak, shrimp, salmon, snapper, and lobster ravioli with Edward making notes while they ate.

"I like the ravioli," offered Lexi.

"You would have liked them better if we made them fresh on the premises, like we used to do, instead of being something frozen and brought in," Edward said. There was bitterness in his voice as if someone had filched a favorite toy and he couldn't get it back.

"Wow, you are a perfectionist, aren't you?"

8

CASH

At her words, Cash snapped his gaze to Lexi. Damn it. He was doing it again. He *was* acting the perfectionist. But he was also angry because before him on the table was the evidence of betrayal. It angered him, so perhaps that was why his next words came out frostier than a winter's day.

"I'm a businessman, Ms. Winters," he said. "One thing my father taught me is that you provide your customers value for the money they spend with you. This food, it's adequate, but what it does not do is add value to the experience of our guests at this hotel. What it is, quite frankly, is a tourist trap rip-off. Apparently, we priced the food too high for what it is."

"Don't people expect to pay extra at a tourist location?" she said. Her voice was pure innocence. And yes, damn it, that was what many people accepted. But his father had a different philosophy and Cash agreed with him.

"If you exceed people's expectations," he said, "then they'll feel they got a bargain regardless of what it costs. And they'll come back to you for that experience."

Lexi stared at him with fascination, as if he spoke words she didn't expect.

"Don't businesses make a profit by giving people as little as possible for as much money as they can charge?"

"No," said Cash firmly. "Businesses make money off the differential between what you pay your workers and what you charge for your workers' goods and services, less expenses."

"Careful, there, Mr. Teach. You sound like a Marxist and not like the good little capitalist you are."

"It's a stupid capitalist that doesn't recognize that equation."

"So what makes it worthwhile for the worker if you are exploiting them so much?"

"I'm not exploiting them. I'm giving them a framework in which to earn a living. In most cases, they couldn't do it on their own and live a lifestyle they otherwise couldn't afford. For instance, on small islands like this, the people live on small farms and subsist. However, most likely they don't have electricity for their houses, or cell phones, or other modern conveniences. Others want more, and I give them a chance to get it."

"So none of the 'little people deserve what they get' attitude for you, eh?"

"Look," he said with more force than he intended. Heat rose from his belly. "Just because I'm rich it doesn't mean I'm a bastard."

Instantly her face transformed, and he saw something he didn't want to see there.

Fear.

Damn.

"I didn't say you were a bastard," Lexi protested. "And frankly, I don't understand your attitude toward me. First you can't leave me alone, and then you give me a difficult time."

"I shouldn't have said that. The past twenty-four hours rubbed me raw."

She didn't say a word and focused on her meal. For once in his life, Cash sat speechless. He and Tiffany never had arguments, not real ones, and he didn't know how to react. He meant it when he said he should have been more careful with his words. Now Cash was embarrassed. Lexi didn't look at him, and he regretted that he'd spoken to her in anger. Now he didn't know what to say, and he covered the silence by taping a few words into his notes about the meal. Then he checked his messages. Tiffany still hadn't returned his last text.

Must be busy. Cash's thoughts curled with bitterness. He was at once annoyed with her for ignoring him and annoyed with himself for caring whether she texted or not.

"Hmm, that's interesting," Lexi said. "I've never heard you say you were sorry."

"Wha—" he started. But then he realized it was true. His father taught him not to apologize. It was one of his unspoken laws.

"Son," he'd say, "If you did something to apologize for, then you weren't watching what you were doing."

"You knocked me over, spilled coffee all over me, caused me to sprain my ankle, and stalked me through the hotel. Now you talk to me like I've pissed you off. And I'm not worth an 'I'm sorry'?"

"Wow," he said. "That's quite a speech."

"Thank you for the meal," Lexi said as she stood and gathered up her purse, "but I need to get going."

"Your rendezvous?" he said. An odd sensation of disappointment spread through him.

"I didn't mean to hurt or upset you, Ms. Winters," he said. "Please, stay."

She shook her head. "Like I said—"

"But you told me you didn't need to meet up with this guy tonight. How about if I show you the highlights of the islands, eh, to make it up to you? A club or two? Come on. Have a little fun."

She turned her head away as if considering it.

But her lowered eyes said his little speech wasn't working, and he wanted it to. He wanted, no, needed, a win after the frustrating twenty-four hours he'd had. For a woman like Lexi, he'd have to give her what she wanted. This wasn't his territory, not when it came to women, but he could fake it.

"Or," he said in an inspired growl, "do I have to command you to come with me?"

Her eyes snapped to his.

"What?"

"Isn't that what you want? Someone to tell you what to do?"

Her eyes blazed. Would she stomp off? He may have gone too far in trying to impress her with his faux Dom skills. But she didn't move. Instead, she leveled her eyes to his as if to challenge him.

Good. He could handle that.

"It most certainly is not."

Their eyes locked and they shared a moment where they peered into each other. It almost upended him, because for the first time in his life he glanced into the soul of another person. The easier part to see was how she controlled so much of her life, from how she dressed to how she acted to fit the perfect role.

That is what she was doing on the plane, he thought. *She wasn't trying to lie. It was to fit expectations. To play a little game to impress a man. Did she even know what she wanted?*

Cash had an inkling that he did.

"Are you sure? Because you are still standing here." He stood and held out his hand to hers. "Come on, Ms. Winters, I have a few things I'd like to show you."

Her eyes swept the table.

"Can't a girl get dessert?"

He leaned toward her and whispered in her ear.

"Dessert, Ms. Winters, is for good girls."

"And if you don't think I'm good?" she said sarcastically.

"If I'm lucky, you aren't. And if I'm very lucky, you're both. But we'll have to see that, won't we, Ms. International Woman of Mystery?"

9

LEXI

WHAT WAS SHE DOING?

You're bouncing along behind the pirate's great, great, great grandson as he drags you towards God knows what, to do whatever evil thing he has in mind.

He's not really a pirate's descendant, she argued with herself.

Whatever gets you through the night.

What would get her through this night? Why did she agree to this?

Maybe it was the way he stared right into your soul?

That was a moment she would never forget. When their eyes connected for the first time in her life, she felt that someone "got" the essential Lexi Winters. That he understood what she wanted and needed even if she didn't know herself. What's more, she peered into his.

She laid him open and vulnerable, and he hated who he was. She made him question himself and ripped the fibers of his soul bare. It wasn't a wound that couldn't heal. No. Her gaze upended him and unlashed his moorings, and he struggled to find an anchor.

For the briefest of seconds, she wanted to soothe him and to restore the confidence that used to be part of him.

But now she questioned all of that as they climbed a hilly street toward an unknown destination.

Clubs lined the road; light spilled from the windows or security lights on the outside. The bright pastels of the buildings bathed in this illumination stuck out against the dark of the night around them. They seemed like a Toulouse-Lautrec with dark outlines and bright colors. A breeze fluttered through the street and sung through the vegetation that sprung up everywhere. It brought fresh air without respite from the island humidity. Lexi shivered as Edward pulled her toward their destination. Her ankle protested, but his promised surprise spurred her.

They had stopped at his hotel room before they left. Edward had delivered, through whatever magic he had, a suit for himself and a little black dress for her after he spent a few minutes on his phone. She almost lost her nerve and took off, but he pointed to the bathroom when he handed her the dress, corralling her in his room. When Lexi stepped out again, he whistled his appreciation, which appealed to her pinged sense of self. The humiliation of Trevor and that gym bunny still clung to her, and she wanted a moment when a man appreciated her.

"Sit," he had told her. Lexi's stomach grew a bunch of butterflies as he knelt at her feet and slipped on a pair of sandals.

"I would have liked to have seen you in heels," he said huskily. "But since I twisted your ankle I can't hope for that now."

Lexi thought she would swoon right at that moment. In any of her brief relationships, no man had taken so much care for her comfort. Not that she had a relationship with

Edward. But if she had a man this thoughtful in her life, she wouldn't be single. By the time they were ready, they both looked as if they were going to a cocktail party, though when she questioned him, he replied no.

"It's a surprise," he said.

Now his steps slowed, and the thump, thump, thump of the bass from some music bled into the street. Here was no island steel drum gaily singing happy notes. The music inside was somber and sensual.

Edward knocked on the door. Two beats, a space and two more. After a moment, the door swung open.

"We're expected," said Edward. He leaned forward and spoke in the man's ear, and the dark-skinned man nodded.

"Yes, sir, we've been expecting you."

Was it her imagination or did that "sir" sound like it started with a capital "s"?

"Stay two steps behind me," he said to Lexi. She didn't have time to ask why as he entered the hallway that was almost as dark as the outside. Sconces lanced light every few feet down the red painted hall, but that was all she could see behind Edward's broad back.

But something else greeted her ears. Moans, groans, and pants came from speakers set close to the ceiling. It was eerie, and she wondered what they were. They sent a shiver down her, and her heart sped up. She wanted to turn around and leave. Only it occurred to her that she didn't know where she was, or how she could get back to the hotel.

Edward turned right into an archway, and Lexi followed. She found, to her shock, sights she'd never imagined. To the left was an ordinary, though curved, bar of what looked like glossy black wood. Against the wall in the circular room, booths faced a sunken stage in the middle of the floor. On the stage sat an x-shaped cross. Lexi swallowed hard when she saw the half-naked woman bound to it, her arms and legs spread wide. She wore a leather bustier and a black lace thong, leaving nothing to the imagination.

Lexi got another shock when she saw women, and a few men, on their knees at some of the booths facing the stage. They held their heads down, looking at the floor. Some wore collars, others not, but they were all skimpily dressed. The men wore no shirts, and the women wore a variety of leather, some more revealing than others. But there was no question that each of these people was on sexual display.

Lexi didn't know whether it appalled or aroused her, though, in the most secret part of herself, she was leaning toward the latter.

She saw now that a man in a pair of leather pants and boots was leading Edward and herself around the circle. Lexi became painfully aware that people in the booths were staring at her with marked interest, and she felt, for the first time in her life, overdressed.

This was silly, since the dress Edward gave her crawled up her thigh too high and too low in the bosom for her taste. But others eyed her with interest, and she wondered how many of these men shadowed by the dark lighting of the bar undressed her with their eyes.

This naughty thought excited her.

As they moved around the circle, she also noticed that some of the young women sat on the laps of the men. They stared out toward the stage, while the men fondled them shamelessly.

"Good girl," she heard one silken-voiced man say to the woman on his lap. Lexi flushed at those words as if he spoke them to her.

"Here you are, sir. What would you like to drink?"

"A Dark and Stormy."

"Very good, sir."

The man walked away, and before Lexi could express her dismay that he didn't order anything for her, he yanked on her arm.

"Sit on my lap," he ordered in her ear.

Lexi stiffened, not knowing what to do. One of the people kneeling on the floor turned his gaze to her, earning a thwack on his shoulder with a whip.

"You have a lot to learn," hissed the man with the whip so low that Lexi almost didn't hear him. "Don't embarrass me with your disobedience. One more time and I will have to punish you."

"Yes, Master," said the young man.

Lexi wondered why this handsome young man would allow someone to treat him like that, but then she spotted the impressive bulge in his leather pants. He was hard and almost quivering at the words whispered in his ear. He enjoyed this and was a willing participant.

This happened in the space of seconds and, aware of the eyes on her, she didn't want to embarrass Edward with her lack of knowledge.

"Yes, sir," she said indicating she would play along.

Edward sat, and she backed onto his lap facing the stage. He folded his arms around her as they watched.

A man in a black robe paced back and forth behind the woman. Every once in a while he'd flick a flogger against her bare ass. He leaned forward and whispered things into her ear, and she would tremble.

He ran his finger down her spine, and her breathing hitched. The black-robed figure lifted the thin cord that held her thong to her waist and traced delicate lines on her puckered hole. She moaned a little, which earned a hard thwack with the flogger.

"Stay still," he said sternly. His voice carried around the room due to its acoustics. From a pocket in his robe, he pulled an object widely rounded at the end with a protrusion. He stuck it in the sub's mouth.

"Suck on that," he said. A few small gasps escaped through the room. Lexi covertly shifted her eyes to see some of those who were kneeling, watching the scene intently.

10

CASH

THIS WAS MORE THAN CASH EXPECTED. THE SIGHTS AND sounds bombarded his brain. Besides the subs on the floor, he saw subs sitting by or on the laps of their Masters. One sub rocked gently on her Master's lap, and it didn't take much imagination to figure his cock was spearing her.

That almost sent Cash into overdrive.

It took everything Cash had in him to remain cool and collected. But obviously, Lexi was more acclimated than he, because she sat quietly on his lap, staring ahead and not making a sound. She barely reacted to the scene before her, the subs on the floor or their seated masters.

If there was one thing he wanted out of this evening, it was that Lexi didn't take him for the barely tutored amateur he was in the world of BDSM.

Now she was sitting on his lap, and her warm ass there had the expected result. His mouth got dry, and his cock grew stiff. The waiter brought the drink and set it before them.

"Anything else, sir?" the man said.

It took everything he had not to stare at the nipple

piercings the man wore. Thoughts raced through his head about rings like that on Lexi's nipples. And though he hadn't seen them, he imagined them, round and pert. How he would love to tug her imaginary nipple rings with his mouth.

"I'm good, thanks." His voice came out hoarse and he took a sip of his drink.

"Yes, sir. Just remember we do have public and private playrooms we rent out by the hour."

"I'll remember."

Lexi's muscles stiffened. God, how easy it was to read her. She didn't like the idea of a playroom.

Well, idiot, you barely know her. Why would any woman let you take her into a torture room to play?

No. He couldn't rush this. In fact, he wasn't sure what he wanted from Lexi now. She was here, just as he wished, compliant, and so far, obedient.

A heavy-set woman in spike-heeled and thigh-high boots and a full bustier walked to the table.

"I'm Ruby. Nice to meet you."

"Same here, Ruby," Cash said. "I'm Edward."

"Your sub is gorgeous. And so well behaved. How long have you had her?"

"Oh, a while now. How long is it, slut? You can speak."

"I hardly know how to answer, sir. It seems like just yesterday we met."

She spoke sweetly but sank her nails into his thigh as a warning. Was it appropriate to offer her name to Ruby? Or not? He didn't know.

"Well, if you are ever into a threesome, let me know."

"That's a kind offer," Cash said. "I'll keep it in mind."

Ruby wandered off, and Lexi became stiffer on his lap. In fact, between the wood in his pants and her stiffened thighs, he was getting very uncomfortable. But he'd brought her here, and he would see this through to the end.

"What do you think of the scene below?"

"He seems to be taking his time."

The man in the robe was. He had inserted the object from his pocket into his sub's rosebud, and now was striking her ass with the flogger. As he left red stripes on her butt, she jerked in the restraints but didn't make a noise. After each lash, he stroked his hand over the reddened area, and her head jolted back.

"Do you like this, slave?" he said. "Tell me how much you like it."

The woman let out a lusty moan of obvious enjoyment.

"Again?" he asked.

"Please, sir," she said almost as a plea.

Around him, the breaths of the different occupants in the booths quickened. Some masters called their subs to sit on their laps or beside them. The lights in the room seemed to darken leaving only the two people on the stage illuminated. Cash guessed things were about to get intense.

The speed of the man's strikes increased, and the sub on the cross grunted and moaned lustily. Despite Cash's initial impressions about the scene on the stage, he enjoyed it. And then to his shock and delight, Lexi rocked her ass against his erection. Holy shit! Feeling her that close but separated by the fabric of his suit pants jacked his arousal higher.

The man reached a crescendo in his abuse of his sub's ass and stopped.

"Your ass is such a pretty red. I'd love to bury myself in it."

The woman moaned her agreement.

"But you've been bad, which is why you got this punishment. Tonight, you won't come."

The sub whimpered.

"And that pains me too because I love your ass. Remember, when I have to punish you, I suffer too."

"Yes, Master. I'm sorry, Sir."

"But I will allow you to service me."

"Thank you, Master."

He released her ankles and rubbed them gently. Then he did the same to her wrists.

"Face me and get on your knees."

The woman did so.

"Open your mouth."

Incredibly she did. He parted his robe revealing his hard cock. He thrust it into her mouth.

"Suck me," he ordered.

Cash struggled to control his breathing. He remembered Lexi's mouth around his fingers, and he imagined her lips wrapped around his cock. The visual of the sub sucking her Master's cock was almost too much for him. It wouldn't take much to explode in his pants like a teenager. But though he heard the grunts and groans from the booths near him as some of the subs and their Masters took their pleasure, he saw others remaining steely calm. Cash was lost. There was some protocol he wasn't mastering at the moment because Lexi's hot ass commanded his thoughts.

But he wanted to impress her, and he wouldn't give in to his body. He needed a distraction.

"Like that?" he whispered hotly in her ear. "Do you imagine being on that stage sucking a man's cock, your Master's dick, swallowing it to the root? Taking his seed when he unloads into you?"

Lexi's breath hitched, but just barely.

"She's there, in the zone, taking her pleasure from giving him pleasure. You'd like that, wouldn't you?"

He put his hand on her throat, and she swallowed hard.

"I'd bet you'd be good at it too," he whispered. "That hot little mouth of yours around a cock, hollowing your cheeks as you swirl the tip of your tongue on the sensitive underside."

Lexi stilled and her breathing evened out. Damn, she was relaxing into his words. Did she hit subspace with just watching the scene? She laid her head back on his shoulder, exposing her neck to his mouth. Damn, how he wanted to lick it, to find the places on it and behind her ear that would make her groan.

He was harder than steel now and his cock found the hollow between her cheeks. This was driving him crazy. Now he understood the part about the Dom controlling the situation. Someone this compliant was too tempting. With the wild thoughts coursing through his mind, and the need through his body, he was about to shove her onto the leather seat and take her.

Fuck. Cash recognized he was close to losing it. On the one hand, his body said go, go, go. On the other, his brain desperately tried to tell him that to take her without Lexi's conscious permission was an uncrossable line.

He found himself stuck in the middle of an exquisite dilemma. Everything about Lexi was calling him to take her and yet he couldn't. His body hovered in the middle of this pleasure torture. It was awful. And wonderful. *Can* and *can't* mixed, in an overwhelming combination that brought him a sexual high he'd never experienced before.

Below him on the stage, the man fucked the woman's mouth furiously, but Cash doubted that man enjoyed his pleasure as much as Cash did by having, yet not having, Lexi. Oh, something had to happen. He couldn't stay like this.

But he couldn't violate Lexi either.

The man on the stage grunted and shoved his cock in his sub's mouth a few more times. His orgasm was obvious to whoever watched. His cock throbbed in her mouth as she swallowed his cum, then suddenly the lights went dark.

"Lexi," he said, "you can sit on the seat now."

She didn't move, but didn't complain as he gently pushed her to the side of him. She put her head on his shoulder. He sat, enjoying her next to him, and came to the conclusion he'd just gotten into a whole lot of trouble.

11

LEXI

THE TRIP BACK TO THE HOTEL WAS A JUMBLED COLLECTION OF
impressions. Edward's speaking in her ear, lifting her,
walking her out of the BDSM club with her arm slung
across his shoulder, jittered through her brain like she was a
drunk person.

Only she wasn't drunk. Oh, she was in an altered state,
though she couldn't, and at this moment didn't want to,
name it. She rode a floaty high where the sound of Edward's
voice was the only thing that broke through the haze. Lexi
found she liked that warm and sure voice very much.

She stretched out on a bed, as soft as heaven, whose
silky sheets shot delicious pleasure through her skin as it
touched them.

Did someone drug her drink?

No. Lexi didn't drink at the club.

Oh, that club. She witnessed such strange things.
Topless men and barely clothed women on their knees on
the floor. Lexi's mind exploded to see people displaying
themselves like that—like toys or possessions. And the men

and few women in the booths? They seemed powerful with a magnetism that sucked you in.

But no one drew her the way Edward did.

She shivered with the memory of Edward's hard dick pushing between her butt cheeks. How she wanted at that moment to wiggle her ass on him, to make him pay attention to her hot and wet sex that wept for his cock. At that moment she would have done anything he asked.

Lexi would do anything to please Edward up to and including his using her body in whatever way he chose.

And that was so wrong.

Women weren't playthings.

They were not the toys of men.

The whole idea went against everything she'd learned and believed about herself. She was an independent, self-sufficient woman who didn't rely on a man for anything. Lexi would build a career, and her 401K, even pay off her student loans. One day she would find a man who was honest and loyal who appreciated all of her while treating her like the equal she was. They would fall in love, marry, have two point four children, and buy a house with too much of a mortgage. But she and her husband would love each other, and treat each other with dignity and respect. They would watch their children grow up while they grew old, and spend the end of their days with their grandchildren.

That was the plan. It was the blueprint for her life.

It was everything her parents taught her to expect.

Because what she saw this night had none of that. What she saw were men and women subjugating themselves to another, and enjoying pain and humiliation.

Opening themselves to a public display of their sexuality.

And reveling in it.

This wasn't right. It's not what her parents taught her.

But it was exciting.

Enticing.

Forbidden.

The Dom lavished his attention on the woman on the cross, inflaming her mind with words while reddening her ass with his whip. He then caressed the reddened bottom with the utmost attention, and emotions stirred in Lexi she didn't know she had.

Lexi wanted to be that woman.

Her vivid imagination conjured the sting of the flogger on her ass, not too much, but enough to send shivers through her. And then a gentle hand soothing the raw skin with soft swirls, and sending little shocks through her body. Pain and pleasure mixed and jumbled, scrambling her brain, bringing a euphoria that let her climb to a height mere alcohol could never reach.

And then Edward's hard cock pressed between the globes of her cheeks, as she squirmed with desire.

Not that she would move. That would break the moment between them. She sat utterly still, pretending to be the perfect submissive, hoping that Edward would do something naughty in this place where so many wicked things happened.

Moans and grunts rose around her. Masters commanded their slaves to be quiet with urgent, hot, and demanding whispers. She loved this exhibition hidden behind a veil of personal secrecy.

But Edward displayed perfect control. Didn't make a single move on her. The thought was disappointing. And arousing. He was teasing her. That had to be it. He wanted her to beg him to give her his cock.

But there was a catch to that.

He didn't ask her to beg.

No. He left her on the precipice, letting anticipation jack her senses rubbed raw by the sexual displays of the club. Never

*making a demand. No. He commanded her to sit on his damned
cock and didn't offer it.*

Torture.

Wonderful torture.

*His cock twitching under her, and leaning her back against
his muscled chest, captivated Lexi. When he settled his arms
around her waist, she felt safe and protected, desired and
cherished.*

*She almost came when the sub on the cross nearly did. But
despite the tingles between her legs, stomach, and her spine, no
friction existed to set the sparks to flame. He sat damnably
unmoving and she could not.*

Because he did not ask her to.

Fuck.

Despite the thick comforter she lay under, she shivered.

Lexi became more aware of her surroundings and realized she was alone.

Edward didn't just drop her here, did he? The thought
plunged her into a deep dark well. Why would he leave
her? Was she not good enough for him? Did she not
please him?

A thousand similar thoughts raced through her mind as
she shuddered in the bed. She was alone, and no one cared
about her. Certainly not Edward Teach, or whatever the
fuck his name was.

How could she let him do that to her?

But, quite simply, he did nothing.

They shared an hour or two at a club. She sat on his lap.
He didn't take advantage of her sexually. Instead, he brought
her back to this room and left her alone.

Tears formed in her eyes as she contemplated her
wretched love life.

He didn't even want to go to bed with her.

Even when she sat on his rock-hard cock she didn't entice him enough to take her.

If she needed an affirmation that no man would want her...this was it. First Trevor and now Edward. She'd taken her swing at bat and struck out twice. Was it too much to assume she would strike out again?

Noise at the lock shocked her. She clutched the comforter tighter and then she realized she had no clothes on except her bra and panties. How did she lose her dress? When?

Shock and shame spread through her. He must have taken off the dress, eyed her body, and walked away.

The door opened, and Lexi's heart rattled in her chest. Alone in a strange hotel room, she was at the mercy of whoever opened the door.

"Hey," Edward said in a gentle voice. His gorgeous body strode into view, and Lexi stared stupidly at him. "How are you doing?"

"I'm fine," she said. But her voice wavered, indicating she was not.

He walked to the bed and casually sat on the edge. His chiseled face tightened in concern. Edward twisted off a cap and handed an energy drink to her.

"Drink this," he said.

She swallowed hard as the depths of his stunning blue eyes drew her in. He still wore the dark business suit, but without the red tie he wore earlier. The crisp white shirt was in a "v" at the neck, showing off a few chest hairs, which she found incredibly sexy. Lexi took the drink and sipped.

"More," he commanded. "I tell you, Miss Lexi. I've never seen a sub hit subspace so quickly."

Lexi stared at him. Is that what it was? That floaty feeling? Wow.

But she couldn't let him know the depths of her ignorance on the whole BDSM thing.

"So I've heard."

"Have you always been like that? Or did someone train your natural proclivities?"

Lexi stiffened and did not know what to say. Neither answer sounded good to her. It alarmed her that her lack of knowledge would soon become evident. Then it would be game over.

She lifted her chin. "I don't kiss and tell," she said. "And I hope you don't either."

"Who said anything about kissing?" he said with a smirk. "Though I came very close to kissing and more."

"You did?'

"Yes. But what kind of Dom would I be if I took advantage of you when you didn't agree to play?"

"So you are an honorable kinkster?"

He frowned then, and Lexi saw her joke fall flat as she regretted speaking disrespectfully to this powerful man. She looked down at her hands.

"Sorry," she said.

"Hey," he said. "As you told me before, you aren't my sub."

Unbidden, disappointment swirled through her body at his words.

"You should go," she said.

12

CASH

CASH STARED AT HER...FLOORED. WHEN HE SAW THE disappointment and hurt in her cornflower-blue eyes it wrecked him. He sucked in a breath. This was his fault. He'd played a game in which he didn't know the rules, and now Lexi suffered for it.

What the hell was going on? They had done nothing. Just went to a club and saw some kinky stuff. He didn't realize that Lexi would hit subspace, and his all-too-brief Internet tutorial on it left him wondering if he was missing something. Any other time he'd assume she was just some crazy chick. But what the different websites warned was that the sub-drop was powerful and real and required that the Dom take care of and reassure the sub.

He'd drawn her into this game, and he was responsible for her.

"I would. But you are in my room," he said.

"What?"

She scooted back up against the headboard, gathering the comforter to her with shock on her face.

"I thought it would be best if I stayed with you to make sure you got through sub-drop okay."

"Sub—" She stopped and shook her head. "Right. That's kind of you."

"Not at all."

"But who took off my dress?"

He shrugged. "I did."

Her eyes flashed open again.

"But I didn't look."

"Yeah. That line is as old as cavemen."

"Maybe older," he said with a smile. "Here. I got something else for you." He fished out the candy bar in his pocket and hoped it wasn't too mushy from sitting in his pocket.

"A candy bar?"

"Chocolate helps with the endorphin drop. Didn't your Dom ever give you chocolate after?"

She unwrapped the bar carefully and bit off the end. As her pink lips closed around one end of the bar, he imagined her tongue rolling around that piece of dark sweetness. Cash almost moaned as his cock stiffened.

"I told you. I don't kiss and tell."

"And that includes gifts of chocolate bars?"

"And sports drinks. Don't forget those."

"Seriously, how are you doing?"

"Still a little out of it, like I'm beginning to sober up after drinking too much."

"Do you need some aspirin, Tylenol, or Motrin?"

She giggled. "Drug dealing, are we?"

"We have little packets of them at the front desk. I'm sure I can wrangle a couple."

"Right, being the owner and all." She looked around the room.

"Tell me, Mr. Hotel Owner, what are you doing in a

room this small? Don't you have a suite at the top of the hotel."

"You did notice we are only three stories, right?"

"I guess."

"I had expected to stay to stay in my condo, but it's not ready for occupancy so here I am. And we're fully booked, so I had to take this last-minute cancellation."

"Likely story," she scoffed. "You're probably a young Howard Hughes, going from hotel to hotel, living in relative seclusion, doing random checks on rooms, the food service, and God knows, the housekeeping. All to satisfy your need for control."

She laughed, and he loved the sound. When was the last time he'd had this much fun with a woman? Not in a long time. He hadn't enjoyed Tiffany's company since long before his father died.

Cash noticed a smudge of chocolate on the corner of her lip. He leaned forward again and wiped it away with his finger.

She pulled back, surprised, but when he sucked the chocolate off his finger with a suggestive smile, she laughed.

He almost laughed too, but he suppressed it. Cash did grin. "I guess you are right. About part of it. Sadly, this is the only hotel I own. As I said, it was a diversification project and one we never followed through on."

"You keep saying 'we.' Is there a Mrs. Edward Teach hanging around?"

Instantly the fun between them was sucked out of the room. An image of Tiffany flashed through his mind. He had almost asked her to be Mrs. Sean Cashman. Now he realized that was a foolish idea. He leaned back and took a deep breath.

"No. I'm not married. Or rather, I'm married to my job, so there is no room for a relationship."

"That's too bad, Edward. You're a man who needs a relationship."

Edward scoffed.

"What makes you say that?"

"You made sure I was comfortable and got me a sports drink and chocolate. That's a man who wants to care for someone, and who wants someone to care back."

Cash stood and shook his head.

But before he spoke his phone rang.

"Excuse me. It's the manager of the hotel. I'll be right back."

Cash wanted to speak to the manager anyway. Rather than have Lexi move, he'd have the staff switch out the luggage. He'd take her room.

He stepped outside the room into the hall.

"Cash here."

"Mr. Cashman. There is a Tiffany Givens here at the desk looking for you."

Shit! What the hell was Tiffany doing here?

"Tell her I'm out."

"She insists on staying in your room, sir."

Cash's heart sped up in his chest. He did not want Tiffany to see Lexi in his bed. Nor did he want to expose Lexi to Tiffany's shenanigans.

"No. Absolutely not. Do we have a room for her?"

"No, sir. We are all booked. It is the tourist season."

"I tell you what. What room is Lexi Winters in?"

"Let me check. Room 2012."

"Okay, send someone to her room and get all her things and bring them to my room. Switch the billing to reflect the different room numbers."

"Sir?"

"Ms. Winters is in my room at this moment. Have house-keeping clean her room and put Ms. Givens there. Make her wait in the lobby until the room is ready. Better yet, put her in the bar with the hotel's compliments. And tell her I'm out for the evening."

"Yes, sir."

Cash paced in the hallway, wondering what the hell he was going to do now. What was Tiffany doing here?

And what the fuck was he doing with a nearly naked woman, a stranger, in his room? Well, he couldn't stay in it now, could he? That would give Lexi the wrong impression. What could he tell her that would make sense and didn't inform her that Cash's long-time girlfriend was in the house?

But Cash wouldn't stay with Tiffany. The thought nauseated him now.

"Who do you hang out with? Sorority Girl Barbie?"

Lexi's sarcastic words haunted him. Just his meeting Lexi revealed Tiffany's superficial and plastic nature. Not that he didn't know before, but now he *cared*. Comparing Lexi and Tiffany was wrong on many levels, but that didn't stop both his big head and his little one from passing notes.

Lexi was soft and real. Tiff was, well, Tiff. She did and said all the right things, but she seemed stiff, practiced, and rehearsed. Tiff was exactly like every other woman in his social set. Why wouldn't he think that was normal and expected? But Lexi was unexpected. She let him see her vulnerability and uniqueness.

It came down to when he stared into her eyes and saw her soul. He had never experienced a singular moment such as that. And that blew him away.

The elevator down the hall dinged, and the bellman dragged an unwieldy brass luggage cart toward him.

"Mr. Cashman? I have the bags."

"This is it?" he asked. "Only two bags?"

"She hadn't unpacked, sir. And I checked the bathroom too. Nothing of hers there."

"Thanks," replied Cash. He plucked the two bags from the cart. *What woman travels this light?*

A brilliant woman like Lexi, that's who.

Okay. You are moving a woman you don't know into your room. Your girlfriend is cooling her heels in what she thinks is your room. What are you going to do now?

His little head didn't mind this situation. Just thinking about Lexi in his bed gave him a chub. His big head, however, thought he was acting outrageously.

Don't go in there. Have the porter bring the bags in. Don't go in there.

No. Lexi would probably freak out if a strange man entered her room while she was mostly naked in bed.

"Thank you," Cash said dismissing the porter. He wheeled her two small bags into the room.

Lexi looked at him with her big blue eyes, and he melted. And his chub grew stiffer.

Nope. Won't do, bud.

"Your bags, madame," he said.

"Oh, are you my porter now?" she said in a teasing voice. Damn. How he loved the silkiness of it and the promise of sex within it. What he would do to kiss her pink lips.

"I'm whatever you need me to be," he said.

"That sounds like quite a promise. How can I be sure that you'll follow through?"

He opened his mouth to answer, but his phone dinged in

his pocket. Lexi looked toward his pocket when it dinged again, and a third time.

"Sounds like someone is trying to reach you, Mr. Teach."

He knew who it was. The only person who it could be was Tiffany.

"I have to go," he said regretfully. "If you need anything, call the front desk. They'll bring it to you straight away. Drinks, aspirin, magazines, food, whatever. Don't worry about the cost. I'll comp the room."

Lexi blinked, and her face fell. Damn. He didn't want to leave her alone. But if Tiffany interrogated the hotel staff about him, things would not work out well.

The phone dinged again, and he could only imagine the angry expression on his girlfriend's face. He wasn't sure what he felt about Tiffany now, but crossing her would start a shitstorm with her father. He didn't need that right now.

"Sorry," he said. He lunged for the door and yanked it open and escaped the haunting vision of Lexi's wide eyes and disappointment on her face.

Why did it seem that when the door clicked shut his heart did too?

13

LEXI

THE DOOR SHUT AND LEXI SCOOTED DEEPER UNDER THE comforter. Edward left without explanation, and he couldn't leave fast enough. And though she barely knew the man, his sudden departure was a blow to her hollowed-out gut. Would he return? Was this his room or her room now?

What was she supposed to do now?

Not only that, but she'd wasted the entire day and hadn't gotten in touch with the elusive Sean Cashman. That left a few hours tomorrow to find him and get him to sign the document before she climbed on her plane to return home.

But how was she supposed to do that? It was late and it would be rude to call or text him now. And though Edward had treated her to a large dinner, her stomach rumbled. Lexi decided to test Edward's generosity and ordered a pizza, soda, and ice cream through room service. Lexi totaled the calories in her head and quickly discarded the disastrous results. Two men had abandoned her in the past forty-eight hours, and she needed the extra calories to fortify her savaged heart. She'd worry later about how those nano-sized energy bombs would thicken her waistline.

She got out of bed and went to the bathroom. As her feet met the cold tile floor, Lexi cast her eyes around the tile-and-granite room. For a man who owned a hotel he didn't have much. Lexi didn't see a shaving kit, or a toothbrush, or any other personal item. This was strange. He had, however, left his polo shirt and khaki shorts in a mesh laundry bag. There was a bathrobe hanging on the hook but it had the hotel's name on it, so it didn't belong to him.

A knock on the door startled her until she realized it was her room service order. She signed the ticket and took the tray.

"Have a good night, miss," the porter said. "Just leave the tray outside the door."

"Thanks."

Lexi sank to the bed and lifted the lid on the plate. The enticing aroma of baked crust, tomatoes, and cheese rose to her nose. She bit into a slice and instantly felt better. There wasn't anything that couldn't be solved or soothed by a good slice of cheese pizza. Lexi was glad that Edward wasn't here, because he'd probably find fault with it.

He was controlling and perfectionist, two qualities she didn't find attractive. But everything else about him was pure man candy, and as she sucked in the pungent sauce and buttery, gooey cheese she thought of something else she'd like to suck.

Stop, she thought furiously. *He may be handsome and charismatic but he is also distant and secretive. Heck. He won't even tell you his real name. And you know what that means? Yup. Married. Or a criminal. He's hiding something.*

Who cared if his hard cock between her ass cheeks was the sexiest thing she ever felt?

Edward Teach, or whoever the hell he was, must remain off limits.

And that BDSM thing? It would never happen again. It wasn't her and never would be. She was overcome by things she'd never imagined, and overexcited by Edward's super-hot body. But she'd never submit to anything like that in a normal situation.

Still, Edward was sexy, and the memory of his musky scent made her shiver. It was stimulating and oddly soothing at the same time, as if she'd found a home in his arms.

Scarfing down a half of the pizza and the whole of the ice cream sated her need for comfort food. But the scenes at the BDSM club invaded her mind with a collage of sights and sounds. Did that woman enjoy her humiliation on the cross? Because they shut off the lights on the stage, Lexi wouldn't know. But the space between her legs tingled at the thought of being bound helpless, and displayed for public viewing.

What would it be like to give up control? To let Edward bind her and take away her will to resist? To allow him to do what he willed to her body?

Her nipples puckered at the thought and the tingling between her legs became more than insistent.

Lexi's fingers strayed to her breasts and the hardened nubs that strained against the flimsy lace of her bra. She pinched one sharply and she gasped. Damn. She was horny. The memory of Edward's long and hard cock pressing against her bottom incited her to rock her hips. Her flesh pressed against the lace of her thong and the string that ran between her butt cheeks rubbed and teased her rosebud opening.

She laid her head back on the cloud-soft pillow, and her imagination flowered with the rising sexual need that strummed through her. In her mind's eye, Edward stood over her, perusing her body with a stare that promised wicked delights, while he considered his next move.

Slowly he pulled two lengths of black rope from the pocket of his suit and ordered her to pull her legs apart and bend her knees. He took one length and lashed her wrist to her ankles on one side then did the same on the other side. She was laid open to him, and could not move.

Edward unzipped his trousers and let them and his boxers fall from his hips. Deliberately, aware that her eyes were on him, he folded them in half and laid them over a chair in the room. He shrugged off his jacket and tugged on his tie. He looked over his shoulder with a dark and smoldering gaze and Lexi wondered what he was going to do.

It could be anything, and she wasn't in any position to protest. But not being able to move made her hot.

Edward was so very good at making her that.

He moved in slow and deliberate steps toward her, unbuttoning his shirt. It fell open revealing the hard muscles of his chest. He put his left knee on the bed, and swung his right leg over her body. His cock was hard and throbbing.

"You need to take care of this," he said.

She nodded, and he propped another pillow behind her head to raise it. He slapped his cock on one cheek, then the other.

"You're my slut," he said hoarsely.

She swallowed hard because her mouth was going dry. His musk wafted to her nose, telling her that he commanded her. She would do what he wanted because pleasing him was more important than her own pleasure.

"Open your mouth," he said harshly and she did. He plunged inside her as far as she could take. He reached behind and put his hand on her mound, hooking his fingers to breach her entrance.

"Suck me," he said. His cock filled her mouth as he rubbed her

clit with the palm of his hand and invaded her entrance with his fingers. She trembled.

"Don't come," he ordered. "You will not come before me."

She couldn't answer, but that didn't matter. She'd given herself over to him but it was because he knew how to pleasure her, how to tease her sex until she was ready to burst. Sparks shot through her, and her hips bucked against his palm. But just as she was about to explode, he pulled out and took away his pleasure-giving hand.

She gasped.

"Not yet," he growled. "Calm down."

He left her there gasping, his cock dripping her saliva onto her chin. When her breathing evened out and she took a deep breath, he started torturing her with the pleasure of his hand, and thrusting his cock in her mouth. She rose again, and he stopped, and made her calm down again. He did this over and over until she was shuddering with frustration and wanted to scream.

And then she gave up her resistance. She couldn't make this happen any faster by bucking her hips. He was going to do with her as he wanted. She was his toy for play. Lexi floated then beyond space and time, giving herself to him in any way he wanted.

He took his cock out of her mouth.

"You are so good," he said approvingly, and his words of praise almost made her come. He swung off the bed and she wondered what he would do now. His cock was as hard as steel and the head purple. She was relieved when he crawled between her legs and, guiding it with his hands, thrust inside her.

"Fuck, yes," he hissed. "I'm going to fuck you hard, but don't come until I tell you."

He moved within her, filling her, fucking her with increasingly hard thrusts of his thick cock. Her body wanted to come but she had to wait until he gave her the order.

"Come now," he said.

Lexi exploded over and over again, her walls clamping tight around his cock, as he went over the edge, and his seed sputtered inside her.

The orgasm she gave herself left her a boneless mass on the bed. She had no thought of getting up or doing anything. She had never come so hard from pleasuring herself and never knew it could be done.

But one thing she did know.

She liked the idea of Edward Teach having his way with her.

14

CASH

Every muscle in Cash's body was hard and his stomach churned as the elevator delivered him to the first floor of the hotel. He strode purposefully toward the front desk. The young woman who stood behind the counter was unfamiliar and she was on the phone. He waited for her to get off but she kept chatting. Cash realized it was a personal call and he saw red.

"I want to make sure the rooms are arranged as I ordered," he barked.

"Just a minute," the girl said. She couldn't have been more than twenty and she snapped her gum. "Look, I got to go. Some old guy is at the desk."

"Excuse me," Cash said. "Where is the hotel manager?"

"He left for the day."

Cash couldn't blame him. The man put in long hours and needed a break. Still, Cash wanted to make sure whoever was in charge was held accountable.

"Get the assistant manager," he snapped.

"And who should I say is asking?" she asked in a snotty voice.

"Sean Cashman, the owner of this hotel."

The girl's eyes widened and she dialed a number.

"Mr. Cashman wants to see you."

Cash stood and seethed as he waited for the assistant manager to come to the desk. As if things weren't going bad enough, now he found that incompetent people were manning the front desk.

The office door flew open and a man that looked about Cash's age ran out.

"What can I do for you, sir?"

"First off, you can supervise your desk people better," growled Cash. "This young lady apparently hasn't received the training to work the desk on her own. I suggest that you work alongside of her tonight and for the next few nights to teach her proper phone etiquette and how to greet guests properly. Then you can check the system to make sure that the two room assignments I gave to the manager were made."

"Sir?" said the assistant manager blinking.

"Make sure that the room that belonged to Lexi Winters is now under the name Tiffany Givens, and the room I occupy is listed under the name Lexi Winters."

"Right away, sir," the assistant manager said.

Computer keys clacked as he checked the screens and Cash stood with his jaw clenched as he waited for the answer. He glanced at the young woman and decided she couldn't be out of high school. He'd have a long talk with the manager tomorrow.

"I'm sorry, sir. The computer system is down."

"Down? What do you mean down?"

"It happens regularly. Sometimes a reboot helps."

"Then why hasn't it been fixed?"

The man swallowed hard.

"It's because of the cheapskates at corporate," snapped the young woman.

"Cicily," hissed the assistant manager.

"No. If Mr. High-and-Mighty wants to give us attitude, he should know why things happen. We need a new system. This one is from the age of the dinosaurs. But they won't pay for it."

Cash stared aghast at his two employees. What the fuck? When did Cashman Corporation start starving subsidiaries of needed resources? The situation here at this hotel grew even grimmer in Cash's eyes. If other of his subsidiaries fared as poorly, it was a huge problem.

Where was his money going?

"Cash!" said an overly cheery voice. "There you are!"

Cash closed his eyes and took a deep breath. Tiffany. She was the last person he wanted to see. But something was going on with his company, and that could lead straight to her father. It was best if he kept his emotions in check and his relationship with Tiffany smooth until he had more information.

He felt a blush creep up his neck. When did he become manipulative?

"Tiffany," he said with a bright smile. "What are you doing here?"

She bumped her lips against his cheek and smiled a fake smile that displayed her artificially white teeth. "I should ask you the same thing," she said gaily. "I suppose I should be angry with you for taking off to this paradise without me, but I know how difficult things have been for you, darling. So I forgive you."

She forgave him. Yeah. She always did, as if he'd done something to tick her off.

Well, you have practically ignored her this entire year, one part of his brain said.

And she didn't seem to care, replied another. *And she kept herself busy enough.*

His stomach soured thinking of the "sweetie" she had at the other end of the phone only yesterday. Where was "sweetie" now?

"Tiff, that's sweet of you, but as it turns out, I have a lot going on right now."

She hooked her arm around his and steered him toward the pool area. "Well, don't you always," she said with a shrug of her shoulders. "But I simply can't let you work yourself into the ground. And since you came to our favorite spot on the whole planet, I can't let you enjoy this all by yourself. It just wouldn't be right."

"And you always do the right thing, sweetie, don't you?" replied Cash with saccharine sweetness.

"How sweet of you to recognize that," said Tiffany, laying her head against his arm. They walked out on the patio to the pool in the warm, breezy, and starry tropical night. Leaves rustled, the scent of tropical flowers floated in the air. It was a romantic atmosphere and Cash had no interest in any of it.

"This is lovely," sighed Tiffany.

"Yes, it is," Cash said stiffly.

"What's wrong, sweetie? You seem so tense."

Sweetie.

"Nothing. It's been a long day."

"Yes, it has. Let's go to bed."

"You go ahead up to your room. You have your room key, don't you?"

"Why, yes."

"Go on up and I'll meet you for breakfast in the morning."

"What? Aren't we staying together?"

Cash bent and gave her a peck on the lips. She tried to make it a long kiss but he pulled away. "Look, Tiff. Like I said, it's been a rough day. I need some time to think."

"Well, okay, hon, if that is what you want. But don't think you'll get out of going snorkeling with me tomorrow."

"Wouldn't dream of it," he said.

"You've got a date, hot stuff," she said flashing those brilliant teeth of hers. "Call me when you're up."

She was so swift that Cash couldn't stop it. Tiffany pushed up on her tiptoes and threw her arms around his neck. She pressed her lips against his aggressively, and pushed her hips against him.

His first instinct was to push her off, but he stilled that impulse. Until he figured out who was fucking around with his company, he had to play things cool.

But he wasn't enthusiastic about the kiss either. She pulled away, sighed, and slid off his body.

"Well, baby, we'll have to work on that. Maybe tomorrow." She winked at him and turned on her heel. Her hips swayed as she walked to the door, then looked over her shoulder with a sultry look. She was working him hard, but he wasn't taking the bait.

"Good night, Tiff," he said.

When she sashayed through the door, he gave a sigh of relief.

But then his phone buzzed insistently in his pocket.

"Yes," he snapped.

"Cash." It was Walker Givens.

Christ. What did he want now?

"Have you met with the paralegal?"

What paralegal? thought Cash. And then he remembered that Uncle Walker had sent some poor schmuck to chase him and sign the papers he rejected yesterday.

"No," Cash said. "I've been busy."

"What do you mean? Have you been drinking again?"

"No. But there are strange things going on in the hotel."

"Hotel? Why aren't you at the condo?"

"You tell me. The electricity and water are turned off."

"Why did you do that?"

"I didn't."

Walker swore. "Look, Cash, I'll look into it."

"You do that. And while you are at it, find out why someone has gutted expenses at the hotel so much, they're working with an antiquated hotel management system."

"Cash, I can tell you are upset."

"Damn right I'm upset. This goes beyond cost cutting, and I want to know who authorized all of it."

"I'll get in touch with our accountant."

"You do that." Cash ended the call and slipped the phone into his pocket. He dropped to one of the chairs by the pool and stared up at the sky. He wondered if his father was out there playing with stars.

Dad, where the hell are you when I need you so much?

15

LEXI WOKE WITH A STARTLED GASP. THE DREAM STILL GRIPPED her, of the man in the business suit doing wicked things to her body. The memory of it faded fast, but she did not see the familiar surroundings of her bedroom, and for a second she was confused.

Then she remembered yesterday's early morning rush to the airport, how Edward tripped her, and the first class ride in the plane. It was one thing after another with Edward, and the day culminated at that BDSM club.

But he took off. Where was he now?

Not here.

Her phone buzzed with a text notification. Lexi's heart danced when she thought it might be Edward, but it fell to her stomach when she spotted Mr. Givens' name.

Givens: Have you got in touch with Mr. Cashman yet?

Lexi stared at the phone, not knowing what to say. Sorry, boss, I was hanging out at a sex club instead of performing the job you assigned me to do?

Nope. That wasn't going to happen.

Lexi: Sorry, no. He's unavailable.

Givens: Well, make him available. Whatever you are doing now, drop it, and go find him. It's important we get these papers filed by Tuesday. There's no time to waste.

Lexi's mouth twisted with consternation. If anyone asked her, she'd say that Mr. Givens was acting more than unreasonably. But no one was asking.

Lexi: I'll get on it right away.

Givens: See that you do.

She threw her phone on her blankets in frustration. There were times when Mr. Givens was demanding, but he went far beyond that this time.

The pizza in the refrigerator called her name and she scooted off the bed. Cold pizza was a great fast food breakfast, she reasoned. That, and a cup of Coke from the can she didn't drink last night, helped her experience her humanity once again.

A shower, and a change of clothes, fully restored it.

Phone in hand, she tried Sean Cashman's number again, and an automated voice invited her to leave a message. But if he was going to be this elusive, leaving a number would alert him that someone was looking for him. No. She'd have to be more imaginative than that.

She'd do an Internet search on him. But then the icy realization chilled her that the only luggage that was here were the two bags she'd checked in. Where was her carry-on? Lexi was sure she left it in the first room she was in. Not her laptop! That thing held everything personal about her life, from the passcodes for her bank and various online accounts to precious pictures that she'd never printed...and her wallet.

Lexi flew out of the room, and hit the elevator button several times as if it would make the doors open faster.

What should she do? Go to the room and see if her bag and laptop were there?

Then she realized what an idiot she was. She'd left her key in her original room! Edward kept her so busy that she didn't even notice.

And did she even have a key for the room she was in?

Hell no!

Now she couldn't get in to save her life. Was she the biggest idiot in the world or what?

Lexi pressed the button to go to the lobby and flew out the door as soon as they opened. Her feet slipped on the granite floors and she slid into the desk.

"Excuse me," said the young woman there. Her voice was huffy and Lexi noted her name tag said "Cicily."

"I'm Lexi Winters and my room was moved yesterday and one of my bags never made it to my room."

"And?" Cicily said.

"I need help getting my bag back."

"What room did you have?"

"I don't remember."

"And what room are in you in now?"

"I didn't look. Can't you just look up the information in your computer."

"Do you have ID?"

"No. It was in the bag that's lost."

"Sorry," Cicily said. "Can't help you."

"I want to speak with the manager."

"He's in a meeting."

"Where is the owner of the hotel?"

Cicily looked at her stonily. "Not here. We're owned by some huge corporation that doesn't give a flying fig what happens here." The clerk looked at her watch.

"I've got to go," she said.

"What?"

Cicily locked some drawers with her keys and walked away without another word.

"Hey," Lexi yelled. But the woman kept walking and didn't look back.

Lexi stood there fuming. What the hell was she going to do now? She spotted a brass bell on the counter and hit it furiously. She was pissed. This was no way to treat a customer.

No one came to the desk.

Angry and frantic, she rushed into the restaurant and looked around for a waiter. Not seeing one, she went to the bar.

"What would you like?" the bartender asked.

"I'd like to see the manager. The person who manned the front desk wouldn't help me and walked away."

"Just a minute, miss."

He dialed a phone behind the bar, and spoke so quietly she couldn't hear the words.

"The manager will be here in a minute. Would you like a drink?

"Orange juice?"

"Sure."

An older gentleman, bald, short, and with some pudge, hurried into the restaurant. He appeared tired and stressed, exactly the same state as Lexi.

"What can I do for you?"

"I'm Lexi Winters. I'm here to meet with Mr. Cashman, who is also supposed to be at this hotel."

"Yes, miss?"

"Well, last night the owner of the hotel switched my room. At least he said he was the owner. But a porter brought my things from my room and forgot my carry-on.

And that carry-on has everything in it. My laptop, wallet, the key to the room. Only I'm not in that room anymore, and I don't remember the room number. Only Edward didn't give me the key, so I can't get in there anyway. And I can't contact Mr. Cashman. He's not answering my calls. So it's all a big mess."

"So sorry, Miss Winters. Let's see what we can do to help you."

"Thank you, Mr....?" She stopped her rambling because she realized she didn't know the man's name.

"Camilo Veranes. Have a seat. Alejandro, have chef bring her breakfast, on us, of course."

Lexi almost protested that she already ate, but she reasoned that a slice of pizza wasn't really breakfast.

"Is Mr. Cashman in the hotel?" she asked.

"Mr. Cashman? No, miss. He went snorkeling with his girlfriend. But he did say he'd back in a few hours. Shall I leave a message that you want to see him?"

Mr. Givens had said nothing about Sean Cashman having a girlfriend. But then why would he? Lexi was here to get papers signed.

"Yes, please," she said. "Oh, and one last thing. There's a guy running around here saying he's the owner of the hotel. Only he gives his name as Edward Teach."

Camilo arched an eyebrow.

"I know," sighed Lexi. "It's a fake name."

"No. I know Mr. Teach very well," said the manager. "Shall I leave a message with him as well?"

"No. I mean... Is he in the hotel?"

"Not at the moment, miss."

"There are some of his clothes in my bathroom. Perhaps you might have housekeeping pick them up and take them to his room."

"I'm afraid Mr. Teach doesn't have a room. But I will let him know you have his clothes."

"Thanks."

The manager left, and the bartender put a drink in front of her. She stared at it. Tomato juice with a celery stalk.

"A Bloody Mary?" she said. "Whoa, that's too much for me."

"I figured. It's a Virgin Mary. All of the taste, but none of the punch. You don't look like you can take any more punches today."

"No. I can't. And if I don't get in touch with Mr. Cashman today, I may have to apply for a job here."

16

CASH

The water was clear and warm. Sunlight danced on it from above, and colorful native fishes swam below and around him. Swimming beside him, Tiffany looked gorgeous in her designer swimsuit. But then again, Tiffany always presented a stunning image. She worked harder on her appearance than most people did at their jobs.

He knew a lot of men that would love to have Tiffany as their girlfriend. But the longer Cash was with Tiffany, the colder he got over the idea. Despite her stunning appearance and cultivated perky personality, Tiffany seemed—not real. He wouldn't call her fake exactly. But Cash got the sense that the face Tiffany presented was a cobbled-together person. It was as if she cut and pasted one thing from magazine A and partnered it with magazine B to create a person.

Maybe it was because he'd met a genuine person, instead of soulless Tiffany. Lexi was right. Tiffany was a walking, talking Sorority Girl Barbie, and he didn't know if he could take it anymore.

She caught his arm and used the hand signal for up. Tiffany couldn't hold her breath as long as he, but she'd insisted on following him down to the lower level. They swam up and broke the surface. On reflex he blew the water out of the air hose, but the less experienced Tiffany didn't and caught a mouthful of water. She sputtered and coughed out the seawater.

"Darn it, Cash," she said crankily. "Why do you have to dive so deep?"

"Whoa," Cash said. "Somebody didn't eat her Wheaties."

"I didn't like sleeping in that hotel room alone," she complained.

"You've slept in that hotel plenty of times."

"I don't understand why we can't stay your condo."

Cash pursed his lips. He didn't understand it either. He had half a mind to catch today's flight out to get back and start his investigation. There were a lot of strange things that had happened this weekend, and he was going to find out the cause.

Plus he wanted to get things back on track for the hotel. He needed to order the new computer system and dig into the profit and loss statements to see what was going on. Yes, it was a small piece of the Cashman empire, but it was a place that held a lot of good memories for him growing up. As a boy, before his father bought the condo, Cash and his father stayed there often.

"Maybe you should go home, Tiff. You don't seem to be enjoying yourself."

Her red lips formed a pout. How on earth did she manage to keep her lips that shade of red after diving?

"You don't want me here?"

Good lord. This was the last thing he needed.

"No. I'm just concerned for you. You were the one that

wanted to go snorkeling, but face it, you're having a miserable time."

Tiffany threw her arms around his neck.

"It's only because I've missed you, Cash. And it seems we're growing apart. I'm worried w're losing what we had."

Cash gazed into her blue eyes, made bluer than her natural pale blue by her contacts. Was anything about this woman real?

But she'd lobbed a figurative ball over the net and it was his turn to return it.

"We've both been busy," he said. It took effort to keep a biting tone from his voice. "I admit it. I've spent too much time at work, but Tiff, be honest here. You haven't seemed to mind."

Her eyes widened. "That's not true. I've just been giving you space. I know you hate a clingy woman. And honestly, I thought—" She stopped and bit her lip as if she didn't know if she should go on.

"What did you think?"

"I thought we had the rest of our lives together. It didn't matter if we cooled things on the relationship for a while if I'd have you forever."

This was more like the old Tiff, the girl he knew before she grew up to appreciate mani-pedis, facials, and body waxes. For a moment he almost sucked in. But the image of her talking coyly on the phone on her patio by the pool filled his mind again. Cash didn't like to think of himself as a jealous person, but it was a spike to his heart to hear her speak that way to another man.

"You're right. I've spent a lot of the past year assessing what I want. The first six months after my father died I could barely function."

"I know," she said softly.

"And after that I threw myself into the business. Even now there are portions of it that are slipping away from me."

"That's why Daddy says this merger is so good for everyone. You wouldn't have to involve yourself in running the business, and you could enjoy the money the sale would bring."

A slow burn spread in his chest.

"Your father talked to you about the merger?" he said tersely.

"Well, no. I heard him talk about it to Preston Lowe."

"Preston," hissed Sean. "He talked to our CFO about the sale of the company?"

"Of course. It was Preston's idea."

Abruptly Cash pulled away from Tiffany and strode out of the water toward the beach. Preston Fucking Lowe. Cash never liked that guy. He was hired after Cash's father got sick. His father relied on Walker Givens' advice more heavily than usual then, and it was Givens that had green-lighted Lowe.

"Wait, Cash. Where are you going?"

Tiffany ran after him. "Cash, why are you upset? This sale is a good thing. We'd have time and money to travel, instead of having all your assets tied up in the company."

He whipped around.

"Tiffany. You don't know what the fuck you are talking about. Go back to the hotel and wait for me. Or better yet, catch the next plane out of here. If you don't understand that the business means everything to me, then you don't know me at all."

Cash grabbed the towel, shorts, t-shirt, and flip-flops he'd bought in the gift shop. Tiffany followed behind him, her feet stomping the sand as they turned in the snorkeling equipment they rented.

"Sean Cashman," she huffed, "are you seriously going to tell me to go home?"

He pulled on his shorts over his bathing suit and then the t-shirt that had the name of his hotel, Crown Bay Hotel, splayed across the front. Tiffany gave him the evil eye.

"That might be best," he said evenly. He walked away as she called his name.

That Tiffany supported the idea of the sale of his business was absolutely the last straw. What was she thinking? What was he doing considering marriage to her?

But the more unsettling thought was that the world had shifted under him and threatened to roll out of control. Not just Tiffany, but her father and the company chief financial officer, Preston Lowe, hid things from him and pushed agendas he did not approve. Cutting back on Cash's personal expenditures? Making decisions about the hotel that hurt operations? And what else? That had to stop.

Cash didn't want to go back to the hotel and face a pissed-off Tiffany. He didn't even want to think of Uncle Walker trying to sell his business out from under him. No, this was something he'd deal with when he returned to New York and went to the office on Tuesday. Now he wanted to put these things out of his mind.

He wandered through the streets of the island town reacquainting himself with the sights that had become familiar when Cash was younger. He found himself on the same street as the BDSM club, *Second Nature*, and decided to visit the owner, his friend Enrico. He'd met Enrico a number of years ago when Cash and his father visited the island after Cash's mother died. Though Enrico was an island boy, they formed a friendship and Cash would renew it whenever he returned to the island.

He knew of Enrico's hobby turned business, but passed

up Enrico's standing invitation to visit until last night. Now he just wanted to talk to someone who was removed from his problems, and Enrico fit the bill.

Cash climbed the stairs cobbled together from island rock, passed the entrance to Enrico's club to the top, which looked out onto another street. To the left a sandy pathway let to his friend's apartment. Enrico answered dressed in shorts and opened bathrobe, and a day's growth of beard. Bleary-eyed, he gave Cash a weak smile.

"Damn," Cash said. "I didn't mean to wake you."

"Copa, mehson. My house is yours." He stepped aside to let Cash in. The blinds were closed allowing tiny spears of light to slice into the darkened, sparsely furnished room. In the background a cranky air conditioner rattled as it sputtered cooler air into the apartment.

To the left was a small kitchen area separated from the rest of the room by a half wall on which sat a Formica countertop. Enrico moved to the refrigerator, stared into it while blinking his eyes in an attempt to wake up. Cash felt bad. He shouldn't have bothered Enrico at this early hour.

Enrico dragged out a bottle of orange juice and set it on the counter.

"Sit," he said. "Juice?"

"Thanks, no," Cash said as he sunk onto a stool. "What I'd like is if you can explain how this BDSM thing works."

17

LEXI

THE HOTEL MANAGER, MR. VERANES, WAS THE BEST. HE GOT her a new card key and told her the entire staff was looking for her bag. He even sent someone to get her bathing suit and her portfolio where the papers for the merger waited for Sean Cashman's signature. Thank goodness she'd held onto her phone. Lexi spent the morning sitting by the pool making calls to her credit cards, waiting on customer service queues and making sure there were no unauthorized charges on them. The staff kept bringing her drinks and between the heat and humidity, and the potent alcohol, she had to slow down to only water with lemon. They wouldn't let her on the plane smashed.

She looked at the time on her phone. 10 a.m. She had to make her plane for 6 p.m. and that meant leaving there by four in the afternoon. That gave her six hours to track down the elusive Sean Cashman and accomplish her mission.

Only the said Mr. Cashman was missing in action and no one seemed to know where he was.

Her phone dinged with a text message. With dread she

looked down. But instead of Mr. Givens it was her best friend Samantha.

Sam: How's sun and fun in the VI?

Lexi's laugh garbled in her throat. This trip had been frustrating and strange.

Lexi: I won't have job tomorrow because Sean Cashman is MIA.

Sam: You'll nail it, grrl. You never give up. But tell me! Hook up with any cabana boys?

Lexi's tongue stuck out the corner of her mouth while she answered. Sam deserved a little teasing for being so nosy.

Lexi: No cabana boys. But I did meet Christian Grey in the flesh.

Sam: LOL. Liar.

Lexi: No lie. We went to a BDSM club last night.

Sam: WHAAAATTTT!!!! You kinky bitch.

Lexi: Shush, you. We just watched.

Sam: WATCHED???? Watched what?

Lexi: Can't say. Don't want to get shut down by the FCC for sending salacious material.

Sam: Bitch! Don't plan on going anywhere when you get back until you give me details.

Lexi: I don't know. I think I signed a confidentiality agreement. I'm legally bound not to reveal details.

Sam: Bound? I call bullshit! Lexi Elizabeth Winters, you ARE going to tell me EVERYTHING!

Lexi: [devil's head] LOL.

Lexi ignored several of Samantha's continuing texts trying to grill her on last night's events. She was going to pay for it when she got home, but seeing Sam's reactions gave her the laugh she needed for the day.

Lexi: Sorry. Must pay attention to cabana boy now.

Sam: WHAAATTTT!!!!

Heels clacked on the patio flagstones and Lexi looked up from her phone. There stood a woman that even another woman would call gorgeous. Her breasts jutted out in her skimpy top as if gravity had no purchase on her full globes. The bikini bottom was more of g-string and left nothing to the imagination. Her perfectly waxed body displayed nary a single stray body hair from her eyebrows to her feet. The woman's hair fell into unruly waves on her shoulders. Her fingers and toenails shined in perfect gloss and different shades of pinks, contrasting with her tan as if color coordinated. Even her tan was perfect and could only be the result of many hours perfecting it under a sun lamp.

She was the type of woman that nearly every woman compared themselves to and aspired to be. And, because she was the reminder of everything a woman wasn't, she was also what every woman hated on sight.

The woman huffed and lowered herself gracefully to the pool lounge chair as if instructed by Miss Porter's School of Grace and Charm on the proper way to do so.

Aware she was staring, Lexi lowered her eyes to the phone once again.

"Is there something I can get you, miss…"

"Givens," she said haughtily. "And you should remember that, because I will marry the owner of this hotel."

"Yes, Miss Givens."

Lexi took in this piece of information.

"Excuse me," Lexi said. "Are you related to Walker Givens?"

The woman leveled her sunglasses toward Lexi.

"Do you know my father?"

Like a dark plague that haunts my soul.

And the daughter's name? She was sure she'd heard it. Yes. Tiffany.

"I work at his firm."

Tiffany shrugged and pulled a phone from her beach bag.

"Well, it's good that you can enjoy the company discount for now."

"Why, what do you mean?"

But Tiffany didn't answer because her phone rang. Instantly she picked up the call with eager anticipation in her face. "Yes, oh hi, sweetie. Yes. I'm sitting at this dreadful pool missing you terribly. You wouldn't believe how pushy the staff is at this place. They wanted to come into my room, but I said no. Hell, I'm not going to let anyone in with the jewelry I have. Can you imagine that there aren't personal safes in the rooms? What a trashy place. It will be good when we get rid of it.

"Yes, Cash took me snorkeling. No, he didn't discuss an engagement. He seems put off by something. You sure he doesn't have another girlfriend? Maybe you should hire a better private investigator."

Lexi sunk in her seat, burying her nose further into her phone. Whoever Sean Cashman was, Tiffany was playing him hard. Having a private investigator follow him? That was dirty and not the fun kind, either.

"I don't know where he is," Tiffany said. Her nose scrunched up in consternation. "The hotel manager is no help at all. But he'll show up eventually. And I'll take him to a club and make sure he has too much to drink. Whenever I talk about his father, he puts a few too many away."

Lexi swallowed hard. Whatever this woman planned seemed nasty.

"I'll be engaged to him by the end of the night. I've been

waiting too long to take the name Mrs. Sean Cashman, and he won't put me off anymore."

Lexi sunk even deeper into her lounge chair. She wasn't trying to eavesdrop but this woman was indiscreet. And what Lexi heard was far above her pay grade. She thought about leaving but then reasoned that if she was to catch the elusive Sean Cashman before her deadline, this woman would provide the access key. And Tiffany was her boss's daughter, so in a sense she was just roping her into team Givens.

Yeah, Lexi, she thought miserably. She'd hitch her job to Givens' daughter's access to Sean Cashman, but she felt miserable about it. The poor schlub seemed to be drowning in the machinations of the Givens family.

Lexi had heard of the firm's most valuable client, but had never seen him. Sean Cashman wasn't inclined to show up at the office for convos with the firm's head man. But by this time she was inclined to think that Mr. Cashman must be some tired middle-aged businessman, with a paunch and bad breath, easily led by Lexi's boss and her boss' daughter.

It made her feel sick to her stomach.

If she could, she'd just climb back on that plane and find another job. Only the problem with that plan was, jobs were difficult to find in New York City and she'd practically had to beg and offer her firstborn child to get this promotion. Well, not exactly. But she put in the outrageous hours that Givens expected so that she was tapped to pick up the work of his last paralegal.

Sean Cashman's problems were not her problems. Hers was getting his signature on the contract sitting in the portfolio at the side of her chair. And she'd wait here until he showed up to get it.

The drink server came by and put down another water with lime.

"I have a note for you," he said.

Lexi, her natural curiosity piqued, opened the note and swallowed hard.

Come meet me in your room. I need to talk to you.

—Edward.

ENRICO COCKED HIS HEAD AT CASH'S QUESTION.

"What do you mean?"

"I met this girl."

"Yeah, mehson, I saw her. Stunning."

"She is, isn't she? Well, she's into what you are. But I haven't a clue as to what to do."

"You sure?" asked Enrico as he handed Cash a glass of OJ, "that she's into the scene?"

"Well, you saw her. She wasn't fazed by a single thing. Though she's not what you call compliant."

"What do you mean?"

"Well, on the plane I tried to draw her out, find out what she was into, but she said she wasn't my sub."

Enrico nodded. "That's normal. And healthy."

"Healthy?"

"We all have boundaries," Enrico said. "A sub with a poor sense of boundaries is messed up. And what we do for play has too many opportunities for someone to end up hurt, or in extreme cases, killed. So you want your partner to know who she or he is and what their limits are."

"Killed?" Cash said, shocked. He couldn't imagine doing anything that would kill a person.

"Yeah, mehson. We play with whips, chains, and ropes. There are other things too, like breath and knife play, things that are on the edge for seasoned players. There are isolated cases that make the news from time to time. And a death makes it harder to convince the vanilla world that kink isn't degenerate. We work hard to teach newbies how to play safely. We even have a term for it. RACK. Risk aware consensual kink."

"Really? What? You have classes in kink?"

Enrico shook his head. "No, mehson. When a newbie Dom or sub shows up to play, we invite him or her to community functions and see who they are. If a newbie Dom has potential, someone in the community will mentor or teach them. A newbie sub is mentored by an experienced Dom. There's a ton to learn. It's part artform, part craft, with physical and psychological parts. And since the Dom is the leader of the pairing, he or she has more to learn than the sub."

"Like what?"

"The biggest thing a Dom has to do is learn to listen."

"What? Learning how to handle the equipment isn't important?"

"See, right there, you weren't listening. Now how can you control a scene if you don't know what your submissive wants from you?"

"I don't know. I thought it was some spanking, some flogging, and—"

"Yeah. The shit they show on television. Violence and pain. Using a sub for what you want instead of what they want. Well, pain is part of it for some submissives, but not for all. Others enjoy the mindfuck more. Others just enjoy pleasing a powerful person. But the thing to remember is that a good sub is difficult to find. It is as personal as finding a spouse. Even harder is finding someone that enjoys what you like to dish out. That's the magic right there."

"You make it sound like a love affair."

"In some ways it is. Other ways it isn't. You can find someone that compliments your style of play, but on other levels a relationship wouldn't work. There are plenty of Doms and subs married to other people but get together to play."

"That sounds fucked up."

"Hey, you don't judge me and I don't judge you. Anytime you step out on a relationship is not good. But most times people play with the consent of their spouse. Otherwise, it is cheating plain and simple."

"I'm glad you have morals."

"Look. You want to talk about this, I will. But I won't stand for judgments. You came to the club. You saw what was there, how people treated each other. At the heart of true BDSM is respect for each other. It's a given that a sub shows respect for his or her Dom, but it works the other way too. A true Dom appreciates what the sub gives him or her. If he doesn't, he's just another asshole."

"Showing respect by beating someone's ass in public."

"What? It doesn't fit your definition of true love?" Enrico's voice turned caustic and Cash got the idea that he'd upset him.

"Hell, I don't know—"

"I get it, mehson. Not a romantic bone in your body. Strong men are like that, right? Stupid about what makes a partner happy?"

Cash scrubbed his face. Enrico pushed all his "I'm an idiot" buttons hard.

"Bro, I can see where the mindfuck thing comes in. You're good at it."

Enrico's eyes glittered with amusement.

"Sorry. I just want to show you that there is more to the BDSM thing than whips, chains, and calling your partner a slut. At least when it is done right."

"So, you're telling me that I shouldn't mess with a sub that knows more than me."

"No. Not at all. If you're new it's better to have a sub who knows how the game is played. Most of it is an illusion anyway, playacting, fulfilling a fantasy that excites you and your partner. But it is serious stuff, with potentially harmful consequences."

"So, back to the mentoring thing."

"Yes."

"How about you?"

"Me? No, mehson. We're too close. I don't want to know the freaky things in your head, and you don't want to know mine. But I'll tell you what I can do. I'll dig around my contacts in New York and come up with a couple names."

"That sounds like a great idea. Thanks." Cash took out his wallet and handed Enrico his business card. "My email's there."

Enrico took the card and nodded.

"So you won't come to the club tonight?"

"I don't know. I'll text you before I do."

"So tell me. What is up with you and Tiffany? You two have been an item for a long time."

Cash stood. "I haven't figured that out yet. I've known her forever. And there was a time when I thought we'd get married. But I think my priorities have changed."

"Yeah," Enrico said. "I think that's what's known as growing up."

"You're such an ass," snorted Cash.

"Yeah. Have to keep the rep going. Can't go soft now."

"I should go. Come up to New York sometime. I'll show you around."

"I just might when the tourist season is over."

"Sounds like a plan."

Cash stepped out into the heat and humidity of the island. The sun warmed his bones and seeped into him. It made him feel good on the outside, but not inside, not in the deepest part of him. Cash now had an uncomfortable dilemma. He wanted to explore things with Lexi, but it wasn't fair to her with Tiffany in the picture. And he had too many issues and questions about Tiffany to sort out in a single afternoon to send her packing.

No, despite the fact that Lexi drew him like no other woman, he had to place his company first. There were thousands of people that worked for Cashman Corporation, and Cash had to put their welfare above his.

His father would expect no less.

He had to find out why Walker Givens and Preston Lowe had a hard-on for selling his company. Cash needed to get to the bottom of the operational changes that were implemented without his permission and if there was a problem, he needed to get his company on track.

He didn't have time for a relationship with anyone.

There was nothing for it. He'd have to come clean with Lexi. Once she found out he wasn't the Dom he pretended to be, she'd probably lose interest in him anyway. He hated it, but it would be for the best. Lexi deserved the type of man that made her happy.

When he got to the hotel he went to Veranes' office and knocked on the door.

"Come in. Oh, Mr. Cashman. We have a little situation with your Miss Winters."

"Oh?"

"It seems her canvas bag with her laptop didn't make it down from Miss Givens' room."

"No clue where it is?"

"Housekeeping tried to find it, but Miss Givens wouldn't let them in her room."

Cash sighed.

"I'll see what I can do. Where is Miss Winters now?"

"She's sitting by the pool. And, sir, she asked for you."

"What did you tell her?"

"That I would pass along the messages."

"Here." Cash pulled a sticky note off Veranes' desk and wrote on it. "Give her this note. And where is Miss Givens?"

"Also by the pool."

Cash was glad he'd come there before looking through the hotel for either of them. The last thing he needed was facing both of them at the same time.

"Tell Miss Givens that I want to see her in her room in about twenty minutes."

"Yes, sir."

Cash walked quickly to the elevators to go the second floor to wait for Lexi. He wasn't sure what he was going to tell her but he had to make it quick. Tiffany was not a woman to keep waiting.

19

LEXI'S HEART RACED IN HER CHEST AS SHE TOOK THE ELEVATOR to the second floor. She shouldn't be nervous, but when she thought of the handsome hotel owner, wetness pooled in a sloppy mess in her panties. She was appalled at her own arousal, but thoughts of Edward swirled around his sexy body, his voice, and thoughts of the things he'd do to her body.

She shouldn't have done this. Lexi needed to stay around Tiffany to capture the attention of the elusive Mr. Cashman. And the clock was ticking.

But as soon as she saw the note, the compulsion to do as he said filled her. It was as if she'd checked her self-determination at the door in favor of the dark promises that she wanted Edward to whisper to her.

As soon as the elevator door opened she saw him. He leaned against the wall with his arms crossed as if he contemplated the sins of the world. Edward looked up at her, but instead of the smile she expected, he regarded her with a serious expression.

"Hi, Lexi," he said.

She didn't like this at all. If he wasn't going be nice to her why did he ask her up to her to see him?

"Hi, Edward," she said coolly. "Out and about on the island on a Sunday?"

She walked past him to her room and used her new key to open it.

He followed and the door clicked shut, sealing them off from the world. Lexi went to the air conditioner and turned it on. She felt flushed and she fanned her face with her hand.

"Gee, this sun here is vicious," she said without looking at him.

"How are you doing?" he asked. His voice sounded dry and cracked.

"I'm fine," she said firmly. "Though my carry-on bag is missing. The porter didn't bring it last night."

"I'm sorry. I'm having the staff search for it now."

"Yes. That is what Veranes said. You didn't need to bring me up here to tell me that."

"You're right. And I didn't. I have to talk to you."

Lexi turned around and face him.

"About what?"

"I'm not...not..." he stuttered, "what you want."

"What is this?" snapped Lexi. "Is this the big brush-off? Where you tell me you are too broken for a nice girl like me, and that I should forget you."

"Oh god," he groaned. "That's not what I mean."

"Oh no? What's the excuse? 'It's not you, it's me'?"

Edward stepped forward and grabbed her wrists. He stared deeply into her eyes.

"Stop this," he commanded.

His eyes reached into her soul and touched a secret place deep inside her where she wanted to give everything to this man. His firm words made her shudder as his sheer power swept over her.

"You are the most beautiful woman I've ever seen."

"I doubt that," she said.

"That's only because you doubt yourself. But you shouldn't. You're perfect. Beautiful, smart, elegant. Any man would be lucky to have you."

"Just not you," she said bitterly.

"I have obligations. A company to run. This is a very bad time for me to get involved with someone else."

She scoffed. "The old 'it's not me, it's you' speech."

He closed his eyes as if he were battling a demon in his soul.

"I meant what I said. You deserve a better man than me. Someone who could give you what you want."

"Sure, sure. I get it."

"No, Lexi, you don't. I'm not—"

"What? Free? Are you trying to tell me that you are married?"

"No, Lexi! I'm not married. But we barely know each other. I have to go back to New York soon—"

Now Lexi was confused. Edward had said nothing about living in New York. She searched his face for answers but got none. What she did get, however, standing this close to him, was a good dose of his masculine scent. Her knees weakened under her.

Damn, she wanted him. Her body quivered with the nearness of him.

"New York? But you are the owner of the hotel. I thought that you lived here."

Edward shook his head. "No, Lexi. I don't. I come here occasionally."

"Then that's good. I live in New York too. But you have to know that. We came on the same plane together."

"From Newark. People go to Newark from around the area."

"Fine," she said as her tempered flared. "We both live in the same place but can't see each other. I get it." She met his eyes, challenging him to give her a better answer.

And it was swift. He lowered his head and pressed his lips to hers. Fire spread through her as he reached around her waist and pulled her to him. His mouth possessed hers as his raw power rolled off him, engulfing her in his passion.

His hips met hers as he hugged her tighter, nearly stealing the breath from her as his hard cock jutted into her. He pulled away and instinctively her mouth followed but he put two fingers to her lips. His other hand drew hers to cover his rock-hard cock. It thrilled her to know that she could make him desire her that much.

"That's what you do to me, Lexi," he said hoarsely. "You make me want everything you have, all you can give."

Lexi rubbed her hand against his bulging length and he groaned.

"What do you want me to give you?" she said.

His eyes flashed.

"Get on your knees," he said in a husky voice.

Trembling, Lexi sank to her knees and gazed up at him. He met her eyes and didn't take them off her as he lowered his zipper and pushed down his pants and what he wore under. His cock stood against his stomach.

His cock was as gorgeous as he was. It was long and thick, and Lexi shuddered in pleasure at the thought of it in her mouth.

"You want this?" he said.

"Yes," she squeaked.

"Yes, what?" he said firmly.

"Yes, sir."

"Touch it," he commanded. He pulled her hand up and curled her fingers around his shaft with his hand. "Yes, that's it. Put your other hand on it. Jack me, Lexi. Let me know how much you want this cock."

Lexi moved her hands. She loved the feel of velvet in steel within her hand.

"Your hands are so soft, like cotton. I love fucking your hands, Lexi. You are so good at this. Open your mouth and let go."

Lexi opened her mouth and he guided his cock to her mouth. He put the head on her lips and traced them with the tip. His precum smeared on her lips.

His musk was stronger and it overwhelmed her.

"You want this cock?"

"Yes, sir."

"What will you do for this cock?"

"Whatever you want." She breathed, hardly believing his dirty words and how much she loved hearing them. She felt sexy and powerful, as if she was the only woman in the world that could make him this hard, make him want her this much. Her panties captured copiously flowing cream and the heat of it lit her sex like liquid fire.

"We will meet when and where I say. It can't be any other way. You won't call me. I'll call you."

He held the head of his cock just beyond the touch of her lips. She took in the pungent scent of his precum and wanted, no, needed to taste it in her mouth. Her lips trembled when she spoke.

"Whatever you want."

He stared at her, his eyes stormy and filled with desire.

When he stepped back, she gasped in surprise. Lexi thought for sure that he wanted her to wrap her lips around his cock.

Instead he lifted her to her feet.

"You are so precious, you know that?" he said. "When will you be back in New York?"

"My plane leaves today."

He nodded.

"Mine leaves tomorrow."

"Oh." She was confused. What was happening? Was that it? He didn't want her to do anything else?

He pulled his phone from his pocket, unlocked it, then handed it to her.

"Put your number in."

Lexi did so, even though her hands trembled. Then she held the phone out to him. He pocketed it without looking at it.

"Good girl. I have to go now. I'll have Veranes call you when he finds your laptop. And if he doesn't, I'll get you a new one. You know, just like Christian Grey got one for Ana." He winked at her.

She blinked, not understanding the reference. But she couldn't let him know that. "Oh, right."

He pulled up his pants and zipped up. Then he smiled a megawatt smile, the kind that only all-American pretty boys could generate.

"You are stunning, Lexi Winters. I can't wait to see you again."

He kissed her swiftly, this one without passion but carrying the promise of more kisses to come. And then he was out her door faster than she could say goodbye.

20

CASH

IT WAS WHEN HE ENTERED THE ELEVATOR THAT IT STRUCK HIM how foolish he was. He'd left Lexi without accomplishing what he set out to do—let her down easy. No. Instead he entangled himself more with the luscious creature.

His hard-on refused to settle, especially when he thought of how sexy it was to rub the tip against her lips. It was so hot he almost blew right then and there. But everything he read about Doms indicated that they exercised control in setting the scenes with their subs. Instinctively he knew he would ruin things if he took advantage of her submission at that moment. It felt right not to push things further, to not use her for his gratification when he didn't have the time to see to hers.

But he was unprepared at how seeing her kneel before him jacked his arousal. Power coursed through him when this beautiful woman would do anything he asked. It was unlike any feeling he had before with a woman.

Admittedly his experience with women was thin. Being with Tiffany all these years left him few opportunities to explore the possibilities with other women. Not that he didn't have opportunities. There were a couple of school semesters when they gave each other a break from their relationship. It was because, as Tiffany said, they knew they had forever, so it didn't matter if they had a couple of dalliances. She never asked him about his nor he of hers.

But there was no one, Tiff included, that gripped him like Lexi. It was a strange feeling. His relationship with Tiffany was one of shared history, and enjoying doing the same things. At least, he thought she enjoyed the sports, the skiing, and the travel to other countries they did together. But the sexual excitement or the romantic feelings he'd seen in the media didn't seem to apply. He decided that they overdramatized things to make the movie or show more interesting, but normal people didn't feel that way.

And now here was Lexi, who released a floodgate of emotions he didn't know he had. It was exhilarating and frightening at the same time. When she got angry at him, he got angry too, but not at her. At himself. He'd be a total idiot to let this woman slip away from him. He would just have to find a way to make it work.

He walked off the elevator to go to Tiffany's room. He hoped she'd done as he asked. With Lexi, he was sure she'd be in the room when he asked. And that was the difference between Tiffany and Lexi. He was beginning to suspect that Tiffany paid lip service to Cash's wants and desires, while he was absolutely certain Lexi wanted to make him happy.

Clearly, he couldn't stay with Tiffany any longer than it would take to find out what was going on with his company. Then he'd be free to pursue a relationship with Lexi.

He came to Tiffany's door and knocked on it.

She swung it open.

"Well, there you are, sweetie," she said with a huge

smile. "I was beginning to think you ditched me for an island beauty."

"No. I visited an old friend. You remember Enrico."

She wriggled her nose in distaste. He never noticed before that she did that.

"Yes. The guy who taught you to snorkel."

He touched the tip of her nose. "There you go. You do remember."

She looked him up and down. Her eyes narrowed at the shorts and t-shirt he wore.

"Is this how you intend to take me out to eat?"

"You know, I left so quickly, I didn't even pack. I've been buying things out of the gift shop."

"Well, I suppose we should go to a proper store and get you something to wear."

"Really, I have a suit downstairs."

"A suit? For island dining? I don't think so. You'd be terribly overdressed. We'll get you some nice slacks and a couple of shirts. Would you like a drink? I have a few things here to make one." She moved into the kitchenette area and ice clinked in a glass.

"No. Thanks."

Cash cast his eye around the room trying to spot Lexi's bag.

"Hey, how's the service been for you? Was the room nice and clean?"

She walked toward him from the kitchenette and handed him a glass.

"It's dreadful here. You know that, Cash. I found some-one's bag."

"Oh, where is it?"

"Oh, here somewhere." She swept her hand across the room indicating Lexi's bag could be anywhere.

"Where? I'll take it downstairs."

"Oh no, Sean Cashman. You've left me hanging for most of the trip. I'm not going to let you get away again."

That's what happens, Cash thought sourly, *when you show up uninvited.*

"No, really. What if a guest is looking for it?"

Tiffany sighed and then smiled. She took the glass from his hand and set it on the table and wrapped her arms around his neck.

"Darling. You work too hard. And you are not paying attention to me. Now, I suggest that we go shopping and get you some decent clothes. Then we'll find ourselves a nice place to eat our lunch and we can plan out the rest of our little vacation. I hear a new place across the bay has a fabulous restaurant and dancing too. It's been forever since we went dancing."

"I'm leaving tomorrow."

"Then I'll leave with you. But we have nearly a whole twenty-four hours before then and I'd like to spend it with my favorite guy in the whole world."

He smiled, though it was more like a grimace.

"Okay. Then let's go. But let's take that bag downstairs. I hate to disappoint a guest."

"Oh, if you must. I probably put it in the closet."

Cash found the bag just as she said, and gave a sigh of relief; the laptop sat inside. Lexi's wallet was there too. The porter just overlooked it when he picked up the bags. He was glad Lexi's things hadn't been pilfered.

Not that he minded the idea of buying her a new laptop.

In fact, there were a lot of things he wanted to buy for her.

"Found it," he said.

Tiffany shrugged, but she picked up her designer bag

and they left the room and headed for the lobby. Tiffany chatted on about something, but Cash wasn't listening.

The elevator door opened and Cash walked ahead of Tiffany. As he headed toward the front desk he heard a familiar voice.

"You can't tell me where Mr. Cashman is?" she said. "Look, my boss sent me here with some very important papers to sign. I need to find him."

Cash rounded the corner and confirmed his suspicions. It was Lexi standing at the desk asking for him.

No. It couldn't be. Lexi didn't work for Walker Givens, did she?

"Lexi?" he said.

She turned her head to him and flashed a smile. When she saw her bag in his hand her grin got wider.

"Oh, you found it! Thank you, Edward."

Tiffany brought up his rear.

"Edward?" Tiffany said. "Who's Edward? Cash? What is this woman talking about?"

Lexi looked to Tiffany, then him, with her eyes wide.

"You're Sean Cashman?" she said. Her voice was as thin as tissue paper.

"Of course he's Sean Cashman," snapped Tiffany. "And who are you again?"

"Lexi Winters. I work for your father as his paralegal."

"You do? You must be new. I haven't heard of you."

"But I've heard of you. You're Sean's girlfriend."

"Why yes, I am." She smiled and her brilliant white teeth stood out in contrast with her bright pink lipstick.

Cash watched his life implode in front of his eyes. Lexi's face turned absolutely red with anger. Tiffany remained clueless.

"We'll trade bags," Lexi said. "Here are the papers you

are supposed to sign." She slammed a leather portfolio case on the granite counter of the front desk. "I'll take my bag now, thank you very much, Mr. Sean Cashman." She held out her hand for the canvas bag.

"Lexi, this isn't what it seems."

"It isn't? You haven't lied to me about your name? Or the fact that you were in a relationship? Is anything you told me about yourself true?"

"Lexi, please let me explain."

"Cash," Tiffany said. "What is going on?"

"Give me my bag, Mr. Cashman, and I won't bother you anymore."

Cash reluctantly held it out and Lexi swiped it out of his hand with fury.

"Lexi, please."

"I've got a plane to catch, so goodbye, Mr. Cashman. And please, do feel free to lose my phone number."

Her shoes slapped the granite floor loudly as her feet took her to the elevator. To Cash, those footsteps sounded like the world ending. The floor opened up below him, just as it had so many times this past year, as he watched the elevator doors close to take her away from him.

21

LEXI

By the time Lexi reached her hotel room, her body quaked with two things.

Anger and desire.

She wanted to slam Edward, no, *Sean Cashman*, against the wall and crush his testicles with her bare hands.

And she wanted to kiss those balls too. Sean's scent still teased her nose, and each time she breathed, she thought of his hard cock inside her. Heat pooled between her thighs and snaked through her core, hijacking the thinking parts of her brain.

She told herself it was the interrupted blowjob and the desire that flooded her as she knelt and he touched his cock to her lips that stressed her. She reminded herself he made her beg for it and then teased her. That ticked her off so much that every one of her muscles shook from head to toe. The shock of finding out who Edward was was the cherry on top of the volcano of her growing rage.

Fuck, fuck me, she thought as her hands shakily guided her card key in the slot. It wouldn't open.

"Fuck!" she exploded as she tried the door again. That fucker better not have locked her out of her room.

"Is there something I can do for you, miss?" said a maid. Her badge identified her as a supervisor.

"Yes! My key won't work."

"Let me see?" The woman took it and inspected the number. "The lock system is glitchy. Here, I'll let you in with my key. The master keys always work."

"Thank you!"

"I'll let the desk know you had trouble, and get them to make you a new key."

"Don't bother. I'm checking out."

"I hope we haven't failed to serve you properly."

"No. It is time for me to leave. I'm catching a plane this afternoon, and I should get going."

"I'll call a porter for you to get your bags."

"You don't have to."

"No worries. We wouldn't have a job otherwise. Are you leaving soon?"

"Yes, now."

"'I'll call him then."

"Thank you."

The woman poked at her phone and then worked her key in the lock. Relief flooded Lexi as the door opened.

She swept the room picking up personal items and throwing them in her bag. As she zipped her luggage, her phone rang. Her stomach clenched when she saw it was Mr. Givens.

"Lexi, is that contract signed?"

"Hello to you, Mr. Givens. I gave it to Mr. Cashman."

"What? It's not signed?" he said gruffly.

"He's busy with Tiffany. She's here." It was difficult to

keep her voice neutral and not edge her words with sarcasm. Lexi hated that she cared that much for the snake.

"Oh, yes," Mr. Givens said. The bluster in his voice eased. "Well, that's important too. They haven't spent much time together lately. But once he signs the contract, he'll have time to devote to my daughter, and maybe give me some grandkids."

Lexi's eyes flew open. Children?

"Of course, after they marry," he said.

"Of course," parroted Lexi. What a lowdown fucking skunk. Tiffany? His fiancée? Well, Tiffany was welcome to him! And good luck to her, because she'd need it.

"Check with him before you leave and ask if he had a chance to look it over."

"Okey dokey," Lexi said. No fucking way did she want to set eyes on Sean Cashman again. But the reality of her situation hit her. Technically, Givens could fire her for refusing to follow the order of her employer. That was no joke. Okay. She'd have to just speak to him once before she left. What happened to that stupid contract after that was Givens' problem.

"Okey dokey?" said Givens incredulously. "Have you been drinking, Ms. Winters?"

Lexi rolled her eyes.

"No." Not that she didn't want to. In fact, when she got on the plane she'd order several glasses of wine.

"No. I don't feel well. I may have picked up something down here, a stomach bug or food poisoning."

"Well, don't bring it into the office. Take tomorrow off and see a doctor. If he clears you, you can come back to work."

"That's very generous of you, Mr. Givens," she said. She almost puked in her hand speaking those words. The bastard stole her weekend, and was "giving" her one day off in return? And he might let her come to work if a doctor cleared her? She needed to find a new job.

A knock on the door rescued her.

"I need to go, sir. The porter is here to get my bags."

"Don't forget to check with Mr. Cashman about those papers."

"I won't. Goodbye."

She clicked off the phone, even more irate. A moment of clarity hit her, shimmering off her like a waterfall. All around her were jerks, well, except for her best friend, Samantha. Lexi needed to get a better playbook, a better plan for getting what she wanted and deserved. She didn't need jerks, like Trevor, Sean, and Mr. Givens, who tried to use her. Somewhere in New York City, there had to be people who would appreciate her work, and her as a person. Hell, New York was a city of over eight and a half million people. Her life didn't demand definition by these three.

With this new resolve, she opened the door for the porter and pointed to her bags. She shouldered the canvas bag because she didn't want to lose it again, and took one last look around while the porter waited patiently.

"Let's go."

Lexi tapped her foot the whole time the elevator descended to the first floor. When the elevator opened, she took a deep breath. When Lexi finished speaking with *Mr. Cashman,* she could leave for the airport. There she could drown her sorrows with a drink or two before she boarded.

"Where do you want these, miss?"

"Is there a place you can put them at the door."

"Yes, miss. I can leave them with the doorman."

"Please do." She fished a five out of her wallet handed it

to him. "And please ask the doorman to call me a cab. I won't be long."

"Very good, miss." Lexi stalked to the desk, like a jungle cat hunting prey, and stopped in front of it. The young woman there was staring at her iPhone, and Lexi had to tap the bell to get her attention.

"Excuse me. I'm looking for Mr. Cashman."

The young woman glanced up from her iPhone. "Who?"

"The man that owns this hotel."

"Oh, that one," she said. "Don't know. Don't care. He's trouble."

"Is there a way to page him? I have a message from his lawyer."

"Lawyer? Is he in trouble with the law?" She looked happy at the prospect, making Lexi uncomfortable.

"No. And I'm not at liberty to discuss this with you. But it is urgent I speak with him."

"I'll take a message for you."

"No. I need to speak to him in person."

The girl rolled her eyes. "Oh, okay. I'll page the manager." She spoke grudgingly, as if she was performing a favor for Lexi. Pursing her lips, Lexi turned and scanned the lobby. She swung her eyes toward the gift shop and spotted a crown of blond hair crossing through the store window.

"Never mind," she snapped to the front desk clerk. "I see him."

Lexi screwed her courage and purposefully stepped to the gift shop. Yes. That was Edward, or rather, Sean Cashman. He stood at a rack with men's shirts and rifled through them. Lexi pulled open the door and stalked toward him.

"Excuse me, Mr. Cashman," she said abruptly.

Cash jumped and then caught her eyes.

"Lexi," he said hoarsely.

"Mr. Givens asked me to ask you if you signed the papers I gave you."

Cash's eyes turned stormy. "No. I'll tell Mr. Givens I will discuss them with him upon my return."

"Very good," she said crisply. She turned on her heels toward the door.

"Lexi—"

She gave him a glance that would shrivel any man's private parts to the size of pebbles. "Mr. Cashman."

"Can we talk?"

"Gee, with whom should I talk? Edward or Sean?"

"You're right. I wasn't honest with you."

"Then we agree on something. Good. I've gotta go now."

"Lexi, please. I want to ex—"

Just then Tiffany burst from one of the dressing rooms, sporting a dress with a tag on it. She worked the walk like a runway model, from the dressing room to the rack where Cash stood.

"Cash, what do—" She stopped when she saw Cash and Lexi staring at each other. "What is going on here?" she said. Suspicion edged her voice as if she expected Lexi was trying the steal Cash.

"I was relaying a message from your father to Mr. Cashman. And leaving now."

"Yes," said Tiffany. "You do that."

"Goodbye, Mr. Cashman. Have a good life." Lexi flounced out of the gift shop swishing her ponytail with indignation.

22

CASH

HOW THE HELL DID HIS LIFE GET SO FUCKED UP? As LEXI walked away—again—his heart dropped to the floor. He wanted to run after her, to explain—what? That was the kicker. Cash never intended to get involved with Lexi, and now here he was, in lust with her, and possibly falling in love. Thinking about that was a shock, but Tiffany threw a bucket of ice water over him by speaking.

"Cash?" she said, "is there something I should know about?"

He leveled his gaze to the beautiful but vapid woman before him.

"Tiffany, I'm sorry. I just can't do this right now."

"Do what?"

"You and me. I've got to go."

"Go? Where?"

"Bye, Tiffany. I'll catch up with you in New York."

Tiffany called his name as he walked away. He thought briefly, there wasn't a single woman he hadn't acted an asshole toward. He'd have to apologize to Tiffany, but he had to get to Lexi. Of all the idiotic things he'd done, letting her walk away was the stupidest. He didn't know how he could make up for his lying to her, but he had to try.

"Cash?" Tiffany said following him, clacking her stilettos on the lobby marble floor.

Cash flung himself out the front door to see Lexi closing a cab door.

"Lexi!" he called.

But the cab drove away too fast for Cash to catch up.

"Sean Cashman," Tiffany said. Her face was red and her tone indignant, but he didn't care. Not right now.

"Get me a cab and charge it to the hotel," he ordered the doorman.

"Right away, Mr. Cashman."

"Sean Cashman," Tiffany spouted. "What the hell is going on?"

"Tiffany, I swear to God, if you don't back off—"

"Are you threatening me?" she screeched theatrically.

"No."

"Sounds like a threat to me, Sean. You've been acting far too unstable for too long. I worry about you, darling, but now I absolutely insist that you seek help. I simply won't marry a mentally unstable man."

Sean laughed at the ridiculousness of her words. "Sure, you worry about me so fucking much that you are sleeping with someone else behind my back."

"Sean! I don't know where this paranoia comes from, but I am not cheating on you. I value our love too much for that. Please, darling. Seek help. You need it desperately."

"Me? It's you that's delusional if you think I'm going to marry you."

"We've planned it for forever."

A taxi drove up and the doorman opened the door for Cash.

"Plans change," he said. He climbed into the taxi and the doorman shut the door.

"Airport," he told the driver.

Cash tapped his fingers on his knees as the cab took them to the ferry. A part of him told him he'd acted recklessly leaving Tiffany behind. And she never spouted off at him, not with words like that. Need help? Paranoia? Where was that coming from? Cash was sure what he heard when Tiffany was on the phone Friday night. She was fucking someone. And curiously, Cash didn't care.

He supposed that he should, but what spark and sizzle that had existed between them didn't exist anymore. Cash wasn't exactly sure when they lost the fire, but somewhere between college and his father's death, their relationship became boring. Routine. Expected.

After being with Lexi, he couldn't go back to Tiffany. Maybe he and Lexi didn't have a future today, but he was sure he and Tiffany did not.

But when they got to the ferry, it had already left, and it would be an hour before another departed. Cash signed for the trip on the driver's phone app, and climbed out. When was her plane going to leave?

He searched Cashman Air to find the next flight at 4 p.m. But it was three now. With a sinking heart, he resigned himself to the fact that there was no way he could catch that flight.

Cash checked the next flight, which took off at 8 p.m., and decided to take that one. At least he could get into the office tomorrow and start working on what was going on in his company.

A taxi drove up, and Cash groaned when he saw Tiffany get out.

"Hi, Cash," she said brightly as if nothing had changed

between them. "I booked myself on the eight o'clock flight. I just adore first class on your airline. And I was so lucky to get a seat too. But I'm sure you can get our seats changed so we can sit together."

Cash suppressed a groan.

"Well, actually, I'll ride in the flight deck."

"What?" she said with a pout. "You can't do that. Isn't there a law about that?"

"For regular passengers, yes. Employees of the company can ride with the pilot-in-charge's agreement. I'm pretty sure he isn't going to tell his boss no."

Technically, the law didn't allow a person to sit in the pilot's cabin without a valid operational permit. But he reasoned he needed to study each aspect of the operation because of some irregularities he'd noticed. At least, that was what he'd tell anyone who asked.

"Can I sit with you?"

"No. I've already explained that only employees can ride in the pilot's cabin."

"Oh, well. I guess I'll just have to settle for a late dinner with you tonight."

Was Tiffany that crazy? Or did the shock of his telling her their relationship was over push her over the edge? He pinched the bridge of his nose.

"Tiff, I'm calling it a night when I get in. By the time I debark and make it to my apartment, I'll be ready to turn in."

"Cash," she wheedled. "You're no fun. But I'll stay at your apartment tonight, since it takes so very long to get to the Hamptons from Newark."

"If you want, I'll pay for a hotel room for you in the city, but you aren't staying at my apartment."

Tiffany huffed and Cash got the wild idea to cancel her

plane reservation and make her go back tomorrow. This situation was getting out of hand. But, of course, that wouldn't work. He was too entangled business-wise with her father to annoy Walker Givens, and the one thing, or rather person, Givens cared about, was Tiffany.

"Fine," she said with a sigh. "I can tell you need some time alone. But don't expect me to wait for you, Sean Cashman. I'm getting a little tired of being ignored."

Tiffany at first gave him the stink-eye as they settled into the passenger section of the ferry. But when that didn't work, she sidled up next to him on the bench and leaned her head on his shoulder.

"Perhaps," she murmured, "I haven't paid enough attention to you. I can understand why I've upset you." With that, Tiffany slid her hand to his crotch and palmed his bulge.

"Tiffany, stop."

"Oh, come on, baby. Isn't this wicked fun? Here." She pulled off her sweater and laid it across his lap. "No one will see."

"No," he said flatly.

"Well, tell me what you want, baby. Tiffany is here to give it to you."

Cash stared hard into Tiffany's eyes. *Can you do what I want, Tiffany?* he thought. *Will you let me do whatever I desire with you? How about letting me take control of your orgasms and make you squirm, beg, and plead to have them? Will you let me take your soul, Tiff, and hand it back to you at my pleasure?*

But staring at the stunningly beautiful but hollow blue eyes, he knew Tiffany didn't have the capacity to give what wasn't in her.

"What you don't get, Tiffany, and I'm sorry to say this so plainly, but I don't want you. Not anymore. You're a great gal, and any man would be lucky to get you. But I'm not ready to settle down, and if I did, I doubt it would be with you."

Tiffany jerked up and her eyes blazed with indignation. "You're telling me to go away? When everyone in our social set knows we're getting married? Well, I'll inform you of one thing, Mr. Sean Cashman. You will not humiliate me in that way. I've invested everything I have into this relationship, and I'm not willing to throw it away because you get a wild hair to...to sow your wild oats." The last four words she huffed out indignantly.

"If everyone in our social set knows we're getting married, it's only because you told them. And you had no business doing so. Period. I didn't give you a ring, and to tell you the absolute bald truth, this past year I barely missed you. What kind of marriage would that make? And when I heard you talking to your 'sweetie' on Friday, that clinched it. It's really very obvious, whether you want to believe it or not, that we've grown past each other. It was a nice dream when we were younger, but we all grow up, Tiffany."

The ferry bumped against the dock, signaling the end of the ride.

"Grown past each other?" she said. "We'll see about that."

23

It was dark. Or Lexi was blindfolded. Her breaths, threatening to run away from her, reverberated in soft huffs in the quiet room. Lexi was on her stomach. A rolled towel placed under her breasts and a pillow under her hips reduced the unwelcome discomfort from her large breasts pressing into the mattress. Ropes pulled her arms out and held them in place. Her knees were bent and tied to spread her legs apart and her intimate reaches exposed. She tested the bindings and found her lower half covered in an intricate weave that kept her calves in the air and roped to her waist. She relaxed into it, safe and secure. But it gave her a chill that her womanhood was open and vulnerable to whoever was in the room. Her cream released in a wet gush and her breathing sped up anticipating unnamed pleasurable tortures.

She felt movement on the silk sheets and heard the soft breaths of another person. Softness unexpectedly touched her spine, and she jumped. It must be a feather, and whoever wielded it was a master of it. It traveled the length of her spine and her neck, to behind her ears and down again.

Lexi gasped.

"Careful, now," said her torturer in a low sexy rumble. "No sounds."

She swallowed hard and nodded her head in agreement. He worked the feather between the crook of her knees and her sex clenched, and she had to bite her lip to keep from huffing her excitement. How could touching such an innocuous place bring her closer to the edge? She wanted to whimper, but all she could do was center on her breathing to keep from making a sound. And this drove her deeper into herself, to focus on sensation and reaction. She didn't need to worry about whether or not she pleased someone with what she was doing or with her looks. Her torturer took pleasure in this, drawing her reactions, and orchestrating the next assault on her senses to jack her higher.

The feather swept up her spine again, almost with the intensity of light spanking on her exposed bottom. She jerked within her restraints.

"Sssh, sshh," the man said. His finger pressed into the small of her back, this time drawing a gasp. Every inch of her body fired with electric sparks and just this barest touch jolted her. Indeed, she arched her back, and a small sound escaped her throat.

"Oh," he said with disappointment in his voice. "Just when you were doing so well. Now, I'll have to punish you."

A tear came to her eye at her shame in disappointing him. She bit her lip and nodded her head.

A firm hand slapped one cheek of the globes of her ass. Fire spread through it, and then soothing swirls of care from that same instrument of torture.

"Count," he ordered.

"One," she said. It was up to him how many strikes he made to her bottom, but she suspected that she wouldn't care in a few more. Her boundaries loosened, and she flew as her endorphins rushed to protect her from further pain. Indeed, he did strike her again, but she barely felt it.

"More," she groaned. She wanted to climb higher, and the more pain he administered, the higher she went.

"That's it," he rumbled menacingly. "You are getting it now."

Yes!

The sound of his zipper coming undone filled her ears. She was wet, swimming in herself, and she wanted this. In one smooth thrust, he filled her and she jerked her hips closer to him. But he stilled, causing her to try to squirm, but the ropes prevented it.

"You are so fucking wet," he said. "Speak!"

"You make me wet. You make me want you. Fuck me. Fuck me hard."

"You want this cock?"

"I want nothing but your cock. Fuck me."

So he began his final assault, fucking her hard, his breaths slamming one after another out of his chest as he jackhammered her sex. Her breaths raced out of her at a furious pace. Caught and plateaued in subspace, she cried out in frustration.

"More. Fuck me, dammit!"

She woke with a jolt, breathing hard and with an impossible pool of wetness between her legs. What the fuck? Did she just have a hot BDSM dream?

Apparently.

And what's more, she was still horny. Squirming, in fact, to have a hot cock between her legs.

When did she become so wanton?

When she met Edward, AKA Sean fucking Cashman.

Lexi hated that Sean played her. She was smart enough not to fall for the tricks of men who only wanted one thing.

But then she thought about his die-for body, and his sexy eyes, and sensual mouth, and before she realized it her fingers found the sensitive flesh between her legs. Lexi replayed every second of that dream that seemed all too real, and imagined Edward/Sean filling her, taking her, mastering her body. Her toes curled as the shock of orgasm crashed through her. She may have cried out.

The knock on her bedroom door confirmed it.

"Are you okay?" Samantha said.

Lexi's face flushed as she gathered her comforter around her like a fabric fortress to ward off the prying eyes of her best friend. Samantha took to bursting in unannounced, and it was a grace from God that she didn't now.

"I'm fine," croaked Lexi.

The door creaked open. "You don't sound fine. Hey, girl, you look flushed. And you're sweating. Girl, did you catch some island bug?"

Yeah. And his name is Sean Cashman.

"No. I just had a dream I was still on the island on the beach. One of those dreams that seem real."

"Uh-huh," Sam said with suspicion her voice. She walked to the bed and put her hand on Lexi's forehead. "You're hot."

"Stop flirting," deadpanned Lexi.

"Please. If girls were my thing, you'd be my thing. We've established that, haven't we?"

"Yes, we did. In tenth grade when we spent New Year's together and kissed each other at midnight."

"Well, you turned out to be the person who loved me most that year, but nope, I firmly play on Team Hetero. But seriously, I think you are running a fever."

"Doesn't matter," Lexi said. "I have to go to work anyway to get fired."

"What happened on that island?" Samantha said. Her eyes widened in shock.

"I didn't get the job done. But don't worry. I'm sure I'll get severance, and I have some bucks put away for the prover-bial rainy day."

"I'm not worried about that, silly. You've covered me enough times I owe you. I am more worried about your shiv-ering ass. Take the day off."

Her phone dinged a text, and she picked it up.

Mr. Givens: Day off canceled. I need to speak to you ASAP.

Hell. What did he want? She planned to go into the office, check out the lay of the land, and get her résumé off the company server. After that, she'd claim a vicious migraine and leave. Lexi wanted to get as far away from Givens and Cashman, et al., as fast as she could.

She stuck her phone in Samantha's face. "Can't. The bossman speaketh. If I call in sick, he'll think I'm putting off the inevitable."

"What the hell happened on that island?" Samantha demanded.

"What happens on St. Johns, stays on St. Johns," Lexi said.

Samantha stuck her tongue out at her. "Brat," she said. "Don't think you are getting out of giving me the juicy details. Dinner and drinks after work at Romallo's."

Lexi groaned. Dinner and drinks at Romallo's meant beer and greasy pizza, and right now her stomach pitched at the idea of it.

"Get off my bed," Lexi said. "I have to get a shower and then the subway."

"Oh, no, you don't. I'm calling you an Uber."

"Don't be silly."

"Nope. I don't want my best friend arrested for being a nuisance to the public health."

"Oh, for heaven's sake," Lexi said with exasperation. "When did you become my mother?"

"Fifth grade, when I nursed you back to health during that case of the measles."

"That wasn't measles. It was poison ivy, and you made me run through it to get the soccer ball we were kicking."

"You remember everything," groaned Samantha. "So don't forget Romallo's." She winked. "I call shower first! Early meeting."

"What!" Lexi said indignantly. She flung the covers from her, but Samantha had already fled Lexi's bedroom and slammed the bathroom door shut.

Of course, that was the reason Samantha called the Uber, so Lexi wouldn't be late what with Sam taking the bathroom out of the established order. As the Uber crawled through Manhattan traffic, Lexi reflected how very lucky she was to have Samantha as her best friend. But, Lexi thought as the car pulled up to her office building, she wasn't so fortunate working for Walter Givens. She suspected that was going to change today.

Lexi squared her shoulders and entered the building to face her fate.

24

CASH

HIS SECRETARY GREETED HIM AS HE WALKED INTO HIS OFFICE. Ann was a thick woman in her forties who usually wore her hair in a bun and dressed in business suits. She ran his office with frightening efficiency. As he entered, she gave him an acid glance as if someone had forced her to swallow lemon juice straight. But then Cash supposed his current brusque attitude didn't do much to cultivate warm and fuzzies in even his closest staff.

"Get me Walker Givens on the phone." No "please," or "thank-you." He didn't have that in him now.

"Uh, that's not necessary, sir. Mr. Givens and his daughter are in your office."

Marvelous. Just what he wanted to face first thing in the morning.

"When did they arrive?"

"About fifteen minutes ago," she said.

"And?" Ann's expertise included scoping out and giving the "weather report" on the people who came into his office. It was one of the reasons that he paid her as well as he did.

"I can't describe it. Weird."

"Weird?"

She shrugged. "Stranger than usual. They both walked into your office like they owned it."

"Okay. Tell Mr. Lowe I want him in my office ASAP."

"Yes, Cash."

Cash entered his office.

"Ah, Cash," Givens said.

"Darling," Tiffany said.

"Good morning," he said brusquely. He walked around both of them seated at his desk and sat in his chair. He leveled a steely gaze upon "Uncle Walker." Cash was not feeling the familial vibe today.

"What can I do for you today?" he said.

"Tiffany told me you had reservations about your relationship with her."

Cash flicked a glance at Tiffany, who looked away. Somehow, she looked like the cat that swallowed the canary. What was she up to?

"I told her, plainly, that it's over between us."

"Really?" Givens said arching an eyebrow. "That's a little abrupt, isn't it?"

"I think it's a decision I put off since my father's death. But now, a year later, I'm ready to move forward with my life."

"But it's so abrupt, sweetheart! Don't you think?" Tiffany spoke sweetly.

"Yes," Givens said. "We worry about you, Cash. You haven't been acting yourself." Givens steepled his fingers. "And if you'll allow me to speak frankly, you haven't made decisions in your best interest."

"Like deciding not to marry Tiffany."

"And ignoring a lucrative business deal."

Cash nodded, keeping a lid on the anger seething inside

him. Not making decisions in his best interest? Or Walker Givens' best interest?

"Frankly, Cash, I'm beginning to think that your father's death has unmasked a certain instability in your personality."

"And you base this psychological observation on what? Not following your decisions in my life and my company?"

"Please, Cash. It's not like that," Tiffany said. "We just want the best for you. We love you. You are part of our family. And I'm so very concerned. You should see a doctor."

"I don't need a doctor," Cash said brusquely.

"Have you, at least, looked at the contract?" Givens said.

"I'll tell this to you once more, and then we drop the matter for discussion. I am not selling Cashman Industries. To anyone. For any price. And, no, I am not marrying Tiffany. Not that I asked her, and I'm sorry that things didn't work out. But I've decided that Tiffany is not the girl for me."

"Oh, and which girl is that?" Tiffany said shrilly. "That paralegal from my father's office?"

Cash's head jerked up.

"What?"

"Cash," Givens said. "I'm sorry. This is my fault. I told Lexi to be persuasive. I didn't realize she'd go overboard. Her actions were highly inappropriate."

"You're blaming Lexi for this? For my not wanting to marry Tiffany?"

"Oh, darling," cooed Tiffany. "She turned your head is all. I heard all about it from the front desk clerk. What was her name? Stephanie. Yes. She told me you put Lexi in your room. Though, honestly, darling, I thought you had better taste than that. But I forgive you. And in a week or two, you'll forget all about her."

"And you don't have to worry about seeing her again. I've discharged her from her duties," Givens said.

"You what!" roared Cash.

"I can't have someone with that kind of poor judgment working for me."

"Get out."

"Cash, you're upset and not thinking rationally."

"Get the fuck out of my office. And while you are at it— you're fired."

"Now, Cash," Givens said in a paternal voice.

"Both of you. Out of here."

A knock on the door interrupted him. Anne came in and again she had the sucking-a-lemon expression on her face.

"Preston Lowe is here."

"Please ask him to wait."

But Preston didn't. The smarmy businessman walked in, wearing a two-thousand-dollar Italian suit, smiling broadly, like he was working a room at a charity ball.

"Walker, Tiffany, how good to see you."

"They were just on their way out," Cash said gritting his teeth.

"Well, I hope they could talk sense into you. Once we get this company sold, we can all rest easy."

"You've talked to Walker Givens about the sale of the company? Without discussing it with me?"

"Cash, the Ramjet division has taken all your time. I couldn't get a conversation in with you about the need to sell the company. And it's a strategic merger, which will put a lot of cash in your pocket."

Cash stared at him, then Givens and Tiffany, all three conspirators working to rip his life apart.

"Preston, wait for me in my outer office."

"You still don't get it, do you? Without this sale, you'll have no money. Cashman Industries is near bankruptcy."

Cash put his hands on the desk to steady himself and swallowed hard.

"Bankruptcy? How is that possible?"

"It was in poor shape when I arrived," Preston said. "We tried everything, cut every corner, but overall we couldn't turn a profit."

"Without discussing any of this with me?"

"You were so withdrawn and depressed," Tiffany said. "After your father died, you buried yourself in your work. You didn't want to hear the details. And because of this we have serious concerns about your mental health."

"And what? Betrayal wasn't high on your list of mental health triggers?"

"Whoa," Preston said holding up his hands. "Right there is why your potential reaction concerned us. You need to put your paranoia away. Cashman Industries is in serious shit. And if you care at all about your employees, you'll think seriously about this deal, because it is the only way they will keep their jobs. Otherwise, the company will die, and your dream of putting Cashman engines in space will die with it."

Cash stared at the three manipulators in front of him. All three were slinging around terms like depression, mental health, and paranoia, and he shivered with the realization they were building a case to wrest his decisions from him. He had to slow down and play this right because these sharks were circling, waiting for any opening for the final takedown.

He sighed.

"You know what? You're right. I am just surprised is all. But you have underestimated me. It is supremely disappointing the company is doing this poorly, but I guess I'm not surprised. I want to see for myself, of course, before I finalize any decisions.

"Of course," Preston said. "I'll email you a summary."

"No. I want everything, all the financial reports, profit and loss statements, and the like."

"It will take me some time to get it together."

"Then do it. I'll not sign anything until I examine all the records."

"But you will sign?" Givens asked.

"If things are as dire as you say, of course."

"Oh, darling," Tiffany said brightly. "It is for the best. And after we settle this company business, we'll go on a nice, long cruise, and get reacquainted."

"Yes, Tiffany. Why don't you go home and start planning it?"

She jumped up and went around the desk to throw her arms around his neck.

"I will. It will be the best cruise ever."

"Go on. I'd like to talk to my lawyer alone for a minute."

"Sure, sweetie. I have shopping to do anyway." She gave him a peck on the cheek.

"I'm sure you do."

"And Preston," Cash said. "I'll see you later."

An unhappy expression crossed Preston's face. "Sure, Cash."

"Good. I look forward to those reports."

The door shut behind them and Cash stood and stuck his hands in his pockets.

"I don't know what Tiffany told you about Lexi. But I can assure you that she did not know who I was until she was about to leave the hotel."

"So you cheated on my daughter."

"Your daughter and I have an arrangement in this

regard, Uncle Walker. We never made you privy to it, because frankly, it's none of your business."

"She's my daughter."

"I understand. You want the best for her. But Tiffany and I decided a long time ago that until we tied the knot, we'd have our little dalliances, as long as they don't mean anything. Do you understand?"

"So you are saying that what happened with you and Lexi—"

"Was just for fun." Cash hated lying through his teeth, but he was in a serious situation here that called for desperate measures. "It was terrible of me to take advantage of your employee like that, and in the future, I promise to display better judgment. But, Uncle Walker, you expose us all to liability if you fire the woman. She could claim sexual harassment, and that wouldn't look very good for either of us. And it might throw a monkey wrench in this deal. Companies looking to merge hate pending lawsuits."

"I see your point," Givens said.

Cash knew he would. If there was anything a lawyer understood it was the threat of legal action.

"So, I expect that you will hire her back, with a substantial bonus for the misunderstanding."

"Of course, son. I'll take care of it right away."

25

LEXI

LEXI HAD NEVER BEEN SO HUMILIATED IN HER LIFE. NOT ONLY did Walker Givens fire her, he did it in front of his insufferable daughter, Tiffany.

"You had no business seducing a client of this firm," he said, "let alone my daughter's boyfriend. Get your things and get out. We have a business meeting to go to."

With security watching her, she barely had a chance to get her personal items from her desk. She couldn't grab her résumé off the computer, but that wasn't a big thing. She'd write another résumé, one that didn't reflect her work with Givens and Associates. She wanted to forget this waste of a workplace as soon as possible.

Lexi had hours before meeting Samantha at Romallo's, so she did the only thing that made sense that didn't involve jumping off a bridge. She turned up the music on the sound system and cleaned her apartment from top to bottom. The place hadn't seen a serious spring cleaning since they moved in. Lexi wasn't surprised at the hidden gunk in the kitchen cabinets and counters, behind the appliances, under the rugs and in the furniture. And the walls needed a good cleaning soon. But that was just the start.

She put all her aggression into scrubbing the tiles and tub in the bathroom. Something gnawed at her like an animal trying to escape a trap. As she furiously ground the sponge into the ceramic surfaces of the bathroom, her one thought was of Edward, oops, Sean decadently touching her body. Her morning dream lingered in her mind and sent frissons of tingles through her skin. Her nipples pebbled unbidden in her bra.

Was she really like that? Did she want someone to tie her up, tease and sexually torture her to get off? Up to this point, she was a vanilla girl, living in a vanilla world, and just French kissing seemed like racy stuff.

Not anymore.

She was a woman possessed. Thoughts of him commanding her, kissing her, stroking her, spread an unquenchable fire through her. She was a woman possessed, driven by a fierce need to take everything that this man could dish out. Lexi swallowed hard as her instincts for self-preservation fought with the inferno within her body. A man like Sean was nothing but trouble. She was well rid of him. It might take a while, but she'd get over him.

Lexi scrubbed the tub so hard she thought that she might scrape the enamel from it. The hot water ran over her hands reminding her of Sean's hands on her body, how he entered her and made her forget who she was.

She turned off the water. The bathtub sparkled but her heart did not. Lexi had never felt so lost. She had lost her job, Sean, and herself. What would she do now?

Hours had passed since she started her war on the apartment's dirt. She left the bathroom and inspected all she had done, drew a deep breath of the air she'd scrubbed of every pathogen. Still it seemed she had accomplished nothing but attach a badly leaking bandage to her soul.

Why did he affect her like this? They barely did anything at all. He took her to a BDSM club. Teased her. Made her wrap her hands around his cock. Put the tip of it to her lips. Only that. Nothing more. But her body burned like some of the great cities of the world had burned— Rome, London, Atlanta.

The morning's dream still swirled in her mind and her body shivered from electric jolts of desire that wouldn't leave her. She swallowed hard and knew there was only one thing to do. Lexi checked the clock on the cable box to find she had an hour to get ready to meet Samantha. So she stripped, climbed into the tub, and ran the water. It was almost a shame to dirty the tub, but she needed this.

Taking the body bath, she squirted it in the running water to make bubbles and she sank into the hot water. It did some good for muscles she'd overworked during her cleaning binge but did nothing for her insistent arousal. With a sigh she put her fingers between her legs and indulged in a fantasy.

She, and a businessman dressed in an expensive dark power suit, sit at a table in a fancy restaurant. Lexi wears an ebony chiffon dress. The sheer dress reveals her black lace bustier under dress fabric. She keeps a modicum of decorum by draping a large lace shawl over her shoulders. Her back is to the room while he looks over it. No one can see she has teased her breast out from the confines of the bustier so that her nipple lies on the edge of the fabric. Her date is eating a salad and not paying attention to her. He told her to do this, to display herself like this while he eats, and she's never felt so wicked. Her arousal pools between her legs as the air conditioning of the room chills her peak's hardness. Because he told her, she does not eat, just sits with her head looking at her plate. If she behaves, she'll get better from him than whatever food this place serves.

He calls the waiter over to pour some wine and before he arrives he forbids her to move, to cover the nipple. The waiter, a young man in his twenties with dark hair and eyes, walks to the table, and swallows hard when he sees Lexi's display. His hands tremble as he pours the wine, and the sharp outline of his cock appears in his slacks. She closes her eyes a second, battling to control herself. An electric arc snakes from her groin up her spine, and Lexi concentrates on not moving a muscle. The effort to remain still causes the energy of her arousal to double even though her master says not a word. He thanks the waiter casually, as if nothing unusual happened and no wanton woman left her nipple out for public display.

"What do you think of my date?" her master says. "Is she not exquisite?" The waiter blushes, and her master smiles at the corner of his lips. He's enjoying this game.

"Yes, sir," stutters the waiter.

"You needn't bring the dessert tray," he rumbles in a suggestive voice. "She's my dessert. She has the most delicious cream I've ever tasted."

Now the waiter's eyes nearly bug out and his cock strains against the fabric of his pants. He is like Lexi, under the control of the beautiful man at the table, and caught between fear and desire. Fear that the powerful man at the table will call him out for his inappropriate erection; desire for the woman who sits serenely with her nipple pebbled for him to see.

"Yes, sir," the waiter says. "Very good, sir."

"If you'd like dessert too, we have the penthouse room. Come there after your shift. We'll wait for you."

The young man's face nearly melts, and he trembles in trying to hold onto his composure.

"Yes, sir. Very good, sir."

He walks away stiffly.

"You don't mind sharing, do you?" her master says with a twinkle in his eye.

"Not at all," Lexi says. "Will I get to suck his cock?"

"We'll see," he says. "We'll see how good you are for the rest of the dinner. Come sit next to me."

Lexi moves the chair next to him, and before she sits, he reaches up and moves her shawl.

"We can't have a precious treasure like that on display for everyone to see."

"No, sir."

He picks up some mashed potatoes and gravy on his fork and brings them to her lips.

"Open," he says.

She does and he slides the fork in her mouth. The gravy spills on the corners of her lips and she licks it up.

"So good," he says as he does it again, but this time he leans forward. "Spread your legs, darling," he whispers. She does and he inserts his finger inside her as she sucks the fork so as not to make a sound. He pulls the fork away and lays it on the plate. He kisses her neck, and for all the world, all that appears to be happening is a man kissing his beloved. But his fingers work her passage, stoking her desire to a fever pitch, and she has to bite her lip to keep from making a sound.

"Now you may cum," Cash whispers, and she breaks apart with a thousand stars exploding behind her eyelids.

Lexi opened her eyes as the water chilled in the bath. She'd spent too long in there, indulging her indecent desires. But the worst part about it all was that when she came, it was Sean that whispered in her ear.

She had to admit it.

Lexi burned for Sean Cashman.

26

CASH

THE DAY WAS AN UNHOLY AND UNPRODUCTIVE GRIND. He ignored the phone calls from Tiffany and only responded by text to her father. He waited to hear if Givens had hired back Lexi, but all he got was "haven't been able to reach her."

Annoyance roiled in his gut. He gave Givens one job, to fix what he broke, and he couldn't take care of that.

The meeting that morning soured him for the day. Where did Walker Givens, Tiffany, and Preston Lowe get off acting like he was too emotionally fragile to handle business? No. This smacked of a concerted team effort to wrest his company from him. Unfortunately, Lexi got caught in the middle.

Cash tried to call Lexi, but she didn't answer. He supposed if a woman found the guy she was flirting with involved with someone else, and then got fired, she wouldn't take calls from him. This did not stop him from worrying about her, though, and in a way that he never did about Tiffany. While he did not doubt that Lexi was a capable, independent woman, he didn't want her to experience pain or trouble. He hated that she suffered loss because of his mixed-up relationship with the Givens family.

Smack dab in the middle of this he received an email from a friend of his island buddy, Enrico.

Mr. Cashman,

Enrico said you might have some questions. I'll be at Romallo's pizzeria tonight at five. I'll be glad to speak to you then.

Sincerely,

Master William

Well, that's an odd message, thought Cash. But his experience with Lexi had awakened something in him that he didn't understand. This man might be able to give him some answers. He sent a message that he'd meet him at the restaurant.

Preston Lowe didn't deliver the requested information by the end of the day. This made Cash even more sure that he was hiding information from him. He called the head of the IT department.

"Josh, I need all the books generated by Preston's department. And I don't want you to inform him of it."

"Is there a problem, boss?"

"No. His secretary apparently isn't well, and I need to get this stuff ASAP. Can you get it to me?"

"Sure. Whatever is on the servers, I'll send to you."

"No, don't do that. I'm on the move. Copy and put them in a separate secure file, password marked on the server, and label it 'Christmas Party.'"

"Christmas Party?" His voice sounded incredulous.

"Yes. And send me the password by text to my phone. Don't use the email."

"What's with all the cloak and dagger, boss?"

"Nothing to worry about, Josh. But I'm counting on your discretion."

"Oh, I see, high corporate politics."

"You're not getting a word out of me, Josh. But I'm not playing here, and you shouldn't be either."

The ultra-serious tone of Cash's voice sobered Josh.

"Yes, boss."

"Good."

Cash opened his door and heard Ann speaking.

"I'm sorry, Miss Givens. He's in a meeting and I can't disturb him."

Good woman, thought Cash.

"But I haven't reached him all day," whined Tiffany.

"I'm sorry, Miss Givens. I'll tell him you came by."

Tiffany huffed but left through the front door.

"Is that the first time she came here?"

"No, Cash. She popped in at lunchtime. You'd already gone."

"Gee, you must have forgotten to tell me."

"Did I? I'm getting old, Mr. Cashman. My mind must be slipping."

He winked at her. "Well, I won't discipline you for that. Sometimes a little forgetfulness is a good thing."

"Thank you, sir. You are very generous."

"Thank you. I'm leaving for the day."

"Oh? A little early, aren't you?"

"I have personal business to take care of."

"And is that personal business called 'Lexi'?"

"Shame on you, Ms. Osterman, for prying into your boss's personal affairs."

"Oh, so you admit it is a personal affair."

"No," Cash said sadly. "Ms. Winters wants nothing more to do with me, and I don't blame her."

"Do you like her?" Ann asked.

"Oh, it's a little more than that, but I messed it up good."

"Seems like Ms. Givens had a hand in it."

"Maybe a bit, but trust me, I stepped in this one real good."

"Well, Cash. You'll work it out. I have every confidence in you."

"Tell me, have there been any rumors about Tiffany hanging out with anyone in the company besides me?"

"I harvest rumors before they get ripe. But no. Nothing on Tiffany."

"Keep your ears open. Preston Lowe seems too in sync with both Walker and Tiffany. It's not right."

Ann cocked her head, considering Cash's words.

"Okay, Cash. I'll keep a discreet ear out."

"Thanks. I'll see you in the morning."

"Good night, boss."

He arrived at Romallo's twenty minutes early. It was the typical New York restaurant with red brick walls fitting too many tables in too small a space. Cash ordered a pizza and pitcher of beer, assuming that when the mysterious Master William arrived, they would have a long chat. Then he realized that he and the mysterious Master William didn't exchange details on how to recognize each other. What did one look for to spot a Dom? An uptight and stiff Christian Grey? Someone who looked as if he had a bunch of rules?

He chose a seat that took in the entire room and sat with his back to the wall. He looked over the patrons, but none had the bearing he saw in Enrico's BDSM club. In twenty minutes people came and went, the pizza arrived, and Cash poured a beer for himself. He watched the door.

At precisely five o'clock a tall, dark-haired man arrived. He looked a little older than Cash, perhaps in his thirties. He dressed in a black suit—by its slim cut through the body, Armani—and wore a crisp white shirt under it. Cash glanced in the mirror hanging on the opposite wall and checked out his Brunello Cucinelli suit, easily three times the cost of the Armani. Cash liked the Brunello Cucinelli line because it flattered his broad shoulders instead of trying to pinch them into the slimmer suits of today's styles. At a certain point, it became hard to tell one expensive suit from another unless one was very conscious of fashion. But Cash had learned the hard way which clothing line flattered his football player's body, so he was aware of what was what in style for men's suits.

The man in the Armani was too, and when he glanced at Cash a wry smile played on his lips. It was the type of smile that communicated he knew exactly who he was dealing with and how he would do so. Cash raised his eyebrows and signaled for the one he assumed to be Master William to join him at his table.

"Mr. Cashman," the man said.

"Master William. Please, have a seat." Cash said the words easily though he felt a bit at a loss for not knowing the man's last name.

"Thank you. And you are prompt."

"A habit I've cultivated in business. Arrive early, and you never have to make excuses if you are late. Would you like a beer?"

"Thank you."

William settled into a seat while Cash poured him a beer from the pitcher.

"Please, help yourself to the pizza."

"You are a cordial one, aren't you?"

"No one wins with rudeness."

"I agree. Enrico speaks highly of you."

"He's a great guy."

"And yet you surprised him with your recent interest. Do you mind me asking why now?"

Cash mulled over what he'd tell this stranger.

"I met a girl. She's into it."

"Is she? Dom or submissive?"

"Wait? What?"

"A female master, otherwise called Mistress."

"No. She's a sub."

"I see. And what did you do together? Did you tie her to the bed?"

"No. I took her to Enrico's club. We watched a scene. She sat on my lap."

"That's it?" William's voice said he didn't believe Cash.

"I had her kneel and kiss—it."

"That sounds remarkably restrained."

"We were getting to know it each other. It didn't seem right to push things."

William cocked his head as if evaluating Cash.

"You did want to fuck this girl."

"I wanted to give her what she wanted. And that's what we did."

"You showed restraint."

"It seemed the right thing to do."

"Hmm," William said. "At first I thought Enrico was supporting a friend's request, but now I see it. You have potential, Mr. Cashman."

"Oh?"

"You show restraint; you don't take things too far, too soon; you care about what your sub feels. Those are the makings of a good Dom. So tell me about this girl. Am I likely to know her?"

Cash shrugged his shoulders.

"What's her name?"

"Lexi."

"Hmm. I don't know of any Lexi, but some women change their names for play. What does she look like?"

"Well..." Cash said. And then he stared. Entering the restaurant was Lexi along with a dark-haired woman.

"She looks just like that."

"HEY, GIRLFRIEND, WHAT A SENSE OF TIMING YOU HAVE."

Lexi looked up from her phone, where she was reading things on her browser she had no business looking at.

"It's a feature, not a bug," she said.

"Nothing buggy about you, my friend," Samantha said. She yanked at the heavy glass door and plastered a big smile on her face to present a relentlessly cheery facade to lift the spirits of her best friend.

"You won't say that in a month when the rent's due."

"Hush, you. You are young, beautiful, and live in New York City. The world is yours for the taking."

Just not, thought Lexi, *one already taken billionaire.*

Did Lexi have to look up the society news about Sean Cashman and Tiffany Givens? No, she did not. Did she? Absolutely. And what she found sickened her stomach. Cashman and Tiffany attended every major charity event for the past six years, arm in arm, looking like God's gift to the overclass. Tiffany was always bright and shiny in Cash's presence, not a lip un-glossed or a hair out of place, and Lexi didn't blame her. To keep Cash's attention required a substantial investment of time and money, and Tiffany had both.

Samantha swung a protective arm around Lexi after they entered the restaurant swarming with patrons and surveyed the floor.

"No tables," she said.

"There—" Lexi said. She stopped speaking when her eyes hit Cash's handsome face. She tried to work her mouth to tell Samantha they needed to leave, but her mouth filled with cotton as her heart raced in her chest. She stood frozen like a deer in headlights as his gaze caught hers. Cash looked just as surprised as she felt.

"I see it," Sam said, and pushed them both relentlessly forward toward the empty table next to Cash's while Lexi fought lightheadedness. *Please don't let me faint. Please don't let me. Fuck. Why the hell should I?*

A wave of self-preservation swept over her, picking up her battered self-esteem and encasing it in a life preserver. Who the fuck was Sean Cashman anyway? A spoiled, rich, pretty boy, who got far too much of what he wanted, and far too little of what he deserved, namely several swift kicks to his rear. She lifted her chin defiantly, forced a smile, and turned her head toward her friend.

"What shall it be tonight? Bottles or pitcher?"

"I'm springing for a pitcher," Samantha said wryly. "What are you drinking?"

"Wine."

Samantha shrugged. "Have a seat. It's my treat tonight. I'll go order for us."

Without waiting for a reply, Samantha pushed off, leaving Lexi to sit at the table under the relentless eyes of Cash. She sat with her back to him, but that didn't stop her from sensing his eyes boring a hole in the back of her head.

Lighthearted conversations and the laughter of other patrons filled the restaurant. At another time she would enjoy the smell of baking pizza crust, and the sharp, distinctive scent of olive oil and basil that snuck into every crevice of the shop. She anticipated melty cheese on fresh-baked crust, sprinkled with hot red pepper. Lexi would scarf too much of it, and have one too many beers, enjoying one of humanity's real treasures.

But not tonight. With Cash sitting behind her, every muscle tensed as if she was balancing on a high wire. Unconsciously she pushed her back rigidly straight and her breath strangled in her chest. She should have left, not try to show her disinterest by sitting casually in front of him with her back to him. Because from the evidence in her panties she was not disinterested.

Fuck me, thought Lexi.

Samantha returned and sat heavily in her chair. "Okay," she said waggling a restaurant pager in Lexi's face. "We're order number twenty-three, and the waitress will bring our drinks shortly—and what the hell happened to you?"

"What?"

"Why do you look like someone shoved a stick up your butt?"

"Do I?" Lexi said. On the one hand, she wanted to leave, and on the other, she'd be damned if Sean Cashman dictated where she ate.

"Did you see a ghost or something?" Sam said with a mischievous smirk. "Like that time I saw old man Luigi the day after that he died and—" Sam trailed off, and concern spread over her face.

"Are you okay?"

"Fine," Lexi said tersely.

"If you don't feel well, we can leave."

At that moment the waitress arrived with a carafe of wine and a pitcher of beer and set them and the glasses on the table. Lexi immediately poured one glass of wine and chugged it. Samantha's eyes opened wide. Not that she hadn't seen Lexi do this on other occasions, but tonight she looked shocked. Lexi poured another and Samantha put her hand on the top of the wineglass.

"Slow down, cowgirl," she said with real worry in her voice.

"What are you worried about? We are walking home. I don't have a place to go to tomorrow, and I can use a good drink after cleaning the apartment from top to bottom. Really? Do you ever vacuum under your bed? It was disgusting."

Lexi pushed Samantha's hand away and chugged the next glass as well.

"You cleaned my room?"

"Someone had to do it. The toxic fumes coming from it nearly earned us a visit from the EPA."

"I don't know if you've heard," Samantha said, "but the EPA doesn't do home visits."

"They would have made an exception in our case, trust me." The last words came out slightly slurred, proof positive that Lexi could not hold her liquor.

Good.

She poured the last glass out of the carafe and downed that one too.

"Damn girl. If you wanted to do shots, we could have gone to Sullivan's. That's a waste of an utterly unremarkable red wine."

"Naw. Why get pawed by total strangers when we can get stared at by total assholes."

"What the hell are you talking about?"

Lexi stood. "I said assholes!" She turned to Cash and the dark-haired man behind her. Cash looked horrified, and the man he sat with wore a confused expression. He couldn't figure out that Lexi was drunk and pissed, and ready to do battle with the man that broke her heart.

Was her heart broken? Lexi was in no condition for accurate self-reflection. She did know that the alcohol fueled the fire in her blood when it came to Sean Cashman, and the fact that she couldn't have him sparked an inferno of hurt and rage.

"Lexi," Samantha said urgently. "Sit down." She reached for Lexi's arm, but Lexi shook off her hand. The alcohol was hitting her good and hard now, and rational thought walked away in disgust.

"What the hell are you looking at?" she snapped at Cash.

Cash stood, wiped his hands with a napkin purposefully, and took two steps to their table.

"What's going on, Lexi?" Cash said. His tone was deadly serious.

"You know this guy?" Samantha asked.

"Yeah. I kissed his dick," Lexi said dramatically. "This is fucking saintly Sean fucking Cashman!"

"Oh," Samantha said.

Cash leaned in and whispered in her ear. "Sit down."

Lexi shook her head violently. "I will not. Who the fuck are you giving me orders?"

"The man who'll spank your bottom if you don't."

Lexi gave a harsh laugh and poked her finger in his chest. "Who the fuck do you think you are, Mr. Big Shot Sean Cashman?"

"Lexi," Samantha said urgently. "People are staring."

"Let them stare. Let them all stare. They should get an eyeful of the biggest jerk in New York City."

The dark-haired man came to stand next to Sean. While he wasn't as tall as Cash, his presence was commanding and soothing.

"Lexi," he said calmly and evenly, yanking her attention away from Cash. "You might need some air."

Words stuck in Lexi's mouth. Here this stranger was acting perfectly reasonable toward her when all she did was to rudely call attention to both him and Cash.

"I think you might be right," she said blushing. "Sorry."

"That's quite all right, Lexi," the man said. "You seem to have had a difficult day. It happens to all of us."

Tears sprung to Lexi's eyes. Oh god. Not only was she drunk and a fool, but she was also a crying drunk and fool. Could she humiliate herself any more?

"Let's go," suggested the dark-haired man. Lexi didn't know what embarrassed her more, her tears or this man acting so unreasonably kind to her when she didn't deserve it.

The experience of Cash, the stranger, and Samantha escorting her out of the restaurant was surreal.

"Did you say," Cash said, "that you had nowhere to go tomorrow?"

"Still jobless, Mr. Cashman," she said bitterly. "Courtesy of you."

The dark-haired man looked at Lexi, then at Cash. "This might be more than I'm qualified to handle."

28

WILLIAM TURNED TO WALK AWAY.

"No, wait, William. Please. I told her boss to hire her back."

William raised his hands. "There are some things above my pay grade. It's too bad. You have potential, Mr. Cashman, and Lexi does appear to be a natural sub, but there are layers here I have no right to tease out."

"Potential? Sub?" said Lexi's friend in utter confusion.

"You, on the other hand," William said cupping his fingers on the woman's chin, "I'd love to see what you are about." He pulled a business card from the breast pocket of his suit. "Give me a call."

With that William smartly turned and walked down the sidewalk. Lexi's friend stood staring at the card.

"Who the fuck was that?" she asked.

"You might as well go, too," Lexi said to Cash. Her knees seemed curiously weak, and she swayed forward, and he caught her.

"Where is your apartment?" he asked. "I'll walk you both home. Or we can get a cab."

"I think it is better if she walks," Lexi's friend said. "She needs to walk this off. Geez, I'd never seen her act like this. My name is Samantha. Sam for short."

"I guess you got my name––Mr. Asshole."

Samantha laughed. "I like your alias better, Mr. Sean Cashman."

"Cash," he said.

"Cash? You want money?"

He chuckled. "No. That's my nickname."

"Nice to meet you, Mr. Sean 'Cash' Cashman."

The restaurant door opened, and the waitress stood there with two pizza boxes.

"Did Mr. William leave?" the waitress asked.

"Yes," Cash said.

"Damn. I wanted to give him his pizzas."

"His pizzas?" Samantha said.

"His standing order for when he comes in at night."

"We'll take them," Samantha said swiping the boxes from the surprised waitress. "He told us to take them. We're on the way to his place anyway."

"Oh, I suppose that's okay," she said with doubt in her voice.

"We'll be back," Samantha said. "We love this place."

Lexi turned to walk back to the restaurant, but Cash pulled her by the waist.

"Not now. It's time to go home."

"But we didn't finish the beer."

"You've had enough spirits for one night."

"You're no fun," whined Lexi.

"Come along, girl and let's get you into bed," Samantha said.

She wrinkled her nose. "Not with him!"

Lexi swayed again, and Cash was afraid she'd fall.

"I won't stay. Just let me get you home."

"Let him help, Lexi. I have pizzas in my arms."

"Oh, well, if you're holding pizzas. Lead on, Macduff," she said drunkenly. She lurched forward, and Cash pulled her back against him. Lexi leaned heavily on Cash, which he didn't mind at all. In fact, she buried her face in his suit jacket.

"You smell good," she murmured.

"Don't mind her," Samantha said. "She doesn't get drunk often, but when she does, you'd think she was the biggest lush you ever met."

"I don't mind," Cash said, "since I'm the cause of this."

"Oh, I wouldn't give you too much credit. Whatever happened between you and her, it doesn't compare to the shellacking she received from her last boyfriend."

"Last boyfriend?" Cash didn't like the sound of that. It horrified Cash that he had a hand in upsetting Lexi when she was raw from a breakup.

"Trevor MacGregor. Made a big play for her. They'd been dating for months until she found him banging a gym bunny in the showers."

"Fuck Trevor MacGregggrrr," slurred Lexi indignantly.

"No, darling," Samantha said. "You don't want to do that anymore."

"Damn right!" declared Lexi.

"So, you tried to get Lexi's job back?"

"She should have it back. I explained it all to her employer. Lexi didn't have a clue as to who I was until the last hour she was at the hotel."

"Well, she's too upset so I suspect she didn't get the 211. Wait." Samantha patted Lexi's side pocket and pulled out the phone. "There are a dozen phone calls from Mr. Givens.

She must not have answered the phone. Lexi gets like that when she's upset."

"I'm not upset," murmured Lexi into Cash's chest.

She was drunk, and she'd put on a humiliating scene in the restaurant, but Cash didn't mind Lexi under his arm and pressed close to his body. He felt responsible for her condition, though he supposed that he shouldn't. Still, the contours of her sexy body leaned against him, and he couldn't help his arousal. His cock half-filled from her hair's scent. God, how he wanted more of this woman.

"Girl, you ain't nothing but," Samantha said. She pressed keys on Lexi's phone and listened to it.

"What a douche," opined Samantha, "but he did tell you to get back to work."

"Let me hear it," Cash said.

Samantha's expression turned skeptical. "It's a private conversation."

"And yet you listened."

"Not the same thing, rich boy. I have her power-of-attorney, just like she has mine."

"You do?"

"Sure. We signed the papers when we were twelve."

"That's hardly a legal agreement."

"I know. That's why we did them again when we turned eighteen."

"Besties foooorrrrreeeeevvvverrrr!" sang Lexi.

"Please, girl. Don't sing. You know how that hurts my ears."

"Look. He's my lawyer. If he isn't representing me properly, I need to know."

"Oh, he's not representing you properly." Samantha hit the speaker and then replay.

"*Ms. Winters, this is Mr. Givens, and this is my twelfth call to you today. There was a misunderstanding regarding your termination. I expect you at work tomorrow."*

"What a jerk!" snapped Lexi.

Cash agreed. If Givens wanted to avoid a lawsuit this was not the way to do it. He was half-tempted to hire a lawyer to press a wrongful termination suit in Lexi's behalf.

"Text him and tell him Lexi is taking the day off tomorrow."

"What you got planned, rich boy?" Samantha said.

"Me? Nothing. Lexi is in no condition to go in tomorrow and face Givens' nonsense."

"Hundo P to that, rich boy."

"What?"

"They do keep you locked up, don't they? It's the new version of 'true dat.' Well, here we are."

Cash looked up at the nondescript red brick apartment buildings in New York that most of the world ignored. They weren't flashy like a brownstone or a Fifth Avenue apartment.

"What's the damage here?" Cash asked as Samantha walked up the stairs.

"Why do you want to know?"

"Sorry. Didn't mean to pry."

"It costs too much," Samantha said, "which is why I take all the free pizza I can get."

"I can imagine."

"Can you, rich boy? When have you had to struggle for anything? Worry about how to juggle the bills so you can pay them before they shut off a service?"

Cash quirked an eyebrow.

"I can't help what the world is like, Samantha. Just like you, I live in it."

"Hmph. I'm not sure I like that answer."

Samantha jiggled the door and pushed it open.

"Come on, baby girl," Cash said. "Let's get you inside."

Lexi was barely sensible, so he nearly had to drag her up the stairs.

"Itsy bitsy spider," she sang off-key. "What was that again? Oh, up the water spout."

"Elevator?" he asked Samantha.

"No. We're on the first floor, though."

"Good. Lead the way."

"Down came the rain and washed the spider out! Out came the sun and dried up all the rain, so the itsy bitsy spider wasn't the same again."

"That doesn't sound right," Cash said.

"She's never been solid on her nursery rhymes. You should hear her Jack Sprat rendition."

Lexi groaned. "I don't feel so good."

Samantha opened the apartment door and whistled.

"She must have been fucking upset. Look at this. It's in move-in condition, and we moved in three years ago."

Cash scanned the very ordinary and small apartment. "Where's her bedroom?"

"Bathroom," croaked Lexi. "I need the bathroom. Oh god."

Cash managed to get her over the toilet before disaster struck.

29

LEXI

THE ROOM SPUN AROUND HER AND LITTLE MADE SENSE. THE aroma of pizza wafted by her nose, which sickened her rebellious stomach. Light flooded the room, and she threw her hands over her head.

"Here," said a deep rumbling voice. "Take this."

A hand shoved two tablets into hers. "Take them."

She nearly dropped them as she brought them to her mouth. But she stuck them in.

"Good, now sit up." That rumbly voice sounded familiar.

"Edward?" she said. Then her eyes flew open. Not Edward. Cash! She wanted to demand what he was doing here in her room, but her fuzzy tongue couldn't talk around her pills. She was in her bed, wasn't she? What idiotic thing did she do last night that brought Sean Cashman into her inner sanctum?

She sat up abruptly.

"Easy," Cash said gently. "You had quite the night last night."

She took the glass of water he offered. "What the hell are you doing here?" she said.

"Samantha had to go to work. She didn't want you to be alone. Something about going overboard on a cleaning binge a sign of disturbed mental health?"

"Only would Samantha think that way," huffed Lexi. "I don't need you here."

"I'm sure. But I need to speak to you, so I beg your forgiveness and hope you'll allow me to have my say."

Lexi gathered the comforter around her. Cash handed her a package of saltines. "That's to ease a queasy stomach. Afterwards, if you allow me, I'll take you to lunch."

"Lunch? What about breakfast?"

"We can go to a diner if you want, but it's past noon now."

"Hell. How bad was I last night?"

"Let's say your nice clean bathroom isn't as clean as you had it."

Lexi groaned.

"I'm sorry."

"What are you apologizing for? You had a rough time of it between my shenanigans and Uncle Walker's."

"Uncle Walker's?"

Cash winced. "Slip of the tongue. I've known him forever. He and my father were college roommates. As close as brothers."

"Ew. That, like, makes Tiffany your cousin?"

Cash chuckled. "We used to laugh about that. Kissing cousins."

"Oh," she said. She didn't like this semi-incestuous relationship between Cash and Tiffany as if that was any of her business. Which it was not. She pushed against the headboard of her bed and held her comforter against her.

"Well, have your say, and then get out."

"Well, that was rough."

"What do you expect me to do? You lied to me, Cash."

"Yes, I did. Things got away from me. From a little joke, it turned into something else."

"Joke," huffed Lexi.

Cash raked his hand through his blond hair. "Sorry. Bad word. My point is, it just snowballed, and I didn't stop it when I should. Sorry, I apologize. It was never my intention to hurt you."

"Hurt me! I lost my job because of you."

"No, you didn't. If you listen to your phone messages, you'll find Uncle Walker rescinded his termination."

"Yeah," Lexi said sullenly. "I'll bet you had something to do with that."

"Yes," Cash admitted. "I told him the truth. You had no idea who I was until you were about to leave the hotel."

"Great. Wonderful. Now I'm stupid as well as a slut."

"No one thinks that of you, Lexi."

"But what we did." The heat of a blush spread through her body.

"What did we do, eh? Visit a club, tease each other a bit."

I knelt in front of you and kissed your dick.

"You can make light of this if you want. I can't go back to work there. I'm too humiliated."

"That's your decision. I have contacts. I'm sure one of my acquaintances will have a job open for a paralegal."

"Really?" Lexi said icily, "So instead of working for someone you know, I'd work for another person you're 'acquainted with'? No, thanks. I'll find a job."

"Lexi," Cash said in appeal.

"Is this all you have to say? Sorry, so sorry I humiliated you in front of my employer. And your girlfriend. Your fiancée? Let's remember that."

"Tiffany..." started Cash in a tortured voice.

"I'm sure you are about to tell me that she means nothing to you. And that you are only together for the children or some such nonsense."

"That's ridiculous. You know I don't have children."

"Do I? What do I know about you, Sean Cashman, AKA Edward Teach? Are you seriously telling me that Tiffany is no longer part of the picture?"

"It's complicated," Cash said. His face looked as if someone was hammering nails into his hands. This seemed like a fitting and appropriate punishment for the man who dared to come to her and offer the same sleazy excuses as every other cheating man.

"It damn well is complicated. But the only thing complicated about it is you trying to shoehorn me into a life that already has enough complications. Oh, don't think I haven't forgotten 'I'll call you. That's the only way it can be.' What a crock! What a fool I was."

"Lexi, please."

"No. I will not please. Not anymore. Get out of my apartment and out of my life, and don't darken my door again."

Cash stood, looking as if someone had shot his best friend and his dog on the same day.

"I suppose I deserve that, Lexi. It's too bad because... well, it doesn't matter anymore. I sincerely wish you a good life. Take care of yourself."

Cash rose from the bed and walked to the door, and Lexi's heart broke for real this time. It shattered into a thousand pieces as he touched his hand to the door handle, and she couldn't help a whimper escape from her throat. She wanted to scream, "No, don't leave!" But this was for the best. The man had another life, a woman he was to marry, from a world that she could only dream about.

But Cash stopped with his hand on the door handle, and he stood there.

"Lexi," he said facing the door. "Are you really going to let me walk out this door?"

She swallowed hard, and tried to speak but couldn't. He stood utterly still, waiting for her final judgment. Tears hazed her vision as she tried to stifle the horrible feeling that she was about to lose everything that was precious in this world.

"Because," he said, "if you do, I'll have to punish you."

30

CASH

CASH FOUND IT IMPOSSIBLE TO WALK OUT THE DOOR AND leave her behind. Things were incredibly fucked up. But it was his fault. Lexi was the fulfillment of a dream he didn't know he had. Cash might as well cut off an arm before leaving her and ending things between them. As he stood with every muscle still, he tried to figure out a way to salvage the situation.

Only a fool would try to bribe her. Lexi wouldn't allow it. Cash would have found her a job, called in favors owed, even fund the damn thing himself to ameliorate the damage he did to her professional life. And she wouldn't accept it. How many people he knew had the kind of fortitude to refuse that? Not many. No one, in fact.

Cash came from a world that revolved around money. Rank of importance tallied on their balance sheets, not their character. Tiffany was one such person, arranging the people in her life that put her at the best economic advantage. She was the product of her upbringing. But hollow-souled Tiffany didn't possess an honest feeling to share with another person.

Tiffany's beauty and social skills were no longer sufficient. He needed a flesh-and-blood woman, one that would shed an honest tear while trying to do the right thing.

Lexi sobbed and her tears wrecked him. It was as if his soul connected to hers and her grief poured into his. It was breaking her heart to watch him leave. And it was breaking his.

This was wrong. But how could he stop this injustice from happening?

"Lexi," he said, facing the door. "Are you really going to let me walk out of here?"

He waited for a beat and died a little inside as he waited for an answer that did not come. The floor opened at his feet, the perpetual black hole that threatened to swallow him since his father's death. He couldn't let her go, and couldn't make her want him, and he was an impossible mass of emotions that galloped toward the edge of sanity. His breath strangled in his chest and he desperately sought a way to bridge the gap between them.

Lexi does appear to be a natural sub. William's words resurfaced in his mind. Was it possible? Appeal to Lexi's inner nature? Or would that be wrong too?

He had to try.

"Because," he said, "if you do, I'll have to punish you."

He waited a second that seemed an eternity too long. Every muscle and nerve in his body strained to catch a single sign that Lexi would take this final thin rope to salvage what they had together.

A gasp escaped Lexi's throat.

"Sir," she said.

Relief washed through Cash. There was a chance to set this right again. But he had to play it right. He turned slowly and caught her eyes.

"On your knees," he said. "On the floor."

Lexi pushed the comforter off her body and slid down to the floor.

"Eyes down," he commanded. God, he hoped he was getting this right. He didn't need to fuck up again.

Lexi bit her lip as she did what he said.

"You've been bad, giving Master a difficult time."

"Yes, sir," she said.

"Did I give you permission to speak?"

She shook her head.

"You've also abused your body with alcohol, making yourself sick. I will not allow this. Nod if you understand."

Lexi looked as if she would protest and he gave her a stern glance.

"Must I remove my belt and apply it to your lovely bottom?"

Lexi squirmed, looking entirely displeased.

Cash sunk to his knees and faced Lexi.

"I find I must entrust quite a bit of my soul to you, Lexi Winters. In a very short time, you have stormed my heart and stolen it."

She bit her lip. He wanted to kiss the consternation on her face away.

"I want you in my life, Lexi Winters. I must have you in there."

Lexi searched his face as if trying to determine if he was telling the truth.

"Do you want to say something?"

She nodded.

"Go ahead."

"What about Tiffany?" she asked.

This was going to be difficult, and he hoped that Lexi would understand.

"I'm in a difficult position with the Givens. Walker Givens has been pressuring me to sell the company. He tells me if I don't, I'll lose everything. I only learned that piece of information today. I still have to get to the bottom of it. But I have to act like I'm on board with their plans. If I don't, they may try other, less savory, methods to get what they want. For the time being, I can't change my relationship with Tiffany because that will tip off them off I don't buy their plan. She is going to act, walk, and talk like we are getting married. I may even have to give her a ring."

Lexi looked away as if wheels were turning in her head. Cash was sincerely afraid she'd kick him out for good this time.

"And how long do you think this will go on?"

"No more than a month."

"A month," she said thoughtfully. "Okay. Thirty days. I can live with that. But if you try to go over that, it's over between us."

"I can understand that," Cash said. "I haven't told you the truth, and you have every right to be cautious."

"And one more thing," Lexi said. "No ring. Tell her what you want, but I don't want that woman flashing a diamond around announcing she's yours."

"Is that a hard limit, Ms. Winters?"

"You'd better believe it is. And there is another hard limit too."

He smiled.

"What is that?"

"No sex between us while this charade is going on. I want to keep some of my dignity while whatever this is plays out."

Cash nodded. "That is a difficult request to make of your

master, but I understand. But that doesn't mean there won't be any play between us, Lexi."

"What kind of play?" Lexi said with a gulp.

"You'll find out. Get cleaned up and get your clothes on. You need food, and from what I see in it, your refrigerator is nearly empty. And going forward, I won't tolerate that either. You are to eat properly. And if you don't, I will punish you."

"Gee," Lexi said, standing. "You're big on this punishment thing, aren't you?"

"Not so much. I'm more into pleasure," Cash said standing as well. "And I must say, it is a pleasure to look at your body."

Lexi flashed him a smile. "Well, as long as you look and don't touch, I suppose that's okay."

"Oh, you said no sex. And I'll honor that agreement. But I never agreed to no touching." Cash reached out and pinched a nipple between his fingers.

"Now, wait. That's suspiciously like sex."

"Why?" he teased. "Because I touched your nipple? But if I touched your bare arm, would that be sex?"

"From you, yes," Lexi said with exasperation.

"Then I'm a very fortunate man to have you as mine."

"I never said I was yours."

"So bratty. Are you looking for a spanking?"

"No. I...I just don't want to get hot and...and stuff."

"Hot, and stuff," Cash repeated. Damn, he'd like to get her hot and...nope. He pulled back on that thought. She had every right to insist on keeping a boundary between them while Tiffany was still in the picture. But he couldn't lose his control of her either. She'd already put demands on him that he suspected no Dom would accept. He couldn't stray far from the role that drew her to him.

"But, Lexi, dear, that's what this is about, isn't it? Piquing your interest and mine?" He stood very close to her and whispered the words, and she shuddered.

"You're going to make this impossible, aren't you?"

"Are you a betting woman?"

"No."

"Well, I'm a betting man. I bet that before the month is over, you are going to beg me to take you to my bed."

"Never happen."

"Are you sure?"

Lexi crossed her arms. "What's in it for me?"

"What do you want?"

"I want a ringside seat when you kick Tiffany to the curb. I want to hear it all and see it all."

"You play for keeps, don't you?"

"Yes, I do. So you'd better get used to it."

Cash's phone rang, and he saw it was his secretary calling.

"Go, get cleaned up."

"Yes, sir," Lexi said with a wink.

The ringing had stopped, but Cash called her back.

"What's going on, Ann?"

"Cash," she whispered, "are you planning on coming into the office today?"

"Well, yes. Later."

"Don't," she hissed in a whisper.

"Why?"

"There are some process servers here, Cash."

"Go ahead, take the papers, Ann."

"They say they need to give them to you personally."

"They lie. Any one of my agents can sign for them."

"That's what I thought."

"If they don't want to leave them with you, they can give them to my lawyer."

"That's just the problem, Cash. They are from your lawyer."

31

Lᴇxɪ ʜᴀᴅ ᴡᴏʀᴋᴇᴅ ᴜᴘ ᴀ ᴍᴀᴅ ʀᴀɢᴇ ᴏᴠᴇʀ Sᴇᴀɴ Cᴀsʜᴍᴀɴ, ᴀɴᴅ then when he spouted a few magic words, she fell under his spell again.

"Lexi," he said as he faced the door. *"Are you really going to let me walk out of here? Because, if you do, I'll have to punish you."*

It wasn't the promise of punishment but the fact he wouldn't walk out the door that touched her. She had raked him over the coals, and instead of fleeing like a cowardly dog, he displayed the strength of character to stay. And he gave her an opportunity to accept him without losing her dignity.

Lexi shook her head. How could she think getting punished would not cost her her dignity?

Because he gave her a choice. A strange one, but he made it her decision. Cash made it clear that he wouldn't abandon her because of an angry disagreement. Or that she made him less of a man because she delivered a few harsh words.

What he said was "Is this what you really want?"

A man-child like Trevor MacGregor would melt down,

spit out ugly names, and tell Lexi she wasn't worth the spit to shine his shoes. But Cash? He was calm, self-possessed, and knew what he wanted.

Her.

And he did despite facing trouble with his company and the Givens, father and daughter. She'd watched Walker Givens enough to know he was a ruthless man. He didn't just treat his employees harshly. Any person who stood in his way was an obstacle to run over or remove. She didn't know how, but Cash had become an obstacle.

She would never understand a man like Walker Givens, but she did get Cash. He wasn't afraid to face a challenge and wouldn't back down when things became difficult.

In other words, he was a real man.

How many of those were walking around these days?

Well, one was walking around in her apartment, and she should get out of the tub if she wanted to spend more time with him.

She wrapped her towel around her and stepped into her bedroom and smiled at him while she stood in the doorway. But he was looking at his phone, with a perplexed expression on his face.

"What's wrong?"

"Walker Givens sent me legal papers."

"What kind?" Lexi said. Her professional paralegal instincts told her this was not a good development.

"I don't know," he huffed.

Lexi had a bad feeling about the papers. Givens may have sensed that Cash didn't plan on fulfilling his agreement with Givens and sent something to push Cash into a corner.

"I'll go in to find out what they cooked up. Nothing in

those papers can go forward until you receive them. You said I had my job back. I'll just show up," Lexi said.

Cash shook his head.

"No, Lexi. You shouldn't do this. Givens is not a man to mess with."

"And I'm not a woman to take things sitting down. I don't tolerate people playing me. So I will do this, as much for me as for you."

"And if I order you not to?"

Lexi raised an eyebrow. "Sir, the bedroom is one thing, when we get there, but you have a way to go before you can command my personal life. Might I remind you that you are an almost-engaged man, and not to me? Don't make demands that don't fit the current state of our relationship."

"Hmm, you make it sound like I'm at your beck and call."

Lexi thought about that a second and decided that sounded right. If a woman submitted to a man in the way Cash wanted, what did she get in return? Because what woman would willingly accede to a man if she didn't get something valuable in return? It had to be more than sex because for most women, sex was the cherry on a top of a great relationship, but it wasn't the reason for it. But to have a man's undivided attention? That was pure gold. That had to be the draw of a BDSM relationship.

"No, sir," she said. "But if you want more with me, then we have start somewhere. Food is always good."

He gave her an intense stare that said he wanted to possess all of her, but it couldn't be like that right now. First, he needed to work through this thing with the Givens and his company. And second, he had to learn more about this BDSM stuff. It was good to play games, but it seemed they could be heading into serious territory.

"Okay," conceded Cash. "Food."

"But later. I have to get to work now."

"I can't dissuade you?"

"No."

It was adorable that Cash wore a worried expression as he put her in the cab he insisted she take. But it wasn't as if Givens would harm her. Besides, there was freedom in knowing that she would leave this job, and the sooner the better. Lexi wasn't naive. She understood that in the business world people played rough. But she couldn't fathom or suffer a man who would throw a man as close as a son to the wolves.

She was late for work and she didn't care. She breezed in as if nothing had ever happened and stepped to her desk outside of Mr. Givens' office. Maria, Givens' secretary, gazed at her in wide-eyed surprise, but Lexi just smiled.

"Good morning, Maria," Lexi said.

"I thought you—"

"Took the day off?" Lexi said. She spoke easily, hoping to smooth over the fact that Givens had fired her the day before. "I should have. I got wicked sick yesterday. Spent a part of it over the toilet. Maybe I caught a bug from that island trip."

"You should have stayed home," Maria said, wrinkling her nose officiously. "We don't need anything like that here."

"How can I when Mr. Givens blows up my phone? Look at this," she said waggling her phone at Maria. "Twelve phone calls. Just what happened yesterday?"

"Nothing different," Maria said.

Nothing different, Lexi's ass. Lexi was going to find evidence on the company server.

As Lexi turned on her computer, she kept up her conversation with Maria.

"Who filled in for me yesterday?" she said conversationally.

"Gracey, Mr. Pullman's paralegal. And it ticked Mr. Pullman off! Put his work back an entire day. Mr. Givens had me call a temp agency for today, and then later told me to never mind. It's a good thing that I always wait until he tells me to do something the second time. That's the only way I can get any work done, otherwise I'd spend half my day doing one thing, then spend the rest of it undoing it."

Lexi found Gracey's folder and opened it looking for yesterday's work, wrinkling her nose in distaste. Gracey made no secret of the fact that she wanted Lexi's job. It would be like her to brown-nose Mr. Givens by working the weekend, and for free. Poking around didn't yield any results, so she figured Gracey had hidden it. It was possible to do if you named the file with a too-long file name so it wouldn't show in the directory. Determined, Lexi ran a search with Cash's name and the date, and a bunch of files came up. She began to look through them, but it didn't take long until she found it.

Lexi had to restrain a gasp. This went beyond anything that she thought Givens would do. Pressure Cash? Yes. This? No.

Lexi stared at the text.

Wherefore Article 7 of the employment contract between Sean Cashman and Cashman Industries specifies:

Termination.

(a) Disability. If, as a result of the Executive's incapacity due to physical or mental illness, the Executive shall have been absent from his duties hereunder on a full time basis for ninety (90) consecutive days, the Company may terminate its obligation hereunder, except for those obligations provided for in Section 8(a) hereof. The determination of whether the Executive is

disabled due to physical or mental illness shall be made by a licensed physician satisfactory to the Executive and to the Company.

And that Sean Cashman has been sufficiently absent from his duties as Chief Executive Officer for twelve consecutive months following the death of his father James Patrick Cashman as to indicate an inability to perform such duties as his contract requires specifically as in Section (2) of the Employment Contract to use his best efforts to advance the best interests of the Company.

And that there is sufficient reason as attested in Affidavits A and B to reasonably suspect that Sean Cashman may suffer from a mental illness triggered by the death of his father. Whereas Mr. Sean Cashman has refused to voluntarily submit to psychiatric examination we ask this court to compel and command Mr. Sean Cashman to present himself to the company's licensed psychiatrist to determine whether or not Mr. Sean Cashman is mentally ill and therefore unable to discharge the duties of his office.

Furthermore, Cashman Industries asks the court to put the employment contract in abeyance until such time as Mr. Cashman is examined and a determination made as to his mental status. In the meantime, his duties will be temporarily assumed by the next officer of the company in the company's chain of command.

Lexi scrolled until she found the scanned and signed affidavits but they did not surprise her. Tiffany Givens had signed one and the other was signed by the CFO of Cashman Industries, Preston Lowe.

It was fiction, legal garbage, but it sounded good. If Walker Givens got this to a friendly judge, Cash's control of his company would be wrested from him before he could mount a defense.

And his company would be sold.

32

CASH

Cash did not like Lexi's striding back into Walker Givens' lair but what could he do? Lexi was a sub, or as William put it, a natural sub, but she wasn't any man's slave. But Cash wanted to keep the sliver of hope between them, so he declined to tell her "no" as her blue eyes blazed with determination. Cash walked her to the curb and put her in a cab. Then he turned and walked in the opposite direction from everything he knew.

Though trekking in an unfamiliar part of town he found himself back at Romallo's and decided lunch was a good idea. He bought a couple of slices and a bottled water and sat at the same table he did the previous night. Cash checked his messages but found none from Ann, his secretary, or Lexi.

"Look who's back."

Cash glanced up to see William standing over the table. Unlike last night he wore a white chef's apron over a black tee.

"The pizza's good," Cash said.

"I'm sure," William said. "My family's recipe goes back to the old country."

"You own this restaurant?"

"It's a family concern. Our parents live in Florida now, but my brothers run it with me. It's a good location, and we try to keep the customers happy."

"Well, I'm not happy," Cash said.

"How so?"

"You left me in the lurch last night."

"That was not business," William said.

"I understand. You were doing my friend a favor by seeing me. And Lexi and I straightened it out."

"You did?" William said surprised.

"Not exactly. But she's given me thirty days to do so."

William quirked a dark eyebrow and inspected Cash as if looking for flaws.

"And who's the Dom here?"

Cash pushed out a chair with his foot.

"Take a seat, and I'll tell you a secret."

"Okay. I've got a minute." He pulled off his apron and sat at the table.

"I'm not a Dom."

"You could have fooled me," William said sarcastically.

"No, I mean, I've never had such an inclination. But Lexi—she's into it."

"So you've said, but I've checked with other people in the scene, and they don't remember seeing her."

This surprised Cash. When William walked away from them last night, Cash thought he had no interest in him and Lexi.

"New York is a big place."

"True. Did you spend last night at her apartment?"

"Why?"

"You're wearing the same suit as last night."

"I did. On the couch. Why is this important?"

"There are a bunch of men who think themselves as Doms because, quite frankly, they are assholes. They think acting the alpha male and roughing up a girl equates to being a master, but in true BDSM, the mastery is of yourself. What I evaluate is, can the man control himself? Make good decisions for his sub? Put her first?"

"You mean the difference between sadism and using pain for pleasure?"

"It's a fine distinction, but yes."

"I've done some reading."

"Good."

"But I'm out of my depth. I don't know where to take this, so I'm going slow. I don't want to mess up with Lexi, but I might if I don't learn what I need to."

"And is Lexi aware of your inexperience?"

"No."

William shook his head.

"Honesty is the cornerstone of the lifestyle. Look, Cash, you have to have that conversation with her."

Cash ran his hand through his hair. "I was hoping that you'd show me the ropes."

William gave Cash a rueful smile.

"I might take you on, but I'd have to train both of you, and you might not like what I'd do with Lexi. Doms can be very territorial about their subs."

"So I can't convince you?"

"Possibly. I've seen Lexi's friend here, and she's quite striking. But she's always with someone. I've even seen her here with a different man or two. Is she dating anyone?"

"I don't know much about Sam. But I can find out."

William pulled out a business card from his wallet. "Perhaps one night you can come to my club, and we'll talk. While I have no doubt you can do anything you set your mind to, I'm still not sure the Dom lifestyle is for you."

"You might be right about that. But for Lexi, I'll give it a good shot."

"Call first so I can put your name on the doorman's list."

"Okay."

"I've got to get back to work. Call me."

Cash's phone rang, and he groaned when he saw it was Tiffany. What did she want now?

"Hi, darling. Where have you been all day?"

"Taking a personal day. I'm still waiting on that information from Preston."

"Oh," she said, and Cash imagined her red lips forming a perfect O. At one time he'd have thought that affectation charming. But now the only vision that came to mind was Greek Harpy Tiffany ready to devour the first hapless sailor who sailed too close.

"I thought we'd have dinner together."

At the same time she suggested they eat together, a text flashed from Lexi.

Lexi: Avoid process servers at all costs. Find another lawyer, one versed in contract law and civil cases ASAP. I'll talk to you soon as...

Lexi's rapid-fire texting stopped abruptly and Cash's jaw set with worry. Though, aside from Walker Givens' acting like a jerk to her, she was safe. Right?

"Cash!" Tiffany said. "Did you hear what I said?"

"Sorry. I got distracted."

"Darling, please pay attention. You disappeared yesterday, and we have a lot to talk about."

Yeah, he was sure. Just as he was positive she wanted to peg him to a location so the process servers could descend on him. It was impossible to evade them forever, but he wanted to find out what Lexi'd found out before he decided how to handle that.

"We'll get together for our usual Friday, okay? I've got to go."

"Cash!"

He hung up the phone and sent a text to his secretary on her cell phone.

Cash: Refuse legal papers. In fact, turn on voicemail and go home. I'll contact you when I want you back in the office. Tell people you have the stomach flu.

He waved over the waitress and ordered a beer, and went through his list of contacts to call for legal advice. It occurred to Cash his contact list was very thin. Aside from those at work, Walker Givens, and Tiffany, he had few people to call. He wondered when that happened. When he was at college he had a ton of friends, but over the years, between his involvement with the company and the Givens family, they fell away.

Plus he needed someone that didn't mix with anyone Walker Givens associated with. And since Cash's father and Walker Givens traveled in the same circles, he just couldn't rely on any of his father's old friends.

It occurred to Cash that in the past couple of years, since his father's sickness and death, he had become isolated. And he was even dependent on the Givens, father and daughter. Was Cash too absorbed in his angst, or did the Givens deliberately draw him in and other people out so Cash had no one else? Perhaps both, but now he realized how unhealthy that was. He had no people in his life, other than Lexi, to turn to for advice.

And he'd just met her.

Also, he had nowhere to go right now, no place where

the process servers might not find him. His apartment was probably being watched and Lexi wasn't home right now. The gym was out, as well the gentlemen's club where he kept a membership. Givens belonged to that one too.

And his phone needed a charge.

Cash needed a charger, so he set out in search of a phone store.

33

LEXI

WALKER GIVENS SWEPT INTO THE OUTER OFFICE FROM whatever meeting he'd attended.

"Maria," Givens said. "Get in touch with Top Notch Security. I want to talk with Justin Crone."

"Yes, sir," Maria said. She clacked her fingers on her keyboard.

As soon as Givens entered, Lexi stopped texting Cash and swallowed hard, wondering what Givens would do when he spotted her. He did a double take, stopped at her desk, and stared at her pointedly.

"I thought you weren't coming in today. Or ever."

Lexi wanted more than anything to leave this place and not come back. But if she had a chance to find more information to help Cash, she would do it. She reasoned since Cash was a client of the firm she was not in a conflict of interest with the firm, though. It did seem to her that Givens might be in one, regarding Cash and his company. Who did he represent at this time? Who paid him? Could he be the lawyer for both if he initiated a motion against Cash? That didn't seem ethical. In fact, it seemed downright shady.

But then Walker Givens hadn't shown himself to be an upstanding citizen.

"Sorry, Mr. Givens. I was very sick yesterday. I couldn't answer the phone. But when I saw how many messages you sent, it seemed best I came in."

"We managed without you for the day. But don't make a habit out of this. And I hope you learned your lesson about mixing personal concerns with business."

"Yes, sir. Sean Cashman is off my radar. Totally. And I apologize for what happened, sir." Lexi was lying through her teeth, but didn't regret it. Since the days of Machiavelli, and perhaps earlier, snakes like Givens lived by the maxim that all was fair in business.

"Hmph," grunted Givens. He fished a pile of file folders from his attaché case and dumped them on her desk. "Go through those. I've marked the ones that need motions. The others need research."

"Yes, Mr. Givens."

He strode into his office, and Lexi riffled through the folders greedily, but disappointingly none were about Cash. The motions showed Givens' legal strategy, though whether or not he'd get away with it was another story. Perhaps he hoped to leverage the legal action to persuade Cash to sign the sale papers for the company before a court could issue an order for a psychiatric examination.

Lexi pulled up the legal papers on Cash again. She couldn't give a copy to him, on the outside chance that a judge would consider that serving him the papers. But she checked on the filing date, and Gracey had submitted them just before 5 p.m. yesterday. But due to the complexity, someone had had to draw them up over the weekend. The research itself would take at least four good hours, especially on such a thin case. She wondered who'd prepared the brief to support Givens' claims. Then it took several hours to draft the complaint and pleadings. It wasn't exactly the sort of thing that you'd craft from a form.

And surprise, surprise, Gracey didn't file this electronically, but in person, probably to get the imprinted copies necessary for serving the motion to Cash. Givens was moving this along as fast as possible.

Lexi was hung between leaving and telling Cash what she knew, and staying and learning more.

Her office phone rang.

"Ms. Winters, come into my office, and bring your pad."

"Yes, sir."

Lexi pulled out the company iPad from her desk and fired it up. After a knock on the door, she entered his office.

It was overlarge, with a desk that was bigger than her double bed. Rows of law books filled the wall-to-wall bookcase behind the desk, and two leather Queen Ann chairs sat before the desk.

On the right-hand side of the wall was a long leather sofa, and on the left a small wet bar. A stack of bundled mail sat on his desk, indicating it was the first time this morning he'd entered his office. He propped his phone headset on his shoulder while he picked up the mail and looked through it. With two fingers, and without looking up, he motioned for Lexi to sit in one of the chairs at his desk.

"I see, Crone. Find him. Understand? Did you check out the gentleman's club? That address I gave you? Okay. I expect to hear from you later this afternoon. And no excuses."

Givens spoke in his usual take-no-prisoners attitude, and if Lexi weren't worried about Cash, she'd feel sorry for Justin Crone.

He hung up the phone abruptly.

"I have Mr. Crone looking for Mr. Cashman. He seems to have disappeared."

Lexi kept her face a neutral mask. If she hadn't worked for Walker Givens for as long as she had, she might not have been able to manage it. But working for Givens demanded that she learn the art of keeping a passive face. Otherwise, he'd pounce and deliver an oration about her faults and failings.

Lexi searched for the correct thing to say. If she said too much, Givens, perceptive as he was, would get the idea that she knew something about Cash.

"You wouldn't have any idea of where he could be?" He delivered the words in a heavy-handed tone of parental disapproval.

Lexi recognized this voice. It was Givens' lawyer interrogation voice. It dripped with authority, disapproval, and judgment. Because most people automatically tried to please an authority figure, Givens was used to people melting under its spell. Fortunately, Lexi had a weapon, a total lack of knowledge about the subject at hand.

"No, sir. I *do not*." She added an emphatic tone in her voice and even managed to convey a smidgen of indignation with her reply.

"Because," he persisted, "I would have to terminate your employment if you were lying to me, Ms. Winters. And I would have to warn prospective employers about you. I would hate if you forced me to do that."

Lexi would not let him frighten her. "You don't need to worry, Mr. Givens." *I won't use you as a job reference anyway.*

"Good. I have several items to go over with you regarding the work I gave you today."

Lexi spent the next half hour with Givens as he gave his instructions on his pending cases. Givens was one of those men who forgot nothing, and Lexi had to concentrate hard to get all the information typed into her pad. It disappointed her that he didn't mention any actions regarding Cash. He didn't trust her.

As Givens droned on with his third "one more thing," the door to his office opened abruptly. Lexi didn't need to turn to tell who'd entered. Tiffany Givens wore the most godawful perfume, and it permeated the room.

"Well, I can't find him, and he refuses to meet with me," huffed Tiffany.

"I have Justin Crone on the job."

Tiffany plopped into the other chair before her father's desk. She shot a disparaging glance at Lexi.

"I thought you quit, or got fired or something," she said with disdain.

"Ms. Winters generously understood that I was unnecessarily harsh with her yesterday," Givens said. "I hope you understand as well." He stared pointedly at Tiffany, and she squirmed uncomfortably in the chair. It was interesting the control that Givens had over his daughter. Up to this point, Lexi had thought Tiffany an uncontrollable force of nature.

Lexi stared at her pad, not reacting to either father or daughter, but she got it. Givens' actions were as clear as glass. He didn't believe that Lexi didn't know anything about Cash, and he was keeping her around as a possible source of information.

"Well, sir, if we've finished, I'll get on these items right away. I don't want to intrude on a visit by your daughter. We so rarely see her here." Lexi shot a saccharine-sweet smile at this horror of a woman and stood.

Tiffany narrowed her eyes at Lexi. She was no fool and recognized insincere words when she heard them. "It was a pleasure to see you again, Lexi," she said just as insincerely.

"I do hope you get a chance to use the employee discount before that hotel gets sold."

It was a parting shot, intended to remind Lexi of the humiliating incident at the hotel. And Lexi did blush remembering that moment when she saw Tiffany and Cash together and the horror she felt. Tiffany lifted her chin in mock victory, but Lexi just smiled.

"I hope so too," Lexi said, "but I might not be able to get the time off. There seems to be a new influx of work that will keep us all terribly busy." She flashed another ingratiating smile at Tiffany and walked toward the door. But as she did, Lexi got to thinking. Why would Tiffany offer up an employee discount to Cash's hotel? Givens and Associates was its own entity, wasn't it? They weren't employees of Cashman Industries. Or were they?

34

CASH

HE HAD ENOUGH CASH IN HIS POCKET TO PAY FOR A NEW charger and realized his supply of bills was growing thin. Cash wasn't using his credit cards in case Givens had them traced. He didn't put anything past "Uncle Walker." When he walked past a branch of the New York Library, he figured this was as good a place as any to hang out until he heard from Lexi. Cash sincerely hoped that she was okay, because it worried him that she was in the heart of the lion's den working on his behalf.

After finding an electric plug to charge his phone in the reference section, he pulled down a copy of the phone book. He used the resources of the public library to search for a new lawyer.

A librarian helpfully showed him the stacks where he could find out information on the local law firms. Who knew there were directories for this? He made notes in the small leather-bound notebook he kept in his inside suit pocket. His father had had Cash's name embossed on the outside in gold, and the fifteen-year-old Cash felt it was a stuffy gift and not at all fun. But after his father died, Cash found it in his room at his father's house and started carrying it each day. It was a small comfort to have something his father gave him close to Cash's heart. Now the journal served its true purpose as Cash searched for an advisor to help him.

He made notes about people who sounded like good fits. After gathering six names of firms, he decided he needed a place from which to make calls. But the library wasn't the place to do this, and he wished he'd heard from Lexi.

As if she divined his thoughts, a text popped up on his phone.

Lexi: Don't go to my apartment. Givens has a PI looking for you, and I worry he will follow me.

Well, hell. What was he supposed to do now? He'd have to get a hotel room, and he needed cash for that. Having no other choice, he searched on his phone for different branches of his bank. He decided that, to be on the safe side, he'd take the subway to another part of town, to throw "Uncle Walker's" bulldogs off the trail. Cabs kept records of pick-ups and drop-offs, so he couldn't take one of those.

Cash used the subway to take him to a smaller branch of his bank across town. No one would suspect him of traveling to that section of the city.

The ride, like any on the New York subway, was brutal. He remembered to stuff his phone and his wallet in the lower inside jacket pocket before he boarded, so no one inadvertently "found" the two items during the ride. Two passengers gave him suspicious glances for his expensive suit and shoes, but he stood big and buff enough to present a challenge to most people on the train. But most New Yorkers just wanted to get on with their day with the minimum of trouble. Soon enough Cash found himself on the street where one branch of his bank did business.

The branch manager was polite but seemed overly concerned in keeping Cash for as long as possible. Cash threatened to close his entire account if the banker didn't deliver five thousand dollars within five minutes. The man smiled at him as tight as a vise before complying with Cash's request. A small branch like this wouldn't keep a large cash reserve on hand but he only needed walking-around money for a couple days, so he withdrew five thousand dollars. While he was at it, he transferred a substantial sum to a new account and claimed a new debit card. Hotels usually required a credit card, and it would take Givens' investigators a couple of days to figure out what he was up to. At least Cash hoped that.

"Your discretion on these matters is essential," warned Cash. "If I find out you gave out this information improperly, I will close my accounts. Then I will inform the CEO of your company by letter of the lack of service I received from you."

"I understand," the man said tightly and with a bit of attitude. But that was too bad. Cash was fighting for his professional life. He made sure the man knew the consequences of violating his privacy.

Cash left quickly and scoped out hotel choices via his phone. He picked a chain hotel about half a mile from midtown and paid for a week with his new debit card. If he liked it, he'd stay longer if needed, but he didn't think he'd need to do that.

His phone chirped with a text.

Unknown texter: Hi. This is Sam. Lexi thinks Givens put a trace on her phone. Can you meet her tonight?

What kind of craziness was this? What did Lexi learn to suspect that Givens put a trace on her phone?

Cash: Where?

Sam: A bar called Sullivan's.
Cash: Address? Time?

Sam sent the information and Cash thought that if Givens had someone tracking phones, he should change out his phone. All that needed to happen was Givens' accessing his phone account and turning on phone location, and it would be all over.

So his next stop was a phone store where he changed his phone and his number. As he paid the money to buy the new device, he thought ducking Walkers Givens was getting damn annoying.

He uploaded his contacts, just in case he needed them, and bought a couple of burner phones as well in case he needed to make contact with Givens. He had the clerk wipe his old phone, then outside the store, crushed it and tossed it in the trash.

After taking care of the hotel and phone situation, he ducked into a clothing store and bought casual clothes. His suit, a spare set of jeans, and several t-shirts were stuffed in the shopping bags. Then he changed into a pair of dark jeans and t-shirt, sneakers, and a light jacket. Now he looked the part of a casual New Yorker instead of a high-powered businessman.

Another subway ride brought him to his hotel where he checked in. He spent the next hour calling lawyers from one of the burner phones. He chose smaller mid-range firms that seemed qualified to handle corporate business issues. Most returned his calls within an hour, but he only set appointments for the next day with two with them. Hopefully, when he met with Lexi, he would get more information about the type of representation he'd need.

With an hour to go before he met Lexi, he caught a cab to Sullivan's, a typical Irish bar with a kitchen. Signature wood paneling covered the walls, and a long wooden bar dominated the room. He found the darkest corner he could, ordered some fish, chips, and beer, and waited for her to show up. Sam's texting him out of the blue made him nervous. He didn't really know if it was Sam who texted, or someone pretending to be Sam.

Maybe he was paranoid.

It's not paranoia if they are after you.

These words were small comfort when his company hung on the predations of a man he no longer trusted.

With the day's activity behind him, Cash couldn't relax and he had nothing to occupy his mind. Worse yet, he'd long since finished his meal and pushed away the baskets lined with paper that once held his food, and Lexi had not yet arrived. Now he worried about her and wondered if she was okay. He also belatedly realized that since he changed his phone number, Lexi had no way to get in touch. He glanced around the bar and spotted two men entering. They were checking out the bar, and the hairs on the back of his neck rose. These weren't two men looking for a drink or two. They were searching for someone. Cash did not want to take the chance it was him they were after.

He wasn't sure what to do. Sit pat and hope that with his new wardrobe they wouldn't recognize him, or try to leave casually and hope they didn't notice him?

Cash, he told himself, *you aren't very good at this cloak and dagger stuff. You should stick to avionics.*

Lexi didn't arrive but unexpectedly someone he did know walked through the door. He scanned the room, then walked straight to Cash's table.

LEXI WAS BESIDE HERSELF. THE MORE SHE FOUND OUT ABOUT what Walker Givens was doing, the more she wanted to stride into his office and wring his neck.

Her suspicions were correct. Through the corporate filings online she found that Givens and Associates were a subsidiary of Cashman Industries. It only occurred a few years ago, long after Givens established the firm. Something must have happened to shift the financial fortunes of the firm, and she suspected that Cash's father bailed out Givens by buying Givens and Associates.

No way Givens could represent Cash as an individual and not generate a conflict of interest with Cashman Industries.

Lexi grew angry that Walker Givens was duplicitous enough to pretend he had Cash's best interests at heart. His primary responsibility was to the company first, Cash second, if he fit in that category of a client at all.

Still, what motivated Givens to sell out his best friend's son? She wished she had the services of a company like Top Notch Security to investigate, but she'd never have enough money for that kind of investigation. She'd had to rely on her research skills, and that would only get her so far.

A man walked into the office, and Lexi didn't like the pensive aura he exuded. Maria announced over Givens' office intercom that Justin Crone had arrived.

Lexi sat on the edge of her seat, wondering how to listen in on the conversation.

"Maria," the intercom blared. "Get us two cups of coffee."

"Yes, sir."

Maria dutifully left the office for the kitchen, giving Lexi the chance she needed. Concocting the excuse of looking for office supplies in Maria's desk, she moved toward it and sat at the desk, sliding the chair closer to the door. She was in luck. Crone had not closed the door all the way. Lexi sucked in a breath and concentrated on picking up Crone's words.

And what she heard was not good. Phone traces and surveillance were two words that she caught.

"What are you looking for?"

Lexi nearly jumped as Maria stood in front of her with two cups of coffee in hand.

"Oh, sorry. Needed a pen." She pulled one hastily out of Maria's top drawer.

"Open Mr. Givens' door," Maria said with a huff. Lexi smiled. Technically, she was Maria's supervisor, but Maria conveniently forgot that, choosing instead to insist that she reported directly to Mr. Givens. Lexi allowed Maria her illusions because she didn't want to upset anyone in the office today.

Lexi opened the door for Maria, then walked back to her desk, and pulled out her phone. And that was when she frantically tapped the message to Cash conveying her worst fears that Givens had a PI looking for him.

"You aren't," said Maria condescendingly, "supposed to use your cell phone in the office."

Normally, Lexi would roll her eyes and ignore her. Not today.

"My roommate was worried I came back to work too early. I just told her I was fine."

At that moment Justin Crone appeared from Givens' office and glanced at Lexi with interest. Then he walked out of the door without saying a word.

Lexi shivered, and fear for Cash curled in her gut. But to help Cash she had to pretend she was here for work.

She tapped down her frustration as she sped through the work Givens had given her that day. At least she'd appear the pliant employee while she spied on her boss. She filed the motions electronically and performed cursory searches on the law for the three cases that needed it. The briefs she would prepare tomorrow. It frustrated Lexi she couldn't find out more about Walker Givens and why Cashman Industries bought his firm.

Maria left at 4 p.m. with a brief good night. That left Walker Givens still in his office. It wasn't unusual that he worked late, though Lexi wondered what he was working on.

But the door to the office opened and Givens stepped out.

"Still here, Ms. Winters."

"Just catching up, Mr. Givens," she said. "You've heard the old saying, one day away and a week's work to pay."

"Is that what they say?" he said, sounding unconvinced.

Lexi shrugged.

"Don't stay too long," he said. "We have a busy day

tomorrow. I expect we'll be in court for motions filed on your day off."

Right. Day off. What a jerk. And then the alarm bells sounded in her head. Tomorrow? When Cash hadn't received the papers? What the hell was Givens up to now?

As soon as Givens left, she called Cash, but the message shot to voicemail. Hell, what was she supposed to do now?

She couldn't even think of digging around more. She had to find Cash and talk with him. She called Sam.

"I can't find Cash," she said. Her stressed voice warned Samantha against spouting the usual truisms—he's busy, or he went home, or some other nonsense.

"Why?"

"I suppose he's trying to hide from Mr. Givens' process servers. Oh, it's a mess, Sam. Givens has worked up a case to wrest temporary control of Cash's company from him."

"Let's get a pizza at Romallo's and talk."

Sam was there with a pitcher of beer and two glasses when she arrived. Sam had gone through half her glass.

"Beer," Lexi said, "does not preserve an hourglass figure."

"Stress contributes to poor skin tone."

"So you're drinking to improve your skin?"

"You know it."

The pizza arrived, but it surprised Lexi to find the man from the night before, William, bearing it.

"One of Romallo's famous meat pizzas, ladies," he said with a wink to Samantha.

"I only ordered—" started Sam.

"But you like everything, don't you? Pepperoni, *meatballs*, and *sausage*."

The way he slid *meatballs* and *sausage* off his tongue

almost sounded obscene, and Sam stared at him with her mouth open.

"As long as you don't charge us for the extra meat," Lexi said with a smirk. Usually, it was Lexi who got the flirts, but this guy dead-on took his best shot with Samantha.

"No. No charge at all. I'm doing a taste test of new recipes, and would value your opinion."

"You don't make your own sausage," accused Samantha. Her eyes narrowed with suspicion.

"Indeed, we do. *Long, fat ropes* of sausage according to an old family recipe."

Samantha's cheeks blazed red as she cycled every dirty thought in regards to *sausage*. Lexi had to bite her tongue to keep from laughing.

"But where is your friend, Mr. Cashman?" William asked.

"I thought he was your friend," Samantha said. "He was sitting with you last night."

"Mr. Cashman and I were discussing a certain arrangement."

"Such as?"

"Would you really like to know?" William said in a voice so sexy and low, Lexi thought she'd fall off her chair. Samantha's breathing hitched and her eyes got very wide.

"I'm not sure," she said. "What kind of arrangement?"

"I could describe it, but it would be so much better if you observed for yourself at my club. Especially if Mr. Cashman joined us," he said, turning his head to Lexi.

"I don't know where he is," Lexi said.

"Strange, he was here for an early lunch."

"He was?" Lexi said. "Did he happen to mention where he was going?"

William must have caught the undertone of stress in Lexi's voice because immediately his face showed concern.

"Is everything okay between you?" he said.

"There is trouble with his business," spouted Samantha. "His evil uncle is trying to take his business away, and he's trying to avoid process servers."

"Worse," said Lexi miserably. "The uncle has private investigators looking for him."

"Sounds like Mr. Cashman could use a hand. Give me a few minutes and I'll see what I can do. In the meantime, *mangia,* as they say in the old country."

William stepped through the kitchen doors, and they ate their pizza, though Lexi found it hard to swallow. Every part of her tensed with worry, and that included her stomach. Even her beer didn't go down well.

"Ladies," William said with a smile as he approached the table again. "Enjoying the pizza?"

"It's delicious," Lexi said politely but without enthusiasm.

"Good. I want you well fed before you go to the club."

"And which club is that?" Samantha said.

"Give me your phone," he said. Reluctantly Samantha handed him the device, and he pulled up a map program and typed in an address.

"Just follow the yellow line," he said with a wink to Samantha. He turned to Lexi. "And before you know it, I'll have you reunited with Mr. Cashman."

"Where he is?" Lexi said. "I'll—"

"You'll do no such thing," William said with deadly seriousness. "Yes, The PIs located Mr. Cashman, but I'll get him out now. Do as I say, Lexi. It's safer for everyone that way."

"TAKE OUT YOUR PHONE," WILLIAM SAID. "AND GIVE IT to me."

"What?"

"Those men over there found you with it."

Cash stared at the two men who'd followed him into the bar. "How?"

"We'll talk on the way."

"It's a brand new phone."

"Judging by that suit you wore last night, you can afford it."

"That doesn't bother me. Finding me so easily does though." He handed the phone to William, who discreetly handed it off to a younger man as he brushed past them.

"Who *are* you?"

"Right now, your lover. Act drunk."

"Come on, sweetheart," William said loud enough for others to hear. "Don't be difficult like the last time. Let's go home, and I'll tuck you into bed."

Cash, as instructed, played at stumbling to his feet and

mumbling, while William threw a protective arm around him.

"Keep your head down. They are looking for an over-dressed man in a five-thousand-dollar suit. Not some gay lush being hauled off by a codependent lover."

"Damn, don't you have all the romantic words on your tongue."

"You don't even know."

Cash gave a little stumble as they exited the building, but William gripped him tight.

"Had much practice at this?" William said.

"The usual, prep school, college."

"Ah, the rich man's vices."

"Alcohol?"

"No. Private schools."

"It doesn't help to make friends with a rich person when you disrespect his educational institutions."

"You can straighten up. We lost them. They're happily tracking Ricky while he leads them a merry chase."

"He's going to be okay?"

"No problem. Ricky's been evading the parents and school authorities for years now."

"The parents?"

"He's the youngest brother. I had to make him sit down and get a GED to keep the parents happy."

"Again, who are you?" Cash asked and smiled.

"No anyone someone like you needs or wants to know."

"Well, thanks. I should be getting on my way then."

"No way, hombre. Ms. Lexi is waiting for you at my club."

What did "Master William" think he was doing dragging Lexi to his BDSM club?

"What the hell?"

"She's fine. She's with her friend, Samantha. And I've instructed my employee to keep them in an entry room until we get there."

"And you got involved how?"

"They came in for a pizza, and I couldn't stand the look of distress on your Ms. Lexi's face."

"Bullshit." Cash was glad that William had helped him out of a bad situation, but he didn't like that the "Master" chose to stick his nose in Cash's personal life. Up to this point, William was reluctant to expose Cash and Lexi to his BDSM world. Now all of sudden he was into it?

William laughed. "You are right. It seemed the perfect opportunity to see if Ms. Samantha might have an interest in my lifestyle. You can't blame a guy for trying."

Cash's ire settled but didn't completely dissipate. His protective feelings toward Lexi extended to Lexi's friend, who'd generously allowed him to sleep on the couch last night.

"You really like her?"

"Been burning with an unrequited need to tie her up and stripe her impertinent bottom red for the past year now."

"Funny. You don't strike me as the shy type of guy. Why didn't you ask her?"

"You have to admit you can't come straight out and ask a woman, 'Do you prefer a flogger or a riding crop when I whip you?'"

Cash shrugged. "It might work better than "'Haven't I met you before?'"

"No, it really doesn't."

"Sounds like you've tried it."

William shrugged. "In my younger days, I wasn't so smooth."

They walked down the sidewalk, and an uneasy silence settled between them.

"How did you meet Lexi?" William said, trying to start a conversation.

"We were on a plane. She was reading *Fifty Shades*. It was a conversation starter."

"You lucked out then."

"I think so. Even if the BDSM thing doesn't work out, maybe we have something else to build on. For the first time, I *like* a woman. She's unlike anyone else I ever met."

"I wouldn't count on her wanting to sustain a relationship with you if she's truly into the lifestyle and you aren't. What happens in the playroom is an important part of a practitioner's sex life."

"Seriously. You have a playroom?"

"At New York apartment prices? No. But I have the club, and that's where I spend most of my off time."

"Pizza and BDSM. You sound like a well-rounded man."

"Oh, there's more to Guglielmo Ianucci than that. But those, right now, are the main things. Here we are. Down that alley."

"Guglielmo?"

"Italian for William."

Cash wondered if he should walk down an alley with a Guglielmo Ianucci. He wasn't a prejudiced man. At least that was what he thought about himself, but hanging out with people that might be part of the mob, which he suspected of "Master William," could create complications.

But Lexi was in that man's club and he wanted to talk to her to make sure she was safe. It hit him then just how important her safety had become to him.

"So, what kind of club is this?" asked Cash. "It is a private club for members or the type of club where only a dozen of your best buds hang?"

"You are asking if I run this club for money? Yes, I do. But we vet our select clientele thoroughly. I know each member personally. And, also, we value our privacy. Coming to this club is a privilege. And we don't appreciate people who don't honor that. I will ask you to sign a confidentiality agreement before you enter the club proper."

"We'll see about entering the club. I do want to talk with Lexi, though."

"That's up to you, but I'll still insist you sign the agreement before you leave."

They stood outside a door with a keypad and William entered a code.

"Just so you know, we change the code each day. People we don't want in don't get the daily code."

"Seems like a good precaution," agreed Cash.

They walked into a reception area painted in a dark purple with a black carpet. A young man sat behind a black desk. He wore a leather jacket and pants with no shirt underneath. Immediately the young man got up and then sunk to his knees with his head down.

"Good boy," William said approvingly. "Get up now, and get three sets of confidentiality agreements for our guests."

"Yes, Master William."

"Carlo is one of my trainees. He is learning how to be a good submissive. He hopes one day to find his Dom."

Carlo brought the agreements to William.

"Is there anything else, sir?" Carlo asked.

"No. Please make the rounds of the club and make sure our guests have everything they need."

"Yes, sir." Carlo trotted off down a long hall to do as the Dom bid.

"I should hire you as my training manager," quipped Cash.

"Do you allow corporal punishment?"

"No. The authorities take a dim view of that."

"Then that wouldn't work. Besides, I have enough jobs. Lexi and Samantha should be in here."

William opened the first right-hand door off the hallway Carlo had walked down.

"Cash!" Lexi said.

"Ladies, I hope you are comfortable," William said.

"Just a little bored," Samantha said. "What took you guys so long?"

"We walked," William said. "Here, ladies. I need you to sign these before you leave. Of course, you can leave at any time, but I hope you'll stay awhile and take a look around."

"What kind of place is this?" Samantha asked. "You didn't say before you rushed off, though your receptionist's clothes, or lack of them, is provocative."

"This is a BDSM club. We serve a select clientele."

Cash watch Lexi's breath hitch and her pupils widen. Samantha looked intrigued as well, but she tried to hide it by looking away from William.

"Is this," Samantha said, "something you do when you're not slinging pizzas?"

"Yes," William said.

"You hurt women?" Samantha said. Her voice rose with those words.

"Only a little," he said with a smile. "Mostly, they feel pleasure. But it's a unique kind of pleasure and not everyone appreciates it."

"And you want me to see this?"

"I'd very much like you to see it. And talk about it if you want."

"What about it, Lexi?" Cash said. "Do you want to see what Master William has to offer?

37

LEXI DREW IN A DEEP BREATH AS HER HEART RACED AT THE memory of the first time she went to a BDSM club with Cash.

"I guess it wouldn't hurt to take a look around."

"Lexi!" Samantha said. She looked around, and Lexi noticed Cash and William watching them with interest.

"Where is your spirit of adventure?" whispered Lexi into Sam's ear. "Did you encourage me to try new things?"

"I didn't mean this!" Sam said in a low voice.

"Try it, you might like it," challenged Lexi.

"Who are you and where is my roommate?"

"Bok, bok, bok," Lexi whispered in her ear.

"I'm going to get you back for this, Lexi Winters," Sam hissed.

"What's it going to be, ladies?" William said.

"Let's see those agreements," Lexi said. "I'm a paralegal. I only sign after I read it." Samantha's eyes grew wider, as if she couldn't believe Lexi was about to take a walk on the wild side.

"Well, here you go, Ms. Lexi."

Lexi read the agreement written in layman's terms. The agreement demanded the signer not to disclose the club's location or anything seen or heard at the club. Guests were to respect the privacy of the other guests, and not involve themselves in an activity without the express consent of the participants. It forbade uninvited or non-consensual touching, and they were to promise to respect the physical and emotional boundaries of other guests. If the guest didn't honor the agreement, security would escort them out and the guest would not be allowed back.

It all made sense to her.

"Do you have a pen?" Lexi asked.

Cash smiled at her while she scribbled her name, and Lexi handed the pen to Samantha, who bit her lip as she signed her set of papers. Cash was the last, and Master William smiled widely as they handed him the papers.

"Good. Give me a minute to put these away and change, and I'll be right back."

Samantha swallowed hard. "Change?" she said when he left the room.

"Will we be overdressed again?" Lexi said to Cash.

"I can always take off my shirt," Cash said with a grin.

"Let's not go overboard."

"Did someone express concern about clothes?" William said. He reappeared wearing leather pants, a tight black tee, and leather jacket. "I wouldn't want you ladies uncomfortable, nor overexposed, not until you want to be. So for you, Ms. Lexi, I brought a perfectly respectable leather dress, nothing fancy or too short and a simple leather mask. And for you, Ms. Samantha, something a little special. I hope you don't mind. Let's let the ladies dress, Cash."

William placed clothes and shoes on the table. He shepherded Cash out of the room and closed the door. Sam stared at her dress, which was black lace over a flesh-colored underdress. "Wow," she said. "I didn't know dress-up was part of this."

"I guess," Lexi said, "it's all about the fantasy."

They changed quickly, backs to each other, and when they turned, they both giggled.

"Okay," Lexi said. "This is way more fun than Halloween."

Lexi's dress was as William said, but cut low in the front. As long as it covered her assets she didn't mind. Samantha's dress was truly stunning, highlighting every curve but revealing nothing. "Don't forget this," Lexi said holding up a black lace eye mask.

"What do you think?" Samantha said as she tied it on.

"Gorgeous. Like Batgirl, right?"

"Batgirl didn't wear a skirt or anything that sexy."

"That's right. Black leather catsuit."

"No, that was Catwoman."

"I can be Catwoman."

"With claws?" Samantha said.

"Kitten always has claws. Meow."

"Oh gawd," Samantha said.

Lexi opened the door, and William's and Cash's heads snapped up. Cash gave her a smile that was brighter than the sun. William's eyelids lowered as he stared at Samantha, and her cheeks flushed.

"I like leather on you," Cash said.

"Hmm," Lexi said stepping toward him. "I guess you'll have to keep me supplied in it. I don't earn enough for this kind of wardrobe."

He reached to touch her mask with his fingertip. "Are you suggesting that I take you as a kept woman?"

"Only if you can catch me," she teased.

"Oh," William said, "and one more thing. While the scenes can get intense, there is no sex at this club."

"No sex?" Lexi said.

"The authorities take a dim view of sexual activities in a place of business, so no explicit intercourse, anal or otherwise, and no oral sex. If you feel the need, take it elsewhere."

"Gee," Samantha said. "Where's the fun in that?"

William smiled mischievously. "Let me give you the grand tour. Oh, and one more rule. Don't interrupt a scene or be disruptive by being too loud. The participants enjoy the intense concentration they have for each other so we need to respect that. But tonight you are in a for a treat."

"Oh?" Samantha said.

"It's Shibari night," he said with a sly smile.

"Shibari?" mouthed Samantha, and Lexi gave a little shake of her head. She didn't know what it was, but the name sounded intriguing.

"What's Shibari?" Cash asked.

"It is the Japanese art of rope binding. It's an art form all its own."

"No spanking?" Samantha said.

"Well," William said, "some play includes spanking, but the object of Shibari is to create sensual feelings by the combinations of ropes and ties. It is giving submission to the person doing the tying."

Lexi's throat got dry. The thought of Cash binding her, making her vulnerable, sounded sexy in a way she'd never imagined.

"That sounds great. Is there a scene now?"

"Let's see. We should be in full swing, as it were." William winked at them while he put his hand on Samantha's arm. He leaned in and whispered in her ear, and she blushed but relaxed.

Cash and Lexi followed William and Samantha into a large former factory room with red brick walls. The industrial windows displayed scenes of men and women in different situations, some bound, chained, or cuffed. Each of the windows had a spotlight shining on it. One picture caught Lexi's eye, of a woman with her hands in leather cuffs before her, biting on the end of a whip draped on her shoulders. She stared intently forward, pupils wide and her mouth looking hungry. Lexi couldn't take her eyes off it until Cash steered her shoulders away.

Lexi shivered as they walked forward to a circle of people gathered in the center of the room. Several spotlights shone down on the two people in the middle. Lexi gasped. On a mat in the middle of the floor, a man hovered over a woman with her arms tied to her knees. An elaborate weave of bright red rope was wrapped around her hips and thighs. The man bent by her head and spoke to her softly. She nodded her head but didn't speak. Her face relaxed in utter bliss and Lexi recognized it as the same feeling she got with Cash when they were in the BDSM club in the Virgin Islands.

The man pulled down on a large hook hanging from the ceiling, and he put it underneath, in a space between her tied wrists and her knees. He gave a signal with his hand, and a winch raised her slowly from the floor. She hung suspended one leg pointing out from the knee and the other pointing to the ground. The man stood by her head and spoke her, touching her jaw gently. She shivered and then gasped, and Lexi wondered if she'd had an orgasm.

Fuck. This had to be the sexiest thing she ever saw.

She glanced at Cash, whose eyes glazed, and his breathing hitched slightly faster. Lexi looked at Samantha, who seemed to be in a trance as William stroked her arm gently and whispered in her ear.

The spotlight snapped off, and another flooded a section of the room that the crowd walked toward. Lexi saw a blindfolded woman, dressed in spiked heels and a baby doll nightie, sitting on a wooden chair. The man leaned in and spoke to her, though so quietly they couldn't make out the words. Lexi imagined Cash whispering in her ear, inciting a flood of heat with his words, and a pool of liquid fire sank into her panties.

The Dom moved the woman and crossed her wrists, then gently wrapped them together with neon pink rope. That done, he whispered in her ear again and her perfectly painted and glossed red lips formed a smile. He pushed the bound wrists to her chest slowly, sensuously, and wrapped another length several times around the back of the chair. He tested the ties, pulling on them, and made sure they weren't too tight.

"This," whispered William, "is relatively simple rope work, as he and she are still learning. But look at the expression on her face. She's already entered subspace, and the more he binds her, the higher she flies."

Lexi noticed that Samantha had leaned into William and as he put his arm around her, she didn't protest.

The Dom lifted one spike-heeled foot and wrapped it around one ankle with utmost deliberation. Her mouth gasped, but otherwise, no sound came from her lips. He wound the rope under the arch of her heel and bent her knee. He pushed up, showing her satin-covered crotch, and tied her shoe and ankle to the leg of the chair. Then he did the same thing to the other, and now the space between her legs was exposed, and Lexi noticed the wet spot that spread on the woman's panties.

Her own breathing sped up, and she swallowed hard, but there was no moisture in her throat to satisfy the dryness there. This was crazy.

Insane.

And the hottest thing she'd ever seen.

"What do you think, ladies? Want to give it a try?" William said.

"YES," LEXI SAID HOARSELY. "I MEAN IF CASH DOES IT."

Cash smiled at her in amazement and William smiled too.

"We can arrange that."

"But I've never—" started Cash.

"I'll be right there next to you, demonstrating on Ms. Samantha, that is, if you so permit, Ms. Samantha."

Samantha's breath hitched. "Sure. I mean, if Lexi does it too."

"Let me set things up," William said. "I'll be right back."

Cash leaned into Lexi. "You sure you want to do this?"

"Why not? It looks harmless enough."

"I'm not sure," Cash said. "Enrico told me that all BDSM practices could be dangerous."

"The only danger I see right now is you trying to back out," Lexi said teasingly. She tossed her hair, and Cash's cock twitched in his jeans.

"Is that a challenge?" Cash asked.

"Yes. We'll see who is begging whom to go to bed in thirty days," she said with a sly smile plastered on her face.

Cash grabbed Lexi around the waist impulsively and kissed her neck.

"Oh, geesh," Samantha said. "Get a room."

"Ladies and gentlemen," a voice said over the intercom. "Master William is stepping into the spotlight tonight to give a beginner's class in Shibari knot tying. With him is a friend, and the lovely ladies, Ms. Lexi and Ms. Samantha."

Murmurs of approval ran through the small crowd, and a spotlight snapped on in the hall. All turned and walked to it, while William stepped into the lighted circle.

"My friends," he said, "many of you have asked for a practical demonstration of Shibari. Mr. Cash, Ms. Lexi, and Ms. Samantha, please come."

They stepped into the area, and William arranged the women to stand side by side. Beside him was a large black gym bag and he put his hand inside and pulled out two long skeins bundled with the rope twisted around the middle. He handed one to Cash.

"Do as I do," William said.

Cash paid attention as William pulled Samantha's arms straight out and then mirrored his movements.

William addressed the group around them and untied the skein and shook it loose. Smoothly he doubled the rope. William impressed Cash with the ease with which he snaked the rope through his hands as if the fiber was an organic part of his hand.

"We are starting with simple wraps. As you all know, more advanced forms present as intricate weaves, but before we get there, we need to master the basics."

"Shibari originated from Hojo-jutsu, a method of restraining captives and a form of torture. It evolved into the erotic bondage form called Kinbaku, which translates as 'the beauty of tight binding.' This happened in the late 19th and early 20th centuries. In the US we use the term Shibari more than Kinbaku, meaning 'decorative tie,' though we start with Kinbaku and move into the weaving forms that denote true Shibari.

"Different terms are applied to the person taking the binding. M-jo is the term for a submissive woman, m-o, for a submissive man, though those are personal terms. In professional stage art, the person performing the binding is a rigger, while rope captives call themselves models."

"When working with your m-jo, as in all BDSM practices, it is important to take inventory of any physical problems or health conditions which could be aggravated by binding. Samantha-mi, do you have any conditions that binding would aggravate?"

"No."

"No, what," he said in a low voice.

Samantha looked panicked for a second, and she glanced at Lexi, who mouthed "sir."

"No, sir."

"Excellent, Samantha-mi. Lexi-san, do you have any health conditions that pressure would worsen?"

Lexi looked at the floor. "No, Master William."

Cash thought Lexi never looked so sexy or gorgeous at that moment. He could hear his heart beating in his chest.

"Beautiful," William said, and Cash wasn't sure he meant Lexi, Samantha, or both. But most definitely, both women, standing in the spotlight and wearing the costumes and masks provided, appeared sexy and mysterious. And in Lexi's case, absolutely fuckable. Cash's cock tingled and twitched. Who knew Cash would like leather this much?

This was going to be a difficult scene to get through.

"When we wrap the rope we will do it with our models' comfort in mind. It is important to leave the space of two fingers between the rope and the model's body. Drawing the rope too tight will cause injury, possible nerve damage that could potentially be permanent. So as in any BDSM practice, the dominant needs to take care he does not hurt his sub. And all of you know how precious our subs are."

William looked directly into Sam's eyes, and her breathing hitched. She lowered her eyes.

William held out his hands and took Sam's fingers into his and urged her to hold her arms straight out. With a sensuously slow draw-down on either arm, he positioned her wrists together. Cash immediately saw what William was doing. The little touches on sensitive parts of Samantha's body would draw out her desire. It would be a slow build to tease out her excitement. Cash wasn't sure this was part of traditional Shibari, but he could see it was part of William's Shibari.

And Cash couldn't wait to start.

He mirrored William's moves on Lexi, who swallowed hard as his fingertips brushed down her arm. Her skin pebbled in goosebumps and her lips trembled.

This was wonderful. Why had he not learned about this way of arousing a woman before? Simply kissing a woman and touching her nipples or her mound seemed amateurish now. What's more, Lexi's reactions to his touch brought him a rush of pleasure. She savored every simple brush of his flesh against hers. His heart filled with warmth at this luscious woman who waited, trembled, for his fingers on her body.

William glanced at Cash, and gave him a sly smile and nodded encouragement.

"We," William said, "call this loop the 'bite.' Hold it off to the side or use it as the lead, depending on how we make our first wrap. It is just a simple turn around the wrists, and again, making sure the rope is flat and not tight on the skin. The more wraps you do disperses the point of tension on the skin, reducing but not eliminating the danger of damage. It is important to remain focused on the sub and notice any signs of discomfort, wiggling, attempts to self-adjust. And also watch for your sub dropping into subspace, which may make them susceptible to injury."

William stood to the side to give the spectators the chance to observe his movements. He wrapped the bite under and around the first wraps, and then looped the longer running length and made a square knot with the first bite. William made a second knot with the first and second loops. His practiced fingers moved smoothly, and a bead of sweat tickled Cash's forehead as he worked to keep up. Lexi gave him a smile of encouragement.

"Come here," she whispered. He leaned forward, and she brushed her lips against his forehead, swiping the sweat with her tongue.

Cash stared at her, his eyes wide, blown away by this act. It was simple and elegant and spared him embarrassment from sweating in front of this group.

He had never felt so cared for in his life.

Immediately, Lexi lowered her eyes again, appearing once more the perfect submissive, and Cash knew he was in love.

He slid his fingers along her jawline, and she gave him a gaze of absolute adoration that made him feel powerful and bigger than life.

Cash drew in a deep breath, expanding his chest, and straightened his spine. Whatever happened, he'd make sure that Lexi was proud of him this night despite his being a newbie Dom.

He concentrated on the wraps that William displayed.

Before long each women had her arms over her head and bent down her back and secured so that her arms weren't moving anywhere.

He loved this. Cash imagined pushing Lexi against the wall and sucking her tits until the nipples pebbled and she squirmed under his tongue. His cock stirred, excited by the idea, and he struggled to keep his composure.

Lexi's breathing slowed, and her eyelashes fluttered, and Cash recognized this reaction from the night he took her to the BDSM club.

Subspace.

Samantha didn't look like she was there, but her eyes were shining. She was enjoying the absolute attention of Master William, who took extra delight in "checking" the ropes, giving Samantha little touches that made her cheeks flame. From the look in her eyes, she was under Master William's spell.

And Lexi was under his.

And then everything went to shit.

39

LEXI

As Cash worked the wraps on her body, Lexi sank into the luxury of his working the knots and caressing her skin with his fingers. The people watching them faded into the background. Samantha and William were mere shadows in her mind. All that existed was her and him, and the intense intimacy between them as he stole her body's movement and released her mind.

Cash smiled, and it was if the sun shone down only on her. He whispered in her ear how beautiful she was and it was as if an angel sang to her soul. She soared high above the clouds, floaty, warm, and wonderful.

And it crashed in a rush as loud banging rang through the building, and men in uniforms rushed in, pointing guns, and yelling. Lexi, disoriented and confused, tried to sort out the noises and the movement. Her mind snapped to the present, the chilly refurbished factory room, and finally pieced together that police had raided William's club.

"Everyone down on the ground! On the ground! Hands behind your head!"

The club members dropped to the ancient polished hardwood floor with grumbles and groans.

"Fuck!" William swore. With a knife in his hands, he attempted to cut the ropes off Samantha, apologizing to her over and over. Sam looked at him in shock, comprehension coming slowly.

"Drop that knife!" snapped a uniformed officer. William held his hands up and let the knife lose where it clattered on the concrete floor.

"On the ground! Hands behind your head!"

Cash put his arms around Lexi and helped her to her knees.

"Get the fuck away from her," snapped another officer.

"But she needs help. Let me untie her, for fuck's sake."

"Shut up and do what we tell you or we'll add resisting arrest to your charges."

"Who is Guglielmo Ianucci?"

"Here," William said raising his hand. "Is that who I think it is?"

"Stand up, slowly," said a menacing voice.

William stood. "Phillips. What the hell? What's going on?"

"Search warrants."

"What? Damn it, Phillips, for what?"

The cop looked away. "Prostitution and facilitating."

The cop named Phillips glanced at the club members flattened on the floor, waiting for the officers to do their work. One woman sobbed. "For god's sake, Alice," said the man next to her. "It's going to be okay."

"I've never been to jail."

"We don't know if they are going to take us to jail. Just tell them your name and then don't say a word."

"Be quiet over there."

Lexi thought the man gave Alice excellent advice. They should all stay quiet. She sighed. This was going to be a long night and one that wouldn't end up well if she didn't make it to work tomorrow.

Which she probably wouldn't if they booked her.

As a paralegal, she knew that protesting her innocence wouldn't do a damn bit of good. But she didn't want to get ahead of herself here.

One by one, police took club members out of the club room and into the atrium.

"This is fucking bullshit," hissed William. "Samantha, I'm so, so, sorry. This wasn't supposed to happen."

Samantha didn't speak, and William looked supremely unhappy. But Sam was always good in a crisis and waited this out even if she wasn't talking to William. Lexi, knowing Samantha well, guessed what the other woman was thinking. Samantha shook with anger because the police had burst in during a vulnerable moment. Would she blame William? Samantha didn't let slights go easily and this seemed likely to Lexi. She was also sure Lexi would hear about her part in this when they were alone.

It would not be a happy conversation.

The police took Lexi and Samantha before William and Cash. As the police officers helped Lexi to her feet, Cash's eyes met hers. They blazed determination and fury, but what could he do? She could guess that she and Sam would get arrested for prostitution. Lexi's and Sam's clothing was provocative, and some would say, slutty like prostitutes.

It didn't matter that they were doing this for fun. The police acted first, and asked questions later, if at all.

It was a huge mess.

They took her into one of the rooms in the hallway that

led from the reception area to the club room. "Is she high?" one officer said. "She looks high."

"Go ahead, drug test me," growled Lexi.

"Yeah, we'll do that."

A cop took pictures of her with her arms tied, before an officer released her. He was not gentle. He cursed as he attempted to undo the knots, and tugged too hard, cutting off the circulation to her hands.

William walked by, cuffed and pushed along by another cop. When he saw the officer manhandling Lexi, his face grew red.

"Madonna," he swore. "Be careful, asshole! If you don't know what you are doing, you can hurt her."

"Shut up, you kinky bastard," the officer said as he escorted him and a handcuffed Cash. Cash flashed her a look of utter regret, and she looked at her feet as embarrassment spread through her. The cop gave William a push. "Now you care she'll get hurt? Move it!"

Finally one of the other officers brought William's knife. They cut her lose but didn't give her a chance get the circulation moving through her fingers before they cuffed her.

Lexi and Samantha were the only two women in the transport, and Lexi wondered what happened with the other women at the club. The cop secured her to the bench and shut the door.

Samantha scowled at her. "This is fucking great. I've never gotten arrested for anything in my life."

At any other time, Lexi would have quipped a snarky remark, but not today. This was serious. This arrest would embarrass her before her friends and family and could ruin her professional career. No one would want a paralegal on staff arrested for prostitution. Just the arrest itself would cast a pall on any future employment prospects because she was sure Givens would fire her now, and with cause. Which meant no unemployment benefits.

Staring at the ruins of her life, a sick feeling spread through her gut at just how fucked she was, and she trembled.

40

CASH

Cash was furious. He wouldn't do or say anything that would trip a resisting charge, but he wanted to rip Officer Phillips apart. Cash would find out what was going on with this bogus raid. He had money that Walker Givens had no clue about, and he'd make it his personal mission in life to redress the wrongs done this night.

"Where are the drugs?" growled Phillips to William.

"You know damn well we don't use drugs here, Phillips. What the hell, what is this about?"

"Those women looked drugged."

"They weren't drugged, just enjoying themselves."

"Yeah, right," snorted Phillips. "Tied up. That's fucking enjoyable."

"There is nothing illegal about it."

"Watch it, William. This is serious shit you're in. The order for this search came from the mayor's office."

"What the hell?"

Cash's stomach turned. Tapping the mayor's office meant someone with money had pulled strings, and he could only imagine it was Walker Givens calling in a favor from a high-ranking official. It didn't necessarily have to be the mayor, but Givens, through his law firm, had many connections through this city.

He was going to fucking kill "Uncle Walker."

"Leave him and the girls out of this," Cash said. "It's me you want, so take me."

"Those aren't my orders. And shut your trap."

The seconds passed as if they were eternity's precious pieces that couldn't be spent. Officer Philips had walked away leaving Cash and William standing in the club room. William's face wore a grim expression.

"I don't understand how this happened," William said.

"I do," Cash said. "And I'll make it right."

"How can you do that?"

"Rich boy, remember?"

"You don't need that kind of trouble. Imagine the publicity, the *Daily News* articles, blogs around the city talking about the secret dangers of fetishes, even pieces like 'the 1%'s new obsession.' Your rich friends will hate you for it, and your golf club will revoke your membership. Charity events will drop your name from the invites."

Cash snorted. "I've never cared about any of those people or those things."

"And yet, they are part of your life. What would you do with yourself?"

"I'll find new hobbies, make new friends."

William snorted.

"To go it alone in this world sucks, Cash. And you aren't used to it."

Damn. William pegged it right. But along with his money, Cash had a reserve of social currency. Despite this past year where he isolated himself, Cash still had friends in places with the ability to smooth anyone's life into the fast and easy lane. They weren't what he called close personal friends, but they were people who gladly traded favors.

But would they engage in a showdown with Walker Givens? He thought not.

"Come along, both of you," said an officer.

Cash walked side by side with William as they traveled up the hallway to the exit. The doors to small rooms on either side were wide open. Cops took pictures and riffled through desk drawers.

"Fuckers," muttered William.

Then they passed the room that contained Samantha. She stood still while a cop asked her questions. She scowled and didn't speak. She stared at the policeman with her eyes blazing. Cash admired her spirit, and his anger flared that she had to go through this.

They passed another door. Lexi glanced from within at Cash and William and her face flushed, and she looked at her feet.

"Uncle Walker" was going to pay for this.

The trip to the police station was uneventful, but his arrival was not. As soon as they entered the hallway, Cash spotted Walker Givens and Tiffany sitting on a bench in the hallway.

Tiffany stood and flew toward Cash.

"Oh, darling, this is horrible. But Daddy will get you out of this."

"I'm sure."

"Give us a minute," Givens said to the officer, who frowned but stepped back toward the door.

"What's going on?" snarled Cash. He was in no mood to be pleasant to either Givens.

"You tell us, son," Givens said. "I got word from a friend

that you were here. Some people you were with got arrested on prostitution charges."

"I don't know what exactly you did," said Cash in a low whisper, "but I won't let you get away with it."

At that moment, an officer hauled Lexi and Samantha into the building none-to-gently. Tiffany's eyes flew open wide.

"Cash! You didn't! Not with that woman! Daddy! You must fire her at once."

"Don't worry, daughter. Already done."

"You bastard," growled Cash.

"That's not the issue," said Givens smoothly. "What's at issue is whether or not whether these charges will go to trial. I can speak to the Assistant District Attorney, point out that someone misread the situation, and have the charges dropped."

Cash hated no one as much as he hated Walker Givens at that moment, though Tiffany, who stood with a proprietary hand on his arm, ranked a close second.

"And what's the price?" Cash said as his stomach roiled.

"Simple. Come home with us, let's get your head straight, and, of course, you'll never see Lexi Winters again."

"I forgive you, darling," Tiffany said brightly. "I'm sure that, that woman seduced you. But that's nothing we can't get past."

Cash gave Tiffany a glance that would have withered a normal person into a sunken shell, but not Tiffany, who grinned at him predatorily.

"Fuck you," he said.

"Cash!" she said with shock.

"And fuck you too, Walker Givens. I don't know what my father saw in you as a friend, but you are a piece of trash I need to sweep off the floor."

"Really, Cash? You are going to play it that way? And what about your little friend? You could possibly ride out this shitstorm, with a few dings to your reputation and your company's, though you might lose any government contracts. That would be unfortunate and would make you sell, and for less than the offer we have now. But you'll be okay.

"But Lexi? She doesn't have money or connections, and once this goes public, she'll never get a job as a paralegal again."

"You bastard."

Givens smiled. "Just displaying that instability again, aren't you?"

It was a good thing that Cash was wearing handcuffs, because the need to wipe that smirk off Givens' face almost overwhelmed him. And the truth of it was, Walker Givens would ruin Lexi to prove a point, and no matter what happened, Lexi would hate Cash for it. Hell, she might never speak to him again now.

"Okay, I'll do it. On two conditions."

"What?"

"You make sure Lexi gets the most glowing recommendation on the planet."

"And the last," said Givens coldly.

"You also make sure the charges against Lexi's friend get dropped too."

Givens unhappily nodded but was not willing to let this deal go on minor details.

"I have a condition as well," Givens said. "Right here you will tell Lexi Winters you will never see her again. And you will make her believe it."

"Okay," gritted Cash. Lexi probably wouldn't want to see him anyway. And he wouldn't blame her.

He nodded to the officer who stood behind Cash, and that man went in the direction they'd taken Lexi. In a couple of minutes, Lexi walked down the hallway to where they stood. The officer uncuffed Cash.

"What's going on, Cash?" Lexi said. She was beautiful despite the stress that registered on her face.

"Everything will be okay," he said. He took a deep breath. "I'm sorry that I misled you, Lexi. I wasn't fair to you, or Tiffany. But I can't see you again."

"Cash?"

"I've got to go. Goodbye, Lexi."

He couldn't look back or bear the forlorn look on her face that began to form as he spoke. He turned quickly and stepped down the hall. As he, with Walker Givens on one side of him, and Tiffany as the other, stepped into the New York night, he fought the sting in his eyes. He denied tears were forming.

It wasn't a good lie, but it was the only one he could hold onto.

41

LEXI

LEXI SAT IN THE DREARY HOLDING CELL WONDERING WHAT GOD she'd angered. Her best friend since forever, Samantha, pressed against her, withdrawn and silent. For all her sass and snark, Samantha's present circumstances shocked her. Charged with prostitution and sitting in a holding cell with women that looked as if they'd slit their throats shook her to her core. Lexi didn't blame Samantha for not talking to her. Lexi got them into this mess.

The horrible cell writhed with sweat and less desirable bodily odors. Lexi wrinkled her nose trying to shake the smells free. Not a single woman that shared this space wore a friendly smile, but Lexi felt bad for them. She'd gotten a mouthful of the treatment these women suffered. They weren't given the benefit of the doubt, and endured the scorn of police officers that had seen and heard the same protestations of innocence one too many times.

"If my boss hears about this—" Samantha said.

"They have to give us a speedy arraignment. And at the arraignment the prosecution has to show cause for the charges. I'm sure William and Cash—"

"Shut up about those two," snarled Samantha. "Rich boy and pretty boy were nothing but trouble."

"Pretty boy?" Lexi said arching her eyebrow. "You do like him."

"Hell, no. Not after tonight. And if I ever encourage you to take a walk on the wild side again, you have my permission to smack me. Hard."

"That sounds like something William would like to do."

"Shut up," hissed Samantha. She glared at Lexi.

"Sorry," Lexi said. "This is a mess."

"You think? My God, Lexi, if the hospital finds out about this they will fire me."

"It won't be that bad. How many floor secretaries can handle an ICU and ICCU, at the same time? You are a magician, and they are damned lucky to have you."

"They are damned lucky they can get another secretary for less money than I make."

Lexi instinctively put her arm around Samantha and thought about what they had for bail money. They had their "butter and egg" money, a large jar where they stashed their bottle return money, and anything they sold on consignment. It was something they'd decided to do, when they moved in together, as a rainy day fund. And boy, was it a rainy day now.

"We'll get through this." Lexi would have liked to add a story from their misspent youth, but she suspected Samantha would not appreciate it now. Perhaps later, when the horror of their present circumstance had passed.

Samantha lowered her head and mumbled something.

"What was that?" Lexi asked.

"I liked it," Samantha said in a small voice. "What William did." She raised her head and look defiantly at Lexi. "That makes me some sort of sick puppy, doesn't it? Maybe that's why I can't keep a regular boyfriend? There is something broken in me and a normal guy just doesn't do it for me."

Lexi drew Samantha in closer. She wasn't used to Samantha's displaying this much self-doubt, and it disturbed her soul.

"You can't make that determination from one rope-tying session."

"Winters!" said a sharp voice.

Lexi disentangled herself from Samantha.

"Come with me," the uniformed officer said.

"What about me?" Samantha said.

"Nothing for you."

"Lexi?" Sam said.

"If I don't come back, I'll see you at the arraignment. Don't worry. You won't have to stay here long."

Lexi wasn't sure about that line she'd just handed her best friend, but Samantha looked so wrecked that she'd say anything to reassure her. The entire situation sucked. It wasn't just the bogus charges, the booking procedure they would have to endure, or the upcoming arraignment. Though her rational mind told her that she did nothing wrong, deep inside she felt like she'd failed Cash. She wanted him near and Cash telling her it was going to be all right. Like that night in the hotel after the BDSM club on the island, she needed him to smooth her anxieties.

But she didn't get that then either.

No, he ran off to damned Tiffany.

Okay, she'd only known Cash, what, four days by then? He had a whole other life before that, that didn't include her. She was crazy to harbor intense emotions for him, and even more so to think he shared her feelings.

The officer led her out to the hall and she saw Cash, but

also Walker Givens and Tiffany. The sorority Barbie stood too close to Cash, and Lexi wanted to rip the blonde's arm off him.

Tiffany glared at Lexi as she walked down the hallway to where they stood. Another officer uncuffed Cash. He stood so close that Lexi smelled the mix of his cologne and him, and that melted her panties. But his expression, as if he'd lost everything important, made her heart tremble. That Walker and Tiffany Givens hovered nearby was a bad sign.

"What's going on, Cash?" Lexi asked.

His face was hard as he looked at her. He gave her the barest of smiles and an icy tremor shivered through her.

"Everything will be okay," he said. He took a deep breath. "I'm sorry that I misled you, Lexi. I wasn't fair to you, or Tiffany. But I can't see you again."

Lexi stared at him in shock. What the fuck was going on? She knew to the bottom of her soul that Cash didn't think or talk like this. What were the Givens doing to him?

"Cash?"

"I've got to go. Goodbye, Lexi," was all he said.

He turned his back to her immediately and Tiffany gripped his arm as they, and Walker Givens, walked down the hall and out the door. Lexi stood there bewildered at this turn of events. Cash left her in the police station? Everything would be all right? Hell, no. Nothing was right, especially Cash walking away from her.

Officer Phillips unlocked her handcuffs.

"You are free to go."

"What?"

"The charges are dropped."

"What about my friend?"

"Who?"

"Samantha Porter. The woman with me?"

Phillips scrunched up his face. "I'll check. Have a seat."

Lexi did, shivering in the air conditioning in the short leather dress she had on. Thirty minutes dragged into an hour, and then another, but she didn't see Phillips again. She began to worry. Her phone and keys were back at William's club with her clothes and shoes, and she had no way to get in touch with anyone. And Lexi couldn't walk the streets in a bondage costume, not if she wanted to arrive home safely.

She tried to pry information from the bored-looking officer at the desk, but he wasn't inclined to respond to Lexi's pleas. Lexi turned away, frustrated. The police ignored her, and the people wandering in and out of the station stared inappropriately at her in her revealing leather dress.

Maddening.

Anger flushed through her and Lexi wanted to do violence to Sean Cashman. He dared to take off with a few empty words, leaving her to deal with this impossible situation on her own. But that would surely land her behind bars again. She huffed and decided she would not think about that jerk, and would get something done.

She walked up to the precinct desk again.

"I need to use the phone."

The police officer shrugged. "It's for official use only."

"I don't have my cell, or purse, and I'm dressed in this ridiculous costume—"

The woman shot her a look as if she didn't believe her.

"Ever heard of cos-play? One call, I promise, and I won't bother you again."

The woman grumbled but handed her the handset.

"What number?"

"Romallo's Pizza," Lexi said hopefully.

"This phone is not for ordering pizzas."

"You sure? Because I could have one delivered."

"Romallo's don't do those."

"Hand to God, whatever you want."

"A three-meat pizza."

"Sold."

Lexi stood, while butterflies flickered wildly in her stomach before the restaurant picked up.

"We're closed," said a gruff teenaged voice.

"I'm a friend of William, and the police raided his club, and my and my friend's clothes are there, and I'm not even sure what is going on with him, but they haven't let William out of the jail, so please, please, please, bring a lawyer, our clothes, and a three-meat pizza."

Lexi achingly realized how desperate and undignified she sounded, but for Samantha she'd suffer any indignity.

"I don't know who you are—" said the kid, sounding annoyed.

"I'm Lexi, and I was at the club with Sean Cashman and my friend, Samantha."

"Sa—Oh, holy Mother of God." More swears and rapid-fire Italian followed that, and over the handset Lexi caught what sounded like feet hitting the floor.

"Um, what's the pizza for?" the teen asked.

"For the nice policewoman letting me use the phone."

"Okay. We'll be there. Hang tight."

The line clicked off before Lexi could ask any questions.

"Thanks, they said they'll be here."

"Right," the officer said with disbelief in her voice.

Lexi wasn't sure what would happen next, but what she didn't expect was a crowd of dark-haired men and women noisily entering the precinct. One of them held not one, but several pizza boxes. One man, slightly older and taller than

William, glared at the officer at the desk and the teen held up the pizza.

"Where," growled the man, "is my brother? And if you can't tell me that, I want to see the duty officer in charge. Now."

42

TIFFANY SAT CLOYINGLY CLOSE TO CASH WITH HER THIGH pressed against his as the stench of her perfume threatened to gag him. Cash clenched his jaw, ignoring the urge to push her away. While she chatted, he tuned her out, thinking about the events that led him to this point.

Walker Givens, a man he used to trust, had a hard-on for Cash to sell his company. "Uncle Walker" insisted that Cashman Industries was in poor shape when Cash's father died, though Cash was sure his father would have told him so. His father didn't keep secrets from Cash. Something else happened, and it must involve Walker Givens. But what?

"Cash!" Tiffany said. "Have you listened to anything I said?"

"Sorry."

"I said we should make plans to visit the condo on the islands next week."

"The services are off," he said mechanically.

"What?"

"Electric. Water. Because I haven't been there for a while."

"Well, get them turned back on," she said. "I don't want to stay at that horrible hotel again."

"Horrible hotel?" Cash said lifting his eyebrows.

"Well, they had no rooms when I arrived. It was horrible."

"That's because you didn't book a reservation. The fact is, despite the shoestring budget it is on, the hotel is doing very well and the rooms are booked for weeks in advance. The only way Lexi got a room was because your father booked her into the company room we keep reserved."

"Lexi! You seriously will not bring up that tramp's name, will you?"

"Tiffany," Givens said in a warning voice. "Cash has had a difficult day. Why don't you give the man a break?"

Tiffany glared at her father, but crossed her arms, and thankfully, shut her mouth.

Cash wished he had that much control over Tiffany. But to accomplish that he'd have to hold Tiffany's financial purse strings, and he wasn't willing to marry her to do that.

No.

He would not marry Tiffany Givens.

Nor sell his company.

How to get out of this mess wasn't as easy as chucking these people from his life. There was too much he didn't know about the situation to figure the correct course of action.

He glanced out the window and alarm raced through him as he realized they had driven past his apartment building.

"Where are we going?" Cash said.

Givens looked out the other window as he spoke. "You'll stay with us tonight."

Tiffany possessively gripped his arm again, and Crash

gritted his teeth. The oppressive atmosphere in the limo turned into a darker pit of suspicion he had to claw free from.

"Why?"

"We have a court date in the morning. It would make it easier for everyone if you stayed with us."

"What kind of court date?"

"Oh, darling," Tiffany said in her most saccharine voice. "You haven't been yourself lately. We are only trying to protect you."

"Tiffany!" barked Givens.

"What kind of court date?" repeated Cash in a low growl.

Givens swung his cold gray eyes toward Cash. "You haven't been yourself." Givens' parroting of Tiffany's words like it was a goddamn script ratcheted up Cash's irritation.

"What do you mean?" The tone of his voice came dangerously close to menace and his hands clenched on his knees.

Keep your cool, Cash, he told himself.

"We discussed this yesterday," Givens said. "And now the police found you in a BDSM club? Run by the mob? Cash, clearly you are a danger to yourself and others."

"Oh, gee," Cash said with sarcasm. "Wasn't that all Lexi's fault?"

"Clearly," Givens said icily, "you two had a sick thing going on."

"Because I don't do the things you want?"

"Cash, darling," Tiffany said. "We're here for you."

"*Clearly* not."

"Cash, I warn you," Givens said. "All it will take is one call, and I'll have your little friend thrown in jail again."

Cash stared out the window again. This was a fucking

nightmare. At every turn, Givens had him corralled and cut off. And Lexi was in danger of arrest because of him.

"We just want you to get the help you need," Tiffany said.

Cash pinched his nose.

"And what kind of help would that be?"

"You should get a psychiatric evaluation," Givens said.

Wonderful. While they proposed a sale of his company to his competitor? Cash saw it now. They couldn't count on him to agree to the deal, so they arranged to take away his authority to make or deny the sale. He curled and uncurled his fists on his knees.

Nor did it escape him that Preston Lowe did not deliver on his promise to supply the company books to him. Preston was Givens' hiring suggestion to Cash's father, so he had to assume Preston played Team Givens.

He didn't know who was worse, father or daughter. Walker Givens was his father's best friend, though now Cash seriously doubted how or why that could be. Until recently Cash thought of Walker Given as a second father figure, but he perceived Givens as grasping and greedy. Tiffany was a product of her upbringing, but she and Cash shared so many things over the years, he didn't understand why she was so coldly calculating toward him.

Cash examined his situation from every angle, but he could not find a solution that didn't screw Lexi. And the last thing she needed was for him to cause more trouble. And he needed time to straighten the situation out, time which Givens took away by playing "the poor boy is crazy" card. As much as he hated the idea, Cash would have to play along with "Uncle Walker" until he could find an opening and make a move.

"Cash," Tiffany said. "Are you okay?"

Like you fucking care.

"It's been a long day," he said.

"Yes, baby," Tiffany said patting his arm. "It has. Once you get some sleep, you'll feel better."

They finally rolled into the Givens' long driveway in the Hamptons, a place he'd spent many hours as a boy and teen. As the brick mansion loomed up, its three stories above him, Cash recoiled at walking in there again.

As they entered the wood-paneled atrium, Cash sighed. "Which guest room do you want me in?"

"Don't you want to stay with me?" Tiffany said. She batted her contact-enhanced baby blues and Cash turned his head away.

"I'm tired, Tiffany."

Givens pressed his fingers into the security pad by the door, turning on the alarms sealing them in. Opening a door or window would trigger the shrill alarm.

"Take whatever one you want, Cash. We'll see you in the morning."

Tiffany leaned in for a kiss, but he stood unmoving as she pecked his cheek.

"This is for the best," she said.

You keep saying that, but I won't believe it or you ever again.

He watched father and daughter walk up the stairs to the second floor. Tiffany leaned over the railing.

"You coming up, Cash?" she said.

"I thought I'd sit and read a while," he said.

Givens put his hand on Tiffany's shoulder. "Don't worry. He's not going anywhere," he said. "Goodnight, Cash."

Cash nodded. Not going anywhere. Damned straight. He jammed his hands in his pockets, and his mouth drew a tight line as he wandered into the first room on the right off the hallway. The four walls of the library held floor-to-ceiling bookshelves. He and Tiffany spent much of their time in the backyard by the pool when they were here.

Cash pulled out his phone but only stared at it. Who was he going to call? Not one fucking person. His hand dropped to the side of the couch and hit the remote for the gas fireplace. Cash turned it on and watched the flames snake and slither over each other but found no comfort in the light or heat, though his eyes grew heavy.

In a haze, he heard tears, and they seemed to overlap another set.

"Oh, God," said a tear-filled voice. "I can't move my legs."

"It's okay, Charlotte."

"The baby—"

"He'll be okay, I promise."

Women's tears always got to Cash. He couldn't bear to hear them. Most men didn't like them, but despite whatever facade he displayed, they wrecked him.

Cash tried to draw near to see the crying woman, but it proved more difficult than walking through quicksand. An unknown force pushed him to the side. The woman gasped, though she sounded farther away than before.

"The baby's coming, Walker."

"It will be okay, Charlotte. Charlotte?"

The woman's cries stopped.

"Charlotte!"

Charlotte fell silent, but in her place, he recognized Lexi's strained voice.

"Damn it, Cash," she said, and her sobs started again.

"Lexi!" he tried to say, but no words came. Lost, he had no light to see with, no bearings to go by, except Lexi's sobs.

Cash jolted to wakefulness, and the hiss of the fire dragged him to awareness. What the hell did he dream? If felt real and both the women crying, Charlotte and Lexi, rattled him.

He stood, shook out his arms as he tried to disperse the strangeness that crept over him. Cash's eyes caught several shelves of pictures and, for the first time in his life, he stood close to examine them.

In the middle shelf were pictures of Walker, Cash's father, Cash and Tiffany at Cash's and Tiff's college graduation. Everyone looked so happy. When did that turn sour? And there were other pictures of the younger selves of Cash and his father. A sharp sensation stabbed at his heart. Walker Givens had been a part of his life, and Tiffany too. When did that relationship turn cold?

Tucked behind a bank of photographs sat one hidden behind the others. Cash drew it out and realized with surprise that it was his father's wedding photo. Givens was there—best man, of course—another woman, and then the woman in a wedding dress. This was rare. His father had few photos of Cash's mother. Cash stared at the features that were a feminine version of his own. It was all there, the blonde hair and blue eyes and slightly upturned nose.

He pulled the picture from the frame and flipped it to the back.

Charlotte and Thomas, Walker and Rissa.

Damn. It had been so long since he thought of his mother.

Charlotte.

She died the day of his birth. His father gave him few details, and he accepted that. But now, after that strange dream?

What had happened the day he came into the world?

Rissa was Tiffany's mother, though it didn't appear they were married yet. Cash flipped the picture again, discomforted by an impression left on his first pass of it. He stared at it for a long while and then found the shadow was in Walker Givens' eyes.

Maybe it was a trick of light, but Uncle Walker stared at the new Mrs. Charlotte Cushman with desperation and desire.

What the fuck?

43

"HERE YOU GO, MISS LEXI," WILLIAM SAID. HE GENTLY pulled away her comforter and guided her into bed. "My man, Carlo, will sit with you."

"Thank you, but not necessary."

"Miss Lexi, you hit subspace quickly and shouldn't be alone right now nor for the next several hours. Let Carlo take care of you, bring you food and water, and keep an eye out for you. Just for a little while."

"I'm fine, really," she said. Lexi saw things clearly. For a middle-class woman like her, a man like Sean Cashman was way out of her league.

"Sure, you're fine now. But in a few hours? You can't predict how well you'll climb out of subspace, and the rest of the night was rough. I can't in good conscience leave you alone. But don't worry. Carlo prefers men. He won't try to take advantage."

Lexi laughed half-heartedly. "Like I'm that attractive," she said.

William cocked his head to one side.

"Miss Lexi, don't doubt for a second how beautiful you

are. I personally know men who would treat you like the precious jewel you are. The raid by the police wasn't supposed to happen. But don't worry about a thing. I've put out the word the Ianucci family protects you and Ms. Samantha."

"Is this where you say, 'When I need a favor, I'll come to you'?"

"No, Miss Lexi. You owe me no favors. You came to my club expecting a safe place, and I did not provide it. It is I who owe you."

"Who is with Samantha?"

"My sister, Angela. She's five years younger than me, but she'll take good care of Samantha."

"You must be very close to your family."

"We are all close, though Mom and Pop don't like my extracurricular activities. So they hang out in Florida, and we take turns visiting them during the winter."

"Really? They live there year round?"

He shrugged. "If they lived here, Pop would want to work the kitchen, and his heart isn't so good. So Momma tells him she doesn't want to leave, and he won't leave her side."

"That's sweet."

William laughed. "Don't say that to him. He claims it's because he has to make sure Momma doesn't feed her lasagna to another man."

"Ah. Lasagna blocking. Wise man."

"All's fair in love and lasagna."

"Except when it comes to Samantha. She doesn't want to see you."

William looked away, and his face darkened. "That's why I'm not in her room. I may be a Dom, but I don't force a woman to do anything she doesn't want."

"I'm glad. Samantha thinks of herself as fearless, but tonight was a first for her. It frightened her." Lexi stopped speaking because she'd never reveal Samantha's confession that she liked the Shibari rope tying.

"I'm sorry I frightened her."

Lexi bit her lip. Being found by the police while tied up freaked out her best friend, but she couldn't admit that either. Samantha and William would need to have that discussion.

"I've known her since the first grade. When she's ready to talk, she will. But don't count on it being anytime soon."

"I figured. She's a stubborn woman, isn't she?"

"Yes."

"Ianucci men can't seem to help but pick stubborn women. It's in our DNA."

"I'm glad to hear you know what you're in for...that is, if she lets you in the door again."

"And what about you and Mr. Cash? Are you going to?"

Lexi drew her comforter closer to her chin.

"The Givens, both of them, have their claws into Cash."

"The Givens?"

"Walker Givens, attorney for Cashman Industries, and his daughter, Tiffany. She thinks Cash will marry her."

"Sounds bad."

"They'll haul him into court tomorrow to force a psychiatric examination. And while that happens, Givens and the CFO will allow the sale of Cash's company."

"They are stealing his money?" William said with concern.

"No. Not directly. He'll get money from the sale. But what is worse is that they're stealing his father's company from him. I suspect that's far worse than anything else they'll do to him."

"So, Cash is in the hands of evil people."

"He is in the hands of his people, William. Walker Givens was his father's best friend. Preston Lowe, the CFO, seems to be cut from the same cloth."

"So these people share history with him. Where's the loyalty?"

Lexi shrugged. "Rich people seem to look at the world or people differently, but I could be wrong. Walker Givens and Tiffany don't care about Cash, but that's none of my business. He went with them, William. Said he misled me and couldn't see me again. So, that's that."

Lexi thought of Cash's broad shoulders walking away from her, and her lip quivered. Damn. Why did she have to get emotional about this?

"Way to go, William, getting Lexi upset."

Samantha stood in the doorway of Lexi's room with a bottle of red wine and two glasses.

"It's not his fault," Lexi said.

"Don't defend this *goombah*. And you," she said staring fiercely at William, "need to leave. And take your posse."

"You shouldn't be alone."

"I'm not alone. I have my best bud here, and we are going to drink this bottle of wine. Then we'll eat the frozen pizza heating in our oven, eat a whole quart of ice cream, and think of horrible ways for men to die. So you'd better leave right now before I act on any death-dealing ones cooking in my head right now."

"Fine," William said, setting his jaw. "If you need anything, call the store. Carlo, Angela, let's get going." He walked out of Lexi's bedroom, and after a conversation Lexi didn't hear clearly, the door shut.

As William made his exit, Samantha crawled under the

comforter and poured two glasses of wine. She put her head against the headboard after she took her first sip.

"What about that pizza cooking?" Lexi said.

"Big talk on my part. I just wanted to insult him by choosing cardboard over his pizza."

"Mission accomplished. What about the ice cream?"

"We're out, remember? You need to go to the store."

"So our snack is wine."

"It's vegetable matter, so that makes it salad. And that's a good snack."

"It's fermented."

"So, we're having fermented salad. Still a healthy food choice. Drink up."

"You made him feel bad."

Samantha snorted. "Who? William? Big bad Dom can't take getting his feelings trammeled? Too damn bad."

"Don't be angry with him. It's not his fault."

"It was his club that got raided."

"But why? No one did anything illegal. And we know that Walker Givens had Cash followed. What if it was Givens who called in a favor from City Hall? He has a lot of influence."

"So why do you care? Mr. Cashman left you for Givens and that tramp of a daughter of his."

"One. How do you know that? I didn't get a chance to tell you anything."

"Carlo filled me in. That boy gossips worse than a drag queen."

Lexi pursed her lips. "Two. How can you call Tiffany a tramp? You never met her."

"The girl's a walking disaster. Hanging onto her daddy, then Cash? The girl obviously doesn't have a life of her own. She needs to grow a set and learn adulting."

"You expect Tiffany to grow balls? Is adulting even a word?"

"No, tits. Grown-ass woman parts. And if it isn't, it should be."

"Ah, well. That's asking too much, as she will not let go."

"And you'll let her get away with that?"

"Samantha, I told you. He walked away from me, not the other way around. I'm not going to throw myself on the pyre of love for Sean Cashman if the boy doesn't even want me."

"Girl, have you looked at him? That's no boy, but a man."

"When he acts like one, I'll believe it."

"You need more wine. Maybe it will clear your head."

44

CASH

CASH STOOD BY HIMSELF AT THE TABLE FOR THE DEFENSE. They were first on the docket though Cash didn't have to wonder why that was. Walker sat at the plaintiff's table, looking through papers. Tiffany and Preston Lowe sat in the gallery, and it surprised Cash when Preston tried to sit next to Tiffany. She gave him a look as if to warn him off, so he settled for a seat in the same row.

"All rise," the bailiff said. "The Honorable Robert Marshall presiding."

The judge took his seat at the bench.

"Cashman Industries vs. Sean Cashman. Are all the parties here?"

"Walker Givens, representing Cashman Industries Corporation. But excuse me, your honor. Wasn't Judge Miller supposed to sit on this case?"

"Judge Miller had a family emergency. I'm pinch-hitting. Do you have an objection?"

"We can continue the case, but it will go back into case assignment. Probably will take a month to get another date."

Givens' eyes narrowed. "I have no objections, your Honor," Givens said.

"And," the judge said, "who is representing Mr. Cashman?"

"I'm here, your honor."

"And do you have counsel?"

"I didn't even know about this proceeding until last night. I haven't had time to secure counsel."

"What do you mean? Weren't you served? Attorney Givens?"

"I assumed the process servers delivered the papers."

"You assumed wrong," the judge said. "Mr. Cashman, how did you know about this proceeding?"

"Attorney Givens told me last night."

"He told you?" the judge said incredulously.

"Due to the urgent nature—" started Givens.

"I don't care how urgent you think it is. We have processes we follow. Mr. Cashman. Who is your attorney?"

"Up until last night, I assumed it was Attorney Givens. He's been the family lawyer for years."

"Explain yourself, Attorney Givens. Why is this young man under the impression you are his lawyer when you represent the plaintiff in this case?"

"The interests of Sean Cashman and Cashman Industries were the same until recently."

The judge shook his head. "This is irregular."

"But your honor," Givens said, "this is for Cash's, I mean, Sean's health and sanity. His depression—"

"Spare me your testimony. It's inappropriate. Son, do you want time to find a lawyer to represent your interests?"

"Yes, your honor. I would appreciate it."

"But," Tiffany said standing suddenly, "Cash needs help."

"And who are you?"

"Tiffany Givens, Cash's fiancée."

"For the record, Your Honor. I never asked Tiffany to marry me. In fact, I've told her several times—"

"Oh, Cash," Tiffany said, dabbing at tears in her eyes. "You are so confused."

"Enough," snapped the judge. "I will not take testimony in this matter until you have representation, Mr. Cashman."

"At least," Walker Givens said, "order a psychiatric hold on Sean. He is a danger to himself and others."

"Why?"

"He got arrested last night."

"Mr. Cashman?"

"I did."

"On what charges."

Cash shrugged. "It's a mystery to me. No one pressed charges."

"You mean the police picked you up and let you go without pressing charges?"

"I'm afraid," Givens said, "that was my doing. I didn't want Cash to spend time in a violent environment."

"Are you saying you used personal influence to interfere with the judicial process?"

"I wouldn't say that."

"It seems, Attorney Givens, that if you had concerns about what Mr. Cashman would do, you'd leave him in a secure environment. And what did you do with him after you arranged for him to avoid charges?"

"Your honor, that's a mischarac—"

The judge cut off him off with a wave of his hand.

"Mr. Cashman, care to fill me in on where you went last night?"

"After my release, Mr. Givens drove me to his home in the Hamptons."

"Did you want to go there?"

"No, sir."

"I've heard enough. I'll continue this case two days from now. There will be no psychiatric hold. And when we gather again, Attorney Givens, I expect you will have a good explanation for your actions. Court adjourned. Bailiff, call the next case."

Cash's and Givens' eyes met. The lawyer appeared calm and collected, but Cash recognized the dark fury behind his icy expression. Cash smiled, but it was not a warm one. It was cold, purposefully arrogant, and calculated to anger Walker Givens.

Givens looked down to his briefcase and shoved his papers inside. He snapped the latches shut, and the sound seemed to echo around the room. Givens glanced over his shoulder toward Cash once more and nodded his head almost imperceptibly. And with that little shake of his head, Givens acknowledged the gauntlet dropped, and the battle between them engaged. Now, there was open warfare between them, and Cash realized he had to be very careful. Givens was an excellent lawyer. Cash's father would never have hired him if he weren't. And Givens had years of experience within the legal system while Cash and his father relied on Givens to provide that skill.

In this chess game between the two men, Cash was a knight, forced to fight in angular moves. Givens was a bishop who fought on the diagonals of the board. Knights and bishop were equal in power, but bishops had a longer reach and could cause more damage.

The change of judge was a setback to Givens. But Cash only had two days to upend Givens' strategy.

Another set of lawyers entered the courtroom and Cash smiled again at Givens, this time a little wider. But this wasn't a friendly smile. It was one that said, "Bring it. I'm ready for you."

Cash wasn't. But he also wasn't above bluffing.

Givens shrugged his shoulders and picked up his case.

"Come along, Tiffany," he said. Preston Lowe had disappeared.

Probably trying to hide from me, thought Cash. Because the first order of business was to fire Preston Lowe.

Givens and Tiffany walked toward the door, and suddenly Givens stopped and turned to face Cash.

"Don't even think of firing Preston," Givens said.

"What, *Uncle Walker*? Have you taken up mind reading too, along with psychiatry?"

"Let's go, Tiffany." Givens placed a hand on his daughter's arm and steered her toward the courtroom's double doors.

Tiffany glanced over her shoulder at Cash and with a sorrowful expression bit her lip.

"Sorry," she mouthed.

Oh, she was good. But Tiffany had been so good at playing him that he no longer believed anything she said or did.

Why had it taken him so long to smarten up?

Walker Givens' betrayal sideswiped Cash too. Walker and Tiffany Givens both held the figurative long knives to slash his life to shreds. Was he that stupid about people?

Checking his phone, he saw twenty minutes remained to make the meeting he'd set up yesterday. He didn't have time to worry about the past. Cash had to find a lawyer to help handle the future. He pushed through the crowd of people milling through the halls, wondering how fast he could catch a cab in front of the courthouse.

Then he spotted Givens, Tiffany, and Preston Lowe clustered at the atrium of the courthouse. Tiffany had her arm on Preston's. She gazed up at him in adoration.

Just like she used to glance at Cash.

Things snapped into place for Cash. Preston was the "sweetie" Tiffany spoke to last Friday night and the one she made plans to meet on Saturday.

Cash's eyes narrowed as he passed the group and Tiffany, seeing Cash, dropped her arm from Preston's.

"Darling," she called out.

Givens turned, and Preston's eyes swiveled to Cash.

Cash gave them a wave, and he hurried outside and down the steps scanning the traffic for any oncoming cabs.

"Cash!" Tiffany called. Her heels clattered on the sidewalk as she stepped next to him. She gripped his arm.

"Just what do you want, Tiffany?" Cash said.

"What I've always wanted—you."

"What part of 'your father has betrayed me' don't you understand?"

"It's not betrayal, Cash, but concern for you."

"You can put away your fake concern for my welfare."

"Fake!" Tiffany said in the most aggrieved voice she could manage.

Cash stared down at Tiffany in disbelief. "Damn, you are persistent. But no sale, Tiffany. One more time, and the last. Our relationship is over. I've had enough. We had a bunch of good years, and hopefully, after this unpleasantness is behind us, I'll remember them fondly. But now? I can barely look at you. So stay away from me."

Her eyes hardened, and for a second Cash saw the authentic person beneath the beautiful persona of Tiffany

Givens. That person was cold and unable to give or share her heart because she had none.

"Oh no, Sean Cashman. If you think you can get rid of me that easily, you don't know me at all."

Cash waved to a cab that had pulled up the curb and let out a fare.

"I realize that."

"I'll make sure she goes to jail again."

Cash turned to Tiffany for one last time.

"Don't do something you'll regret, Tiffany." His voice dripped warning, and Tiffany's eyes widened briefly.

"Are you threatening me?"

"No. Just passing along some friendly advice."

He climbed into the cab and gave the driver the address. When he turned his head before the cab pulled away from the curb, he found Tiffany staring at him as if she wanted him dead.

Alarm sizzled through Cash as he feared for Lexi. He wondered just how much influence Walker Givens had with City Hall.

45

LEXI

A SINGLE SPOTLIGHT SHONE ON HER, BUT IT WAS THE HEAT SHE felt on her skin because the blindfold she wore did not let in a single edge of light. Lexi couldn't move because soft rope wrapped around her entire body in a cocoon of knots and bindings.

Master wove the rope to support her, to suspend her without undue pain. Oh, there might be pain later as he willed, but not because Master carelessly suspended her artlessly. No. He was supremely careful with her.

Master did not say so, but the way he looked at her, full of lust and want, told her that he was always thinking of her.

That gave her sublime pleasure.

In the mundane world, Lexi was confident, independent, and professional. She ordered her tasks with efficiency, supreme master of her competence in the office. But Lexi moved through her workplace among the rich and powerful as a functionary—a doer of tasks that didn't directly affect her. No one noticed her unless she made a mistake. And anyone with similar qualifications could do her job.

She was insignificant.

But now, she was the most important person in the world

because a powerful man whispered into her ear, and his attention was only on her. And hers was on him. She didn't see but smelled his arousal letting lose the mixture of his musk and spicy cologne that made her lightheaded.

"So beautiful," he said as he tweaked her nipples sharply with his fingers. It was a surprise, but he enjoyed surprising her. The little nips of pain spiked her excitement. "Let me see," he said as he fingered the tender flesh between her legs. Her folds dripped with her cream. "So wet. Good girl. Master loves to feel that you are hot for him. You can't wait until I fuck you, can you?"

"No, sir."

"Beg for it, beg for my cock."

"I need you, sir, need you bad. Please, fuck me. Fill me with your cock. I need it, so much."

"Ah," he said, running his fingertips down her spine. His finger played at her entrance, dipping it within the tight hole, promising delights but not delivering them. She whimpered as he withdrew his finger, but then he pressed it against her mouth.

"Suck, slut, my finger like it is my cock. Show me how you would make Master happy with your mouth."

Lexi licked her lips and parted them, and he slid his finger, full of her juices, slowly, intimately over her tongue until she took all of it to barely reach the back of her throat.

"Suck it like it's my cock."

Lexi hollowed her cheeks, rolling her tongue under the digit, applying all the suction at her command. He rewarded her with a slight hitch in his breathing.

"Such a good little slut. You want it, every inch of my cock pounding you, don't you?"

"Um," she said in approval.

Suddenly his finger withdrew, but his hands pried apart her thighs.

"This is mine," he said between her legs. "Do not come until I tell you."

He licked her clit, then swallowed it with his mouth, making her want to thrash. Restrained, there was no way to stop the onslaught of his tongue, or his fingers at her rosebud, circling it. His finger sparked thoughts so dirty, so needy, that if Lexi could arch her back, she would. His tongue was everywhere, on her clit, sensitive near to the point of pain, and inside her entrance. Her heart raced as waves of pleasure as sharp as broken glass overloaded every nerve ending. She fought to hold back her orgasm by breathing through the peaks of pleasure shivering through her and concentrating on relaxing her muscles. Masterfully his magic tongue made her inner walls flutter.

He pulled away, and she whimpered.

"That was close. Settle," he ordered. "I told you not to come, and you were about to disobey me."

"Sorry, Sir. I'm trying to be good."

"Let's make this a challenge."

She shivered.

"Come, and I will spank you. Don't, and I'll fuck you. Your choice."

She whimpered again. He'd torture her with his tongue for hours, and she did not know if she could take it.

On and on Master lapped at her tender flesh, bringing her to a peak and withdrawing his pleasures while her heart beat so hard it seemed she'd pass out. By the fourth time fighting back her orgasm, every muscle in her body quivered, and she had no rational thought left.

"Please, please," she begged. "Need you. So much. Fuck me. Please."

He didn't say a word and moved away, and she whimpered at the loss. Then she fell suddenly, and her heart jumped into her throat. But she had forgotten, being suspended so long, that she *was over the mattress, and not that high, and Master was there catching her, lowering her gently to the bed.*

His fingers worked the supporting knots at her knees, freeing them. The ripping noise of his zipper filled the room and then in one plunge he filled her with his cock. Again and again, he pulled back then jammed his cock into her, and her body trembled with the need to explode.

"Please. Got to. Got to. Please."

The rude noise of the alarm on her phone jolted her from her dream, and she looked around wildly, disoriented. Her heart pounded in her chest, and her nether regions flushed wet with excitement.

Fuck.

She swallowed hard and then her head reminded her painfully of the two bottles of red wine she and Samantha downed the previous night.

Fabulous. Horny and hungover. A wonderful way to start the day.

She swung her legs out of bed to start the automatic routine of getting ready for work.

And then she remembered.

She didn't have a job.

Lexi groaned and fell back onto her bed as she thought about different tasks of the day, none of which she wanted to perform. She would apply for unemployment insurance, check her bank accounts, put in some applications online, and call her mother.

"No" she groaned.

Her hand hit a lump in her bed that stirred.

"What the fuck?"

"Damn it, girl," groaned Samantha.

"What the hell? Why are you in my bed?"

Samantha pulled the comforter tighter around her body.

"I fell asleep after our snack. But if you are this noisy this early in the morning, then no wonder you don't have a boyfriend."

Lexi jerked the comforter off Samantha, who groaned in protest.

"I could say the same thing, Ms. Judgmental. Out of my bed. One of us has to go to work."

"Ouch, that hurts," swore Samantha.

"Me taking the comforter?"

"No. My head. I think I'll take a sick day."

"You work in a hospital. Every day is a sick day."

"Ha ha," Samantha said dryly. "I didn't get much rest."

"Too bad."

"Your fault. You talk in your sleep."

"I do not."

"That's what you think."

"Don't blame me for being too drunk to sleep well. That's what you get for taking your vegetables fermented."

"You're mean when you're sober," complained Samantha.

"I can scale new heights of mean. Did you hear about the ham that went to the Emergency Room? They couldn't treat him because he was already cured."

"Oooh, that hurts my head."

"Did you hear about the on-call neurologist that got an urgent call at 3 a.m.? When he introduced himself, the nurse exclaimed, 'Neurology! I wanted Urology. I got the wrong end!'"

"Why are you torturing me?" Samantha said with a half whine that ended in an amused snort.

"I have a great HIPPA joke. But I can't tell it to you."

"You are beyond silly." Samantha turned away, trying to hide her snickers at Lexi's horrible jokes by burying her head into her pillow, but Lexi yanked it away.

"This is what you get for hogging the comforter. The only one staying home today is me. Because I have no job and somebody's got to pay the bills."

"Slave driver."

"I'll make you coffee, though."

"You will?" Samantha said, her voice brighter. "Will I get treated to Domestic Barbie Lexi during your period of unemployment? For instance, will you hand wash my bras?"

"Please, you don't hand wash your bras."

"Why not? You cleaned the apartment because you were broken-hearted over a guy. But your best friend can't get a little TLC for her unmentionables?"

"You're unmentionable."

"How about a pie? You haven't baked a pie in a long time."

"I've never baked a pie. What is wrong with you?"

"I guess," Samantha said, sitting up in bed and putting her arm around Lexi, "I'm trying to say that I'm worried about you staying home alone today."

"Why?"

"Because I've never seen you so wrecked over a man before."

"I'm not wrecked." Lexi delivered her denial with vehemence. She would not let Sean Cashman govern a single moment of her emotions. She wiggled away from Samantha and her insinuations.

"Then why did you call out Cash's name at least six times last night?"

The offices of Boughman, Cushing, and Hiller were in a respectable midtown office building, neither shabby nor ostentatious. The firm had a solid reputation, but the principals did not run in Givens' circle. This Cash had checked with a couple of friends at his gentlemen's club who knew who did business with whom.

"Mr. Cashman, Mr. Wilder will see you now."

Wilder? The name sounded familiar.

The secretary opened the door to the office. Cash's eyes widened in surprise at the man behind the desk.

"Cash!"

"Jamie? You work here?"

He and Jamie played two seasons on the rugby team in college, and he remembered Jamie as a hard-working guy who wasn't afraid to tackle a challenge.

"We lost track after college. Hey, you had your business, I got busy trying to pass the bar." Jamie Wilder came from behind his desk and stuck his broad hand out to Cash, who gave it a firm shake.

"Sorry to hear about your father."

"Thanks," Cash said. His throat thickened and his voice got rough. He cleared it with a cough.

"But, hey, I thought you'd go home to California."

"The fiancée wasn't happy about that idea. She likes to stay close to her family."

"Fiancée?"

"Yeah, Shannon Hiller." He flipped a picture on his desk around to show a beautiful dark-haired, brown-eyed woman. "We're getting married next June."

"Congratulations. She's a beautiful woman."

"Thank you. And you? Did you and Tiffany tie the knot?"

Cash held back a sigh. He supposed, considering all the years he and Tiffany were together, he'd be answering the same sort of question for years to come.

"No. And that's part of the story."

"Take a seat. Would you like coffee or water?"

"Thanks, but I'm good."

"Thank you, Janet. Hold my calls."

The secretary nodded, and the tall, efficient-looking woman closed the door after her.

"So," Jamie said taking his seat again, "what can I help you with? Or more precisely, why is the owner of Cashman Industries seeking counsel from a B list New York lawyer?"

"I'll be honest. You know Tiffany's father?"

"His firm has handled your legal business for years."

"Walker Givens has a lot of influence. I don't want a firm whose partners are his buddies."

"This sounds serious."

"I'm in trouble. I didn't protect myself as I should have. Since my father died, I haven't paid attention to business as I should. I've been more involved in the ramjet division, working on developing more efficient engines for space shuttles, and well, other things slid. Now, I've got the CFO claiming the company has been in financial trouble since before my father died, which my father did not mention at all. Givens and Preston Lowe cooked up this deal with Pittman, our biggest competitor, but I won't sign, so they've become Machiavellian. Givens has manufactured a case questioning my psychiatric competence. We were in court this morning, but the judge had problems with how Givens did things, so it's continued for two days."

"That's not enough time to do anything."

"You're telling me. What do you suggest?"

"What do they have on you?"

"I got arrested last night."

"For what?"

"Wrong place, wrong time. Givens has a hard-on for making things seem as bad as possible, and he had private detectives following me."

"Where were you arrested?"

"Last night. At a club."

"Why would that be a problem? Were you drunk?"

"No. In fact, they don't serve liquor, but it was a BDSM club."

To Jamie's credit, he didn't react with shock as Cash expected.

"What is the name of this club?"

"I never got it. Guglielmo Ianucci owns it."

Now Jamie's eyebrow did go up. "And how well do you know this individual?"

"I met him a couple of days ago. He's trying to date—" He stumbled in trying to reach the right word to describe Lexi. "The roommate of a woman I'm interested in."

"And that's all Givens has?"

"Aside from the fact that I tried to break things off with Tiffany, that's it."

"What did his filings say?"

Cash shrugged. "I never got them."

Jamie steepled his fingers. "Seems like Givens is playing hardball. We've seen things like this before, though admittedly not on this scale. But unless he has something significantly more than this, we can head him off. But I'd have to look at what Givens filed, and I can't do it without filing an appearance as your lawyer."

"You want this mess of a case?"

"Sounds like you need a lawyer, and it will make the future father-in-law happy to have such a high profile client."

"You're not ambitious at all, are you?"

"I am. That's why we'll have all hands on board for you, Cash. You and I weren't that close in college, but I remember how everyone genuinely liked and looked up to you. You're good people. I'm honored to serve as your lawyer."

"You'll be playing against some big fish, Jamie. Givens has influence throughout the city."

"I'm aware. But I like a challenge. So, shall we draw up the contracts?"

Cash hoped Jamie's law was as good as his sales skills, but at least Jamie was a straight shooter. "Yes. Let's do this."

Janet entered and handed Jamie the retainer agreement. The lawyer looked it over and gave it to Cash. It surprised him to see his name and information typed into it.

"That's efficiency."

"That's Janet. She types them before the appointments and has them ready to print."

Cash signed it, and relief settled over him.

"I'll need a retainer, to make it official."

"Sure," Cash said. He pulled out his wallet. "Is a grand in cash enough for now? I'll have my secretary send a check for the rest."

"A grand will do for starters."

This relieved, Cash because losing his walking-around money didn't appeal to him. Though he didn't want to admit it to Jamie, Walker Givens trying to wrest control of Cash's life had upended him. Just the thought of the man he considered as close as an uncle trying to put him away in a psychiatric hospital gave him cold chills. When had Givens turned evil?

"Thanks. I don't carry a checkbook."

"You almost don't need to these days," agreed Jamie. "Okay, then, let me file the appearance."

He typed into his computer.

"You are doing that now?"

"The wonders of technology. Okay, the system recognizes me as the attorney of record. Let's take a look at what Givens filed." Jamie pressed a few more keys, and then he stared intently at the documents.

"Who is Preston Lowe?"

"CFO of Cashman Industries."

"He says you are distant and removed from day-to-day activities since your father died. But you just told me that."

"I did."

"He also says you are depressed and uncommunicative."

"It's hard to communicate with a guy who won't give you the reports you ask for."

"Hmm. Well, Tiffany says much the same thing, withdrawn, uncommunicative, lost interest in regular activities." Jamie sighed. "Okay, I'll set up an appointment with a psychiatrist for an evaluation. It will be one that the court regularly uses for such things. Where can I reach you to give you the appointment?"

"Sorry, I had to ditch my phone because the PIs were following me."

"Hmph. You aren't paranoid if someone is after you. Okay, hang on."

Jamie placed a called. "Avery? I have a client here facing a competency hearing. Do you have any time, today or tomorrow... The sooner, the better. Five today? Great. Yes, the usual fee. Bill me."

Cash set his alarm on his watch to remind him of the appointment.

Jamie scribbled a name, address, and phone number on the legal pad, tore off the sheet, and handed it to Cash.

"Be there. Talk to him. It will take a couple hours, but he's good, and he'll have a report tomorrow. Then we can assess where we stand."

"What?" Cash said half-joking. "You think there's a possibility I'm nuts?"

"I don't think that's quite the term professionals use, but with everything that's happened to you, who could blame you? But, no. I don't think so. Getting a professional to say so will go a long way toward making this go away."

Cash felt better having hired a lawyer, and he was glad it was someone he knew. Jamie would need all of his A game to face Walker Givens.

As he left Jamie's office, a clock on a bank told him it was lunchtime. And he figured he owed a certain pizzeria owner an apology for dragging him into his personal business.

LEXI SAT AT HER COMPUTER UTTERLY DEVOID OF MOTIVATION. Oh, she'd filled out her application for unemployment insurance online. Lexi figured Givens would fight it. Walker Givens wasn't a man to just let her get the benefits due her, especially if he had a vendetta against her because of her relationship with Cash.

Only she didn't have a relationship with Cash. He walked away and left her standing there. If she weren't flushing red in embarrassment at getting dumped in a police station, she'd rage in anger. But she didn't want to. Sean Cashman didn't deserve a single second of her rage, or pain, or tears.

Despite that fact, her insides quivered with those emotions.

So, she stared at the screen with her laptop resting on her knees. Lexi should rewrite her resume, apply for jobs, make a few calls to colleagues at other firms, and look up the latest networking meet-and-greets. Her fingers lingered on the keyboard. Her eyes remained fixed on the last page of the unemployment application for benefits, instructing her to make a claim weekly via computer or phone. And it seemed so fucking cold.

On impulse, she Skyped her mother. Lexi didn't expect her to answer, so it surprised her when she did.

"Lexi, how good to hear from you."

"Hi, Mom. How are you and Dad?"

"We're fine, but what's wrong?"

"What makes you say that?"

"Lots of reasons. The puffy eyes, the blotchy skin, the fact you are calling during work hours."

Busted.

"I lost my job, Mom."

"Do you want to talk about it?"

"Not really. I finished filling out the online application, and then I remembered how Dad said he had to go in person to the office each week. It made me think of you."

"Oh yes. Those were bad times. They talk about the Recession of 2008, but the seventies were bad too. No one could find work. But that's how I met your father."

"Really? You never told me that story."

"Oh yes. We were in line together, and the lines were long, and we struck up a conversation. Despite the fact that he didn't have a dime, he asked me out. He managed to wrangle a couple of egg salad sandwiches from his mother, and a bag of chips and a couple of cans of soda. Then he put the food in his mother's old covered basket with a broken handle. Risking his father's wrath, he siphoned off some gas from his car and drove to my house and then to the local lookout point.

"We ate our sandwiches, watched the lights of the city below, and he recited the balcony scene from Romeo and Juliet, which impressed me quite a bit. When a shooting star streaked the night sky, I told him to make a wish. He looked at me and said in all earnestness he already got what he wanted because I was there with him."

"Wow, Mom, I didn't know he was such a romantic."

"Well, yes," her father said dryly, passing through the kitchen to get a beer. "I had to make getting a mouthful of gasoline worth it."

"And you deserved every ouch you got, you old coot."

"Love you too, Abby," he said with a smile.

Her mother smiled at Lexi again. "That's how people used to fall in love. I don't know how you young people do it with your Facebook and OKCupid."

"No, Mom. Not Facebook or OKCupid. No one does those. Snapchat and Tinder."

"How can you find someone in a 'snapchat'? I feel bad for your generation. I do."

Her father, with a look of absolute mischief on his face, sneaked up on her mother and kissed her on the back of the neck.

"Oh, hi, daughter," he said with mock surprise on his face.

"Henry!" her mother said with fake outrage. "I'm busy here."

"Too busy to get busy with me?" he said.

Oh, god. Because they lived hundreds of miles away she forgot how foolishly in love they still were after all these years. Why couldn't she find a love like that? Why couldn't Cash care for her like that? Tears sprang to her eyes. She hated those tears, and the stab to her heart when she remembered his crystal blue eyes. Lexi despised how her breathing caught in her throat when she saw in her mind's eye his warm smile that beamed like the sun had shone directly on her. It wrecked her to remember how he made her feel as if she was the most precious woman in the world.

And then he left her.

"I've got to go, Mom. I'll call you this weekend."

"Come visit. We'd love to see you."

"I will."

She pulled the top of the laptop to shut it quickly, because she didn't want her parents to see the tears streaming down her face.

Her phone rang. It was Sam.

"Just doing a wellness check," Samantha said.

"I'm okay," she snuffled.

But Lexi couldn't fool Samantha.

"And I'm Taylor Swift. Girl, have you eaten anything today?"

"I had coffee."

"Wrong, wrong, wrong. Don't let your blood sugar drop. You're likely to start crying and stuff, and I do not want to face that when I get home."

"You care so much for my welfare."

"Get dressed and go out and eat. You can't sit in the apartment all day alone."

"Why not?" she said. Lexi wiped the tears from her cheek with a swipe of her hand.

"Because you need to be in a state to comfort me when I get home."

"Oh. Nice to know your care and concern is not totally unselfish."

"Wench. Damn. Why did we let those men under our skin?"

"So," Lexi said triumphantly, "you like William."

"Shut up! I think he's a witch and put a spell on me."

"They call male witches warlocks."

"What? That makes no sense."

"Can I help it if you are deficient in your *Bewitched* television viewing?"

"Fine, warlock then. But no, I definitely *do not like him*." Samantha spoke the last words too emphatically.

"Uh-huh," Lexi said in disbelief.

"You better have my unmentionables washed, or I will not buy you dinner."

"Ooh, I love how you threaten me."

"I've got to go. Eat!"

Samantha clicked off the call, and Lexi sighed. Samantha was right because Lexi's stomach rumbled, signaling its unhappiness at its empty state. Still dressed in her flannel pajamas, she shuffled into the bathroom and groaned at her appearance in the mirror. Her hair was a tangled mess, eyes puffy, and complexion washed out.

"Oh, how the mighty have fallen," she muttered.

Suddenly it was too much even to climb into the shower and put herself together to face the day. It seemed an excellent idea to crawl into bed and pull the blankets over her head.

"What is wrong with you, Lexi Winters?" she scolded. "So you got dumped. Get over it. It's his loss anyway."

But the woman looking back at her stared in disbelief.

Have you seen yourself lately? What man would want you? And what you let him do to you?

"So?" Lexi argued out loud. "It was fun."

Yeah. He had you kiss his dick, and he walked away. Tied you up, and then he walked away again. All this man does is walk away from you. That's fun? Did you enjoy that?

"No. Of course not."

Lexi had to admit that how Cash treated her was not as the precious jewel that William promised other Doms would.

In fact, it was humiliating how often the man treated her like a piece of ass that his rich, privileged one would use and discard. And why wouldn't Cash do that, when he had someone like the ultra-beautiful Tiffany Givens to go back to?

At that moment, staring at the wrecked woman before her, Lexi looked into a crack of her soul and was horrified at what she found. She'd never imagined it true, and it went everything against what her mother had tried to instill in her.

She looked again at her mousy brown hair and washed-out blue eyes, her body that was *not* stylishly thin—and Lexi realized what she'd hidden from herself all these years.

Lexi did not think she was beautiful.

How did this happen? When did it happen? With all the boys she thought cute who didn't pay attention to her at school? The young men at college that were eager enough to have A-student Lexi as their study partner, but took someone else to the football games?

Oh, she thought it briefly when she saw how Cash stared at her at certain moments. Overall, though, Lexi was a C list beauty competing with all the A and B list women in the world. Why wouldn't Trevor McGregor want a gym bunny with abs tighter than hers, whose butt didn't jiggle when she walked?

Why wouldn't Cash want a perfectly sculpted and coiffed Tiffany Givens?

What did she have to do to get and keep a man's attention?

Where were the men that would treat her like a precious jewel?

With a fire that raced through her body and to her heart, she decided to find out.

48

ROMALLO'S CUSTOMERS FILLED THE TABLES, AND A LINE HAD formed at the ordering window set in the red brick wall. Cash waited in line until he reached it. Beyond he got a good view the kitchen. Two large industrial ovens stood at the farthest wall while a long tiered workstation dominated the center of the room. A stove held two large pots on very low flames. One woman stood at the stainless steel table making pizzas, and a younger man worked on other orders. Behind them another man shoved in and took out pizzas, and the younger man cut them into slices with a pizza cutter. It was fast-paced and difficult work.

Cash ordered a meatball grinder, and the woman behind the counter who took his order narrowed her eyes when he asked for William as he paid for the sandwich.

"He's busy," she snapped. "Who shall I say is asking for him?"

"Sean Cashman."

Her eyes narrowed. "I'll see. But I can't make promises," she said with a rude snort.

Cash thought it was an odd thing to say. The woman

disappeared and took several minutes to return, leaving him to stand at the window awkwardly. He leaned against the red brick wall watching customers either place orders or pick them up.

"Meatball grinder," called the woman at the window.

Cash took his grinder, but she didn't say anything about William, so he sat down and navigated the sandwich.

It was delicious, with the roll crispy and the meatballs and cheese nicely heated. He enjoyed the sandwich, but that wasn't why he was there. Cash thought he might have to return at another time.

He caught the rare sound of the kitchen doors popping open, and William stepped onto the floor wearing a green kitchen apron splashed with white flour. He looked at the patrons until he spotted Cash. Then he walked toward Cash, but the expression on his face was not friendly.

And Cash did not blame him.

"Hi, William."

"Hello," William said coolly.

"I won't keep you," Cash said. "I just want to apologize for the trouble I caused you last night."

William crossed his arms over his chest.

"Forget about it. We're handling it."

Really? William just brushed him off with a "forget-about-it"? Cash frowned. "What do you mean by that?"

"Nothing you need to know about. Is there anything else?"

"No. I guess not."

"I thought so," William said. His tone was cold and his eyes flinty hard. Cash got the message. He wasn't welcome.

"I mean it," Cash said. "If there is anything I can do to help—"

"Help?" William said icily. "No. You've done enough."

William stared at Cash menacingly, and it hinted at violence.

Cash brushed the grinder crumbs from his hands. Suddenly, he lost his appetite.

"Then I'll just go."

"No," William said. "Come with me." He pointed to the kitchen doors.

William's serious tone raised the hackles on the back of Cash's neck. Fine. If the man wanted to trade blows to settle whatever score stood between them, Cash would do it.

In a couple of steps, William pointed to another door, and Cash opened it to the service alley between the buildings. He stepped out into a space that was hemmed in by another brick wall and ran toward the parallel street on the next block. Cash stood close to the opposite wall and crossed his arms and straightened. He was taller than William, who stared at him with disdain.

The door shut with a thud shutting off the clamor of the noisy restaurant kitchen. William spread his legs and crossed his arm, and his lips turned downward into a sneer.

"You came to me looking to learn about being a Dom. And you run off leaving your submissive to fend for herself," William said coldly. "You insult her and me with your actions."

William's words struck Cash hard. He was only trying to protect Lexi.

"What is this to you?" snapped William. "Some sort of game? Something the rich boy tries, and when it becomes inconvenient, you drop?"

"It wasn't like that, at all."

"That's how it looks to me. And certainly it looks worse to Lexi, who watched you walk off with another woman."

"I had to do that. They were going to put her in jail."

"Don't give me your excuses. You, with all your money, couldn't protect her? This is why I was reluctant to take you on. You don't get it. There are more Doms than subs, and to get a good one, one that is absolutely devoted to you, that's more difficult than you know. And the Good Lord graced you with a natural submissive? One who would live and breathe for you? And you walk out on her in the arms of another woman after a scene. You don't deserve her."

Cash saw red. He rushed at William and slammed him against the door of the restaurant to hold his arm against his throat. But William just glared at him, in total control of himself, and it made Cash feel ashamed.

It wasn't the harshness of William's words that made Cash angry. It was because the older Dom was right.

Cash stepped back.

"I'm sorry. I fucked up."

"You have."

The words hung between them. Cash wasn't sure if William was giving him a reprieve or if in a few minutes an associate of William's would track him down to beat his ass.

Cash nodded and turned to walk down the alley. His heart was heavy, and his feet were lead, as the weight of how utterly he screwed up descended on him. Lexi deserved way more than a man that turned and ran at the first sign of trouble.

"But," William said, "we've all made mistakes."

Cash glanced over his shoulder

"So?"

"Can you learn from yours?"

Their eyes met briefly, and it was as if William offered him a challenge. But the sting of defeat clouded all his thoughts. He'd lost the woman he was falling for by his stupidity.

"I haven't so far."

"Here," William said. He pulled an object from his pocket.

"Here's your phone, at least. If you need some lessons in how to be a man, give me a call. I put my number in there."

William's words were the last jab to his heart. Cash took the phone. "Thanks," he said.

Cash didn't remember walking away from William, or where he wandered most of the afternoon. He walked. Perhaps Walker Givens was right. Could he run Cashman Industries? He certainly wasn't handling his personal life correctly. How could anyone trust him with an international business? Would his father approve of what he'd done so far? Probably not. He kept walking until an alarm on his watch reminded him of his appointment with the psychiatrist. He plugged the address in his phone and swore. The cab he flagged barely got him to the building on time, and Cash rushed through the opening paperwork, preoccupied with what William said.

He couldn't have taken him down a peg more if he opened his pants and showed Cash that his cock was two inches longer than his.

So when the receptionist told him to go in, he couldn't have been more downcast. He stood and straightened his shoulders and willed away his defeated mood. He put a smile and his face and held out his hand.

"Sean Cashman, though my friends call me Cash."

"Have a seat. Can I call you Cash?"

"Sure."

"I'm Dr. Oliver Scott. Jamie sent me an email telling me your situation. What I'm going to do is conduct an interview and administer some routine tests. It will take about two hours."

"I hope I'm not keeping you from anything."

"When Jamie calls, I know it's urgent."

"So he told you about the competency hearing?"

"A little. Not enough to influence my opinion. But let's get started."

The doctor ran him through some tests, and routine questions, most of which seemed silly to Cash, but he cooperated with answering them.

"Okay, that's done."

"Have you found any screws loose?"

Dr. Scott frowned. "It's a misperception that competency revolves around whether someone has a mental illness. That may be a component. But the actual key is that the person can decide things in accordance with his wants and desires and can act in his self-interest. Drug and alcohol use, anxiety, delusional thinking, depression—to name a few—can influence that.

"So are you trying to tell me if I suffered depression since my father's death, they would have a case?"

"Not exactly. Grief is not a mental disorder. It is a healthy response to a life-altering event. But things like getting arrested may indicate a tendency not to take care of your self-interests.

"I see. And what if I indulged in some behaviors others considered deviant?"

"Such as?"

"BDSM. That's where the police arrested me, a BDSM club, probably at the prompting of Walker Givens."

Dr. Scott scribbled on his pad, and Cash's discomfort returned.

"And why would he do that?"

"He wants me to sell my business to my competitor. But

I've not seen one piece of evidence that supports his claims that my company is about to go bankrupt."

"I see," Dr. Scott said. He wrote some notes on a pad.

"And is this interest in BDSM recent?"

"Yes. I met a woman who is into it."

"And are you the submissive?"

"Lord, no. Lexi is."

"So tell me about Walker Givens."

Cash did, telling him Givens' relationship with his father, and Cash's relationship with Tiffany. Before he knew it, he'd told Dr. Scott the entire story, including some about Lexi.

Scott's face smoothed when he put his pen down.

"Cash, I'll write up my report tonight and send it to Jamie."

"What's the verdict?"

"You probably could use a few sessions with a good therapist because you've had some bad shocks and your emotional support system is thin. These are all things to make a case for depression, which you probably suffer from. But in my opinion, it is not enough to prescribe medication or cloud your judgment."

"And how do you think the BDSM thing will play in court?"

"Such things never go down well with judges, but it's no longer considered a mental illness or even a perversion. As long as it doesn't cross over into non-consensual assault, you don't have a problem legally."

"So what do you think my problem is then?"

"Do you think you have a problem?"

"Obviously. There isn't a single person in my life I'm getting along with."

"From what I can tell, most of the people close to you are

the ones with problems, except the woman you like—Lexi, is it?"

Cash nodded his head.

"That's all on you. Step up and stop letting other people come between you and her."

"You mean, grow up and be a man?"

"Yes."

"You are the second person today who said that to me."

"Then you should."

Cash left the office wondering how he would make up with Lexi. He had demonstrated the worst of himself by allowing Walker Givens to manipulate his life. Lexi needed a man who was more than a puppet to the machinations of a shark like Walker Givens. Cash should have known better, but he took the easy way out and justified it by saying it was for Lexi's own good.

He couldn't be that man anymore. Cash needed to be the strong man that Lexi deserved.

Cash found William's number and dialed it.

HER EXCITEMENT MORPHED INTO NERVOUS BUTTERFLIES AS SHE stepped closer to Romallo's. She bunched her itchy palms at her side.

This is ridiculous, she told herself. *You're getting a pizza.*

She knew this was a lie because in the back of her mind she wanted to talk to William.

As her mouth got progressively dry, she opened the door and walked inside. Immediately the aroma of oregano, garlic, and baking bread assaulted her. It was heavenly, and she relaxed slightly. But waiting in line ramped up her nerves again, and she almost fled.

What would she say to William?

Master William, I want to join your BDSM club?

It sounded crazy.

Can you point me to a Dom that would appreciate me?

That was worse.

Finally, it was her turn at the window.

"What would you like?" the woman said.

"Ah, a small cheese pizza. And also, is William here?"

The woman wrinkled her nose.

"And you are?"

"My name is Lexi."

The woman turned her head and shouted out some words in rapid-fire Italian. Immediately everyone in the kitchen stopped what they were doing and stared at Lexi. Fire crept through Lexi's cheeks, as they stared at her, but then the man working at the center table pointed to a door to Lexi's left.

"He'll be in shortly," the woman at the counter said. She put a pager on the counter. "We'll page you when it's ready."

"How much?"

The woman waved her hand. "No charge." The woman nearly growled as if she disapproved, but before Lexi could protest, she turned away.

Lexi sat at a table and waited. The lunch rush now seemed to settle into a slower but steadier pace. She gripped the pager, but it didn't go off when she expected it would. She hadn't paid for the pizza, and it would be ungracious of her to complain she didn't get it fast enough.

Instead, she sat and scrolled through her thin email and text messages. Lexi wasn't sure what she expected. Maybe a note from one of her former co-workers? Or even something from Cash.

Stupid. He's not going to text you. He's with Tiffany and doesn't need you.

"Hello, Ms. Lexi."

Lexi nearly jumped at William's rumbling low voice. It was almost as if he was a jungle cat purring at her. He set her pizza on the table.

"How are you today?" he said.

"I'm fine," she said.

"You sure? That was a bad night last night."

"Well, no harm came of it."

"Except you lost your job."

"How did you know that?"

"I have my ways of finding things out."

"Well, that isn't my biggest problem," Lexi said. "I can always get another job."

"What is it you do?"

"I'm a paralegal. There is always someone looking for a good one. I only worked for Givens because he offered me the highest salary."

"I'll put my friends on the lookout for a job for you."

"Thanks, I think I've got this, though."

"So what is it that you haven't 'gotten'?"

"I—I—" Lexi stumbled because, now that she had to speak what was on her mind out loud, she didn't know if she could. She lowered her eyelashes.

"You said something about other Doms."

"Ah," he said. "Well, that is a little bit of problem."

"Oh, I thought—"

"Not that I couldn't introduce you. It's just that we don't encourage subs who've been in a difficult relationship to jump right into another one. What we do rouses intense emotions. You have to be in a place to be able to separate the emotions generated by play from your normal emotions. You haven't had that chance yet."

"I guess that makes sense. Well, then I guess I'll just go."

"Now wait. There is one other thing we can do. At times a Dom will take a sub under his wing and give him or her a chance to get on their feet until they are ready for another relationship."

"How does that work?"

"For the purposes of this, I would be your Dom."

"You? I don't know. I mean you're a nice guy and all—"

"You misunderstand. I wouldn't engage in play with you.

I would just make it known in the community that you are under my protection. And you can spend time at the club and learn a few things. And when you are ready, I can introduce you to some people, if you want that."

"That's a very generous offer. Can I think about it?"

"William," called out the woman at the counter. "You have a phone call."

"I've got to go." He took out a pen from his slacks and wrote a phone number on a napkin. "That's the number to the club. Anytime you want to come by, call. And we can talk more about what I've proposed."

"Thanks, William."

A sly smile played on his lips. "What did you call me?" he said in a low voice.

Lexi scoffed and shook her head and smiled.

"You said we wouldn't play."

William shook his finger at her in mock indignation. "Oh, Ms. Lexi. We have so much work to do." He disappeared into the kitchen, and Lexi smiled. As she ate her pizza, she felt better than she had for the past few days. She believed William when he said he'd protect her.

That was what she told Samantha later when her roommate returned home from work with a bag of Chinese for dinner.

"What?" Samantha said indignantly "You went back there? What is your problem?"

"Why are you getting upset?"

"I'm not upset," Samantha said. But she spoke hotly with anger dripping from her voice.

"Gee, sorry I brought it up."

"My God, Lexi. What makes you think he would help you at all? He's a *goombah*, get it? A wise guy. Someone both of us should stay away from."

"I like him."

"Please," snorted Samantha. "There is nothing to like about the man."

"Wait," Lexi said. "Weren't you the one who told me that you liked what you two did together?"

"Good lord, Lexi. Can you not see the red flags here?"

"I'm not talking about dating him. I'm taking the opportunity to learn more about this thing. Even if you don't want to admit that you liked it, I do. And so far, William's been nothing but good to us."

Samantha pushed away from the table and held up her hands in disgust.

"I'm not your babysitter," she huffed as a red flush crept up her neck. "You do whatever the hell you want. Don't call me to bail you out."

Samantha stormed out of the kitchen while Lexi stared after her, dismayed at her friend's reaction. They'd had their tiffs over the years, but they were never this serious, or this angry. Lexi was at a loss as to what to say to fix this.

"Oh, come on, Sam," Lexi said.

"I don't want to discuss it," snapped Samantha. The door to her bedroom slammed shut.

"What the hell?" Lexi said. Samantha might have her own problems with William, but her anger with Lexi was unjustified.

She strode to Samantha's door and pounded on it.

"Go away!"

"No! Open the door!"

"Fuck you!"

This was going off the deep end. They had rules that governed their relationship, which was why it had lasted as long as it did. They weren't ever to call each other bitch or cunt, and they never told each other to fuck off.

"You're ridiculous!" yelled Lexi through the door.

"Leave me alone!"

Those were fighting words.

"No. You can't breach our Non-Interference Directive and tell me to fuck off."

The door was yanked open, and Lexi stumbled against Samantha, who pushed her away. Samantha's eyes blazed as Lexi's back bumped the doorjamb.

"What Non-Interference Directive? I never agreed not to interfere with your life."

"You sure did. In the eighth grade when you mooned over Billy Hillman as the cutest thing that walked on two legs and I called him Hillbilly, remember? We did a pinkie-swear to affirm our commitment not to interfere with our romantic choices and to offer unconditional support."

"I don't see how BDSM and *that* club has anything to do with romantic choices, so I call bullshit on that."

"Well, we'll have to expand our Non-Interference Directive to include variations on vanilla sex."

"Damn it, Lexi, this isn't an ice cream choice."

"You're unreasonably stubborn."

"I should be, since you are unreasonably stupid."

Lexi's jaw clenched, and blood rushed through her head. The word tumbled from her mouth before she could hit the brakes.

"Bitch!"

In a split microsecond, Samantha's eyes widened, and her hands squeezed into fists.

"Cunt!"

Lexi stepped back, mouth gaping open, and hot tears stung her eyes. Samantha had never stared at her with such hate. It was inconceivable and unimaginable that her best friend felt that way about her for even a second. It shocked her to her core.

"Sorry," she mumbled. And she turned and fled down the hall, and scooped her purse and phone from the table by the door with one shaking hand. Her other fumbled on the door handle.

"Lexi, wait!"

But Lexi fled out of the apartment and into the elevator seeking the shelter of open city streets. Her ears rang as she thought about how Samantha had ripped apart the fabric of their relationship by uttering things that never should have left her mouth. She couldn't go back to the apartment, at least not now.

It occurred to Lexi she had no other place to go.

Except one.

She pulled out the crumbled napkin she'd jammed into her jeans pocket and dialed the number.

"*Uncommon Pleasures*."

"Can I speak to William?"

"*Master* William is not available. Can I take a message?"

"This is *Ms.* Lexi. Tell him I'm taking him up on his offer and coming to the club."

Cᴀsʜ sᴛᴏᴏᴅ ʙᴇғᴏʀᴇ Wɪʟʟɪᴀᴍ's ᴅᴇsᴋ ᴀᴛ ʜɪs ᴄʟᴜʙ, ᴡʜɪʟᴇ ᴛʜᴇ Dom stared at him coolly.

"And you expect me to do what for you?" William said.

"I need to be the kind of man Lexi needs. And you can show that to me."

"We tried this before," William said with a quirk of his mouth.

"I know it, and it's my fault it didn't work. I failed Lexi, and I failed you."

"And what about Walker Givens and his daughter?"

"Screw them. I'm done with them. I love my company, but a business doesn't keep you warm at night. Dealing with sharks all day doesn't illuminate your soul. And Lexi is a woman a man can come home to, regardless of how he earns his living."

"I scoped you out, rich boy. You don't need to work."

"You're right. I don't. But I'm not the type of person to jet around the world chasing the next party. My father raised me to contribute to the welfare of the world. I thought I would do it by putting people into space with my engines.

But if I can't do that, I'll find another way. But what I can't find is another Lexi."

"That's the first sensible thing you've said. But you might not like the next steps here."

"What do you mean?"

"If you want to be a Dom, you need to learn what it means to be a sub."

"What?" Involuntarily Cash took a step back, and amusement lit William's face.

"*Mamma mia*, you should see the expression on you. What? You can dish it out but not take it?"

"William, I'm totally straight."

Then William burst out laughing, and Cash stared at him incredulously.

"You have so much to learn," William said wiping a mirthful tear from his eye. "Submission is not sexual."

"But?"

"Look, I know how the media portrays BDSM. And yes, people incorporate sex into their games at home and some clubs. But the act of submission is a state of mind, and if you are going to be a Dom, you have to understand how that works for a sub."

"Do all Doms do this sub thing?"

"No," William said. "But a bunch do. Some start as subs when they are younger and switch to Dom when they are older. All human beings are different; so are the methods we learn to express our wants and desires. But if you work with me, I insist you take this step. I promise you. I won't touch you sexually. And we'll start off easy and work our way into it."

Cash's jaw set as he considered this new development. He noticed William staring at him gauging Cash's reactions and realized this was a test. William was studying him testing whether Cash intended to follow through and learn what he needed to win Lexi back. If he didn't agree, William would have nothing more to do with him. And then where would Cash be? For all he knew, Lexi would be searching for a new Dom now.

There are more Doms than subs. William's words tortured him. Lexi could find another Dom quickly, and someone who wouldn't waffle on whether or not she fit into his life.

So far, William had kept his word.

"Okay. I'll do it."

The phone on William's desk rang. "Yes? Of course. Inform me when."

William hung up the phone and gazed at Cash as if he had evil plans for him.

"You will? Okay." He pulled out a drawer and handed Cash a sheaf of papers. "Read this. It's a limited Sub contract."

"What? Like in *50 Shades*?"

"Not as involved and no, I'm not asking you to give your freedom and soul to me. It's a consent form that outlines what you can expect from me and what I can expect from you."

"Does this have legal standing?"

William shrugged. "More like evidence of what we agreed to should the matter come up, so there's no 'he said, he said.'"

Cash took a deep breath wondering what the hell he was getting himself into. But this was for Lexi.

"Okay." Cash pulled his pen from his inside pocket.

"No. Read it. I have something else to take care of. When I return, I'll answer any questions you have."

William grabbed another stack of paper and left Cash

alone with the contract. It was straightforward, saying that the submissive allowed William to direct his/her activities during the time the submissive was in the club. The Dom (William) had the right to punish the submissive as he saw fit, subject to the restrictions checked off or written in on the last page of the contract. In choosing the no-sex option there would be no sex between the Dom and sub. Etc, etc. It all sounded sensible.

It relieved him to know William established and kept limits between himself and his subs. Not that Cash looked forward to the sub part, but he was confident William wouldn't take things farther than Cash wanted.

William returned.

"Well then?"

"Yes. I can sign this."

"Do you have any questions?"

"No. It's clear. It's clearer than some business contracts I've read."

Cash checked off his limits and signed the contract.

"Good. Follow me."

William led him down the hallway. "This is a private room. Go in there and strip."

"What?"

William glared at him. "Are you disobeying me already? You just gave me permission to direct your activities in the club. Take off your clothes, all of them. If you don't, walk out that door and don't return."

"Okay."

"The correct words are, 'Yes, Master William.' After you disrobe, hold your hands behind your back and keep your eyes to the floor until I return."

"Yes, Master William," said Cash through gritted teeth.

"Good boy," William said. "Oh, and make sure you fold

your clothes and put them neatly on that chair in the corner."

"Okay."

"What?"

"Yes, Master William."

Cash wasn't sure this would work. He didn't appreciate how William insisted Cash say "Yes, Master William," or used the words "good boy," as if he were a dog. This would be more difficult than he imagined.

But Cash did as he instructed and stood naked in the middle of the floor. Minutes ticked slowly by before the door opened. But it wasn't William that entered.

He could tell from the tight leather pants on the legs he could see. He recognized the boots as belonging to Carlo. Cash swore under his breath. Why had he allowed this? He didn't like the idea of Carlo's seeing him naked.

"Master said to blindfold you."

"Why?"

"I don't ask questions, and neither should you. Bend your head, big guy, so that I can slip this on you."

Reluctantly, Cash did, and Carlo fitted a blindfold over him. Then Carlo went to Cash's back. The rope tightened around Cash's wrists, holding them in place.

"You're going to like this," Carlo said.

"What?"

"Again, no questions," Carlo said in a teasing voice. The door shut and Cash heard no one else in the room.

The room was not well lit to start with, but now Cash was entirely in the dark. He tested the rope and found it would not give. His heart began to race as he imagined the worst possible things that could happen to him. What was he thinking? What would William do to him?

The door opened once again and that brought a rush of chilled air that prickled Cash's naked skin.

The door shut and he heard another person breathing. And a second person? He wasn't sure. It was so faint it could be the rasp of only one who'd entered.

Footsteps, the clatter of dress shoes on hardwood, circled him.

"Head down," commanded William.

The sudden injection of sound jolted Cash, but he lowered his head.

"Very good. Do you sense someone else is here? I have another sub I'm training. Like you, the sub signed a no-sexual-contact contract. But that's no sexual contact with me. I never said I would never bring another person into this. Don't speak! I see you want to say something and I warn you I will punish you if you do.

"We are going to have a little conversation here—well, rather, I will speak, and you will listen. You might have guessed that I'm not like other Doms. I'm not so much into the pain aspect of this, though, of course, if my submissive wants it, I will oblige. But that's not what we are doing here today.

"I find the aspects of submission, respect, devotion, and service more rewarding than administering physical pain. Pain is a means to an end, but for me, the end point is that you surrender your trust to me. I want you to look at me, and I want to see your devotion. I desire that you will do anything I ask, to surrender your will to me. There are rewards for this. When you give yourself to me, I am responsible for you. It becomes my duty to protect you and make sure no harm comes to you, at least not past what we've consented to.

"Gaining trust is never easy, and it takes longer with

some than others. We will go slowly tonight. I will direct both of you, never past your limits, and I will ask if you want to proceed. Both of you are not to speak, and the only signal you have to make to stop is making a fist with your hands; to agree, wiggle your hand. Don't worry. I will be watching you both intently. You will learn to trust me, trust that I'm only interested in your pleasure.

"The goal is to let go and just allow the experience to happen. Again. I remind you, no pain tonight. And though there will be touching, no sex, no exchanging of body fluids, not even kissing. Experience each sensation as they happen. Enjoy them. But I give you both one order. Neither of you is to come."

"Are you ready to proceed?"

51

WILLIAM'S STRANGE WORDS CAUSED A SHIVER TO RUN through her body. She had no idea what would happen next, or who this stranger was he wanted her to touch. But William had been nothing but honest with her.

After she signed William's contract, which she read thoroughly, he told her to strip and put on a robe. The robe was smooth and soft silk and caressed her body like a gentle lover's hand.

He left while she did this and knocked on the door when he returned.

"You look lovely," he said.

Lexi blushed.

"Usually, when I start training a new sub, we work one on one. But I have a special situation here, and I think you can help me with training another person."

"I'm not sure I'm ready for that."

"Don't worry. I'll be right there directing both of you. And I assure you that all you'll do is touch the other person unless you want to do more. If that is the case, crook your finger like this to signal me. Because when we enter the room, I won't allow you to speak. Do you understand?"

"Yes, Master William," she said quietly

"Such a prize," he said. "It's too bad I can't keep you for myself. But I have my heart set on another. And well, anyway..." His voice trailed off, and he shook his head. "Are you ready?"

"Yes, sir."

He placed a blindfold on her, so slowly and deliberately it made her breath hitch, and then he took her hand. His folded around hers was strong and comforting, and she relaxed.

"Follow me," he said. "We are just walking a couple of doors down."

When she entered the room, she became aware of the regular breaths of another person. She had no idea who it was, or why they were here, but she trusted William to keep things under control.

William gave a little speech that Lexi suspected was more for the other person's benefits than hers.

She thought William's enjoinder not to orgasm was a little too strong if all they were going to do was touch. But he'd let her "safeword" out of the scene if she found it too odd or intense.

William took her shoulders and walked her forward several paces. He put her hands on the person's body, and Lexi touched hard pectoral muscles. A man, then. William gently pulled her hands down his torso but stopped at his hips. He was tall too. She sensed her face came up to his pecs. William lifted her arms so her hands ran down his arms and she found the man's hands pulled back.

"Yes. I've bound his arms," whispered William. "You are in control here.

"One thing," William said louder, "that new Doms fail to understand, is that the sub has all the power. The sub can accept what the Dom is doing, or safeword out of the scene. What the ultimate goal for Dom and sub is the power exchange between them. The sub gives his or her trust over to the Dom and makes him responsible for her pleasure.

"This is much different from vanilla sex. Instead of two people grasping at each other to get excited enough to come, the Dom nurtures the sexual and sensual sensations of the sub. He strives to bring him or her to a state of emotional release. The sub is then free to enjoy what is happening and knows that his or her Dom's pleasure comes from that release."

Lexi explored the masculine angles of the man before her and liked what her hands found. For a moment her mind fought with her because the one she wanted was Cash, but she resisted. The man dumped her. Lexi barely knew him anyway, and she had every right to indulge in whatever man she wanted. And she was more than willing to let William make that choice knowing he wouldn't let anything bad happen to her.

"Touch him whatever way you like. He can't resist. Just like so many men can't resist looking at your beauty without wanting to touch.

"To kiss.

"To possess."

William's hot whispers sent a blazing streak of fire down Lexi's spine. How could a man do that with just words? He was close but didn't touch her. The idea of two men with her, one whispering dirty things in her ear, and the other standing helpless at her touch, sparked wildly wicked thoughts in her.

Lexi's fingers grazed the man's nipples, which pebbled

under her touch. She let them lightly trail under his arms, down his sides, and his breathing stuttered. Lexi smiled. How did she miss that a light touch could affect a man? This was delicious.

But, of course, in the usual vanilla sex, she waited for the man to give her an orgasm, and if he didn't, somehow it was his fault. It struck her then how unfair that was. How did things get so fucked up between men and women? Lexi liked touching the man's skin.

She brought her hands to his neck and lightly swirled her fingertips behind his ears.

He gasped, and in leaning forward, his arousal grazed her hip. This? This light touching got him excited? A sense of power surged through her.

"Do you want to touch him there?" William asked. This time he spoke loud enough for both of them to hear.

Lexi made the hand sign to indicate "Yes!"

"Can she touch you?" William asked. "Remember, I told you not to come, so think about it."

Lexi held her breath waiting for the answer. Would the anonymous man let her touch his engorged cock? It seemed wickedly delicious thing to tease a man like that. The thought sent a thrill through her, and she felt her wetness gather between her legs.

"He said yes. Go ahead, darling. Do your worst."

Though she couldn't see William, at his light-hearted tone she imagined he was smiling.

She let a single hand snake down the man's hard torso feeling every ridge and bump of his abs. What a delicious man. This was giving her thoughts she shouldn't have.

But her hand found his cock, and she stroked the silken skin. The man shivered.

"Go ahead," whispered William, "wrap your hand around it."

Lexi swallowed hard but wrapped her hand around it. Good lord, it was big. She slid her hand down its length and back up again, and he sucked in a deep breath.

"Again," William said.

Lexi did, but this time used her other hand to cup his balls. Knowing she held his most sensitive parts sent a tingle of fire through her. The flesh between her legs began to throb. She couldn't remember ever taking this much time with a man, but she liked it. With barely-there touches, her fingers ran over the plump orbs and drew more staggered breathes as she palmed the plump head of his cock.

A tiny noise escaped his throat as a pearl of pre-cum wet her hand.

"Careful," William said in a warning voice. "How are his balls, darling? Are they drawn up nice and tight? Nod your head. I can see it."

Lexi nodded her head.

"And does this make you hot?"

Lexi crooked her finger.

"She wants you," William said. "She enjoys touching you. How about you? Do you like this?"

"He likes this and wants more. Do you want to put your mouth on him?"

At William's words, the man's cock throbbed in her hand, but no. Lexi wasn't sure. She'd given blowjobs, but she didn't know this man.

She shook her head.

"Do you want to know a secret, darling?" William whispered in her ear so low only she could hear. "This man wants you desperately. He's willing to do anything to have you, including coming here to learn how to be a good Dom to you. He speaks of nothing else."

A chill ran through Lexi. This man knew who she was? She shook her head violently. If William didn't stop this, she'd "safeword" out.

"Trust me, darling. It's rare to see such a good match. Do you want to see who he is?"

Lexi's heart raced, and she nearly cried out, "No!" But the man wore a blindfold and didn't have a clue who she was. She could walk away. And, she figured, she would rather put a face to what she just did, rather than wonder at night who she'd touched so intimately.

She nodded.

William's hands were at the back of her head untying the strings of the mask. The fabric fell from her eyes. Lexi gasped and stared at a bound and blindfolded Cash. Every part of him strained toward her, including that impossibly large cock whose head wept with desire.

"Darling," William whispered low and close to her ear. "I'd put down money that this man loves you. He's made a terrible mistake, and he regrets it. But I think you'll regret it more if you walk away."

52

CASH'S HEART PUMPED WILDLY AT THE ILLICIT TOUCHES OF Master William's sub. At first, he was afraid it would be Carlo, especially after Carlo's crack that Cash would enjoy what was coming up.

Standing tied and naked in a private room in William's club did strange things to his head. This wasn't the same as standing in the men's locker room, or with Tiffany. Blindfolded and with his hands tied behind his back, he felt unprotected and vulnerable.

When William entered and brought a woman with him, alarm raced through him. What the hell was this?

But he was here to learn to be a Dom. To get tutored on what Lexi needed. He had no idea if she would take him back after he dumped her cruelly at the police station but he had to try.

Cash decided a type of insanity had descended on him while police, Givens, and Tiffany surrounded him at the police station. The added inducement of getting Lexi out of jail pushed him to this latest act of betrayal.

But now, the woman's touch, rousing his dick, was

another betrayal. He wanted to yell out to stop and make her, with her incredibly soft hands, and the silk robe that brushed enticingly against his cock, cease her relentless stroking.

Her caress of his balls made him want to whimper with the tingle she sent through him, but he was mindful of William's enjoinder not to make a sound. Focusing on not doing something made him more aware of his body's responses. It forced him to concentrate on every surge of pleasure that her hands sparked.

It was hell to keep silent.

And it was heaven how utterly focused he was on his body's pleasure. Every trailing touch fired pleasure, building need and passion. That he couldn't react, or move his hands to grasp this alluring woman, jacked sparks of pleasure to a higher level than he'd ever experienced.

William's whispering in her ear was a torture of its own. Cash couldn't hear what the Dom said, and he strained to pick up stray words to figure out what was going on. This strange way of training confused Cash. But it was also very hot.

A tiny noise escaped his throat as a pearl of pre-cum wet her hand.

"Careful," William said in a warning voice. "How are his balls, darling? Are they drawn up nice and tight? Nod your head."

Cash couldn't see her response, but her hands cupped his balls.

"And does this make you hot?"

He spoke to the sub and not Cash. William's words drove Cash insane. He wanted, needed, more than this torturous teasing. His inability to see what the woman replied frustrated him. Seconds moved like minutes, and Cash's cock throbbed, needing more and not getting it.

"She wants you," William said. "She enjoys touching you. And you, Cash? Do you like this?"

Cash waved his fingers as William instructed earlier, though if allowed he'd scream, "Hell, yes."

"He likes this and wants more. Do you want to put your mouth on him?"

At William's words, his cock throbbed, eager and willing. A warm, wet mouth on his cock would be just perfect. Cash was on fire with every nerve cell lit and ready to explode.

But her lips did not brush the head of his cock and Cash held back a needy moan.

William whispered more words into the woman's ear that frustratingly Cash could not catch. They would not leave him like this, would they? His breathing stuttered as he waited, not knowing what would come next.

He heard footsteps and the door opening and closing, and he wondered if William had left him alone again. But then he caught the woman's scent as she walked around him. Cash swallowed hard as she skimmed her fingertips on his skin.

"What should I do?" she whispered huskily. "Should I touch you some more?"

Why did her voice sound faintly familiar? Cash's brain, scrambled by overstimulation, found forming coherent thoughts difficult. The huskiness of her voice did not help in recognizing who it belonged to.

Her hand touched his dick, and he jumped. "Suck your cock?"

Cash remained quiet. Did William leave the room? What would happen if he spoke?

"Or should I leave you here as you left me?" She spoke in a normal tone, and Cash's chin shot up.

"Lexi?"

"Damn straight it's Lexi."

"What are you doing here?"

"I'll ask you the same thing, Mr. Sean Cashman. I didn't expect to find you like this, blindfolded and trussed up like a Christmas turkey."

Cash's face flushed.

"Can you untie me, please?"

"I think I like seeing you like this. At least you won't run out on me."

"I'm very, very sorry about that. Part of this was William's way of teaching me the error of my ways."

"I'm not sure I accept your apology. You were cold and cruel."

"I'm sorry."

"I spent hours in the police station."

"What? They were to let you out right away. That was the—"

Cash stopped. Would she understand that he'd tried in his own fucked-up way to protect her? Probably not.

"The what, Cash?"

She circled him, and he swallowed hard.

"Did you make a deal? With Walker Givens?"

"Lexi, please untie me."

"No. Not until you give me a sensible answer. Because the last thing you told me was that you made a mistake, and you led me on. What is it you want now, Cash? Or does that change with the moment?"

"Oh lord," groaned Cash. He could see why she would think that. He'd been nothing but a yo-yo going back and forth between her and Tiffany. And what woman would want to put up with that?

No sane one.

"I know that I haven't been consistent—"

"Consistent," Lexi said. Her voice rose in disbelief.

"I didn't mean for any of this to happen."

"Says every man everywhere when he screws up."

"God, yes. I fucked up, Lexi. How many times do I have to say I'm sorry?"

"Until I believe it."

"How can you believe it, if I can't show it to you?"

Lexi's breath landed on his chest, and her hand went to his now deflated cock.

"You aren't showing me much here, now."

"Dammit," he growled. "Give me a fucking chance."

"Like you gave a fuck for me, leaving me there in that police station."

"Oh, fuck. What can I do to make it up to you?"

"I'm not sure," Lexi said with uncertainty in her voice.

This was wrong. Lexi sounded confused, and yes, she had every right to be. But what did William say? She was a natural sub? Maybe what she needed was why he came here in the first place. She needed her Dom.

"Suck my cock," he ordered.

"What?"

"Get on your knees," he said sternly, "and suck my cock like you mean it."

Cash's heart thumped in his chest. Would Lexi follow his command? Would she give into her submissive instincts, or would she walk away in disgust? Microseconds stretched into seconds, and he feared he'd screwed up again.

And then her hands slid down his abs, and then his thighs, and she breathed on his cock, and he said a prayer of thanks to whatever god was listening. She rasped her tongue on his tip, and he shuddered.

"Good girl," he said. "Go ahead, put the head in your mouth. Show me how you worship my cock."

In the dark, his hands secured behind his back, unable to reach Lexi's head to grip her hair, warmth and wet enveloped the sensitive head. His dick twitched and filled again.

"That's good," he said evenly. "But you can do better."

Lexi made a small noise but sucked him deeper into her mouth. Every muscle in Cash's body clenched with the fire she sent through him.

"That's right, baby," he murmured appreciatively. "You do that so good." He pressed forward, driving his cock deeper. "Yeah, take that, take it, fuck yes."

He was big and didn't expect her to take it all. "Wrap your hand around it," he ordered.

Lexi moved her tongue on the bottom of his cock, cradled his balls in one hand, and wrapped her fingers around his base. She pulled back and worked her luscious mouth around the head once more and then to the shaft. Cash's balls and stomach tightened.

"I'm going to come. Let go, so I don't—"

But Lexi sucked even harder, sending him over the edge.

53

LEXI GOT LOST IN THE SENSATION OF CASH IN HER MOUTH. SHE fondled his tight balls and jacked the steel within silk of his shaft. He tasted delicious, like everything right in the world, and she loved his cock throbbing in her mouth.

Cash had mistreated her, but she tucked that away for future review. William's words rang in her head.

"Darling," William whispered low and close to her ear. "I'd put down money that this man loves you. He's made a terrible mistake, and he regrets it. But I think you'll regret it more if you walk away."

But with her mouth crammed with his shaft, she didn't care if he cared for her or not. All that mattered were his encouraging murmurs and her desire to satisfy this man who haunted her dreams.

His musk filled her nose, making her lightheaded. Her mouth worked his cock with a fevered frenzy. Her heart beat double-time and her own sex buzzed with heat as his shaft throbbed in her mouth.

"I'm going to come," he husked. "Let go, so I can—"

Lexi wanted it. She craved his cum and wanted to drink

it down her throat. The notion made her imagine herself a wild, wanton, and wicked creature ready to undertake all to satisfy her man. She sucked him rough and deep, willing him to erupt in her mouth.

He plunged into her mouth, filling it with his cum. Lexi grabbed his hips and held onto him, capturing all he had to give. Finally, he slumped against her and pulled away.

Lexi dropped her hands but remained kneeling at his feet. His completion completed her. Not sexually, but in a way that fulfilled her to the marrow of her soul. She sighed.

The door swung open noisily, as if someone was battering it open. Lexi jumped and stood to her feet as William strode into the room.

"I'm shocked," he said in dismay. "Shocked that sex is going on in my club."

Lexi's heart raced, thinking she did something wrong, when he winked at her.

"You two must leave now!" he declared. "Here!" He threw a pile of clothes on the floor. "Get dressed, both of you! And leave!"

"I'd be glad to," said Cash wryly, "if I wasn't tied up at the moment."

"Lexi, release Cash. And then both of you go."

"Yes, Master William," she said with her eyes downcast.

William cupped her chin and raised her eyes to him. "You are a good girl, Lexi. You'll make one lucky man a fantastic sub." He dropped his hand and nodded toward Cash, and Lexi moved behind Cash to untie his bonds.

"And you," William said to Cash. "You'd better not fuck up again. I won't interfere a second time."

William turned and left, shutting the door after him.

Lexi pulled off Cash's blindfold, and he grinned at her.

"My god, Lexi," he husked appreciatively.

Standing before him in only a silk robe roused her self-consciousness. Lexi turned away as she blushed and stooped to retrieve his clothes, but Cash slid his arms around her waist and drew her to him. When she straightened, he turned her around.

"Cash," she said.

"I will kiss you."

"Is that a command?"

"Yes."

"I understand what your problem is," Lexi said.

"What?"

"You don't know when to shut up and start kissing."

Cash slanted his head and brushed her lips with his, and slid one arm around her neck. In the next kiss, Cash pressed past her lips and found hers writhing against it, shooting sparks along her spine.

A knock at the door broke them apart.

"You're aware there are cameras in here, right?" said William through the door.

Lexi jumped away in embarrassment, and she grabbed Cash's clothes from the floor and flung them at him.

"Get dressed," she hissed.

Cash chuckled as he pulled on his underwear and pants, and then his shirt. But he kept his eyes on her even though she turned her back and dressed as discreetly as she could from under the red silk robe.

"You don't have to hide your gorgeous body."

Lexi blushed.

"Let's go," William said after he knocked on the door once more. "I have this room booked."

Lexi left the private room first, with Cash following her. But soon he had his arm around her waist again when they walked to the exit of the club as they followed William.

"It's up to you two what you do going forward. But you don't need this club. Of course, if you ever want advice, you know where to find me. I expect, though, you will find your own way."

"Thank you, William."

"She's yours to protect now. Do it well. And be honest with her. Or you will answer to me."

William pushed open the door, and Cash shot the Dom a puzzled look.

"I wonder what that means," Cash said as the door shut behind him. "Why would he say that?"

"He had taken me under his protection because of all that happened, but I think he assumes you'll take that on now. But Cash, you aren't obligated—"

"Lexi, I confess I've done a wretched job of it, but yes, I will protect you. And take care of you. First order of business is that I'll take you home."

They were near the curb now, and he looked up and down for a cab.

Lexi bit her lip. "Cash, I can't go home."

"Why not?"

"Samantha and I had a huge fight."

"Does that happen often?"

"No. It never happens. But she was so upset about getting arrested, and then I told her that I liked William and she blew like a volcano."

Cash huffed.

"You hungry then?"

"Oh, I don't know. I feel stuffed right now." Cash did a double-take and then stared at her.

"Did you just engage in dirty talk?

"Heck no. It was barely suggestive."

"No," Cash said. "It's my job to figure out whether you should engage in dirty talk."

"So you are taking over."

"What did William tell me? Yes. The sub has all the power."

"You're kidding me, right?"

"Nope."

A cab came at them, Cash whistled. The vehicle skidded to a stop and Cash opened the door. "Your carriage, madam."

Lexi entered the cab and turned to him when he settled next to her.

"Madam? You make me sound old. At least William uses 'Miz.'"

"Are you comparing me to other Doms now? Maybe I should punish you for that."

"What? Here?"

"I should put you over my knee. You didn't listen to me when I told you to stop sucking my cock. That's disobedient."

"That does sound Dom-like—punishing his submissive for giving him pleasure," Lexi teased.

"You are asking for it, aren't you?"

He pulled out his phone.

"What are you doing?"

"Ssh," Cash said as he pressed his fingers on the screen. Lexi looked out of the window and saw they were heading to midtown.

"Where are we going?"

"You do ask a lot of questions, don't you?"

"I think I should know where a man who likes to whip women is taking me."

"Who says I like to whip women?"

"You keep talking about punishment."

"There are other ways of punishing someone."

"Such as?"

"Oh, I could have a delicious dinner delivered to my apartment and make you watch while I eat it."

"That would depend on the food."

"Armenian."

"Armenian?"

"Yes, wonderful aromas and flavors. And rich, very rich."

"That might be torture. I'm not convinced. Plus, I just might steal your food."

"I could always tie you to a chair and make you watch me eat."

"Oh?" Lexi said. Wicked thoughts entered her mind about how she liked restraints. "Do you have a nice collection of ropes?"

"No. But I do have a huge selection of silk neckties."

"Hmm," Lexi murmured as she imagined slinky silk around her wrists and ankles. "How many?"

"Neckties?" said Cash sounding surprised. "Around fifty? I'm not sure. Why? You want to see my necktie collection?"

"Is that like etchings? Only in silk?"

"Are you implying that I'm trying to seduce you?"

"You're talking Armenian food, so yes, I assume you are trying to seduce me."

"So, you have had it."

"What? Armenian food or seduction?"

"Oh, Ms. Lexi, you are a tease, aren't you?"

"And if I am?"

"Then I will have to punish you."

54

CASH

Just the thought of "punishing" Lexi, pulling her across his lap and spanking her round little butt, made his cock twitch again. He'd love to see her wiggle as he smacked his palms on the spectacular globes of her ass.

He put his arm around her and pulled her closer to him. She didn't mind. In fact, she scrunched closer to him, close enough that her head fitted under his chin. Her sexy scent filled his nose, and he looked at her full breasts generously filling her white button-down shirt. Her nipples jutted forward as hard as pebbles, and he wanted to squeeze them between his fingers to hear her gasp.

Cash snapped into a different headspace. He became focused and aware of every breath she took and the rise and fall of her breasts. The flush of excitement in her cheeks, the way she licked her lips with her delicate rose pink tongue fascinated him. He noticed how his frame towered over her delicate one. He felt the power and strength within him. She made him feel this way. How he wanted this woman, to make her his.

"Punishment?" Lexi said. Her sweet-as-candy voice

dripped sex. He stared into her eyes, keenly aware of the little movements of her mouth and how her nipples pebbled under her shirt. Only she existed in the Universe.

Then Lexi put her hand on his twitching cock. "You don't want to punish me," she said a teasing voice.

Every one of Lexi's muscles bunched and her jaw tightened as she tried to take control of this moment between them. If this were another woman, he might let her. But he felt to the depths of his soul that this wasn't what she wanted. She needed his approval and acceptance as if it was a palpable thing: a need that connected them. Lexi wanted him to take control, and he was letting her down by not doing so.

Cash pushed her delicate hand away and put both of hers together on her lap.

"You," he growled, "are not paying the proper respect to your master."

"What?"

"Lower your eyes," he said, "and don't speak."

Lexi's eyelashes fluttered, and her cheeks flushed prettily as she bent her head toward her hands.

"I will let you know when you can touch me. And if I need to punish you, I will. If you want to avoid punishment, you will do what I tell you."

"Yes, sir," she said.

"Did I tell you to speak?"

She shook her head.

He bent his head to her ear.

"I'm taking you to my apartment," he whispered. "And when we are there, you will do exactly as I say. Nod if you understand."

She did.

"Shake your head if you don't want to go to my apartment. If you shake your head, it will disappoint me, but I will not force you to do something you do not agree to."

Lexi sat motionless.

"Good girl," he said soothingly.

The cab pulled up to his apartment building. He gave the driver the money and stepped out, holding Lexi's hand.

The doorman greeted Cash. "Good evening, Mr. Cashman. Good to see you. I have your mail, and a delivery just came for you. Oh, and I'm sorry to say some process servers came while you were away. I took the envelope."

"That's fine, George. I know what it is. And, George, this is Miss Lexi Winters. Admit her anytime she wishes. If I'm not here, arrange to let her into my apartment."

"Yes, sir, Mr. Cashman."

"And take Mr. Walker Givens and Ms. Tiffany Givens off the admittance list. Do not allow them past the lobby. Wipe Mr. and Ms. Givens' entry codes from the security system."

"Very good, sir."

"Thank you, and good night, George."

Cash picked up the bag of food and took Lexi's hand.

"You can relax, Lexi. We aren't in the apartment yet."

"I should have figured you lived in Central Park West."

"My father bought it years ago. Since he passed, I lived here alone. But it's too big for one person, as you'll see."

The elevator opened on a wide vestibule, and Cash moved toward the keypad.

"Put your index finger here and choose four numbers and punch them in. This way you can let yourself in any time you want."

"Are you sure you want to do this? Give me access to your apartment?"

"Maybe I haven't made myself clear. I want you in my life, Lexi, all of it. I know things are running shit now, but if I wait for things to be perfect, then I might not get the chance. There are a bunch of things I have to explain to you, but right now, I want to be with you. And I do believe it's your turn."

"My turn?"

He arched an eyebrow. "For me to return the favor."

"So you are planning to seduce me?"

"Who said anything about seducing?" he said. He keyed in his security code, and the door latch opened.

Lexi followed, and the door shut behind her with a solid thud.

"Now. Take off your clothes. All of them. And when you've finished, go kneel at the couch." He left the mail on the table by the front door, but took the bag of food and stepped down into the wide living area of the apartment. A long curved couch followed the sweeping curve of the open floor plan set two steps below the section of floor that edged the room in a crescent. Cash put the bag of food on the specially made curved glass coffee table. He walked away knowing if he stayed close to Lexi, she'd argue, and he didn't want that. He wanted her obedience. Cash hoped she'd follow through because he had some creative thoughts on how to tease her.

He walked into his closet and took off the jeans and shirt he'd worn for the past twenty-four hours. Cash donned a pair of black slacks and his white button-down. As he learned, setting a scene was as much theater as it was about dominance. Cash wanted to set the right tone for what he planned to do.

He pulled open the tie drawer in his closet and took out a couple of ties. One he draped around his neck. Another he put in his pocket, for later, just in case.

Stopping by the kitchen, he gathered one plate, a single

set of silverware, and some napkins and a glass of water. His heart thudded in his chest as he stepped down into the living room area of the apartment hoping he'd find Lexi kneeling at the couch.

His breath caught in his throat. She was absolutely gorgeous. From her full breasts to her rounded hips she looked delectable. Her brown hair spilled over her shoulders in a cascade. And her skin? He'd never seen anything so smooth and creamy, as if the sun never touched it.

He sat on the couch and set down the plate, silverware, and drink, and pulled the bag to him.

"It's very difficult to get real Armenian food in the city now, but I found one little place where I can get it." He held the bag to her nose.

"The food smells wonderful, doesn't it?"

Lexi nodded her head.

Cash filled his plate from the containers in the bag.

"Now this little appetizer," he said, "is sarma. It's grape leaves wrapped with rice and vegetables, cooked with fresh lemon juice and olive oil. Mmm," he mouthed as he took a bite. "The flavors just burst in your mouth."

He watched Lexi's jaw grow tight. He didn't intend to tease her, just build up the anticipation. But perhaps he should go easy on her. She didn't know what to expect from him.

"You want some?" he said. "You can speak."

"Yes, sir."

"Very good," Cash said. "Hold up your hands."

Lexi held out her hands, and Cash pulled the tie from his neck. He quickly wrapped it around her wrists and, pulling one end through the middle, tied it off.

"Cash!"

"Don't you mean 'sir?' Lexi? I thought you were better

trained than that. Now put your wrists to your knees again and open your mouth."

Lexi's eyes went wide. She must have been thinking the worst. But tonight Cash only intended the best for Lexi. He picked up a piece of sarma and put it to her lips. "Go ahead, take a bite."

She bit into the crunchy morsel.

"Is it good?"

"Oh, yes, sir."

"Do you want another?"

"Please, sir."

"Now this is mantee. It is a puff pastry with melted cheese in it."

Cash fed it, and every item in the bag, to Lexi from his fingers. Pastry crusted mantee, spiced potatoes, marinated steak kabobs he bought tenderly to her lips. He loved how she licked his fingertips. Ms. Lexi performed her own brand of teasing, and it sent sparks to Cash's cock.

"Oops," Cash said. "Some of the juices from the kabob ran down your chin. Sit next to me."

Cash helped her to her feet and then sat her on the couch. Lexi shivered.

"Are you cold?" he asked with concern.

"Oh, no."

"Here, let me take care of that juice." Cash bent forward and licked her chin, cleaning it up with his tongue.

"Oops," he said playfully. "I think same juices dripped lower. Put your legs up on the couch and let me take a look."

55

LEXI

AT FIRST, IT ANNOYED LEXI THAT CASH DEMANDED SHE STRIP and kneel at the couch. Not that she didn't want to please him, but it seemed ridiculous, especially when he returned to the living room wearing clothes more formal than he'd arrived in.

And when he tied her hands and started eating the food, Lexi thought he'd deliver on his original threat to torture her by eating and not allowing her to.

She was hungry, dammit!

But Cash started to feed her from his fingertips, one delicious thing after another. The care he took, and the intense way in which he watched her, made her stomach flip-flop. This was an intimate act of a man caring for a woman. As she took piece after piece of food from his hand, she fell a little more for Sean Cashman.

And it seemed he was warming up. He fed her a morsel of beef kabob, and it was so juicy that it spilled down her chin.

As Cash bent forward and licked her chin, cleaning her

with his tongue, it sent frissons of pleasure through her body.

When he mentioned the juices that had dripped lower, and for her to put her legs up on the couch, she wasn't sure what he was up to until he pulled apart her legs and gazed half-lidded at the tender flesh between them. "Yes," he rasped. "There seems to be some juices here too."

She gasped as he lowered his head and licked her. "Mmm. Delicious. I just think I found dessert."

Lexi clenched her ass involuntarily as his tongue became an instrument of pleasure. He was everywhere, darting between her folds, then lapping the flesh around her clit, sucking that tender flesh into his mouth. It was almost too much and definitely too good. Where they still playing the game? Was she allowed to come?"

He lifted his hands to her breasts and tweaked her nipples between his fingers, and her hips rose from the couch. Fire rose through her belly, racing toward her womanhood, threatening to overtake her with its heat.

"Please, can I come?"

Cash pulled back suddenly, leaving her gasping, needing, wanting that magical tongue between her legs.

"No," he said.

Lexi threw her head back, breathing hard.

Cash pressed his fingers into her wet channel.

"This," he said roughly, "belongs to me. Say it."

"It belongs to you, sir."

"I will say when you can come. I own your orgasms."

"You own me, sir."

"Good. Now that we've got that out of the way..."

He stood and scooped her up into his arms, and she hung in there as he strode through the apartment. Cold air prickled her skin as he carried her into a bedroom. He laid her down gently on the bed as soft as a cloud.

"Watch me," he said.

He pulled something from his pocket, and her eyes widened when she realized it was another tie. Cash leaned over her and lifted her arms up, looped the second tie through the one binding her wrists, and tied it around a slat in the headboard. He inspected his work and tested the makeshift cord to see that it was secure.

Was it wrong that she liked not being able to move? That she enjoyed being at his mercy? Never in her life had she entertained these thoughts. But as long as Cash was in control, she didn't have to think about her own response. Lexi didn't have to worry whether she would get excited enough to come, or whether the man chased his orgasm at the expense of hers. Cash looked her over, his eyes focused on her hands and face, watching for her reaction. Their eyes met, and she thrilled at the connection his gaze sparked. It was a moment where she felt fused to him but at different poles of existence. There was no singular Lexi or Cash. They were one.

The intensity of that perception laid her soul open. Whatever he wanted, she would give—no questions, no reservations.

"How's that? Too tight? Tingling in your fingers?" His voice caressed her ear, as soft as the silk that bound her wrists. The care in his voice sparked flutters of excitement in her stomach.

"No. I'm fine, sir."

"You tell me if your fingers or hands get numb, okay? That's an order."

"Yes, sir," she breathed.

"I wouldn't want my sub hurt. That wouldn't do me any good."

With a feather-light touch he trailed his finger from her jaw, around one nipple, then the other. She gasped as Cash caressed down her stomach and between her legs. He sighed when he put his hand at her entrance.

"You are so fucking wet. Are you wet for me?

"Yes, sir. For you. Just you."

"That makes me happy to hear, but I think we've waited long enough. Don't you think?" As he spoke he pushed his finger inside her, and her back arched with a jolt of desire.

"Whatever you want, sir," she said. And she meant it. If he wanted to tease her for hours, she'd submit to him. If he wanted to take her hard that was fine too.

More than fine. She wanted Cash inside her. She needed to feel his cock fill her, commanding her thoughts and emotions.

More tingles swirled through her tender folds, and her breathing sped up as he finger-fucked her. When he curled his fingers to tap her g-spot, she gasped. Lexi pulled at her bounds, desperate to pull his hips into alignment to hers.

"Please," she whimpered. "Want you."

"Oh, Lexi," he groaned. "You wreck me, you do."

"Please," she whined. "Need you."

Cash pulled his finger from her and leaned over her as he sucked the fingers slathered in her juices.

"You are so delicious," he said. "I may have to keep you tied to my bed so I can taste your nectar whenever I want." His voice was a tease like a slow strip dance, and Lexi pulled on her bindings once again.

"Master!" she called.

Cash's face changed from amusement to deadly serious-ness. His fingers worked his zipper and Lexi breathed a sigh at the sound. She shivered at the memory of Cash's big and thick cock. She wiggled her hips eager.

"I'm going to take you hard," he growled.

She nodded, pulling at the silk that held her wrists fast.

Cash gripped her hips and thrust inside her, prying her channel open to take all of him.

Her breath staggered at the sudden invasion, and he stared at her, the tendons of his neck standing out as if he fought against something. Then Cash clamped his mouth on her hardened nipple and sucked it sharply, sending a shock of fire throughout her body. Her back arched and she cried out.

"Ahhh!"

One hand moved to cup one globe of her ass and the other cupped her other breast. Juts of his hips, and his tongue laving the hot nipple, turned her into a bubbling mess of sensation that ripped pleasure through her in torturous waves. Suck and release, snap of his hips and then pull back, again and again, driving her to a place she never went before. Her breathing sped into labored breaths as she alternately sucked in air, and pleaded with Cash to fuck her harder.

Cash suddenly moved onto the other nipple with a sharp suck that had her crying out. His hand moved to the abandoned nipple, and he pinched the over-sensitized bud as he thrust inside her hard, bringing her to the edge of orgasm.

"Come!" he commanded. He thrust into her again with all the strength of his muscular thighs, battering her inside with fierce strokes. At last she flew over the edge and tumbled into eternity, his heat searing her from inside out.

"Cash!" she screamed.

"Lexi!" he shouted as he pumped his seed inside her.

With a few more jagged and irregular pumps, he fell against her, breathing hard.

"You are so fucking perfect," he breathed.

"Sir?"

"Yes?"

"Can you untie me now?"

56

CASH

"Oh, my god!"

Cash jerked his head toward Tiffany standing in the doorway of his bedroom with shock written over her perfectly painted face.

"What the fuck!" spit Cash. "What the hell are you doing here?"

"I had good news for you. Honestly, Cash. Can't you answer your phone?

"I've been tied up," he said.

Lexi groaned, and he realized his poor choice of words.

"Really," Tiffany said with her eyebrow arched. "It looks like your little friend is the one tied up."

"Cash, please," Lexi said as she flexed her fingers. She gulped in air as her face flushed with embarrassment.

"Sorry, sorry," he said as he quickly untied the silk around her wrists. "You okay?" he said as he rubbed her wrists.

"Oh. I'm just fine," snapped Tiffany. "Even though a little whore climbed into the bed with my boyfriend."

"Jeezus," snarled Cash. "Get the fuck out of here, Tiffany. And why you're at it, get out of my apartment."

Tiffany huffed. "Well, okay. If you don't want to hear the news about your company." She gave a little shrug of her shoulders and turned away.

"What about my company?" Cash said. He pushed off the bed, pulled on his pants, and followed Tiffany out of the room. He closed the door, so Lexi could regain what she could of her shattered privacy.

"Oh, why would you worry?" Tiffany said. "You haven't paid attention to it for months."

Cash crossed the room quickly and spun Tiffany to face him. Anger raced through him for this woman who'd invaded his home and interrupted his private moments with Lexi.

"Quit the fucking games, Tiff. I can have you arrested for trespassing."

"But Cash, I've been here a million times. Who is going to believe I'm trespassing?"

"I've told you we are through. Now get to the point before I call the police and have your ass hauled out of here."

Tiffany laughed. "Oh, darling. Are you really going to try that? As unstable as you've been lately, no one will pay you any mind. Really, Cash, a BDSM club? Is that the sort of sick and perverted things that girl pulls you into?"

"Lexi didn't pull me into anything. I'm losing my patience, Tiffany." He pulled out his phone from his pants pocket.

"Fine. It's really good news, anyway. Your delaying the sale was such a good move. The buyer added another ten percent to the sale and Daddy signed the papers today."

"What! I didn't authorize that!"

Tiffany shrugged. "Daddy remembered some papers that your father signed before he died giving Daddy power-of-attorney for Cashman family personal affairs. He has every legal right to do it."

"Get the fuck out of here."

"But, darling. This means you don't have to worry about the company anymore and we can do that traveling we talked about."

"You are delusional, Tiff. We're through. How many times do I have to tell you that?"

"Cash, you shouldn't be making life-altering decisions while you're in this state. And I forgive you for your indiscretion with that little homewrecker. We can go on just as we always did, only a few billion richer. This is going to be so good, Cash."

Cash pressed the speed dial number on his phone for the doorman.

"George. I have an intruder in my home. Tiffany Givens. Call the police."

"I'm sorry, sir. I can't tell you how that happened."

"Just call the police. I want her removed."

"Yes, sir."

Tiffany rolled her eyes. "Fine, if you're going to be difficult. I'll see you at the competency hearing Thursday. Bye, darling."

She strolled out the door as casually as leaving a party. His bedroom door opened and Lexi walked out wearing one of his robes. It was too large for her, and she clutched the opening tight with her delicate hand. Cash thought she looked adorable.

"I should go," she said. She took the paces to where her folded clothes waited for her.

"Please don't go," Cash said.

"As long as I'm around, that woman will continue to harass you," she said.

Cash crossed the room to where she stood with her clothes in hand.

"Don't say that. None of this has to do with you. In fact, I'll tell you a secret."

"What?"

"You saved me. Tiffany and I haven't been good for a long time."

"Really?" Lexi said, shrugging off his arm. He let it fall, afraid to upset her more by touching her. "How long would that be, eh? From the photos in your room, you two were pretty serious."

"I admit the girl you've seen lately isn't the one that I grew up with. Something changed in her. She used to be fun. Good to hang around with. Comfortable."

"So you're comparing her to an old pillow, and I'm the new one." Lexi's words held a dangerous edge of sarcasm, and it warned him to be careful about what he said. He did not want Lexi to walk out on him.

"Please, Lexi. I know it upset you that Tiffany saw us together. Anyone would be."

"What can I think, Cash? It seems one minute we're right for each other. Then a piece of your life comes crashing down, and everything is wrong. Because all the woman talks about is getting married to you. Making it sound like it was a done deal. Listening to her tonight, she still believes it's a done deal."

"No, Lexi. I told Tiffany we were through."

"Then explain this!"

Lexi pulled out a receipt from his bathrobe pocket.

"I wasn't snooping. It was in the robe. Imagine my surprise when I found a receipt for an engagement ring bought a mere two days before your trip to the Virgin Islands. I can't imagine that you would spend all that money, and then decide two days later 'Hey, the woman I grew up with and planned to marry? Nope. Not happening.'"

Lexi turned her back to him and pulled her arms out of the oversized robe and began to put on her clothes.

"That did happen."

She shot him a glance over her shoulder that told him he didn't understand a key point.

"Cash, you spent half a million dollars on one ring. I can't even imagine possessing half a million dollars let alone wearing something like that on my hand."

"It was my money to spend."

"Damn it, Cash. Don't you understand? I don't belong in a world like that. Sure, it's fun to fantasize about, and every little girl dreams about her prince sweeping off her feet—"

"Then let me be your prince."

She shot him another, darker glance.

"I'm not Cinderella. I don't expect to stick my foot in a shoe and end up a princess. My life is ordinary. I wake up in the morning, drink my coffee, go to work, pay my bills, go to bed, and get up and do it all over again. A five-million-dollar condo overlooking the whole damn city is beyond my wildest dreams. I don't jet to the Virgin Islands to hang out for a weekend. That's your life and I don't fit into it."

"This," he said incredulously, "because you found a receipt to a ring I bought?"

"No. The ring reminded me that I don't belong in your world."

Cash stared at her in disbelief. Where did this come from?

"Is this because Tiffany burst in on us?"

"No. Yes. Damn, Cash. Every time I look at that woman I

know I'll never be as beautiful, or as well dressed. Even if it weren't Tiffany, there'd be another woman from your social set that would be so much better for you than me."

Oh, dear Lord, thought Cash. He flailed mentally, trying and failing to find the right words to say to her that didn't sound insensitive or snobbish. Cash was not a man that cared about social class, but he knew plenty of people in his social circles that did. Lexi was correct that should he introduce her to them, they could very well give her a difficult time. If he took Lexi to a charity ball instead of Tiffany, people might make unkind comparisons.

If they had known each other longer, this would be easier. But it had only been days since he met her.

"It is you I want, Lexi," he said. "Tiffany no longer interests me. None of the women I know hold a candle to you. You've widened my world since I met you and taught me things about the man I want to be. I've been through a long dark year, out of which I'm just beginning to see the light. And you are that light. Give us a chance."

Lexi frowned.

"I'm not the woman you think I am, Cash."

"I don't understand."

"Look, I have to be honest. I've loved everything we've done, but I'm not into the BDSM thing like you are. And I might not mind exploring it as a private part of our lives, but now... Cash, she saw us, and that's huge, and she literally has no filter. How much do you want to bet that she's on the phone to her father telling him what she witnessed? Who knows what she'll say to people, or if I were to become part of your world, what she would say to the people you mix with? The sorts of things she'd call me. I'm sure gold digger is already on her list. She'll tell people that I am a sex slave. I can't handle it."

"Lexi, please," Cash said stepping toward her.

She held up her hands. "I can't, Cash. I just can't."

Cash watched helplessly as she yanked open the front door. She looked over her shoulder one last time and he saw tears streaming down her cheeks. "For what it's worth, I could love you, Cash. But I can't be with you at the expense of my self-esteem."

57

LEXI NEARLY MELTED INTO THE FLOOR OF THE ELEVATOR AS SHE fled from Cash. She had never been so humiliated as when she saw the smirk on Tiffany's face. After experiencing such joy in Cash's lovemaking, it wrecked her to have it shattered by Tiffany's intrusion and hurtful words.

Not that she would care about such stuff in her normal life. But when she found that receipt in Cash's robe, the reality of her situation struck harder than a blacksmith's hammer on an anvil.

A half a million dollars. A half a fucking million dollars. How does anyone buy a ring like that? How does anyone wear anything that ostentatious? But more than that, how much did Cash care for Tiffany to buy her such an expensive ring?

He had to love her—a lot.

Was it different for a rich man? For a man in her economic class, buying an expensive ring was a sign of his commitment and devotion. It represented tons of hours of hard work he had to put in to pay for it. But for Cash with his untold wealth? What did mean to him? Could he buy such a thing so easily only to discard the woman two days later?

And his declaration that he wanted Lexi? Well, apparently he'd loved Tiffany just as much at one time. What did it say about him that he would ditch the woman he intended to marry suddenly?

But the kicker was seeing Tiffany standing in the doorway of Cash's apartment. Despite Cash's precautions, she'd entered easily. It didn't matter how. This woman seemed determined to stay a part of Cash's life, one way or another, and privacy and good sense didn't matter to her. What Lexi could see was Tiffany's spreading vicious rumors at every opportunity.

Lexi meant what she said. She loved what she and Cash did together. But he had too much power over her. All he had to do was to command her, and she did whatever he said. How was that normal?

And Tiffany's finding them with her hands tied to the bedpost reminded her how abnormal that was.

She fled out of the elevator.

"Ms. Lexi?" George said, looking up from his desk. "Is there something I can do for you?"

"I need a cab."

"I'll call one. You just stay right here."

"I'll stand outside," she said.

The doorman shook his head.

"Begging your pardon, but it's safer if you stand inside. Across the park like this, sometimes standing outside isn't safe."

Lexi bit her lip and positioned herself by the door waiting for the cab. Behind her, in the vestibule, the elevator doors opened.

"Lexi!"

She groaned hearing Cash's voice. *Can't he just let this drop?*

"Go away, Cash."

"No. I can't. Lexi, please look at me."

"Damn it, Cash."

Cash took her hand, and she turned toward him. His handsome face twisted with trepidation. He pulled out a red leather ring box from his pocket.

"Lexi, I know we are still new, and there is a mass of problems to solve, but when it gets to the point where— here. Look at this."

He popped open the lid, and Lexi stared at a beautiful emerald-cut one-carat diamond ring with two round diamonds on the side.

"When I think of marrying you, it's this ring I see on your finger, not some half-million monstrosity that impresses everyone but me. This was my mother's ring, and my grandmother's before that. My family wasn't always rich, and my grandfather worked very hard to build our wealth. After my mother died, all my father did was work, so he earned more. But this ring represents who the Cashmans are."

"Cash," she gasped. "You weren't ever going to give this to Tiffany?"

"She'd never appreciate it, which should have been my first tip-off."

He closed the box and pressed it into her hand.

"When you are ready, I'll make a proper proposal. But you keep this because it represents my heart, Ms. Lexi Winters, which you have firmly in your hands."

Lexi looked into Cash's eyes, which brimmed with sincerity. She blinked, blown away, as his hands closed around hers on the red leather box. How could she refuse this man now?

He didn't need to command her with his words, to withhold and give pleasure at his whim to make her fall for him. This one act did it. Sean Cashman owned her heart.

She swallowed hard. The enormity of this moment slammed into her and tears ran in a steady stream from her eyes.

"Lexi?" Cash's voice faltered. "Why are you crying? Did I upset you? Please, baby. Tell me what's wrong."

Lexi threw her arms around Cash's neck, standing on her tiptoes to reach him.

"Nothing's wrong," she said into his broad shoulders. "I've never heard anything so beautiful in my life."

Cash breathed a sigh of relief as she buried her face in his neck.

The flashing lights of a police car drawing up to the front door broke the moment, and they pulled apart, though Cash continued to hold her hand.

"They must be here because of my complaint," Cash said. "Hang on. This should be quick."

The police walked in, and George met them at the door.

"We're here to see Sean Cashman. We understand a Lexi Winters is with him."

"I'm Lexi Winters."

"Turn around and hold out your hands."

"What?"

"You're under arrest."

"Arrest? Arrest for what?" demanded Cash.

"Theft of company property."

Lexi let the ring box drop into Cash's hand. She didn't want Cash's family heirloom to get lost.

"Lexi?"

"I didn't steal anything," she said.

"That's not what your former employer said."

One policeman pulled her arms back and handcuffed her.

"Is that necessary?" Cash asked in appeal.

"It's procedure."

The officer read Lexi her rights and then led her out of the building.

Cash tore through the doors.

"Don't worry, Lexi. We'll get you out. I'll call my lawyer. We'll be right behind you."

Lexi didn't know what Cash could do. It was after midnight, and arraignments were probably in the morning. She'd be spending another night in that damned holding cell.

"This is just fucking great," she said.

But they gave her one phone call, and she only had one person to call. Her stomach clenched as she dialed the number. Lexi hoped Samantha had calmed down because right now she did not need any more grief.

"Hey, Sam. It's me."

"Lexi! Where have you been? I'm beside myself here worrying about you."

"And well you should. Break out the butter and egg money. I'm in jail again."

58

CASH

CASH WAS FUCKING FURIOUS. ONLY TIFFANY KNEW WHERE Lexi was, and Givens had threatened to get Lexi locked up again. Stupidly, Cash hadn't thought he'd follow through.

Damn Givens and his legal connections. He probably had one of his judge friends write out a warrant for Lexi's arrest, waiting to use it when he wanted. And Cash had no doubt that when Tiffany tearfully called her father to tell him what she saw, he pulled his ace card. Cash wouldn't just fire him, he'd get Givens' license to practice stripped. Walker Givens wasn't the only one with connections in this town.

Cash grabbed the cab that pulled up as the officers put Lexi in the police car. He vowed not to lose sight of her, or let them shuffle her around so no one could get to her. He called Jamie Wilder, and it surprised him that a human answered.

"This is Sean Cashman. I have an emergency and need to speak to Jamie Wilder."

The operator took his number and told him she would pass along the message. As the cab dropped him off, his phone rang.

"What's up, Cash?"

"A huge mess. The police arrested the girl I told you about, Lexi. Givens pressed charges on her for theft of proprietary information and got an arrest warrant too. The police have her in custody now."

"And where are you?"

"The precinct where they took her."

"Then you should go home. Her arraignment won't be until the morning."

Cash raked his hair with his fingers.

"I don't want her to think we've abandoned her."

"Are you hiring me as her lawyer?"

"Yes. I'll pay all the expenses."

"Okay, I'll come down and try to see her. But really, we can't do much until the arraignment."

"I'll wait for you," Cash said.

Cash wasn't going home to wait in the comfort of his apartment. Lexi was in this horrible place, and he wouldn't leave until she knew she wasn't facing this alone. First, he leaned on the wall, then sat on a bench waiting for Jamie. He was never so happy to see a lawyer as when Jamie walked into the precinct.

"Don't get your hopes up," Jamie said as he disappeared into the bowels of the station. A half an hour later he returned.

"They gave me five minutes with her. She says she took some confidential information, but it was about you. Lexi was afraid that Givens didn't give you proper representation on the sale of the business, and I think she's right."

"So we can get these charges dropped?"

"If we can have a chat with Givens and get him to do that. Frankly, I'm a little worried that he'll try to use these charges to leverage you to do what he wants."

"How's that?"

"There's a little-known wrinkle in the Patriot Act that makes taking unauthorized information from an employer a federal crime. He must have moved too fast to have that happen. But dollars to donuts he'll threaten that."

"Yes, probably because of the competency hearing Thursday. And another thing, Tiffany told me that Givens signed sales papers of my company to Pittman."

"He's pushing hard. How can he do that?"

"Something about my father signing papers giving him power-of-attorney on personal matters."

"But didn't you fire him?"

"I did."

"Did you put it in writing?"

"No. I haven't had—"

"It's okay. We'll fix this. One thing at a time. We'll get Lexi out, and then we'll tackle Walker Givens."

"Good. Did you tell Lexi I was here?"

"Yes, and she said the same thing I did. Go home."

"On one condition. You'll text what court is holding Lexi's arraignment."

"As soon as I confirm it, I will. Court opens at 8:30, though."

"Okay. I'll be there."

Jamie shook his hand and then Cash turned toward the door, only to crash into a dark-headed woman. It was Samantha, and she was spitting fire.

"You! What did you do to Lexi?" Samantha snapped.

"I didn't do anything. I'm trying to help her. Jamie, this is Samantha—sorry, I never got your last name."

"It's Porter, Samantha Porter," she said, lifting her chin. She glared at Cash as if he were a demon.

"Samantha, this is Jamie Wilder, the lawyer I hired for her."

"You hired a lawyer?" Samantha said in disbelief.

"Yes. And he's going to get her out of jail."

"Well, Lexi doesn't need your money, Mr. High-and-Mighty. Lexi was fine until she met you. Then she loses her job, and gets involved in that *stuff* in that club, and gets thrown in jail twice. You'd better stay away from her."

"Samantha—" started Cash.

"And you, Mr. Lawyer Man, you'd better get my best friend out of jail. And here." She shoved a plastic freezer bag at him with cash and coins. "This is all our butter-and-egg money. This guy? Don't take a dime from him. We'll pay the rest of it."

"I'll discuss this with Lexi the next time I talk to her," Jamie said with a glint of amusement in his eyes. "In the meantime, you keep that. You might need it later for your own bail for causing a public disturbance."

Samantha's eyes grew wide and glanced around the station.

"Yes, well..." she sputtered.

"Go home. She won't get arraigned until the morning. Here," he said, handing her a business card, "this is my office number. Call after eight and my secretary will give you the address of the court and the docket number."

For once, Samantha stood speechless as she stared at Jamie's card. "Thank you," she stuttered as if she couldn't believe that a lawyer could be kind.

"All right, Cash, I've done all I can. I'll see you in a few hours."

Jamie walked away, leaving Samantha with Cash. "Look," she said. "I should go."

"With all that butter-and-egg money? Let me take you home."

"I can get myself home," she said.

"Sure you can. But I'm not sure Lexi will forgive me if I let her best friend brave a cab ride at two in the morning."

"I tell you what. You flag the cab and pay for it. I'll take it from there."

"Okay, I can do that," agreed Cash.

After he put Samantha in the cab, his phone flashed with a text.

Jamie: Meet me at the coffee shop by the courthouse at 7:30. We need to talk.

59

LEXI NEVER FELT AS NASTY OR DIRTY AS WHEN THE OFFICERS brought her to court. The ride was short, but the seats hard. The other occupants, who looked bored, were a seedy mix of half-dressed and overdressed women with runny mascara and their complexions as pale as death.

Good times.

Lexi was at odds and ends. Her clothes from yesterday were the worse for wear, and she needed a shower. She wasn't prepared to go in front of a judge like this. However, judging by the other occupants of the transport, she seemed to be on the best-dressed list.

It was not a comforting thought.

Waiting in the holding cell wasn't fun either because they didn't remove the shackles. Finally, after forever, she was taken to the courtroom. As she entered, Lexi searched the galley and finally saw Samantha and Cash sitting together, looking like an unlikely pair of helpers.

"The State of New York vs. Lexi Winters."

"Appearances," said the judge, who seemed slightly bored.

"Attorney James Wilder for Ms. Winters, your honor."

"Alex Holcomb for the prosecution."

"Mr. Holcomb, you seem to be getting a break from your usual prostitution cases."

"Yes, sir."

"And Mr. Wilder. I don't believe I've seen in my court, Mr. Wilder."

"No, Your Honor. I usually work family law cases."

"Charges," the judge said.

"Theft of company property," Holcomb said.

"And this property would be?"

"Proprietary company information," the prosecutor said.

The judge frowned.

"Weren't there recent rulings saying such is a civil matter?"

"Under the Patriot Act—"

"Spare me. That doesn't apply to New York state law, and this isn't Federal Court."

"Mr. Wilder?"

"The state fails to meet the burden of proof of the charges. They are just supposition by the employer. I ask for the charges to be dropped."

"Your Honor," protested the prosecutor, "the IT logs showed that Ms. Winters accessed information without authorization."

"Was this within the scope of her duties for said employer?"

"Yes, Your Honor."

"And what is Ms. Winters' status with her employer?"

"He ended her employment."

"I've heard enough. Charges dismissed."

"But, your honor," protested the prosecutor.

"Mr. Holcomb, let the civil courts deal with this, as they

should. As it is, this is a waste of the court's time. There are real criminal cases on the docket. Ms. Winters, you are free to go. And bailiff, get those cuffs off her."

Lexi couldn't believe her good luck. "Thank you, your honor."

He waved his hand as the bailiff unlocked her handcuffs.

"Call the next case."

Wilder put his arm on hers and led her out of the noisy courtroom. Samantha and Cash followed, and as soon as they were in a free space in the hall, Samantha flung her arms around her.

"I'm so, so sorry, Lexi. I shouldn't have taken my anger out on you."

"And I shouldn't have said the things I said."

"That's my best bud. Let's get you home."

"Well, no," Jamie said. "We're meeting with Walker Givens to get several things straight. I assumed, Lexi, you will want to be there."

Cash put his hand on Lexi's arm. "You don't have to, but it will make it easier to confirm a few things if you are there."

"Sure, Cash," she said. Though exhausted, grimy, and in need of a good shower, she'd do anything for this man.

Sam looked up at Jamie. "You didn't sleep, did you?"

"This guy is keeping the whole firm busy. But no one's complaining about what we are charging."

"So my butter and egg money wouldn't cut it, eh?"

"I doubt if it could buy ten minutes."

"Ouch."

"Sorry. People like Cash possess much to protect, and it takes a lot of work to do it."

"I guess I never thought rich people had problems," Samantha said.

"Oh, they do, but they turn out to be expensive."

"I'm not complaining," Cash said. "And I can't wait to talk to 'Uncle Walker.'"

"I should go home," Samantha said.

"Aren't you supposed to be at work?"

"I contracted a very nasty case of stomach flu. Right now I'm bowing to the porcelain god."

Lexi patted Samantha's arm. "Your secret is safe with me."

"It better be. I've more secrets on you than you do on me."

"Says who?"

"Ladies," Cash said. "There's just a few minutes to make our meeting. And Sam, since you got arrested because of Givens' nonsense, you are welcome too."

A quick cab ride brought them to Jamie's office. It wasn't as large as Givens and Associates. It was in a nice building and the desks and chairs were gleaning walnut, and the walls paneled in polished oak.

"Mr. Wilder, the partners and Mr. Givens and his party are in the conference room," the receptionist said.

"Thank you, Madge. This way, Cash, ladies."

Jamie opened one of two double doors and walked inside. Lexi, peering in, saw a long mahogany table and a number of chairs around it. She saw Givens and Tiffany sitting facing the door. Another man, whom she did not know, stood against the wall.

"Walker, Preston, Tiffany," Cash said.

"Cash!" Tiffany said. "We've been waiting for you for an hour now. I've never known you to be rude."

"I had business to take care of."

"Well, I certainly hope that you've brought those prenups I sent you yesterday. We have a lot to talk about."

"Tiffany," Givens said in a warning voice. He sat with his hands steepled, looking at Cash with a dark expression on his face.

"Lexi, Sam, please come in," Cash said.

Lexi walked in, with Samantha following her. Jamie took a seat at the table with Givens and Tiffany. At the end of the table were three solemn middle-aged men. She surmised they were the partners the receptionist mentioned.

Tiffany rose. "What are you doing here?" she said, pointing to Lexi. "You should be—"

"In jail?" Cash said. "You don't think I can figure out who turned her in? You were the only one who saw her at the apartment."

"Cash, I'm not going to tolerate—"

"You don't have to tolerate a damn thing," snapped Cash. "I told you we're finished. So let that sink in, because if you show up anywhere near Lexi or me again, I will file stalking charges on you."

"You can't do that," Tiffany spouted.

"Oh, yes, he can," Jamie said, pulling an envelope from his briefcase. Lexi saw he'd marked it #1. She wondered how many more envelopes there were. "Here is a no-contact order signed by a judge. It's temporary, of course, so you'll get to spend a nice day in court next week for two different cases: Cash and Lexi. But that's only fair since you enjoy sending people there."

"We can do without the sarcasm, Mr. Wilder," snarled Givens.

"Preston," Cash said. "I hope you and Tiffany will be very happy together."

"What?"

"Don't make me pull out the envelope of pictures of you and Tiffany in positions that are impossible to misconstrue.

I'm fortunate that Jamie here works quickly. His PI was able to get those pictures last night before she came over to my apartment. But seeing that Uncle Walker here had a couple of PIs on me since I returned from the Virgin Islands, I'd say turnabout is fair play."

"You bastard."

"Oh, and one more thing. You're fired."

"You can't do that," Givens said.

"Yes, I can. I own the company."

"Not anymore."

Cash glanced at Jamie, who pulled out another envelope, marked #2. He slid it across the table to Givens.

"This is a letter explaining to the Pittman people that you acted without authority. Attached is a letter formally separating you from Givens and Associates."

"You're firing me, from my own firm?"

"It's not your firm, is it? You used it ten years ago to secure a loan from my father when you needed cash. He set up a payment plan for you, which you paid until my father got sick. You're in arrears to a tune you can't repay. So, I'm calling the loan."

"Fuck you. Fuck all you Cashmans. You've always had everything and were so fucking gracious about it. Even when your mother died, he never blamed me for it."

"What are you talking about?"

Tiffany put her hands on her father's arm.

"Dad, don't get upset. Your heart—"

"Shut the fuck up, Tiffany. If you didn't push it with Cash, Pittman would have bought the company and given me back my firm."

"Mr. Givens," said one of the solemn-faced men. "You shouldn't say anything else."

"Why shouldn't I?" Givens said. "It's all fucked up, anyway."

"Walker," Preston said with alarm on his face.

"You," said Walker, pointing his finger at Cash. "You messed up things since day one. Yeah, we all were drinking, but your father stayed back to talk some business, so I said I'd take your mother home. And then that truck swerved, and I jerked the wheel. It was dark and I didn't know we were that close to an embankment."

Shock covered Cash's face.

"That was real?"

"What?" Lexi said gently.

"A dream I had," he said softly.

"She would've been all right if she weren't pregnant. She might have suffered a broken bone or two. But she died. Because of you. I screwed up, and she died."

"Uncle Walker," Cash said. "You don't have to say anything else."

"Don't 'Uncle Walker' me! You are just like your father. He should have blamed me...been angry at me. Instead, he said that God took her because he needed her in heaven. What a bunch of nonsense. How could he think that? And I was the worst best-friend in the world, and he—"

Walked stopped and twisted his lips.

"And then I got to watch him suffer because she died. Watched you grow up knowing your father died that night too. It wasn't fair. It didn't need to happen."

Lexi stared at Givens emotionally bleeding out in the room full of lawyers.

"Wow," muttered Samantha, who stood behind Lexi. "That's fucked up."

"Sam," Lexi whispered as a warning. Thankfully Cash,

Tiffany, Lowe, and the lawyers were too focused on Givens to hear Sam's indiscreet words.

"Preston," Cash said. "Take Tiffany and her father home."

"What? Won't you pull out more tricks from that briefcase of yours?" Givens said nastily.

"I don't need to. You've said more than enough. Uncle Walker, maybe it's time for retirement."

"Come on, Dad," Tiffany said. "Let's go home."

EPILOGUE

CASH

SIX MONTHS LATER

"Damn," Samantha said as she dragged the last box into Cash's apartment. The front door closed with a thud. "I can't get over how big this place is. And you've got two other bedrooms here with their own bathrooms? Are you sure you don't want another roommate? After all, I wouldn't want my best friend to get lost in here without someone to find her."

"Sweetie," Lexi said. "It's time to cut the cord."

"Don't worry," Cash said, putting his arm around Lexi. "I'll put a bell on her so I can hear her."

Lexi gave Cash a sideways glance and Cash hid his smile in her shoulder. He had something special to share with her tonight, and he hoped she liked the idea as much as he did.

"Uh-huh. Besides, Sam, your new roommate seems nice."

"But she's not you."

"Yeah, I can see you crying in your pillow every night. Right after you gorge yourself with pizza and ice cream."

"I expect pizza and ice cream tithes every month. My just deserts because you deserted me."

"I feel your pain," Lexi said.

"Before I go, I want to see the ring again," Sam said.

"You've seen it a hundred times already."

"Doesn't matter. I use it as inspiration. You know, the law of attraction thing."

"Girl, everyone got over the laws of attraction years ago."

"I don't care. You got your prince. Now it's time for mine."

"Thank you, Sam," Cash said.

"Don't compliment him," Lexi said. "He's got a big head as it is."

He growled playfully. "The better to see you with."

Lexi held up the ring he'd given her—the engagement ring the women in Cash's family wore for two generations. It looked just right on her finger.

"Gosh, that's huge. Just like this apartment. I'll bet you play a lot of hide-and-seek here."

"Good night, Samantha. Remember, tomorrow we shop for bridesmaid dresses. You want to get a good night's sleep so you can't blame me for the monstrosity you pick out."

"Please, girlfriend, I'm the epitome of style."

"Says the woman who is still wearing leggings."

"Insulting my leggings? Now I have to leave."

Samantha kissed Lexi on the cheek, and Cash too.

"I'm glad you didn't turn out to be the dick I thought you were."

"Thanks?" Cash said. "I'm sure there was a compliment in there someone."

"There is," Lexi said. "You just have to search for it."

"Night, you two. Remember to do everything that I wouldn't do." She winked and nearly skipped out the door.

Alone, Lexi turned to Cash. Finally...finally, she'd agreed to take his ring and move in with him. He appreciated how circumspect and careful she was. But when she made a deci-sion, she stuck with it.

She decided on him, and Cash couldn't have been happier.

"So," Lexi said. She pulled out the open bottle of white wine in the refrigerator and poured two classes. "How did the sale go today?"

Pittman gave Cash a fight about the sale of Cashman Industries. There were suits and countersuits that kept Jamie very busy. But the young lawyer found he liked prac-ticing corporate law more than family law. So when Cash offered him the managing partner position at Givens and Associates Jamie jumped at it.

This caused a few problems with his fiancée, but Jamie looked at the numbers and decided he'd do better working for Cash than his future father-in-law. Between Cash and Jamie, they were able to square away most of the problems generated by Walker Givens and Preston Lowe. But as Cash found, the finances had gone south, but not for the reasons Givens gave. Lowe invested money poorly and failed to pay back some company loans. The work it took to straighten that out was a small nightmare.

But one thing that wouldn't disappear was Pittman's claims that Cash breached the selling contract. It got messy until Cash discovered what they wanted was the food service division of Cashman Industries. Their supplier for airline meals kept driving up prices, and they wanted to own a food service supplier. Cash wouldn't give that up, but real-ized that perhaps a smaller merger was in order. So today, he signed the papers that gave Pittman Industries a half share of the Cashman Food Service, satisfying everyone. That gave Cash leeway to expand the division and create more jobs, and Pittman got a valuable service as a bargain price. In returned they dropped their lawsuits.

It was a win-win.

"How about that?" Lexi said. She had wandered to the table at the apartment entrance where Cash put the mail. "Another postcard from Tiffany."

"What does she say?"

"What she always does. That the around-the-world cruise is fabulous, Daddy is getting better each day, and she and Preston are fabulously in love."

Cash couldn't help but sympathize with Walker Givens after his breakdown in Jamie's office. His mental condition took a sharp turn downward and required a stay in a hospital. The years of guilt and irrational anger toward Cash had worn on his mind for many years, and he grieved as much as Cash when Cash's father died. Along with his fear of losing his firm, it was too much for one person to take. When Cash learned all this, his anger towards Givens dissipated, and he quietly reinstated partial ownership of Givens and Associates to Uncle Walker.

"She doesn't say that, at least of her and Preston," Cash said.

"It's implied. You were too good to them to give Tiffany and her father that trip around the world."

"I consider it enlightened self-interest. With her gone you could concentrate exclusively on me rather than worrying what she would do behind your back."

"What are we having for dinner?"

"Pizza. I'm having it delivered. Should be here any moment now."

"You are such a nice boyfriend."

"Boyfriend?" Cash said ominously.

"Oops. Sorry, sir."

"That's better. But I may have to punish you for that slip."

Lexi put her hands on his chest, kneading his pecs with her hand.

"How?"

"Um. A butt plug?"

She wrinkled her nose.

"Or the ben-wah balls?"

"Hmm. Are you giving me a choice?"

"No, I'm considering the possibilities. But maybe there's something better?"

"Like what?"

"Remember how cute you were in those kitten ears at Halloween?"

"I remember you chasing me through the apartment calling. 'Here, kitty, kitty. Daddy has some cream for you.' It was a good thing the guests had left, except of course for Samantha sleeping in the guest room. She'll never let me forget that night."

The doorbell rang.

"I'll get that," Cash said too quickly. He didn't want Lexi to see the gift until after they'd eaten. And then he'd spring it on her.

The idea made him smile.

"One large everything pizza," William said grinning from ear to ear. "And the special thing you ordered."

It didn't surprise Cash to learn that among William's enterprises was a BDSM supply house. And he was grateful too, knowing his purchases were confidential.

"Thank you, William. I hope everything is going well at the club."

"Just fine, though I wish you and Ms. Lexi would visit."

Cash wished that too. William was an excellent mentor, but Cash had to respect Lexi's wishes. The club unsettled her, so they didn't go.

"She's still getting over what happened. It was a rough few days for her. I can't even try Shibari on her."

"Sad, but you need more instruction on the dummy, anyway. And how is Ms. Samantha?"

William carried a torch for Samantha bigger than the Statue of Liberty's. But as usual, Cash had no good news to report.

"She's fine, and no, she has not asked about you."

"Well, one can only hope. I've got to get back."

"Thanks, William. Talk to you later."

"Good night. Have fun," he said with a smirk.

"Who was that?" Lexi said. "I thought I heard William."

"It was. He couldn't stay."

"What is that box?" she said poking the box on top of the pizza.

"A surprise."

"Show me," she said with a cute pout.

"No. It's for after dinner."

"I want to see."

"Lexi, go kneel at the couch," he ordered.

She smiled in delight because these were his words to start play. Dinner would have to wait. They could reheat the pizza.

Slowly he walked into the living room carrying the box. Lexi sat on her heels, head down and hands in her lap.

She was gorgeous.

Cash sat down and slowly opened the box.

"Lexi, look at me."

He held out the black leather collar he'd had custom

made. Though Lexi and he had discussed collars, she didn't find one she wanted to wear.

She gasped. "It's perfect. Even this little loop in front. It's adorable."

"It's more than that. But first I'm putting this on you."

Cash fitted the collar around her neck with care.

"How's that feel?"

"I like it."

"Good, because there's more."

He pulled out a bell with a clip and hooked to the front of the collar. "There," he said. "I will know wherever you are within earshot."

"What makes me think this is part of a plan?"

"Because it is." From the box he drew out a silk nightie. "Put it on."

Lexi pulled off her shirt and bra and slipped on the garment.

"Very beautiful. Now put these on."

"What? Kitten ears?" She frowned. "What else is in there?"

Cash lifted the top and playfully looked inside but didn't give her a chance to look. He pulled out a specially crafted set of black velvet gloves, in the shape of cat paws.

"Um," Lexi said as she slipped them on, "Very soft. Where do you want me to touch you with these?"

"Guess."

She stared between his legs where his shaft tented his pants.

"There's not much guessing in that."

"And after, I want that delightful tongue of yours to lap at my cream."

"So you want me to be your kitten?"

"Yes, my sweet little kitten. And you are getting Daddy's cream tonight."

"Tonight?"

"As many nights as you like."

"Then, Sean Cashman, I'm on board for a life of night-times with you."

THANK YOU

Thanks for reading this book. I hope you enjoyed it and hopefully the other books in this series.

Jessie.

Made in the USA
Columbia, SC
10 October 2020

22537957R00212